HAVENFALL

SARA HOLLAND

BLOOMSBURY

NEW YORK   LONDON   OXFORD   NEW DELHI   SYDNEY

BLOOMSBURY YA
Bloomsbury Publishing Inc., part of Bloomsbury Publishing Plc
1385 Broadway, New York, NY 10018

BLOOMSBURY and the Diana logo are trademarks of Bloomsbury Publishing Plc

First published in the United States of America in March 2020
by Bloomsbury YA

Bloomsbury books may be purchased for business or promotional use. For information on bulk purchases
please contact Macmillan Corporate and Premium Sales Department at specialmarkets@macmillan.com

Library of Congress Cataloging-in-Publication Data
Names: Holland, Sara, author.
Title: Havenfall / by Sara Holland.
Description: New York : Bloomsbury [2020]
Summary: Maddie loves spending summers at Havenfall, a Colorado inn where her
uncle brokers peace between worlds, until a murder forces her to take on responsibilities
for which she is unprepared.
Identifiers: LCCN 2019031799 (print) | LCCN 2019031800 (e-book)
ISBN 978-1-5476-0379-4 (hardcover) • ISBN 978-1-5476-0380-0 (e-book)
Subjects: CYAC: Hotels, motels, etc.—Fiction. | Murder—Fiction. |
Missing persons—Fiction. | Magic—Fiction.
Classification: LCC PZ7.1.H646 Hav 2020 (print) | LCC PZ7.1.H646 (e-book) |
DDC [Fic]—dc23
LC record available at https://lccn.loc.gov/2019031799
LC e-book record available at https://lccn.loc.gov/2019031800

Book design by John Candell
Typeset by Westchester Publishing Services
Printed and bound in the U.S.A. by Berryville Graphics Inc., Berryville, Virginia
2 4 6 8 10 9 7 5 3 1

All papers used by Bloomsbury Publishing Plc are natural, recyclable products made from wood
grown in well-managed forests. The manufacturing processes conform to the environmental regulations
of the country of origin.

To find out more about our authors and books visit www.bloomsbury.com and sign up for our newsletters.

To everyone who's ever felt like they don't have a place

HAVENFALL

without care for the consequences, have ravaged the world and left most of it uninhabitable to Byrnisians.

Years ago, the Silver Prince used his immense magic to tame the storms and erect a wall around his city-state, Oasis. Ever since, he has ruled in peace, keeping the storms at bay. Almost everyone living in Byrn resides within the city walls, having agreed to cease all elemental wielding—except for the nomads who remain outside and brave the lightning, hurricanes, and burning wind to keep their magic.

Solaria

Little is known about Solaria, a tiny, sealed-off world that is a hotbed of powerful, highly volatile magic. It's thought that the people of Solaria are largely responsible for our world's mythologies around djinni, demons, and vampires. Some call them soul-devourers. It's been said that Solaria has no visible sun but instead has a blazing golden sky. Though Solarians can take many shapes, their beast forms all bleed dark blue blood.

The doorway to Solaria was sealed off years ago after a deadly incident that took place at Havenfall. Solarians are no longer welcome at the inn and they are not part of the Peace Treaty alliance of the Last Remaining Adjacent Realms. There are rumors that Solarians snuck into the other realms before the door was closed, and that they still roam the worlds.

Haven

Haven is what we know as the human world. It is the only realm without natural magic, which is why the people of other realms call

A BRIEF INTRODUCTION TO
THE ADJACENT REALMS

⟡ Fiordenkill ⟡

Most of Fiordenkill is encased in ice and frost. Ethereal in its beauty, Fiordenkill sparkles with ice bridges and palaces of packed snow. It seldom sees the sun, but the sky is bright with auroras and thousands of stars. Soldiers ride on wolves and great bears roam the woods; enchanted fruit grows on the trees, immune to the frost encasing their bright skins.

Compared to people of other worlds, Fiordens are thought to be noble and stoic and sometimes secretive. Fiordenkill magic can heal flesh and make plants grow.

⟡ Byrn ⟡

The massive world of Byrn swelters under the heat of two suns and three moons. Enormous, long-lived storms batter the deserts, the roiling seas, and the lightning plains, so that the ground seems to shift constantly beneath one's feet. Millennia of elemental magic, unleashed it Haven—a safe place, a neutral place. The existence of other worlds have been kept secret from humankind. This is the number one rule that all the Realms must abide by. Humans can't live in the other Realms. Their biology prevents them from surviving conditions outside of Haven for more than a few hours.

Omphalos: The Inn at Havenfall

All the realms intersect at Havenfall, through a series of doorways connected by tunnels hidden beneath the Rocky Mountains. These doorways have been guarded by us Innkeepers for as long as anyone can remember. There is a radius around the doorways within which people from all realms can breathe safely and not sicken, as people usually do in worlds not their own.

The Inn at Havenfall was built on this spot as was the town of Haven—so named because, to the people of the realms, the town and the inn represent our whole world.

There used to be many more worlds accessible from the inn, but over the centuries some doorways have closed due to the inscrutable forces that govern the realms. Only the doorway to Solaria has been sealed shut on purpose, for the protection of the Last Remaining Adjacent Realms.

The Annual Peace Summit

On the longest day of our year, Fiordens witness a blazing, multicolored aurora in their dark sky and Byrn undergoes a simultaneous eclipse of its three moons. This is the solstice. On this day every summer, travelers can pass safely through the doorways into the Inn at Havenfall— the neutral realm that serves as host to them all.

During this special time, the inn holds its annual peace summit, where delegates from all the realms negotiate trade and political agreements by day and dance in the ballroom by night to celebrate the diversity and unity of all the inn's guests.

PROLOGUE

THE FIRST BREATH OF AIR Marcus takes in another realm feels like
lightning. Human lungs aren't built for this world, for Byrn. He doesn't
know how long he has before they give up and he needs to stagger back
through the shining doorway to Haven.

But every new Innkeeper is duty-bound to visit all the remaining worlds,
if only once—that's what his great-grandmother, Annabelle, who ran the
Inn at Havenfall for almost a century, told him before she died. So Marcus
doesn't flinch, not with twenty nobles of Byrn lined up in a semicircle around
the portal, waiting with scaled cheekbones glittering in the orange light. All
of them are gathered, curious to hear the new portal-keeper speak. Behind
them, clusters of metallic buildings shimmer against a sky the color of flame.

Havenfall is all celebration, all pomp and ritual and freely flowing spirits, in stark contrast to this intense formality. Now is Marcus's time. The
book he brought with him is heavy in his hands.

He will only read one page. There is more to the peace treaty that he won't have time to recite: the names of the delegates who died at the inn when the Solarians rioted; the decree to forever seal the gateway to Solaria with old magic; Havenfall's promise to hunt down all of those who escaped. A reminder to Haven, Fiordenkill, and Byrn that even after nearly a hundred years, rogue Solarians still roam their realms.

Some still blame humans, blame Haven, for the bloodshed. Marcus knows that. It's now his responsibility, as the portal-keeper, to keep everyone safe. Not just the Byrnisians and Fiordens, but his beloved Graylin; Marcus's sister, Sylvia; and her children—who will one day inherit the Inn at Havenfall and all that comes with it.

He must remind everyone of their promises to one another. So he lifts the book, the only time this leather-bound volume has ever left the inn's library, and begins to read aloud from its old, crumbling pages—to tell the waiting crowd that Havenfall remembers.

I stop in front of the arrivals board and hoist my duffel bag higher on my shoulder. I look at the aged screen to try to push the images out of my head. Mom's face behind the scratched plexiglass, the flat darkness of her eyes. It's like she doesn't care, can't be bothered about what's going to happen next.

I blink hard, focus on the places and times flickering above me. *Omaha, 2:25.*

That's the bus I'm *supposed* to take. The plan is to stay with Grandma Ellen, my dad's mom, for the summer, and intern at the insurance company she runs. Dad doesn't want me at the Inn at Havenfall—not now and not ever again. He didn't understand Mom's attachment to the place, and he doesn't get mine either. It's like he can sense the glimmer of magic clinging to me when I return, and it makes him suspicious. He says I should be doing something I can put on a college application next year.

And it's true that Havenfall doesn't exactly appear in an online search. My working at the inn won't earn me internship credits anywhere. But these summers are all I have. I've been going to the inn for summers since I was six. And the older I get, the more important it is to show Uncle Marcus what I can do, that I can be useful. If all goes well, this time next summer I'll be traveling to the mountains with more than just a summer bag. Marcus will name me as his inheritor, and I'll move into the inn for good.

So, no. Clearly I'm not going to Omaha. A sparkling insurance-sales career is not in my future.

My insides feel tense, brittle somehow, and my eyes keep drifting back to the blue smudges of mountains outside the windows. Like I'll fall to pieces if I'm not among them soon. I look back at the arrivals board and scan a few lines down, past Boise and Laramie and Salt Lake City to Haven. *3:50.* Gate 8, the last one, at the dusty far end of the depot.

I glance around the room, where sunlight bounces off the high ceilings. There are only two other people in the waiting area now, a young guy in a hoodie sleeping across four chairs and a middle-aged man with thinning blond hair reading a yellowed newspaper. I go to the far side and sit against the wall on the dingy carpet, next to the outlet that I know from experience is the only one that works, and plug in my phone to let it charge for the long ride.

I should text Marcus and let him know I'm coming. But when I start to type, a sense of dread fills me. What if he tells me not to come? To listen to my dad? Just the thought is almost unbearable. I lock my screen and put it on the floor facedown, then dig my fingers into my palms. If I just show up, he can't turn me away. Soon I'll be there, in my room overlooking the valley, dancing in the ballroom, with Brekken under the stars.

Going up into the mountains always feels like I'm leaving the rest of the world behind. In the thinner air, it's as if I'm someone else. I'm Maddie Morrow, Marcus's trusted niece and maybe inheritor of the Inn at Havenfall, if I play my cards right and impress the delegates from the Adjacent Realms. Not Maddie Morrow, the girl with the dead older brother, the girl with the mom on death row.

Shit. I didn't let myself remember those words until now. I got all the way out of Sterling Correctional's visiting hall, onto the bus on the county road, to the depot, and into this corner before I thought about them. And now the memories flood back in with a rush of nausea. The stares and whispers that follow me everywhere: in the halls at school, at the grocery store, even at home, Dad and his wife, Marla, trailing me with their eyes like any second I might snap, like whatever sickness Mom has lives in me too.

But Mom is the worst part of it. Her apathy. When the death sentence was first handed down, I thought maybe, just maybe, this would shock her into admitting the truth. That she didn't kill Nathan eleven years ago. And even if no one but me really believed her, it would be enough to keep her alive.

But when I sat across from her this morning, the plexiglass between us, she was the same blank face she's been for eleven years. She just blinked, slowly, when I told her for the thousandth time—*I was there. I saw the thing in our house. It came in through the window; I saw the glass on the floor.*

She replied the same as always, too, slow and soft. *You were imagining it. We see what we want to see, love, but there are no monsters, just people who do horrible things. I was unbalanced, and I did a horrible thing. Don't go looking for answers where there are none.*

But that's not what happened. I know what I saw that night, even if it was only through the crack between two cupboard doors. Before the overhead light shattered, leaving us in shadows, I saw the monstrous dark shape vaulting toward my brother. Heard the roaring sound that filled the kitchen. Then all at once, the screaming stopped and my brother was gone, the kitchen floor slick with blood.

My mother wasn't responsible for Nathan's death; it was a beast from a banished world. And someone, or something, pressured her into taking the blame. Maybe she feared what might happen to Havenfall if she were ever to reveal the truth.

And what could I do? Because the thing is, you can't tell people a monster killed your brother. People will start to talk about you. *Freak. Liar. Crazy.*

But at Havenfall, people believe me. I've only told a few people, but they believe me. I have to hold on to that. It's all I have.

I check my phone reflexively, half-afraid that Dad will somehow sense I'm not on the way to Omaha. I'll update him when it's too late to turn back. I have only one bar of service, and that's likely to blink out once we reach the mountains, but it doesn't matter. All the people I actually want to talk to are up ahead, at the summit in Havenfall. I'll see them soon, and besides, no one there even knows what a phone is. To them it's just a strange, glimmering, blinking artifact.

I grin as a memory from last summer surfaces. I finally wheedled Dad into getting me a smartphone, and my first night at Havenfall, Brekken and I snuck out to the barn and I introduced him to Candy Crush. I wish I had a video of him—serious Brekken, with his soldier's bearing and noble manners and literally otherworldly cheekbones—hunched over the screen with the tips of his jeweled ears turning red, hissing Fiorden curses whenever he lost a life. I've never taken a picture of Brekken, of course. While Marcus doesn't subject me to the no-phones-on-inn-grounds rule like he does every other human who enters Havenfall, he trusts me not to be stupid. A leaked video could be disastrous, and I'd never endanger my safe place. My birthright. My home.

Anyway, I don't need a picture. I'll see Brekken soon in the flesh.

At 3:55, the bus to Haven finally pulls up. It looks older than the others, with scratches and rust gathering around the wheels. But my heart still lifts as I climb on board. The driver, a slight, wrinkled man, smiles warmly at me.

"How you doing today, miss?"

"Great," I say with a returning smile as I drop my duffel and slide in a few seats behind him, and I mean it. There's a smattering of people on the bus—an old woman in the back, bundled up as though it's winter and not June, a young mother cradling a wailing infant, and the two men from the depot. The engine rattles loudly, and the metal roof above me is dented with what looks like the marks of hailstones.

It takes us four hours to reach the mountains, and I let myself doze off against the window, sinking into troubled half dreams. I dream Mom and Nate are on the bus beside me, just as they were when we visited

Havenfall as kids, my brother fiddling with the silver jacks Marcus gave him when he was born. And my heart leaps for joy.

But when I say Nathan's name and they both turn to me, I see the prisoner version of Mom, with her baggy tan jumpsuit and listless expression. My brother's eyes are wide, and I see something reflected in them, a monstrous shadow—

I'm shaken, grateful when a pothole in the road jars me awake. The sun starts its descent just as we begin to climb into the mountains, painting everything gold. The narrow road hugs a mountainside; to our right are the carved-away stone walls, sometimes covered over with avalanche nets, and to our left, out my window, green pines blanket the valley. In contrast to the sprawl and shine of Denver and its suburbs, the mountains seem like a formidable force against humans, and signs of civilization dwindle rapidly until all we pass are old, half-crumbling mining towns. Decrepit houses and listing trailers are tucked in between the boulders and pines.

The dream lingers, but I breathe out, imagining it leaving me like smog from my lungs. I crack the window, put on my headphones, and focus on the bite of cool mountain air. Crowns of ice gleam in the sun, and the sky somehow feels bigger framed by the jagged peaks. On the horizon, I can see the translucent curtains of rainfall.

We're getting close now.

Omphalos, I think. A Greek word Marcus taught me. It means navel, technically. The center of everything. Where it all starts. Where it all connects.

The roads get steep, and the bus sputters and creaks. My music blocks out the worst of it, but I can still feel the bus vibrating around me, like a panting beast of burden, as it climbs up these twisty roads. The metal frame shudders in a way that the worn polyester seat cushion can't disguise. It doesn't help that the only thing separating us from dropping off the mountain is a metal railing that doesn't look like it would withstand a strong gust of wind. For a second, I imagine what it would be like to lose control. To hurtle through the misty air, plunging past the soft blanket of fog and into the yawning forest of darkness below.

To shatter like glass.

I blink again and pull out my phone—it's time to text Uncle Marcus now that we're getting close. The text goes through, and I hope he sees it amid the bustle of Havenfall's summit—an annual celebration which is just about to begin that marks the peace between our three worlds.

"What's that frown for?"

A gravelly voice to my right snakes through my music. I half-turn away, hoping that it's not me being addressed, but the man across the aisle, the one with the newspaper, is looking at me, lips split to show cigarette-stained teeth. Reluctantly, I take off my headphones.

This guy must be from Haven. He's wearing a necklace with a teardrop-shaped pendant of the same odd, pearlescent silver that supposedly comes only from the old mines surrounding the town. But I've never seen him there before.

I give him a bare, polite smile. "Just happy we're almost there."

He rubs the pendant between his fingers. He has sun-weathered skin and pale eyes. "You going to Haven?"

"Yep." I can't help popping my lips slightly on the *P*. It's a stupid question—that's the only stop left, which this guy surely knows. "Going to visit my uncle."

"You from there? You look familiar."

Wariness curls around my heart, but I push it down and shake my head. Haven has less than a thousand people, and it's tucked away so high, inaccessible but for twisty county highways. It's possible the man might remember me from seeing me around town. But he

10

wouldn't—couldn't—have remembered me from the inn; Havenfall protects against that.

"Like I said, just visiting family."

"Well, I'm pleased to meet you."

"Likewise," I lie, reluctantly shaking the hand he sticks across the aisle. His hand is clammy, his grip too tight. When he smiles, I notice several fillings made from the same pale silver as the pendant.

To my relief, he doesn't ask further questions once I turn back toward the window. We're climbing higher and higher as the sun sets, the air thinning and my ears popping. Clouds creep in from the west, covering the orange sky and casting the craggy mountains in shadow. The driver goes slower as the wind picks up. The towns are almost nonexistent now: the only signs of human habitation are the odd cabin or broken-down car. But the landscape gets more beautiful, even under the gathering blanket of storm clouds. Fog creeps down over the mountainsides, wrapping around the trees and spilling tendrils over the road, but the effect is almost comforting, like we're the only people in the world.

Another oddity about Haven: the weather is strange around here. Locals know it, and it keeps outsiders away. There are other measures, too, other precautions meant to keep this place secret and safe. As we pass the faded road sign that says Welcome to the Inn at Havenfall, I look at the trees on either side. My uncle employs a dozen people to keep watch outside town year-round. I know I won't see them—they're stationed deep in the woods, in cabins or converted deer blinds. There to make sure that no magic escapes the boundaries of the town.

It hasn't happened in years, and when it does, it's usually easily explained—a maid sneaking out a bottle of Fiorden wine without realizing the power it holds, or a bored noble taking a ride through the woods that ranges too far. But once every few years a delegate will decide to try to smuggle magic out for profit. I don't know what the punishment is for that, but I've never seen any of the offending delegates again.

The clouds finally crack and rain drizzles down as we round the mountain and see the town of Haven up ahead, a smattering of buildings clinging for dear life to the mountainside, encroached upon by the trees and the mist. A bright river snakes down across the mountain before disappearing into the valley below us. And my heart leaps to see it, because Havenfall is just beyond the next ridge. The fog sparkles like a mirage. I glance behind me and see all my fellow passengers glued to the window, even the baby, looking out with round blue eyes.

We reach the crossroads just outside town, the place where Marcus usually picks me up in his jeep. Ahead is the general store, a big log building with a generous wraparound porch, spilling welcoming yellow light from inside. Two women chatting in rocking chairs on the porch look when the bus stops and the passengers file off. I'm relieved when Silver Teeth Man exits, his fillings flashing as he gives me one more broad smile, and then disappears into the store. But then the anxiety slides back in. Maybe Marcus didn't get my text. He isn't here.

When the door closes, the driver meets my eyes in the mirror. "Someone coming to pick you up?"

I nod, holding on to the feeling of anticipation. No, it's not anticipation. It's need. Havenfall, my uncle and friends, Brekken—all less than a mile away now.

"We can wait a few minutes, but I can't take this thing any farther up these damn roads." The driver slaps the dashboard with a mixture of exasperation and affection. "And . . ."

He lifts a hand, pointing at the dark clouds coming in from the north, the curtains of rain in the distance. Even if he doesn't know why, he knows that the weather gets more freakish the closer we are to Havenfall.

"Sorry about this." My voice catches as I shift in my seat, trying to call Marcus again. But I don't have service here. It's dead air. "My uncle should be here in a few minutes."

But a few minutes pass, and then a few more. No one comes.

The general store's lights have gone out; the doors are closed. And the storm is near, the scraggly pine trees around us stirring in the wind. My mouth is dry, my stomach heavy. The idling bus grumbles beneath me.

I'm used to being forgotten—it beats the smirks and stares that usually come with being noticed. When you're the loner, the weirdo, the daughter of the Goodwin Lane Killer, it's better to not be seen at all. It's different with Marcus, though. He's always had a place for me at Havenfall. He's never failed to be here at the crossroads when the bus has come in.

At least, not before now.

I dig through my backpack until I find my umbrella, then get up and thread through the aisle toward the driver, wishing I'd thought to pack a raincoat. "I'll just walk into town a little ways," I tell him. "I usually get service once I'm higher up." This isn't true, but I'm suddenly anxious to get off this bus, despite the rain. He must have places to be. As do I.

His brow crinkles again. "Are you sure, dear? I don't want you out when the lightning starts." He gestures at the road. "There's a diner about a half mile up the road that stays open all night. Ask Annie to let you use the phone—"

"Okay." I cut him off without meaning to, but the idea of spending another moment away from Havenfall puts a pit in my stomach. I lift my umbrella. "I'll be fine, I promise."

The driver doesn't look happy about this, but he pulls the lever to open the doors. Cool, pine-and-rain-scented air pushes into the bus, raising bumps on my spine. The smell of Havenfall. But tendrils of anxiety wiggle through me.

"Be careful," the driver reminds me as I stop on the stairs to open my umbrella. "If there's lightning, knock on someone's door, or find a ditch and hunker down."

"Thank you. Will do." I smile at him, meaning the thank-you but not the rest of it. I'll walk all night if I have to.

He stays idling there as I walk up the deserted, darkening Main Street, my old Converse squelching in the mud. The incline here is so steep I can see it, and I internally groan thinking of the hike ahead. My duffel strap is already cutting into my shoulder, and this dollar-store umbrella won't hold up against Haven weather.

But I lift my hand, giving the driver one last smile and wave. Then I start the long trek up to Havenfall. A little walk, a little rain won't stop me from getting to the one place where I actually belong.

2

MOST OF THE TOWNSFOLK OF Haven don't know the truth, I think, about Havenfall and the Adjacent Realms and the Accords that we commemorate every summer with a summit. But everyone knows there's something special about this place—an undercurrent, a breath of wind from another world.

A few different stories float around town, passed along when you're getting your hair cut, in line at the general store, chatting on sagging front porches. That a tiny village once here disappeared from the face of the earth, and no one knows where everyone went. That a cult leader during a camp meeting walked a group of devout followers off a cliff. That Lewis and Clark types came here a little later in the nineteenth century, trying to map the Rockies, only to all vanish. People say the mountain has a will of its own. It can be magnanimous or cruel. If you come here with ill intentions, you'll find yourself beset by rain, hail, and wind strong enough to dislodge rocks above and send them tumbling onto your path. But if you come here for refuge, the fog will swallow you up like a protective blanket and hide you from whatever you're running from.

The point is, people know that this is a place where you can vanish, even if they don't know why. We're hardly in Briar County, Colorado, anymore. We're *elsewhere*.

Giving up on keeping my feet dry, I look up from the ground and take in what's around me as I walk through town. The other bus passengers have dispersed, and I pass a handful of clapboard houses built right into the mountainside, with flimsy wood porches overlooking the valley. Faces appear in windows as I go by. Then there's the post office with its yellowed newspaper notices. That's where gossip is traded, where to go if you want to know the stories about this town. There's a sharp-eyed clerk there, Debbie, who's run the place as long as I can remember. She always greets me by name and asks after Marcus when I stop by to pick up packages.

There's Dr. Abram's house, the doctor-slash-veterinarian who almost certainly isn't licensed but who everyone trusts anyway. There's the shell of an overturned livestock truck that went into a ditch years ago and no one has ever picked up, which now seems to be home to a family of coyotes. I catch a glimpse of a skinny tail disappearing behind a ragged metal panel as I plod by.

The town is diminished, as is Havenfall itself. The inn used to be the crossroads to uncountable realms, each behind its own door, and all but two have been sealed magically shut. There are only three worlds left—Byrn, Fiordenkill, and Haven, which is what everyone from the Adjacent Realms calls Earth; that's how the town got its name. But even though neither the town nor the inn is what it once was, the air still feels laden with possibilities. Havenfall is the neutral zone between all the worlds, a peaceful, magical crossroads.

I pass the long, low brick diner, where I'm supposed to call Marcus. I'm pretty sure it used to be some sort of factory, but now the steamed-up windows illuminate a smattering of people eating in red-vinyl booths. I try to see if there's anyone I know. Sometimes guests from Fiordenkill and Byrn will venture out if they need to have a conversation too controversial for the inn, or if they're curious about the human world. But I don't recognize anyone, so I keep walking.

And besides, I don't want to be out once dark really falls. Even though I know the doors to Solaria have been sealed off since the postwar treaty over a hundred years ago, worry burns through me like a live wire when I remember that we are never fully safe. That plenty of Solarians crossed through into our world before the treaty, and not all of them were found. They're shapeshifters, capable of adapting and living among us—of living in any of the realms. They wear monstrous forms when they're hungry, using teeth and claws to hunt us and devour our souls, but the rest of the time they can look like whatever they choose. Can look human, can breathe our air indefinitely.

The rest of us—humans and people from the other Adjacent Realms—can't make it more than a few days, or a few weeks for the strongest of constitutions, in a realm other than our own before gasping and flapping like fish out of water. We are not meant to travel between realms. Except at Havenfall.

That's why the inn is so special. Its magic makes it different—makes it safe. It is truly the one place everyone can intermingle.

I shudder and walk faster, passing the ancient motel with windows too dusty to see inside, which for some reason has never been knocked down or repurposed, even though Haven types are usually all about resourcefulness and reinvention in order to avoid having to interact with the outside world. A busted car becomes a chicken coop, the skeleton of a burned-down miner's cabin becomes an illicit playground, an old bomb shelter becomes a bar. (Where, as Brekken and I have discovered, they don't card.)

The rain slackens enough for me to close my umbrella as I leave town behind and trudge up toward Havenfall—good weather always seems to wrap the inn like a bubble, no matter what's happening in town. But it's rapidly getting darker even as the clouds slide away, and here's the part of my plan I wish I'd thought more about. There are no streetlamps, and the whispering pines block any light from the inn above or the town below. It's twilight now, but soon I'm going to have nothing to guide me but the moon and stars.

I've been walking on the side of the road for half an hour, squinting at the ground to make sure I don't misstep, when an engine sound from down the road makes me look up.

A motorcycle's headed right at me.

I leap back just as the bike roars around the bend.

My chest jackhammers as I watch the driver swerve, tires skidding over the dirt road, the bike going out from under him. The rider tumbles into the road, rolling over, while the bike shoots across the gravel, the motor sputtering out, and tangles in the brush between the trees.

My duffel is on the ground, my hands over my mouth. I run to the driver, who pushes unsteadily to stand. "Are you okay?"

He's wearing a helmet—one of those shiny black ones that make you look like a Martian—and a leather jacket. He pulls off the helmet and oh—not a *he*, I realize as two dirty-blond braids tumble on either side of a pale, heart-shaped face.

"No thanks to you."

She's pretty, with a thin, wide mouth. A white scar runs down her chin, like this isn't her first fall. Dark circles beneath her blazing, dark eyes. She swipes the back of her hand across her mouth.

"What the hell were you doing in the middle of the road?" She reaches up and touches a silver locket around her throat, as if to make sure it's still there.

"I'm sorry, the fog—" I start to say something about how she could have taken it easy on the turns, but then I register the smear of red across her cheek. "Shit, you're bleeding."

Panic speeds my heart. I yank out my phone, not sure if I should call Marcus or 911. If she's really hurt, could an ambulance even get up here?

Her hand shoots out and grabs my wrist before I decide. Her grip is hot, too tight.

"Don't. I'm fine. Just bit my tongue." She lets me go and spits blood onto the road, then troops off toward her bike, fists clenched. "This bike is my everything, though, so you better hope it still runs."

"Sorry," I mumble, at a loss for what to do. A second ago I was panicked, then mad, and now guilt fills me as I trail after her. "Are you from around here?" I call out. "Is there someone you could call to—I really don't think you should try to ride that thing right now."

She glares at me as she drags her bike from the underbrush back onto the road. Besides the left rearview mirror being cocked at a funny angle, the bike looks fine to me, but then it's not like I know anything about motorcycles, and the way she took that fall . . .

Once her bike's back on the road, she props it on the kickstand and turns to me, crossing her arms. "Worry about yourself," she says. "The real question here is why the hell are you wandering around in the dark?"

Around us, the chorus of frogs and crickets slowly starts up again. I didn't realize they'd stopped singing.

I lift my head, trying to match her manner, though I can't imagine

I'm all that intimidating with my damp clothes and sagging umbrella. "I'm headed to the Inn at Havenfall."

"What a coincidence, me too."

"What for?"

Marcus always hires all sorts of people to work at the inn every year during the summer summit; the meetings, parties, and events require extra maids and stable hands, cooks and attendants. But I can't picture this girl blending into the background like a staffer is meant to. Besides, all the new staff was supposed to arrive last week, a few days before the delegates, to get ready.

"I saw an ad in the paper for a landscaper." She lifts one shoulder in a shrug. "Seemed like a good deal."

"You're late," I snap. Then realize I didn't mean to say it like that, but the adrenaline from a moment ago broke down my filters. "I mean, it's okay. I'm sure it doesn't matter." I feel myself blushing, and quickly bend down to pick up my duffel bag.

Her eyes are narrow. "I would be less late if you hadn't been walking in the middle of the road."

"If you hadn't been taking that bend like a madman—" I stop myself. Becoming irritated won't help things. "You know what, arguing about it isn't going to get us there any faster."

Havenfall's got to be less than half a mile away now, and I can feel it, an insistent tugging like a balloon string tied to my breastbone. I don't want to fight with this girl. I just want to get there, and I offer an olive branch. "I'm Maddie."

"Taya," she says. But she doesn't take my outstretched hand. Dark, unreadable eyes examine my face, and the scrutiny freezes me, makes me want to shrink away. It brings me back to my home in Sterling and the constant stares of everyone there, where I keep my head down and walk fast, hoping to stay under the radar.

But that's not who I am here, not in the mountains and not at Havenfall. So I hold my ground and meet her eyes, even if something about her gaze feels dangerous. In Havenfall, I am brave. I must be, if I want to prove myself worthy of preserving the peace we celebrate with every summit, protecting the portals to the world's lost realms of magic. The *omphalos.*

And in the long run, it's not like she'll remember any of this. Marcus always sees to that. No one ever remembers—except me.

Eventually, Taya turns away with a shrug. She throws a leg over her motorcycle, then looks back at me. "Well?" she says after a moment. "Are you coming?"

Surprise freezes me in place. A few moments ago, I'd have said I'd never be caught dead on a motorcycle, but I'm ever more conscious of how dark it is and how far I have to go. I glance at the motorcycle, and Taya must be able to read the hesitation on my face, because she grins.

"I'm a good driver. I swear. But if you're worried, you can wear my helmet."

"There's no need—" I begin, but Taya has already lifted the helmet and plunked it down over my ears. I cock my head, a little charmed and a little indignant, as she turns and strides back toward her bike, seeming to assume I'll follow.

She pauses and looks over her shoulder at me, lifting one eyebrow. "Unless you'd rather walk. Alone. In the dark. With coyotes."

Unable to think of a way to reply to that, I trail after her. "So, do I just, um . . ."

Taya already has her leg over the bike, and it kicks to life with a growl. "Get on behind me and hold on."

I do as she says, nervous but trying not to hold her too tight. I don't remember the last time I've gotten this close to, well, anyone. But Taya is easy, comfortable as she grabs my hands and situates them so they're wrapped around her, not resting on her sides. I need to scoot up, my chest pressing against her back.

"Sorry," I mumble, glad she can't see me blushing.

"It's fine," she replies distractedly, kicking the bike into gear. Then it leaps forward, and under the roar of the engine I hear her *oof,* because I've instinctively squeezed her tight as the unpaved road spools away beneath us. "Mind loosening your death grip?"

"Sorry," I call again, adjusting my hold and trying to breathe normally. Taya drives us up the road, and I know we aren't going that fast from the leisurely way trees slide by, but it feels like we are. The motorcycle rumbles beneath me.

"So how did you hear about this place?" Taya shouts as she takes us smoothly around the curve of a switchback. The fresh, damp air whips past, and the last of the clouds are scudding away in the sky, revealing a few stars starting to blink through the gathering dark.

"My uncle." I have to try the words twice, because the first time the wind steals them away.

"Think you can put in a good word for me?" Taya asks.

A little flame of pride curls in my chest. "I'll think about it." I risk taking my hand off her waist to point up ahead, where a ridge juts up dark against the sky. "Focus till we get over there."

Taya half-turns her head to glance at me. "What's there?"

"You'll see."

Not much longer. The mountains seem bigger now than they did on the bus. The air is chilly and sharp with scents of pine and wildflowers. More stars are winking into existence above us. And—

We crest the ridge. Even over the rumble of the engine, I hear Taya gasp.

Mirror Lake is laid out before us, a silver crescent slash in the landscape, reflecting the night sky perfectly beneath the black line of the bridge. The water looks like indigo silk sprinkled with diamonds, the round moon's reflection—floating right in the lake's center—seeming to give off its own light. And on the other side, lit by the pale rays of the twin moons and by gold light spilling from inside:

Havenfall.

My uncle has told me that this place has been rebuilt hundreds of times over the centuries, and of course I know it's true—the portals in their caves have been here longer than humans, longer than memory. The caves, and the structures the portal-keepers have built on top of them, have been buried by avalanches, burned down in fires, and twice destroyed in wars spilling over from other worlds—Fiordenkill, Byrn, Solaria, and the countless others that at one point or another opened up in the caves beneath these mountains. The inn that currently stands was built by my great-great-grandmother after the ranch house that stood here before burned down. At least that's what we can tell from the journals she left and the stories Marcus remembers from when he was a child. We don't know who came before her, or why whoever it was chose her.

Still, it's hard to believe the inn hasn't been here forever—it looks so timeless, so natural. The inn is massive, built right into the side of the mountain so it looks almost like it's growing from the earth. A sprawling creation of cedar and slate, girded by staircases and balconies. A waterfall behind the inn turns into a winding stream that circles the inn like a silver ribbon before feeding into Mirror Lake. A wide paved drive in front holds a mixture of cars and horse-drawn carriages, cherry paint and polished wood, chrome fenders and the flanks of horses standing side by side.

Haven—not the town, but the world, Earth—doesn't have its own magic, obviously. That's why the other realms see it as neutral territory. But the spark that lights up in my chest as we crest the ridge is a kind of magic too, I can't help but think.

We coast down the slope toward the lake. Taya's spine is rigid, her knuckles tight on the handlebars. She stops the bike before we reach the bridge and kicks out a foot to hold us upright.

"What's wrong?" I ask. My voice comes out embarrassingly high and breathy. I want to leap off the bike and run. All my tiredness seems to have evaporated. But Taya is still.

"That's a lot of water," I hear her say, quietly.

"We don't have to swim across it. There's a bridge."

"I see that." She turns back to give me an irritated glance, and one of her braids hits the side of my helmet. She swings off the bike, forcing me to grab the handlebars to stay on. Something in her voice lets a chill seep in. I dismount too and pull off the helmet, my legs cramping and my heart beating fast from the ride.

It's easier to look at Taya when she's glaring at Mirror Lake and not at me. She's smaller than I originally thought, shorter than me and slight beneath the bulk of the jacket. Her face is closed off, expressionless.

"It's safe," I say. "Look, all those cars got across it fine."

"You can go ahead if you want," she says, standing stiffly beside the bike. "I'm walking, so I'll be slower."

My stomach twists. She did me a solid, taking me here after I made her crash, even if it was 50 percent her fault. It feels wrong to just leave her now. "I'll come with you."

Her mouth turns down, but she nods, and we walk over the water, Taya wheeling the bike in neutral along the bridge and me trailing behind. She flinches when the old wood creaks beneath us. If she notices how the ground is dry here—despite the all-consuming rain in Haven—she doesn't comment on it.

Halfway across, a gust of wind sweeps down the mountain, making the trees and the bridge sway, and Taya freezes. I almost run into her.

24

"Sorry," she whispers.

"It's okay." I mean it this time, because I know what it's like to have seemingly irrational fears.

"We're blocking the bridge," she says.

"It's late. I doubt anyone else is coming tonight." But my words don't seem to land. Taya is staring straight ahead with a lost expression marring her face. I think of something to distract her. If she's going to be here all summer, maybe it doesn't matter if I tell her a secret or two.

"My uncle says this water shows you as your best self," I say, drifting to the wooden railing to my right. "Do you want to take a look?"

A harsh laugh escapes her. "Not really," she says, but puts down the kickstand and joins me anyway.

As our images form in the water below, I almost wish she hadn't.

I'd forgotten why I always avoided this lake when I ran around the grounds as a kid with Brekken. His reflection matches him perfectly, but for me, Mirror Lake seems to reflect something other than real life and nothing I could ever aspire to be. The Maddie in the water looks serene and happy. Even without a smile this Maddie looks ethereal, like nothing anyone says—nothing the world can do—can touch her.

And that's not me. Not the girl who feels constantly scraped raw by the cruel words that have sunk through my skin and nestled in my heart, braiding with the poisoned strands of lingering memories to create something heavy, dense, and thorny. The Maddie in the water is just another bit of Havenfall magic. A fantasy.

I glance over at Taya, the ease of earlier having vanished, hoping she isn't looking at my reflection. She's not. She looks troubled, her brow furrowed and lips flattened into a line, even though her reflection seems to more or less match what I see.

Before I can think of something to say, she crouches down, picks up a pebble stuck in between the planks of the bridge, and splashes it into the water. It sounds like breaking glass, and I flinch. The water ripples, silver and black, sending our reflections to the depths.

"My parents died in a car crash going off a bridge," she says evenly, without looking at me. "In case you were wondering why."

I wish I had a better response than "That's horrible. I'm sorry."

She shrugs. "I'm fine now. Just not a fan of big bodies of water." Gripping the railing tight, she looks over at me with those uncanny eyes. Sorrow curls in my stomach, heavy and cold. "What about you?" she asks. "Why are you here and not home working, or partying, or whatever it is normal people do with their summers?"

I feel my walls going up, my wariness rising. She's shared a secret and now she wants one in return. Maybe the near-death experience we had earlier has pushed Taya to trust, but not me.

"I feel like myself here," I say, a half truth.

What happened to her family is no one's fault. Mine, though—those secrets are ugly. And looking down at the water, at who I could be, I know I want none of those memories at Havenfall. They are my past, but this place is my future.

It has to be.

3

OVER THE BRIDGE, HAVENFALL LOOMS above us against the starry sky, towering at the end of a winding gray cobblestone path. Two guards materialize from the trees to check our IDs before they let us go any farther. They're human, but one wears a Fiorden fur cape and one a Byrnisian scaled jacket. Taya's eyes narrow in confusion at their strange clothes as she hands over her driver's license. I'm just glad the guards' swords are hidden beneath their outerwear. And that Taya doesn't see the rest of the guards, the ones I know are here, hidden in the trees, to make sure no unauthorized people get into the inn.

They wave us through, and faint strains of music float down to us as I lead Taya up. Excitement builds in my stomach when the inn's gold-lit windows come into view, and it's all I can do not to make a beeline for the door. Instead, I go with her to park her motorcycle in the stables, which Marcus has converted to double as a parking garage.

Taya cocks her head as we claim a stall next to a huge, gorgeous chestnut mare.

"Never seen a hotel like this before," she remarks, pocketing the keys.

In the low light, her locket seems to have the pearlescent shine of Haven silver, of Nathan's jacks, and I wonder if she's telling the truth about never having been to this town. Why would she lie about that, though?

"So where are you from?" I ask, trying to fill the silence.

Maybe I'm imagining it, but Taya seems to tense as we head up the path toward the inn's grandiose front door.

"All over," she says after a moment. "Foster care will do that to you." Her voice is mild, conversational, but there's the hint of a challenge in it. I detect it, because it's the same tone I've deployed on so many "concerned" onlookers in my own life. Tell them the facts, see how they react. The more syrupy-fake pity in their reaction, the more likely they're only talking to you to get the lurid details.

So I take a moment to figure out how to reply, reaching my hand out so it brushes the flowers lining the path. The soil here is rocky, hard to grow anything in, but the gardeners—with the help of a little Fiorden blood magic and a bit of Byrn-born rain in the dry times—have coaxed up small riots of brambles and rosebushes, their colors bright even in the dim of the evening. Birch trees line the path and vines drape picturesquely over the inn's cedar walls. Muffled music and light spill from the windows above our heads.

"Which was your favorite place?" I ask her finally. Interested but casual, not nosy. A question to do with her, not her tragic circumstances. Sure enough, pleasant surprise flickers over her face.

"Roswell," she says with a little smile. "I lived with an older couple. They were a little weird—said they'd seen UFOs, the whole thing—but kind. The town was shit but the desert was beautiful."

"Ugh, that sounds terrible." I fake-shudder. "Nothing but cactuses for miles around." I imagine a flat, sunbaked plain, dotted with prickly plants and scraggly trees, the heat beating down. No whispering pines, no fog-scented wind, no mountains like the ones surrounding us now like silent sentinels, towering and safe.

"It's 'cacti,' actually. And it's not just that. There's hills, sand dunes—"

She stops talking when we reach the inn's carved, polished double doors, which look like something out of a storybook castle. They stand open to reveal the grand entrance hall, cedar-paneled walls rising to a high, sloped ceiling and lit by torches in sconces along the walls. A split staircase frames an archway on the other end, blocked with a green curtain, but the hall is empty except for a side table bearing a crystal flagon of wine and a deep armchair where Graylin, Marcus's husband and the sole member of Havenfall's welcoming committee, sits.

Graylin looks up from his book—*Leaves of Grass*—as we enter. "Maddie! And . . ."

His voice trails off in confusion as he looks at Taya, then back at me, and rises from his chair. He's striking, over six feet tall with dark skin and light brown eyes, and despite spending so many years with Marcus on this side of the divide, he still has an otherworldly air about him. He's a scholar of the Realms and still visits Fiordenkill every so often to give lectures. His walk is fast but light-footed, like he could pass through the woods in winter without leaving footprints in the snow. And even though he's basically family, I still feel an instinctive rush of awe and unease, as I always do meeting anyone from the Realms. But the embrace he wraps me in is familiar, if a little sharp and bony.

"So good to see you," Graylin rumbles in his deep, faintly accented voice. Then he pulls back, his brow creasing. "But I thought you weren't coming this year."

I guess Marcus didn't get my texts, then. "I changed my mind," I say, aiming for breezy. "Hope that's okay."

"Of course."

Graylin studies me, blinking, and the soft look in his eyes makes me realize he probably knows about Mom and the death penalty. There's nothing in all the worlds I want less to talk about, so I speak quickly, beckoning Taya forward.

"Graylin, this is Taya. She applied for a landscaping job . . . ?"

Picking up my cue, Graylin turns to her and smiles. "Of course. Maddie will show you in and introduce you to Willow, the head of house. Won't you, Maddie? But first . . ."

He reaches back, catching the carafe of wine and two glasses in his long fingers. He pours and extends the drinks to us. "Won't you have a drink to celebrate the start of summer?"

Taya glances at me, uncertain, and I smile reassuringly, though a small pang of regret goes through me. We've built a weird little bond in the last half hour that it feels wrong to erase. But that's just my loneliness talking, I tell myself. Someone almost hitting you on their motorcycle's hardly a promising start to a friendship.

I tip the wine against my closed lips and swallow, pretending to drink, and Taya follows suit for real. I resist the urge to lick the flower-scented berry wine off my lips.

The effect on Taya is immediate. She blinks, dazed, and sways on her feet a little. Graylin takes her arm gently and settles her in his chair as she looks around, as if seeing the hall for the first time.

It's necessary for the staff to let go of their lives before and to accept the existence of magic, I remind myself. And then it's necessary for them to drink another glass before they leave at the end of the summer, to forget all they've seen at Havenfall and keep its secrets safe. So necessary that before the door to Solaria was sealed shut, the portal-keepers used to employ Solarians to track down anyone who let word slip about the other realms. Now, of course, that's not an option. So we use the wine—made from Fiorden-grown enchanted fruit—to remove the possibility of any leaks.

Of course, a few whispers have gotten out over the years. Marcus thinks that in ancient times, there were other *omphalos*, other places where the worlds converged, and that our myths—of dragons, vampires, djinni, fae, what have you—stem from other realms. The myths, the stories winding their way through human society, sometimes bear a strange similarity to the Realms. Graylin swears that Narnia's resemblance to Fiordenkill is more than just a coincidence.

"I'm so sorry we didn't pick you up, Maddie," Graylin says, sliding my duffel and backpack from my shoulders before I can knock over the wine. "Did you call?"

"It's my fault. I decided to come at the last minute."

"Well, of course you're welcome anytime. But I will warn you," he adds apologetically. "The Heiress returned this afternoon. So Marcus may be a bit . . . distracted."

"The Heiress?" Surprise colors my voice.

The elegant elderly woman has been a fixture at Havenfall for as long as I can remember; she has her own suite in the north wing. And she likes to be referred to as "Heiress," as if she never had a name—or has ditched it on purpose. She looks human, but moves with languor that seems a little unearthly. She claims to be a former member of the Fiordenkill High Court who wanted to spend her twilight years in the place she loves most, Havenfall. No one really believes that, nor do we know where she really comes from. She has tales and gossip from across all the worlds, and every summer when I'd return to the inn, she'd always have some little treat for me: Fiorden candy that tasted like sunlight or a Byrnisian glass figurine that whistled a song when you held it up in the wind.

That was until last year. When I arrived in June, she was gone, her suite empty, and all Marcus would tell me was that they'd had a falling out.

"Did they make up?"

"I don't know." Graylin's mouth flattens. "They still don't seem on very good terms, even though Marcus and I spent all afternoon moving her knickknacks into the suite. But your uncle won't tell me what's wrong."

"I'm sure they'll find a way to smooth things over," I say, happy to hear that the Heiress is back, but unnerved because it's not like Marcus to keep secrets—not from me, and especially not from Graylin.

Taya stands, a vacant smile on her face, and I find I can't meet her eyes. I know the wine, the enchantment, is necessary to not blow the secret of this place wide open. But somehow, I prefer the scowling version of her.

"You probably want to clean up and join the party. Will you just take, ah—"

"Taya," I supply, and she cocks her head at me, eyes bright.

"—Taya to the staff wing, and Willow can figure out where to put her." Graylin smiles at me. "I'll make sure your room is ready."

He waves us off, and my heart lifts as I beckon to Taya and lead her up the right side of the grand staircase, the thick red-and-gold rug soft beneath our feet. I can hear the music from beyond the green curtain, the strange haunting melodies of the Byrnisian Elemental Orchestra, the laughter of the delegates, and it takes everything I have not to turn and run toward the sound. It feels like I've been awake for weeks, like my visit to the prison this morning was a lifetime ago. I need to call Dad and break the news that I'm not in Nebraska, and my muscles are sore from sitting so long on a bus and straddling a motorcycle. But I'm here, and that's all that matters.

We reach the aged common room outside the staff wing, hearing chatter and laughter before we even round the corner, loud and loose with the influence of forgetting-wine. On the first day of employment, Willow always tells the human staff the basics about the Adjacent Realms and the peace summit, just enough so people can do their jobs and don't get freaked out if they get a glimpse of weather magic or a glimmer of scales. Surprisingly, everyone usually takes it more or less in stride. There's something about this place that makes people accept magic. That draws them in, along for the ride until the second dose of forgetting-wine in August.

In Byrn and Fiordenkill, the portals aren't a secret the way they are on Earth. Most of those who attend the summit are upper-crust, Fiorden nobles or elite Byrnisian soldiers. But there are civilians, too, in each delegation, who come to supplement the inn's human staff in housekeeping or security. Each spot is a huge honor, so I'm told, given out as a prize to the most promising youth among their peoples.

Those chosen tend to treat summers at Havenfall like one big exotic party, bringing wine and sweets to trade with the humans. This year is no exception.

Inside the staff lounge, worn velvet couches ring the wood-paneled room, filled now with mostly humans, but a few Fiorden and Byrnisian staff too. Several open bottles of wine balance precariously on side tables and armrests. Someone's dragged in an old boxy TV, and a young Fiorden boy whose ears are adorned with jewels—showcasing the wealth of his family—laughs uproariously at *Jeopardy!*

The Boulder kids, a group of four college students who've come to work here every year for three years, have coaxed some new maids into a louche version of beer pong, played with Fiorden wooden goblets and Byrnisian purple wine. I'm surprised Marcus let them back for another summer, even if they can't remember last year. One of them,

Jayden, snuck into the caves and stepped through the door to Fiorden-kill. The enforcers on the other side threw him back through the door-way, gasping and frostbitten, barely conscious. It's only because of Graylin's healing magic that Jayden still has all his fingers and toes. Marcus likes to remind me of that—that the magic of Havenfall isn't just flowers and wine and music. It's powerful and dangerous, a current that will drown you if you don't keep a good head on your shoulders.

At a massive desk in one corner sits Willow, the beautiful Byrnisian woman who serves as Marcus's chief of staff. She looks a bit like Amal Clooney, if Amal's skin glittered in a distinctly scale-like pattern under certain lights. If the whispers I've heard are true, she was high up in Byrnisian circles before some sort of affair gone wrong drove her from Oasis, Byrn's last habitable city-kingdom. If she resents being stuck here now, corralling frequently drunk humans into keeping Havenfall run-ning, she doesn't show it except by being ruthlessly effective.

She leaps out of her chair when she sees me, though, and hurries over to wrap me in a perfumed hug. She's been here my whole life and is almost as much family as Marcus and Graylin. Everyone at Havenfall—all the delegates, at least—just accept me. It's deeply weird to go from being the freak at home to everyone's friend. I feel like they see me as a novelty, a sidekick, not an equal to Marcus. But this sum-mer I'm ready to change that notion, ready to prove that I'm fit to move permanently to Havenfall when I turn eighteen—and take over as Mar-cus's successor one day.

"Madeline," she says warmly, holding me by my shoulders so she can appraise my appearance, a survey which leaves her looking, as usual, unimpressed. "You look a bit ragged."

I feel a smile forming all the same. "I'm sorry. I was on a bus all day."

"You can't go to the ballroom like this." Willow twirls a limp lock of my short hair around her finger.

"I won't. I promise." I turn to the side to look back at Taya, who's lingering in the doorway, uncertain. "But first—I brought you another staff member. I know she's late, but she's all right. She gave me a ride here."

I smile encouragingly at Taya and draw off to the side while Willow finds her name in her massive ledger. Soon, Taya has a job assignment—reporting to the groundskeeper to trim hedges at 8:00 a.m. sharp tomorrow—and a room key pressed into her palm.

Before she goes, Taya smiles at me. "Hey, Maddie, right?"

Surprised that she remembered my name after the wine, I nod.

"I'm Taya," she says. "Thanks for the tour."

Then she's gone.

I swallow down the weirdness of that interaction and turn back to Willow, hoisting my smile back on. "How's everything so far?" I ask her.

"Oh, chaos as usual," Willow says, slashing a hand dismissively through the air. "We've already had a minor catastrophe, when Marcus realized we didn't have enough wine for tonight, so I haven't had time to catch up on Realms gossip. Do you think you could sniff some out to save me from dying of boredom in my office?"

She lays a hand over her heart in mock seriousness, and I grin, happiness shooting through me. With the chatter of voices all around and the buzz of the TVs and the bits of otherworldly music floating up from downstairs, I feel buoyed by sound and life. So different from Sterling, where the reigning noise is empty silence punctuated by the thunder of highway traffic rushing by. When I was a kid, when I had just moved in with my dad, there were names too—names flying like knives. *Freak.*

Jailbird. On the playground, on the school bus, the few times I made the mistake of trying to play with kids in the neighborhood. Now I don't get the names so much, just despising or pitying stares that always feel like they're drilling holes in me.

"Where do you want me?" I ask Willow, pushing those thoughts away to get back to the present. Where I'm wanted, needed.

"I'll put you at the bar. Get those delegates drunk and report back on what's happening in my city." Her eyes gleam, hungry for information.

Half an hour and a quick shower later—quick because for all Havenfall's charms, the ancient pipes can never be relied upon to supply hot water—I plop down on the bed, wrapped in a fluffy blue bathrobe, and dial Dad's number. To calm the anxiety that rumbles in my stomach as the phone rings, I look around my room, focusing on each of the familiar objects in turn to calm myself. The shelf loaded with impressive-looking tomes on Realms history, which I must have forgotten to return to the library last summer. The small window and the starry mountain-broken sky I can see through it. The quilt beneath me, made of interlocking diamonds of Byrn silk and Fiordenkill velvet; a gift from Marcus to my mom when I was born. Nate had one, too, but I don't know where it is.

"Hello?" Dad's voice breaks off the melancholy thought. "Maddie?"

I hear the muted hum of the TV in the background. I imagine him in our cramped living room, exhausted after a long day of fixing wiring and repairing power lines, kicked back on the recliner—but worried, now, because of me.

In a second, the wistfulness is gone and the nerves are back. "Hi, Dad." I fiddle with the edge of the quilt. "How's it going?"

"Fine." Dad sounds wary. He knows something is up. "Marla's gone to pick up a pizza and we're about to watch the game. How about you? Have you made it to your grandma's yet?"

I know I should feel guilty about coming here behind his back. I should. But it's hard to feel guilty when such a great relief is filling me up, lifting my spirits. I feel like I can breathe for the first time in months. But I try for a contrite tone when I say, "No. Dad, I . . . I went to Havenfall instead."

The sound of the TV clicks off. There's a long silence, and I twist the quilt between my fingers, trying to parse it. Is he angry? Disappointed?

When he speaks, though, it's with resignation. "Maddie. You should have told me."

"You didn't want me here." Even though I don't mean to, I can hear that I sound defensive.

"No, I didn't," Dad replies. "I don't think it's good for you to be there. There's a whole world for you to explore."

There are whole worlds here too, I want to say. But I stay quiet, knowing Dad doesn't know about the Adjacent Realms, about the magic. He's visited the inn—I have a dim memory of the four of us, Mom, Dad, Nate, and me, visiting for Christmas when I was very small—but only in the winter when it was empty.

"I'm learning things here too," I tell Dad. "Marcus is teaching me about the business side of the inn, how to balance a checkbook and stuff."

That's a stretch, but I want it to be true. This summer, I'm going to focus on learning, on being a help, so that Marcus will let me stay full-time after I graduate next year. What Dad doesn't get is that Havenfall isn't about hiding away from the world. I'm creating a life for myself in the one place I can really make a difference. I failed Mom and Nate years ago, and Havenfall is all that's left of our family. I won't run away from that.

"I had to, Dad," I say, emotion leaking into my voice in spite of my best efforts. "I'm sorry. Don't be mad."

"I'm not mad." He sighs. "I know you've had a hard year, what with . . . the news about your mother. And you're almost an adult; you're old enough to be making your own choices. But I want you to study for your SAT while you're there. You hear me?"

Tears gather at the edges of my eyes. "I will. And I'll tell Grandma."

"No, don't worry about it," he says wearily. "I'll call her. Right after I call your uncle and tell him to keep an eye on you."

I swipe the tears off my cheeks. "Thanks."

"Be safe, Maddie." His voice goes a little quieter, concern entering it. "I worry about you, you know."

"I know."

And I do. I grip the blanket, sitting with the guilt. I know Dad cares about me; I know he only wants what's best for me. We just have different ideas of what that is. He doesn't deserve my lies.

But I remember being a little kid and telling him about doorways and magic, and the way he grinned and ruffled my hair and told me never to lose that imagination. At some point, I started to understand why Mom never told him it was all real. The lie isn't hurting anyone, and telling the truth would mean a coin toss between upending everything Dad knows about the world and having him think I'm crazy. The image of my face in Mirror Lake lingers behind my eyes as I tell him I love him and hang up, feeling guilt and relief in equal measure.

After coaxing my short, messy hair into something resembling a style, I open the closet, considering the bright array of Byrn- and Fiordenkill-inspired clothes that have waited patiently for me since last summer. My usual jeans–Doc Martens–canvas jacket combo won't cut it in the ballroom, so I pull on velvet riding breeches and my favorite Byrnisian jacket. It's dark blue linen with gold buttons and panels of black shining scales marching down the sleeves. Then to balance that out—Marcus always says I should take care not to seem partial to one Realm—I stack jewels in my ears in the Fiorden style. Brekken and I made the piercings the summer we were both twelve, hiding in my room with a needle and candle. It could have been a disaster, but he did careful work, two even lines of piercings along the edges of my ears.

I choose three jewels for each ear—blue, green, and silver, the colors that symbolize peace between the last three Adjacent Realms. I swipe gray powder over my eyelids and mauve over my lips, and for the first time in a long time I look in the mirror and smile.

My bedroom is at the end of the Fiordenkill wing, a big room with a dormer window facing west. The view of the sunset over the mountains is the best in Havenfall, and as a bonus, there's a shortcut—a narrow, out-of-the-way staircase used mostly by the staff, but which takes me past the hallway where the Solarian guest rooms used to be.

Now the hallway is sealed off with pine boards, since no one else wants to sleep in those rooms. It would be cowardly to take the long way around just to avoid passing a covered-up doorway, so I rarely do, but just walking past it on the landing always makes ice cascade down my spine. There's something about the idea that Solarians used to sleep in rooms just like mine, with cedar eaves and windows looking out over the mountains.

The wooden boards have warped with age, opening up cracks between each wide enough to see through. After the Solarians were banished, my great-great-grandmother painted the walls and ceiling in that part of the dormitory a pleasing light blue, scrubbed the floors to a high shine that still glints underneath the cobwebs, but no one was willing to stay there. Annabelle couldn't erase the memories of rough places where claws gouged the walls, bloodstains on the floor.

As kids, Brekken and I once dared each other to peek through the cracks and see what we could see. But when I knelt and pressed my face to the wood, a shadow scurrying across the floor scared me so bad I jolted back and almost fell down the stairs. Brekken caught me and held me to his chest until I stopped shaking, already chivalrous at ten. After that, I looked up what happened in the library. Back when Havenfall's tunnels opened up to three worlds instead of two, back when guards surrounded the grounds both to keep humans out and Solarians in—because unlike the rest of us, they can travel throughout the worlds without getting sick—a political disagreement ended when a Solarian delegate murdered a Byrnisian princess and ate her heart right out of her chest.

After the war that followed, the door to Solaria in the tunnels beneath was closed, and the Solarians' old guest rooms have stood empty ever since. Too many bad memories and mojo. Even the human cleaners, who don't know what happened, are put off by this part of the inn, as evidenced by the thick layer of dust on the floor of the stairwell, thick enough that as I walk past, I leave footprints behind me. *The Solarians are gone*, I remind myself.

But they aren't, not entirely. One killed my brother in Sterling eleven years ago. It might still be out there. Who knows how many more might have slipped through the dragnets.

We don't talk about such things at Havenfall, though. The guests would be horrified if they knew how Nathan died, why my mother ended up in Sterling Correctional when, despite all her flaws, she didn't kill my brother. I've never told anyone except Brekken and Marcus about that, because the important part of the story is something that would threaten the very peace that was brokered here so many years ago, the reason for the summit every year. Marcus just told the rest of the delegates that his nephew had died and his sister had moved away. It wasn't technically a lie.

Marcus always told me the purpose of the summit is to remember the Accord that allied Byrn, Fiordenkill, and Haven. But if you drill down deeper, if you read the Accord, the real reason behind it is darker. It's *Solaria.*

I shake the dark thoughts away. Now isn't the time to get dragged into a dark mood. I have a job to do. And someone to see.

When I come down the stairs, the ballroom is filled with people. They're spread out below me, and even though I've seen this tableau so many times before, I stop for a second and drink it all in.

Havenfall. At last.

The peace summit officially begins tomorrow, but it looks like most of the delegates have already arrived. The denizens of the three worlds practically glitter, the crystal chandelier shedding light on their bright hair, feathery hats, and silk scarves. Staff, human and otherwise, flit between them with trays of prettily arranged snacks and bubbly drinks. Voices and laughter in three languages rise up to me. A handful of guards—mostly humans who report to Sal Fernandez, Marcus's trusty head of security—are stationed at intervals along the mirrored walls. More a formality than anything—Havenfall hasn't needed defending since before I was born—but their presence makes me feel safer.

In the corner, the Elemental Orchestra plays—three musicians using strange instruments with Byrnisian magic. One plays something like a harp, but instead of plucking the strings she plies them with small flames spurting from her fingertips. Another produces tinkling sounds by spinning ice over a wooden frame and smashing it with a mallet, over and over. And a gold pipe contraption wraps the small stage, emitting

41

mournful notes whenever the players send air into it with a thrust of a palm. It looks like a steampunk game of Mousetrap, but the sound is wistful and wild all at once. The elemental magic that flows through Byrnisian blood never ceases to amaze me.

The ballroom is huge, and it seems even bigger because of mirrors lining the walls on either side, while the far windows show a magnificent moonlit view of the mountains and Mirror Lake. I should be looking for my uncle, but I can't stop my eyes from scanning the crowd for someone else instead. For broad shoulders and hair that flames red in the light. His name is stuck in my head like the song of the summer on the radio. *Brekken. Brekken. Brekken.* I don't know what I'm going to do when I find him, but my gut says this is the year to do something, say something, make something happen. Maybe it's the leftover adrenaline from the motorcycle ride, or my fears about not being welcomed back, but I feel brave, maybe a little reckless.

I slip behind the bar and pour myself a glass of wine, figuring I might as well get started on that whole courage thing, when—

"Maddie!"

My uncle's voice to my left. I stop and turn as he emerges out of the crowd—the Heiress at his side.

Despite the press of the crowded room, I can almost see the distance between them, like a block of glass. Marcus is short and trim with an easy manner, curly black hair and beard, and kind eyes. He's always gotten along with everyone, especially the Heiress, despite how mismatched they look at the moment—him in his outdated suit and her dressed like some kind of a dispossessed dowager empress. Tonight the Heiress wears a velvet gown. Her silver braid circles her head like a crown. Her expression is especially cool and untouchable. By contrast, Marcus's hair sticks up especially high, and I know that means he's been nervously running his hands through it.

"Maddie," Marcus says again, giving me a side hug, which is all he has room for in the crowded room. "I just talked to your dad on the phone. I'm so sorry for not picking you up, I completely missed your text—"

"No problem," I interrupt, hugging him back. "Someone gave me a ride." I pull back and smile at him. "Thanks for letting me stay."

One side of his mouth quirks up. "Well, you're always welcome."

I know he probably feels a little guilty for enabling my truancy, but Marcus understands that Havenfall is my world. That, at least, I can count on.

We part and I turn to the Heiress, not sure what to say or how to act. Should I ignore the obvious tension between them? Should I just pretend everything is normal?

"Madeline." The Heiress greets me by my full name as always, giving me a smile that's as warm as ever despite the chilliness between her and Marcus.

So I guess that's where we're at.

"Just the woman I was hoping to see," she says kindly.

"Lady Heiress." I pull a wineglass from the cupboard behind me, making sure to get one of the fancy ones with the gold rims. "May I make you a drink?"

"Why, my dear girl, I haven't seen you in far too long. We have much to catch up on." She clasps my arm briefly, her plump hand dry and warm. "But, yes, a spot of champagne, if you please."

The Heiress claims that she's writing a history of Havenfall. Every year she invites people from all three worlds up to her suite for tea and pastries and long, meticulous interviews. She must have an encyclopedia's worth of material by now. But no one's read any of her supposed epic, and there are whispers that it's all nonsense, that the notes she takes are air and fluff.

43

If she's not writing, though, what is she doing here, in our world? And why did she come back to Havenfall?

As the trio of musicians kicks into a faster number, I hide the disappointment that Brekken's still not here and I pass her the champagne.

"How's the book coming?" I try to sound casual and pretend I don't notice anything wrong between her and Marcus.

She gives the same answer she always gives, an elegant shrug and a little sigh. But then, just when I've opened my mouth to reply, she goes on.

"There are so many worlds that have been closed off forever," she says sadly. "How am I to write about all the Adjacent Realms when their citizens aren't here for me to speak to?"

A chill settles over my skin. The Heiress told me once how beautiful the Solarian delegates were said to have been, whether in human form to parley with everyone else at the summit, or in their beast forms, running through the mountains under the moonlight. She said the Solarians were the most free of all the peoples, and I'll never forgot the raw curiosity I heard in her voice.

"But some worlds are better closed off," I point out. "You don't have to speak to Solarians to know why their door was destroyed . . ."

Because the victims—Fiorden, Byrnisian, human—remember. I remember.

Marcus stiffens beside us. He casts me a wary look that warns, *Watch what you say.*

The Heiress flaps her hand, like it goes without saying, as a Byrnisian couple in chainmail-like silver tunics pass close by. It's frowned upon even to speak of Solaria here at Havenfall, as if putting the word out in the air will summon the real monsters. So I have to keep my true thoughts at bay, even when I will never—can never—forget my brother died at the claws of someone from that cursed world. I wonder again how many there are still on Earth, hidden shapeshifters, preying on human souls.

A short, uncomfortable silence passes, and then the Heiress sighs again and looks out over the crowd. "Of course," she says. "The less said of Solarians, the better."

I still feel cold. I want to go find Brekken, but you can't just walk away from the Heiress, not without being dismissed.

"What happened last summer?" I blurt out. "Why did you leave?"

Even though he's pretending not to listen, Marcus frowns, and the woman turns her steely eyes on me. It takes effort to stand still and not apologize or walk back my question.

"Madeline," she says evenly. Her face is blank, her voice inflection-less, but what she says next sends a current of apprehension through me. "Much like Solarians, sometimes the past is better kept locked away."

4

THE HEIRESS'S STERN PRESENCE SEEMS to have kept people away from the bar—but once she retires to her room for the night, delegates flock toward me, calling out the names of different wines and spirits. I like this work—it keeps my hands busy and the conversations I over-hear are interesting, giving me plenty of details to tuck away and smuggle to Willow. Quickly, my muscles grow accustomed to the task of pouring wine and champagne.

The great thing about Havenfall—well, one of them—is that I'm the least remarkable person here. The Fiordens and Byrnisians come with stories straight out of soap operas—every summer, every summit, there's new gossip about a Fiorden duchess falling in love with a low-born knight, or a lone Byrnisian soldier fending off a lightning storm that threatened Oasis. Fiordenkill has ice storms that white out the whole world, and Byrn has been so ravaged by magical storms that almost everyone there has been backed into the one city standing. Amidst all that, no one gives a shit if I live in a mobile home, or if I have short hair, or if I like guys and girls both, or if my mom's in prison.

Marcus sits at one end of the long, polished counter, talking to two delegates I vaguely know—Lonan, a yellow-haired Byrn man who married a fellow delegate here last year, and Nessa, a Fiorden woman in a daring green gown. I listen in. Nessa is fretting about one of the Fiordens' favorite gossip topics: Enetta, the beautiful but feckless princess of a Fiorden island country who is, unthinkably, late to the summit.

"It doesn't matter when she arrives," I jump in, taking the carafe to refill Nessa's glass.

Marcus raises his eyebrows at me, and I smile back. *Look. I can play the room too. You can trust me.*

"Havenfall is always open to her," I say to Nessa. "I look forward to meeting the princess whenever she gets here."

I don't fully understand the magic governing the doorways, but I know they're more stable during the summer—every year on the solstice, all the Realms come into some sort of alignment. We have our longest day of the year; Byrn has a lunar eclipse of all three of their moons; Fiordenkill has a spectacular shower of shooting stars. Some thread runs through all the worlds on the solstice that allows large numbers of people to pass through the doorways. At other times, they're less safe—people crossing through can cause strange charges in the air of Haven, or make the ground tremble.

Marcus and Willow carefully plan a schedule of departures from the inn at the end of the summit—the rulers of the Realms leave after two weeks, while the lesser ones stay longer, hashing out the details of the broad-strokes agreements made by their higher-ups. It's not ideal that the princess is late, but one person passing through after the solstice isn't enough of a risk to keep her away and squander the goodwill of the Fiorden delegation.

I wave a hand, as if to send the political topic away. "Lonan, where is your lovely bride this year?"

The Byrnisian man looks momentarily surprised to be addressed by me, but then he smiles, and his too-many teeth betray him as not being human. I wonder what he would look like in his home world. "She is with child," he says, jovially, "and you know it's not our way to travel in her present condition."

"May the earth bear her up," I say, remembering just in time that Lonan and his wife possess earth magic. I busy myself straightening the rows of goblets on the back counter, hoping to hear more about the wild princess, but Nessa throws a glance at Lonan and excuses herself. She shouldn't have spoken ill about royalty in front of a Byrn delegate, I realize. But everyone trusts Marcus. Could I ever fill that role, hearing out the troubles of a world I will never see, soothing anxieties and balancing egos with a few well-chosen words?

Last summer, I studied Adjacent Realms politics from books I "borrowed" from Marcus's study. So when the Elemental Orchestra kicks up a faster song and delegates fly from the bar to dance, I take the opportunity to lean across the marble toward my uncle. "Is this the year you're finally going to let me sit in on council meetings?"

"Not yet. Maybe next year."

His smile is thin, but I scarcely notice. Because just then someone appears on the stairs across the room.

Broad shoulders, copper penny hair, and features sharp as a knife. Brekken.

I feel a smile spread across my face.

He looks different somehow. It takes me a moment to realize why, but then it hits me all at once. He's dressed like a soldier, a cloak of fur fastened at his throat. His hair is combed back and tucked behind his jeweled ears—red for his family—and his tunic is embroidered with a pattern of leaves and swords. Brekken came of age this year and joined the High Court's army. It was everything he'd been dreaming of since we were children.

And then, finally, he sees me. Brekken catches my eye as if our gazes have their own gravitational field. His face breaks into a broad smile as he waves. In an instant I forget all the formality. Almost without meaning to, I take a step toward the stairs.

"I need you for a moment longer, Maddie."

Marcus's voice snaps me out of the reverie. Brekken has to wait. Marcus and Havenfall are supposed to come first. I turn to see Marcus's worried expression. His eyes follow my trajectory over to Brekken on the stairs. But in a flash, his smile returns.

"Can you go get a bottle of the Fiordenkill champagne from my office?" he asks.

Disappointment and impatience flare through me. "Of course. Just give me a minute." I take a step away, but Marcus's hand on my shoulder stops me.

"Brekken's a soldier now, Maddie," Marcus says, his voice low and serious.

"Okaaay." I draw out the word. "So what? What are you getting at?"

"So he's bound to the High Court."

"All the more reason to go congratulate him." There's a beat of awkwardness. "Isn't that the *proper* thing to do? I'll get the bubbly after I say hello."

My confusion must show on my face, because my uncle hurries to add, "Yes, but . . . just . . . don't spend all your time together. You know how people talk."

"No, I don't know." My voice comes out sharp and I can't help it. "What will people say?"

And why should I care?

"We are the portal-keepers. We have to stay neutral, Maddie. No one can think we're showing favoritism between the Realms. That is our job. Our responsibility. That is, if you want to run Havenfall one day."

"Of course I want that," I say, waspish. "You know that. More than anything."

Anything except maybe Brekken.

What Marcus is saying makes sense, but he's talking to me like I'm a kid, and it rankles me.

"You're married to a Fiorden," I point out.

"Graylin was never a soldier."

I swallow, trying to stay calm even though it feels like the bottom of my stomach has dropped out. The horrible thing is that Marcus's right; I know how careful he is to split his time evenly between Fiordens and Byrnisians. The whole point of Havenfall and the peace summit is to provide a neutral zone for the Adjacent Realms. Fiordenkill and Byrn are the only two left, making it more important than ever to sustain the peace.

But my stupid brain never connected that with *Brekken*. We can't be together. And now my eyes are burning.

I clench my fist tight. I cannot, I will not, cry in front of Marcus and the delegates and everyone. I know Havenfall isn't perfect, but it's supposed to be mine, the summer refuge that makes up for the shitty rest of the year. Strange that a place with so many rigid rules, regulations, and protocols would have, all this time, felt to me like *freedom*.

"What we do here is dangerous, Maddie," Marcus is saying. He smiles at me, gently, but his eyes are serious. "We need to be all things to everyone to maintain the balance. This place, what happens here, is important and I wouldn't trade it for the world, but I don't want to see you hurt again."

Again.

He pauses, twirling his wineglass in his hands, then looks back up at me. And I know he's trying to find the words for something he tells me every year, in his roundabout way.

This is our history. Our legacy. To be Innkeeper requires courage, diplomacy, and the will to carry out the greater good. Not everyone is cut out to do this work. It won't be easy, but you're strong.

The idea fills my head like an oil spill. It triggers the dread that always eats away at the corner of my mind, the fear that with the wrong words or actions, I could lose Havenfall. I could misstep and turn the delegates against me, or let the secret slip and ruin everything. Since I was a child, this place has been the only place that has ever mattered to me—the inn and its people have felt like home all these years. Without it, I'd have nothing.

Sometimes the past is better kept locked away.

I clutch my key ring, feeling the metal edges of the cat-ear brass knuckles scrape into my palm, focusing on the minor physical pain to chase the other kind away while I go around to the other side of the bar. I need to get some air. I need to talk to Brekken.

If I ran into Brekken on my way to the cellar, that could hardly be read as favoritism, could it?

Anyway, all these delegates have seen us play together as children, weaving through feet in the ballroom, making a mess of the gardens, splashing around in Mirror Lake. It's hard to think everything has to change now.

He comes into view and my heart flips, the dark worries of moments ago bubbling down to a low simmer. I want to launch myself at him and throw my arms around his neck, but Fiordens aren't big huggers, so I stop an arm's length from him, my heart banging against my ribs. Just as well, as it turns out, because he has two glasses of something sparkling in his hands.

"Maddie," he says, and his eyes are the exact shade of indescribable blue as the mountains outside. He's grinning. "I am so, so glad to see you."

"Well, I scarcely recognize you," I tease, though the effect is a little ruined by the breathless way my voice comes out. "What's it like being a soldier?"

Brekken smiles, unmistakable pride lighting his eyes. This is all he's wanted since we were little kids, since he made me practice sword fighting with him with sticks we found in the garden, or we sat upstairs in my room, playacting battles with my stuffed animals. He passes me one of the glasses, and I take a sip to find it's sweet. My chest warms.

"It's difficult," he says. "And tedious sometimes, and cold."

"What do they have you doing?" I ask curiously. Fiordenkill is at peace as far as I know, both with Haven and Byrn and internally, among the snowbound city-states that make up that world.

"Oh, you know." Brekken's smile widens. He can't quite hide how proud he is to finally be a soldier. "Nothing too exciting. Collecting taxes, protecting trade ports."

"Protecting the palace from giant bears?"

Fiordenkill has a lot of the same animals we do—bears, wolves, deer—but they're all on a giant scale. Deer the size of horses, bears twice as tall as me, even on all fours. Or so Brekken tells me.

"Occasionally," he says. "Not often enough. But it's an honor to serve the High Court. And look, I have a sword."

He reaches down and pulls it a few inches from its leather scabbard before letting it slide back down, and I catch a glimpse of silver and rubies.

"You'd better get me one too," I tease. "Or I won't last long in our garden fights."

Brekken grins and starts to say something, but his words die off as he sees something over my shoulder.

I follow his gaze to see a young Byrnisian man gliding in our direction, someone I've never seen before—I know, because I would remember. He looks around our age, maybe a little older, though Byrnisians age slower than humans. He's tall and broad-shouldered with sharp features and gray eyes, and his pale skin and silvery-blond hair have a weird metallic tint, like he's been dunked in molten silver and only mostly rinsed off.

As he reaches us, Brekken bows, and I instinctively do the same. It's only then that I notice an older man behind him, just as tall but unnaturally thin, dressed in black with bangles of Haven silver stacked around his wrists and throat.

"No need for that." The younger man's voice pulls us back up, deep and resonant. "I'm only a guest here, same as you."

"Your Highness," Brekken says, and a shiver of awe drops down my spine as I realize who this man must be. I've heard stories about the Silver Prince. He's the one who created the massive city of Oasis when he was scarcely more than a boy, erecting a magical barrier to shelter its people from the elemental storms that have nearly decimated Byrn. *Imagine if one guy single-handedly stopped climate change,* is how Marcus explained it to me once. The Silver Prince rules that city now, and most of the world's inhabitants with it—everyone in Byrn lives in Oasis, except for a handful of nomads who value their independence enough to brave the lightning and hurricanes and burning wind.

Looking up now into the Silver Prince's deep-set eyes, I find myself doing math in my head, trying to match the stories I've heard to the young man towering over me. He's probably around twenty-three, twenty-four—not that much older than me, but I can almost *feel* the power rolling off him like a force field. His magic must be unimaginably powerful to have kept the Oasis storms at bay. He's never come to the summits before, since he was the only thing standing between Byrn's last habitable city and destruction. I guess the fact that he's here means the storms must have finally calmed.

Willow never thought it would happen. She'd always joke that she was lucky to be banished, that she was going to live longer than everyone stuck in a dying Byrn. Seeing the Prince now, his serenity and power, I can't help but feel a little awed.

"Soldier," he says, dipping his head toward Brekken. Then he looks at me and tilts his head, considering. "And you must be Madeline."

There aren't many humans here other than summer staffers, and it's not a surprise he recognizes me. Still, it's weird. I'm used to keeping my head down and avoiding everyone. So I'm caught off guard to be on a first-name basis with a prince from another world.

The Prince doesn't introduce the other man—a servant, his bodyguard? He just zeroes in on me, those iron-colored eyes holding mine, and says, "You seem troubled."

Brekken looks sharply at me. Fiordenkill and Byrn don't have the same rules for small talk as we do. Most of the Fiordens who come to Havenfall would sooner swallow coals than talk about feelings, and Byrnisians, on the other hand, prize truth and forthrightness.

My stomach turns. I *am* troubled, but I don't want Brekken to know that. Yet I can't be rude to Oasis's and, by default, Byrn's ruler. I can't jeopardize Havenfall's relationship with an entire world.

"It's nothing," I say, forcing a smile to my face. "I'm just tired."

The Silver Prince tilts his head slowly. It's a little unnerving.

"Is that true?" His voice isn't reprimanding, just curious.

The man wearing silver is a silent, eerie presence behind him, his colorless eyes taking in everything.

Brekken moves forward, as if to step between us, but I hook my pinkie around his to stop him. His actions carry more weight now that he's a soldier, and my feelings aren't worth an inter-world incident.

"It's just . . ." I choose my words carefully, trying to find a version of the truth that will satisfy the Silver Prince. "This is the most important place in the world to me. It's not just a party that happens every summer. It's my home."

As soon as the words are out, I regret them. Brekken's eyes widen, and it feels as though I've given too much away.

"Your home?" the Silver Prince asks.

His words are affectless; we could be discussing anything. Still, my skin prickles. *Why is he spending his first visit to the Adjacent Realms—a visit that must have been in the works for years—asking the sixteen-year-old Innkeeper's niece about her feelings? What is that Byrnisian intuition telling him about me?*

"After this summer, Marcus will decide if I can stay for good." I look at myself in the mirror along the wall. The gems in my ears glitter in the low light, and laughter and music weave together all around like a beautiful net. "It's—a lot of pressure is all."

Then, I feel stupid. The Silver Prince saved his people from the elemental storms that obliterated almost the whole of his world. He maintains the barriers that keep everyone in Oasis alive. What do I know about pressure?

But when he smiles, it's sympathetic. "These are dangerous times," he says. His eyes meet mine in the reflection. He seems to give off his own light; I understand why his people follow him. But he gives me the feeling of driving down winding mountain roads. It's awe-inspiring, despite the fact that—or maybe because—it's a long way down. There's a feeling of power coiled inside the Prince. The air crackles a little around him.

"But," he adds, "I sense danger is familiar to you."

I look toward him, surprised and wary. "What do you mean?"

An image flashes, as it so often does—my mother and brother cowering in the kitchen as a dark shadow bears down on them. My brother's piercing scream. But I push it away, panic gathering in me, as if somehow the memory will spill out into the Silver Prince's sight. Like he could see how I hid, how I let a Solarian kill Nathan.

"I understand Marcus's fears," the Silver Prince says, still affectless. "But strife shapes us into who we are meant to be. And places us *where* we are meant to be. Don't you think?"

Even though he's a total stranger, something in me leaps at the words, overjoyed to be seen. I nod, my pulse racing for some reason.

Brekken clears his throat, and the Prince smiles. Even his teeth have a silvery tint. I wonder what his life is like at home in dangerous and wild Byrn. A place ravaged by storms born of elemental magic run amok.

"Well, I must be off," he says. "It was a pleasure to meet you both." He inclines his head at Brekken and me in turn, and then sweeps away.

It's not until he's gone that I think to ask what he meant by *dangerous times*.

Brekken turns to me, a crease between his eyebrows. "Are you all right?"

"Of course." I let out a laugh that, somewhat to my surprise, is real.

Maybe he's right, maybe Marcus is right to be afraid. The Silver Prince certainly seemed dangerous, as does Brekken in a way, with his sharp-cut uniform and eyes I could lose myself in. But that just makes it all the more thrilling, my knowledge of these people and theirs of me.

Havenfall might be dangerous, but I am equal to it. I'm part of it. I belong here, more than anywhere else.

I take a sip of my drink. Fizzy heat rushes down my throat, warms my chest. Feeling emboldened, I pluck the other drink from Brekken's hand and put them on a side table. Then I do what I wanted to do earlier and twine my arms around his neck as a new song begins. I'm already taking a risk ignoring Marcus's request. I might as well take advantage of this bravery while it lasts.

The knot in my gut unwinds as his arms come up around me. The scent of snow fills my nose, and his cheek is cool against mine. It makes me wonder what it'd be like to experience the winter chill of Fiordenkill. I've only seen glimpses of it through the open door in the caves below the inn, but I imagine snow-cloaked mountains, ice shining over lakes, castles with fires glimmering in their windows. With the exception of Havenfall as a safe zone, Byrnisians and Fiordens can't travel outside their worlds without deteriorating, and humans can't visit Fiordenkill or Byrn for more than an hour or so. People have tried to make it before, and the books say it's a horrible way to die—like drowning.

But it's not impossible. Once, when I was a little kid, a Byrnisian runner made it as far as Telluride before collapsing. Marcus had to send in a cleanup crew with bribes and berry wine to ply the skiers who'd seen a scaled man dying in the snow. I daydream, sometimes, that someone will find a way around our bodies' limits. About seeing Fiordenkill at Brekken's side.

Brekken pulls back, his hands on my arms, and looks at me with warm eyes that shift into concern as they travel over my face.

"Maddie," he says, his voice soft and low. "Can we go somewhere else? Alone?"

I nod, something fizzy as champagne bubbling through me. "Took you long enough. Let's get out of here."

5

AFTER DELIVERING MARCUS'S BOTTLE OF champagne from his office, Brekken and I make it out of the inn unnoticed, another bottle of wine clutched in Brekken's long fingers. We slink through the gardens and into the barn, past a few shiny cars and Taya's motorcycle. I laugh out loud when a snort from the chestnut mare makes Brekken jump back.

"It's just a horse."

"We don't have these back home." Brekken looks indignantly at me, then stretches a cautious hand up to pat the animal's cheek. He's clearly doing it for my benefit, and I have to choke back another laugh as the horse snorts and he flinches. "They're so . . . large."

"Says the boy whose army rides giant *wolves* around," I tease.

"Our wolves aren't nearly this big. And they don't have sharp hooves."

I swallow a laugh. I shouldn't be uncharitable—I know that in centuries past, Fiordenkill was at war with Tural, a world peopled by centaurs. You can still find the odd hoofprint in some of the caves beneath the inn. But that world was closed off sometime in the 1700s, so it's hard to take Brekken's fear seriously.

"You and I have very different ideas of what's dangerous."

I think again of the Silver Prince's words as I go to the ladder that leads to the barn loft and climb up, reaching a second floor filled with hay. The walls are covered with rakes and old harrows and tools I don't know the purpose of. A hole in the roof reveals the night sky. I swear there are somehow more stars above Havenfall than there are elsewhere, and the moon always seems to hang low. As if the heavenly bodies can sense the doorways at Havenfall and are huddling in close, hoping to catch a breeze from another world.

As I plop down on a hay bale and wait for Brekken, it occurs to me why Marcus and I disagree. We, too, have different ideas of what constitutes danger. Marcus thinks it's Havenfall, the soldiers and swords, cliffs and deep pools, the doorways in the cellar, the current of politics that simmers beneath everything, even as all the delegates drink and laugh together. And maybe that is dangerous. But not nearly as dangerous as staying in Sterling would be. I hate how everyone looks at me like I'm about to break or explode, making it feel like a self-fulfilling prophecy. Nothing is as dangerous as the loneliness that wraps around me sometimes, as cold and real as an iron manacle.

When Brekken climbs up too, the sudden silence rings loud. He stops and stands framed against the hole in the roof, a soldier's silhouette, and for a second the expression on his face is strange, still and uncertain. We can hear the music and noise from the summit, distantly, but the two of us might as well be in another world. Memories swirl through my mind like petals on the wind: him as a boy, the two of us chasing beetles or climbing trees after birds' nests. The bond between us is still there, but it's changed into something taut and charged, something that steals my breath.

But then he smiles, and unfastens his cloak, and it's like no time has passed between us at all. He spreads it over the hay bale and comes to sit beside me, legs crossed. We've done this every summer for ten years, since he first appeared in Havenfall when he was seven. He was accompanying his delegate mother. It was the first summer after that horrible night. I was still shell-shocked after my mom's arrest, after what happened to my brother.

We were the youngest residents of Havenfall then, too young to be part of the festivities, so Marcus packed us away to my room. Our babysitter was a maid who slipped away after half an hour—but it didn't matter. Brekken and I were already in our own little bubble, entranced with each other. I was more surprised that he seemed fascinated with me too. Not for the reasons I was already coming to expect from people. Not because he'd seen the picture of me in the news, my round face red and wet with tears as a bailiff pulled me from a courtroom, usually accompanied by Mom's mug shot and the moniker "Goodwin Lane Killer."

This beautiful boy—even as a kid he was beautiful—was fascinated with *me*. My freckles and short fingers, my toys and love of horses that I'm pretty sure made him think for a while I was some sort of hero, facing up to those terrifying beasts. That first summer with him was the first time I felt like a person again, running around Havenfall and getting underfoot, teaching him knock-knock jokes (he never quite mastered the format), and exploring the woods around the inn, even though we weren't allowed outside, because everyone thought a Solarian might still be on the loose.

That entrancement's never faded for me, but I've no idea if the same is true for Brekken as he sits across from me, deftly uncorking the wine bottle. I don't know if he thinks about me when he's not in Havenfall, when he's going about his day, riding wolves or sharpening his sword or lying in bed in the barracks. I don't know how he feels about a lot of things. But then he distracts me by reaching into a satchel on his belt and bringing something out. A gilt-paged book only as long and wide as his hand, bound in dark red silk that gleams in the moonlight. The language on the spine isn't familiar to me, but a chill sweeps through me as Brekken translates.

"*Iavalar*. Poems," he says, looking up at me with a smile. He presses the volume into my hands, still warm from being close to his body. "By Stimarya, one of Myr's most famous poets. Some people think her verse sentimental, but I've always loved it."

I blush, running my finger along the smooth edge of the book. "Thank you so much," I whisper. Brekken has always brought me gifts from Fiordenkill, but they're usually little trinkets, jeweled earrings or good-luck charms of tiny carved-stone animals or, when we were littler, pretty rocks or leaves he found in the woods. Nothing as personal as this before. "You'll have to teach me what they mean."

"No need." Brekken reaches over, opens the book and holds it open in my hand with two fingers. "I translated them already."

I look down, my skin heating at his closeness. Sure enough, the printed text of a poem in the strange language of Myr runs down the right page, but on the left, Brekken's careful, compact handwriting fills the page with blue ink. I make out a few phrases—*snow like fleece falls over us; the tender stars hang low*—before Brekken laughs, low in his throat, and shuts the book.

"Don't read them now or I'll be self-conscious." He takes the book and slips it into my jacket pocket, an easy, familiar gesture. "How about you save them for the fall?"

I shift my weight, pleased and embarrassed, and the loft floor creaks slightly under us. Maybe it's Marcus's words earlier—*You know how people talk*—or maybe it's just how Brekken looks in his soldier's uniform, the embroidery on his tunic accentuating the flare of his shoulders and the blue of his eyes.

"Okay. But I didn't get anything for you."

Not when I wasn't sure if I was even coming to Havenfall until that last moment at the bus station.

His eyes and teeth shine as he smiles. "That's all right. I'm here, that's enough."

I lean closer to him without quite meaning to. These three months with him every year are all I get. No pictures or videos to remember him by, and it's not like I can talk about him to anyone at home. *Yeah, I have a crush on this guy. He's a fairy-elf-warrior type. Gorgeous, stoic, not much of a sense of humor, but that might be because they don't have sarcasm in his world. And he doesn't think I'm a freak, so that's a plus.*

He produces a deck of cards from his breast pocket. It has gilt images on the back. "Cards of the Caves?" he asks, and I nod, because this is another of our traditions. A silly game, a kids' game, but it makes my heart beat faster because it's ours.

"So," he asks, grinning as he cuts the deck into two equal stacks and hands one to me. "Anything happen this year?"

He puts one card down. Appropriately, it's Fiordenkill, the white flowering tree on the back suggesting their blood and plant magic.

It's the same question he always asks, but there's no way I'm telling him about *the* thing, not at all. The words—*death penalty*—are cold, heavy, ugly, final. They have no place here under the stars, between us. I put down another card—Tural, from the centaur silhouette. Brekken grins and takes both cards, setting them down at his side. Fiordenkill beat Tural in that war, leading to the centaurs deciding to close off their portal. So it went in history, so it goes in the game.

I shrug off the loss and throw the question back at him. "You tell me." I pat the uniform cloak beneath us. Sleek black fur, like mink, ripples under my palm. "What does a soldier do in a queendom at peace?"

I slap down another card and bite my lip to stop the shudder. It's the picture of a silver goblet filled with wine, or maybe blood. It represents Solaria.

"Soldiers are always needed." Brekken takes a sip of wine, passes the bottle to me. "The High Court . . ." He trails off, his fingers brushing mine. "There always seems to be some sort of issue. Good to have an army on hand." He glances up at me, and I try to ignore the undercurrent of something unreadable in his voice. "What was the Silver Prince talking about earlier? About you being unhappy?"

He puts down another card, an insignia made of the four elements, for Byrn. This win is mine.

My chest tightens. "It's just my uncle." Now it's my turn to look down, not wanting to see Brekken's reaction. "He thinks, I don't know, that I don't understand the risks of being here." I remember the Silver Prince's words earlier, delivered with such surety. *Danger is familiar to you.* "But I do. Understand, I mean. And I don't care."

Brekken looks down, fiddling with the wine cork, flipping it between his fingers. "I always wondered, you know. Why do you keep coming back here, when this is where the Solarian monster got through, the one that . . . ?" He doesn't have to finish the sentence. We both know how it ends. *The one that killed my brother.*

"Well, it's not like Havenfall is more or less dangerous than anywhere else," I say, going for lightness. "There could be Solarians anywhere on Earth—sorry, Haven—if they were here when the door to Solaria closed. And anyway, if there are any of them left, I think I'm safer here than anywhere else." I punch him lightly on the arm. "Seeing as how I have a brave, strong soldier to protect me and all."

Brekken smiles. "I would, you know."

"Would what?"

I'm distracted, putting down another card. Haven—a scale on top of a sword—to his Solaria. Mine again.

"Protect you."

The seriousness in his voice catches me off guard. He's earnest, just stating a fact. He's witnessed a lot of my human feelings over the years—from weeping over Nate to raging at my mom—and still doesn't quite know how to deal with it, doesn't grasp the concept of deflecting with humor. But in a weird way I appreciate it. That means whatever I hear from him is the truth. Not the fake platitudes humans rush to give each other at the first hint of discomfort. *No one thinks you're crazy. Everything will be okay.*

Instead, Brekken slides toward me and puts his arm around me, and I lean in, even though his body is cool compared to mine. I put the cards aside, grateful not to have to think about Solaria anymore, though it feels silly to admit this even to myself.

His voice comes softly. "So why do you keep coming back? You have a whole world to explore."

His words are wistful. Everything about Haven fascinates him, from the cars to the diner food to the idea of the post office. But the ancient protective magic ends at the edge of town; he can't go farther. Just like I can't go into Fiordenkill—it would be a game of what would get me first, the air or the enforcers.

"There are other reasons I come back. The magic. Seeing you." I make my voice deliberately offhand on the last two words, a little dizzied by the wine, or maybe it's how close he is. "Anyway, Marcus doesn't have kids. Who will run this place when he's gone?"

"Do you want that?"

I look up at Brekken. I need to remind myself to blink, not wanting to stare, even if he probably wouldn't notice. Sometimes in the dark days of winter, when I'm mired in my real life in Sterling, and my life is freezing walks to school and finals and lunch hours spent alone in the library, I think about Brekken and he doesn't even seem real. Like maybe I've only dreamed him. Then I get here again and he's larger than life.

Sometimes it feels like *this*—how I feel right now—is the only real thing there is.

"Maybe," I say honestly. "I have a lot to prove first, but I think so."

"Well, I think you'd be wonderful." He looks uncertain, lips parted, like he's on the brink of telling me something else. I have a crazy urge to touch his lips—to feel whether they are cool, like everything from his world, or warm, hot like my hammering chest, my raging heart. "If you took over, what would it mean for . . . for *us*?"

Us. So he feels it too. Maybe. Or else I really have lost my mind.

But I don't think I'm wrong. Not about this.

He's so close to me now, leaning closer, looking into my eyes. In the darkness, his are hard to read. The scent of wine edges his breath, and the stars outline his head like a halo. And I don't know if it's the wine buzz or tonight's emotional roller coaster or if this is something that's been building for a long, long time, but the impulse rises in me like bubbles in champagne. I stretch up, feeling the bale beneath us shift slightly.

"Us?" I ask softly. Our faces are so close, I can feel my breath stutter.

"Yes, us," he whispers, his words like feathers against my skin, and with that, the gap closes between us.

His lips find mine.

The softest brush of contact. He hovers, not pulling away but not going any further either, and I think my entire body might explode.

The whole world seems to stop turning, as if everything is waiting with bated breath.

And then, all at once, we're kissing. His mouth is cool against mine—and then warm. A spark of sensations fly through me. Something seems to wake up in me—my heart jumps, and it's so sweet it almost hurts, the realization that Brekken is kissing me back, one of his hands coming up to cup the back of my neck while he traces my cheek with the other. It sends delicious chills down every inch of my skin. I should do something with my hands too. I move them to his waist, then his back, feeling the solid shape of him beneath his light jacket. He sighs against my mouth. I try to remember to breathe. Can't remember, can't think about anything except how he tastes like wine and snow—

He pulls back, looking into my eyes. I let out an embarrassingly ragged breath, trying to read his expression. My heart and mind are competing for which can race the fastest. What is he thinking? Why can't I tell?

"Maddie." But then he smiles, and the moon lights him up, bringing out the sharp angles of his face, and warmth floods my whole body as he leans down to kiss me again.

I shift my body closer. My foot connects with something. I register a distant clunk, and the scent of wine spreads through the air. But all I care about is the roaring of my blood in my ears and Brekken's breathing, faster and faster, and his heartbeat even, as he drops his hands to grip my waist, knotting his fingers in the silk of my jacket. The silver scales of the coat scrape together, and he fumbles with the buttons, and the urgency is suddenly wild, like a surge of birds taking flight all at once, and I don't care if my jacket is ruined, don't care about the wine pouring out over the floorboards. Let my jacket tear, let wine drip down onto the horses. Right now, all that matters is how Brekken's pulled me into his lap, how I can feel his heart hammering against mine, his body shuddering with it. The whole world—all the worlds—could fall apart outside this barn, and in this moment, none of it would matter.

Tonight, Brekken is mine.

———

I don't know how long we sat there in the loft, lips against skin, pulses cresting together, breath in the dark, whispers and the startled laughter that escaped as cool air touched my skin, as my jacket and Brekken's playing cards fell to the floor, landing right in the blooming stain of wine.

I wanted it to go further. I wanted it to be my first time. But then Brekken felt me shiver with the cold, and he—ever chivalrous— promised we'd pick this up later.

Now, lying awake in my room around midnight, too wired to sleep, I feel engulfed in an unfamiliar glow of happiness. There is no rush, I remind myself. We have all summer. We have this time, and we have each other. We have the beginning of whatever this is, blossoming and unfolding between us.

I've never been the giddy type, but my chest literally aches with the sweetness of it. I roll over in bed, the roughness of the linen pillowcases creating a tingling feeling against my cheeks as I replay the feel of Brekken's lips lingering on mine, his cool, sure hands on my hips pressing me against my bedroom door as he went in for the goodbye kiss, his breath in my ear as he whispered *good night, Maddie.*

Eventually sleep closes in, but the feelings stay with me. Even just in memory, the sensations burn away all Marcus's worries, all my fears about not belonging, of being unwanted. It doesn't matter if we have to keep it a secret. I'll happily spend all three months of summer in the barn loft if it means I get to keep kissing Brekken.

I drift off.

And then a noise cuts through the haze of happiness—as vile and jarring as the dreams it shattered were soft and sweet.

A crash.

A scream.

6

IT'S STILL DARK, THE SKY purple-tinged at the edges outside my
window.

More screams.

I sit up, feeling around for my lamp in the dark. I'm no stranger to
bad dreams, but mine are always the same, with the same ingredients.
Mom in her jumpsuit and dead eyes—beautiful eyes, one brown and
one green, but with no life behind them—being dragged from a courtroom by faceless men in white uniforms, her limbs dragging on the floor
like she's already given up and died. Or our old house, a thin strip of
kitchen—linoleum floor, battered table, walls scrawled with crayon
marks—visible through cracks in cupboard doors. The sound of breaking glass and Nate's scream and my mother's cry. *You can't take him!*
Then spilling out of the cupboard afterward, the broken glass and
blood covering the linoleum, the streak of red leading back toward the

window where a monster disappeared with my brother. Mom in the corner with her head between her knees, keening. Her fingers bloody too, nails broken, like she was trying with all her might to hold on to something before it tore from her grasp.

These are the images I associate with the sound of screams.

These screams, though—they are unfamiliar. Not mine or Mom's or Nate's. And there are so many of them. Why are there so many? What's happening?

Finally my fingertips connect with the lamp, and I manage to turn it on, even though my hands are shaking. I'm still wearing my fancy clothes, my necklace with one of Nate's silver jacks, my jacket—damp and stained now—and even my shoes. I guess I was too giddy to take them off again after Brekken and I snuck back inside a little before midnight, silencing each other's giggles with kisses. As my boots hit the floor, more screams—at least that's what it sounds like—filter up from downstairs.

What the hell is happening?

I grab my phone off the nightstand and run into the hall, but then spin on my heel when I realize how light my pocket feels, the usual jingling absent.

Dread washes over me. My keys are gone. I duck back into my room to see if I've left them on the nightstand, but they're not there either. My stomach turns over.

Something's wrong.

I have to shove through clusters of sleepy delegates on my way downstairs, their willowy frames wrapped in silk robes or cloaks or blankets. People protest and withdraw as I run by, but I couldn't care less if they're in their night things or if they're wondering why I'm not. More guests are gathered at the edge of the railing of the staircase, trying to see what's happening below. The screaming has stopped now, replaced by a confused clamor of voices, muffled shouting. I stop at Brekken's door and knock, but there's no answer.

"Brekken!" I try the handle—locked. "Open up. This isn't funny."

I stand there for a long moment, my heart sinking down through my guts. He's a soldier now. Whatever people are screaming about, what if he went down to deal with it? Or . . . A thought—an ugly thought—twists in the back of my mind.

The look on his face in the loft, like he was considering whether to tell me something. And then later: his hands roaming, my waist, my hips, over my jacket, under it.

My keys, gone.

I push the idea away as I run, horrified at myself.

The lower floors—the common area—are emptier, quiet. That makes it easier to hear where the muffled shouting is coming from— the long corridor at the back of the inn, where Marcus's office is located— and the tunnels with doorways to the other worlds.

It's an unspoken rule that I'm not supposed to go down here, but I don't care about that now. The corridor slopes down and curves gently toward the left, toward the center of the mountain, the old-fashioned lamps along the walls doing little to penetrate the darkness.

Willow is emerging from the passage, her face pale. She jumps when I round the corner. It's clear she's been pulled out of bed, a silk dressing gown tucked tight around her frame, her hair rising wildly in all directions like black fire. She isn't wearing makeup, and the green scales glitter on her cheeks.

"What's going on?" The words leave me in a rush of breath. "Who was screaming?"

I expect her to yell at me, but instead she grabs my arm and hauls me into Marcus's office, shutting the door behind us.

The room is ransacked, chairs tipped over and drawers and cabinets hanging open. All the lights are on, even the harsh overhead that Marcus never uses. It washes the room in colorless light, making the people standing around the perimeter look haggard and sickly: Graylin, Sal, who guards the doorways, and the Silver Prince. Why is he here—why are any of them here? And—

Marcus. He's lying on the desk, eyes closed. Panic shoots through me, hot and sudden. For a heartbeat I'm five again, back in the cupboard, hearing Nathan scream; I'm tumbling out into the quiet, seeing Mom sitting in a puddle of blood and broken glass, looking at me with empty eyes.

"What the hell?" I gasp.

Graylin is saying something, standing next to the desk, a protective arm laid over Marcus's chest. A stunned, lost look in his eyes as they meet mine.

He's saying something, his mouth moving, but I can't hear him with the blood roaring in my ears. I'm moving toward Marcus, the room blurring around me, then my foot trips on something and I'm falling. I catch myself on one of Marcus's built-in bookshelves, wood cutting into my hand, and twist around. Something large, weirdly lumpy, is wrapped in a rug.

"What is that?" I choke out. My thoughts fly in all directions. The office is a mess, papers littering the floor. On the far side of the room, a spill of ashes trails out from the fireplace. Something wet and dark as ink seeps over the exposed flagstones. My heart pounds painfully against my ribs and my ears buzz as I try to process what I'm seeing.

A body.

Blood.

Fear fills me up, and I lurch toward the bundle. Willow steps back, and Sal makes a grab for me, but I've already seized a corner of the rug and yanked it up, held by a wild, terrible fear that it's Brekken, that something's happened to him, that whatever he seemed afraid of earlier closed in.

But instead, as the wrap of carpet unrolls, I see indigo fur, claws, a bloodshot eye, all of it sodden with dark blue blood.

A beast.

A Solarian.

My palms are stained blue. For a second, I've forgotten how to breathe. I'm convinced that this is it. I will die of a heart attack right here, right now.

To see one like this, up close. It's too much.

Someone grabs my arms. Graylin. He pulls me up and away, and I feel his hands shaking. "For skies' sake, don't look, Maddie."

I stare at him, too stunned to think anything at all. Then Marcus's prone form behind him draws my gaze. I don't see any injuries, but he is ghost-white and oh so still, his chest rising and falling almost imperceptibly. The Silver Prince stops pacing to meet my eyes. He looks bone-pale and furious.

"What's wrong with Marcus?" I croak, unable to tear my eyes away from Marcus's closed eyes, his empty face.

"We don't know yet," Graylin says, keeping his hand on my shoulder. "We think the Solarian attacked him." He looks distraught, with dark circles under his bloodshot eyes.

My stomach drops even further. *Soul-eaters.* That's what Solarians are. They devour your soul before destroying your body. *Is that what happened to Marcus?*

Graylin moves his right hand in a complicated motion over my uncle's form, and the air between his hand and Marcus's chest shimmers. Fiorden healing magic. *But can it undo the damage from a Solarian attack?* I don't know. My heart beats unevenly, nausea coiling in my stomach. All I can manage is, "What happened?"

The Silver Prince moves, kneels by the Solarian's corpse and peels back the carpet for a moment. I close my eyes as a spill of curses in a language I don't recognize fall from his lips. The air in the room heats up, and a hot breeze whips my face as he dips his fingers in the blue blood. In his other hand, he clutches a silver bangle stained with something red.

"I killed this beast after it killed my manservant," he hisses, rage and disgust boiling off him and infecting the room. "It *ate* him. Not even bones left."

His manservant.

The thin man with the colorless eyes, watching silently on the ballroom floor as I spilled my fears of not belonging to the Silver Prince.

He's dead? Eaten?

The Silver Prince looks up at Graylin. "You need to question the Fiorden delegation. Find out what the soldier was doing down here."

"What soldier?" I hear myself ask.

The Silver Prince looks squarely at me, suspicion kindling in his eyes. "The one with you in the ballroom."

The soldier. He couldn't mean—No. I find myself shaking my head, as if to scatter the words. I want to pinch myself. I'm still in a nightmare; I must be. None of this makes sense.

"Graylin," I whisper, my voice trembling, threatening to break. "How did this happen? Where did this Solarian thing come from?"

But Graylin doesn't seem to hear me. His gaze is intent on Marcus and the magic streaming from his hands.

Sal is the one who answers, his voice heavy with regret. "The Solarian door," he says. He scrubs his forehead with the heels of his hands. "It's cracked."

"And this thing escaped?" Willow looks more shaken than I've ever seen her. "How? Why now?"

"We can't let them find out," the Prince is saying, but I'm still stuck on Sal's word, echoing over and over in my ears like struck metal. *Cracked.*

Cracked.

Cracked enough to let this monster through, just like the one that tore my brother from this world. I feel suddenly dizzy with the worst jolt of déjà vu.

"The door is *open?*" I croak.

No one answers; they just exchange tense glances. My pulse is a war drum in my ears. This can't be real. Can't be. I'll go to the door. I'll see that it's the same as ever, just a stone wall framed by a dusty archway, and the nightmare will be over and I'll wake up.

"Maddie!" Graylin is reaching for me, but I dodge him and dart into the hallway. I glance to my left, where the floor slopes down into a pool of darkness.

"Maddie, don't go down there." Graylin steps carefully toward me, like I'm a horse that might get spooked. His voice is misery. "Please don't—"

Sick dread cascades over me. I don't want to see it. I want to go back to bed and pretend this is all some Bosch-painted nightmare. But this is my home too and I have to know. I have to.

Graylin is shouting something else at me, but I'm already running.

I move through the inn, oblivious to its inhabitants, to the voices calling for me to slow down or watch out or explain what's happening.

I dart down hallways and around corners and leap down the hidden stairwell at the back, three steps at a time, until I stand at the juncture—the open space where the tunnels to all the different doorways intersect, each of the dozens of tunnel mouths around me inviting me into different worlds.

Though the tunnel mouths are unmarked, I know them all, could navigate them in my sleep. Cold fresh air, incongruous this far under-ground, seeps out from my left. There's the tunnel that contains the door to Fiordenkill. A gust of icy wind, smelling of snow and ocean salt, blasts out and snowflakes get in my eyes, melting and running down my cheeks like tears. If I went left, I'd see a bright white sky, the peaks of a castle. Then another gust lashes me from the right, this one hot and dry, smelling like molten metal. If I went down that tunnel, I'd see a metallic city, silvery buildings against an orange sky, the last city in a ravaged world—not by industry like here, but by magic. Then there are tunnels that lead to closed doors, empty sockets to nothing, yawning portals to worlds that fell apart or were closed off hundreds or thou-sands of years ago.

I thought Solaria was one of them. Dead, safe.

I run forward into the Solarian tunnel as my vision blurs with tears, adrenaline battling with exhaustion as I descend. My legs feel about to give out, and every breath burns my throat. The Solarian tunnel is dark and slopes down, so far down I can almost feel the weight of the moun-tain pressing on my chest. I take out my cell phone to see by. And I see not a stone wall, but something else.

A crack.

A fissure in the expanse of rock, shadows swarming beyond it.

Claw marks score the stone on either side.

The door to Solaria is cracked open.

7

A PALE, LONG-FINGERED HAND CLOSES around my arm, and my
heart seizes. I tear free and spin around to see Willow's face, white in
the dark.

"Maddie," she says, breathless. "Come back. It's not safe to be here."

"How many Solarians got through?" I hear my own voice as though
through water, strange and distant.

"Maddie—"

"How many?"

"I don't know," Willow says, her Oasis accent slipping through in
her fear. "No one knows. Come back now."

I turn back to the doorway and look at the crack in the smooth stone.
My body feels stiff and cold, hard to control. The opening to Solaria—a
crack scarcely a finger's width across, bleeding darkness—calls to me in
the same way that cliff edges sometimes do, whispering dark thoughts

into my head. *Come closer. Step over. What's on the other side?* There's motion in it, malevolent life. I think I can hear something from the other side too, a distant, low thrumming like the breath of some giant beast.

"We need guards here," I say dumbly as Willow drags me back toward Marcus's office. "We have to stop anything else from getting through. We need to seal it shut again."

I don't say out loud the fear hanging in my mind, that something already has gotten through—something besides the monster dead on the floor. *Who was down here tonight?* Someone is dead. And Brekken, Brekken—

I cut off the thought as Willow and I reach the office. Graylin, Sal, and the Silver Prince all look up as the door slams shut behind us. Graylin's hands are raised flat over Marcus like he's a puppet master and the glittering magic in the air is his show. But my uncle is still unconscious. Sal paces with his hands in his pockets. Someone's shoved the carpet-wrapped corpse off to the side, and the Silver Prince sits in the now-upright armchair, his elegant posture at odds with the blue blood on his boots. Tension hangs in the air and in the men's steely expressions. I get the sense that I've walked into an argument and the echoes have only just faded.

The Silver Prince levels his gaze at me—not suspicious exactly, but curious, evaluative. He saw Brekken and me together in the ballroom. Does he remember us holding hands, or the way Brekken stepped protectively in front of me?

I can't let my mind stray to Brekken now, or I won't be able to think, or figure out what to do next. I lean against the wall, trying to focus on the feel of cold stone against my shoulders, as Sal takes his leave, saying something about moving more staff to guard duty, so people are watching the juncture at all times.

"How do we shut the door?" I hear myself say, once it's just Graylin, Willow, the Silver Prince, and Marcus's unconscious form left in the office.

Everyone turns to me. I don't like the looks on their faces. From stricken (Willow) to scared (Graylin) to pitying (the Silver Prince), they all look like they know something I don't. I zero in on Graylin, the most familiar face in the room—except for Marcus, that is, but he's still out cold.

"Graylin, you're a scholar." I hate the edge of pleading I can hear in my voice. "Annabelle and her forces closed the Solarian door a hundred years ago, after the first attack. How did they do it?"

I don't think he has an answer. I can tell from the dismay on his face, but I need to hear him say it.

"We don't know," he replies quietly. "No one knows."

My knees go weak. I press harder against the wall to stay upright, tears burning behind my lids. Part of an Innkeeper's job is to keep meticulous records of *everything.* I've lost count of how many times Marcus has impressed that upon me. "How is that possible?"

"Annabelle didn't want people to have that knowledge," Graylin goes on softly. "She was afraid that if anyone else knew how to close the doors, it would open Havenfall up to infighting and wrongful alliances. She closed the door to Solaria and kept the *how* a secret her entire life."

I rub my eyes, stunned. The door to Solaria is open. Nothing at all between us and a world full of monsters who can take any shape, walk wherever they wish. And because of the shortsightedness of one Innkeeper a hundred years ago, we don't know how to close it.

"The screaming," I hear myself say.

The Silver Prince cocks his head at me.

"I heard it. Everyone did." It occurs to me that I don't know *who* was screaming. Was it the Prince's dead servant? Marcus? No. That's another place I can't go right now. "What do we tell the delegates? The staff?"

Willow worries her lip. "Not the truth, not yet," she says. "That will cause panic."

I've never seen her so discomposed before, and a sharp pang of unexpected pity goes through me. This isn't like the normal problems she faces, drunken fights between delegates or lackadaisical staff sneaking off to do God knows what in dark corners. She can't fix this with a few soothing words or well-placed glares. This was a threat to Havenfall, Havenfall which is as much her home as it is mine. Maybe more so. She has nowhere else to go.

After a few moments of silence, Graylin speaks up. "There was that boy," he says, "last year, who decided it would be a wonderful idea to sneak past Sal and into Fiordenkill."

"Jayden," I supply weakly. I remember the frostbite incident, but I don't see where Graylin is going with this.

"We could say another staff member went through a doorway and got themselves injured," Graylin says heavily. It sounds like it costs him to say it—I know how he prizes honesty. But his eyes flicker down to Marcus, and I see his shoulders settle and square.

He looks at me, and I nod. It's a good idea.

Willow frowns but nods too. "I'll tell them a new recruit got through the Byrn door. Got caught up in a solar storm."

I nod, imagining the Byrnisian solar storms Willow's told me about, where the atmosphere thins enough for the deadly heat of their two suns to pierce straight through. Numbly, I improvise an end to the story: "They made it back through the doorway, but we had to send them straight to the hospital."

"So the summit will continue?" the Silver Prince inquires. His fury has cooled and now he seems the calmest of all of us, his voice light and level even as we stand over the corpse of the monster that ate his friend.

The sound of it chases away the panic a little, and I turn to look at him, studying the sharp, still angles of his face.

His magic tamed the storms that had nearly destroyed a whole continent. Surely with his help we can devise a way to close the door. The only other choice, as far as I can see, is to call the whole thing off—end the summit and send everybody home to their respective realms. But it would have to be *tonight,* while it's still the solstice. And I can't stand the thought of Marcus waking to find the inn empty and dead. We can fix this—we *will* fix this.

"Yes," I say. My voice only comes out even because my panic has morphed into numbness, but the others don't need to know that. "We'll say the commotion was caused by a staff member, and post guards in the tunnels until we figure out how to reseal the door. There's no need to send everyone into a stampede when the Solarian is dead."

Assuming that was the only one that got through. I'm careful not to look at the bloody carpet-wrapped mound in the corner.

Willow looks grim but determined. "All right," she says. "I'll spread the word." Then she's away, hurrying off and leaving the office door open to the dark tunnel.

Anxiety crashes over me anew, but I know Willow carries a knife; she can defend herself. I hurry to close the office door with shaking hands. Somewhere down toward the juncture, I can hear Sal speaking to the guards, his indistinct voice echoing up to us. Now that I have my feet under me, I go to Graylin's side, reaching for Marcus's wrist to search out his pulse. It's there, but weak. A new fear washes over me.

"What if he's not awake by tomorrow?" I murmur to Graylin, very aware of the Silver Prince's eyes resting on us both. "The summit is starting. The delegates need him."

Everything that happens at Havenfall hinges on the presence on the Innkeeper. Marcus makes announcements every morning and evening at breakfast and dinner. He attends all the official summit functions—meetings and negotiations that require a neutral presence to moderate between Fiorden and Byrnisian interests. He resolves disputes. The whole point of the summit is to put the most important people from all the Realms in the same room, to ensure continued peace between the worlds. But that can't happen without Marcus.

Plus—and I can barely bring myself to articulate this even to myself—he's my uncle. The only family on Mom's side I have left, the only person who I can talk to, really talk to, about Mom and Nate. If anything happened to him . . .

Graylin puts a comforting hand on my shoulder. "It's okay. We'll cross that bridge when we come to it—"

"No." The word, soft but commanding, comes from the Silver Prince. He's on his feet now. Looking not at Graylin, but at me.

"What good will come of waiting?" he asks us. "A leaderless society is a vulnerable one. There are plans to be made. We must close the Solarian door."

I look to Graylin instinctively, but he shakes his head. "It can't be someone from another Realm," he says softly. "The laws are clear about that. The Innkeeper—or anyone acting in the Innkeeper's stead"—he swallows, but goes on—"has to be neutral. Has to be human."

I sense the direction of his words, and panic reignites, flaring in my stomach. "Sal," I say. "Sal could do it . . ." *I'm not ready. Not yet.*

The Silver Prince steps forward. His face and voice are softer when he speaks to me.

"Madeline," he says. "I was younger than you are now when I erected the barrier around Oasis. Youth is nothing if you have a clever mind and a strong heart."

But I don't have either of those things, I want to say. If I were strong, if I were clever, everything would be different. My family would still be here. Maybe Brekken would still be here, if I had been sharper-eyed, kept better track of what his hands were doing in the hayloft. I could have stopped him, made him explain himself.

"I'm sure Marcus will wake up soon," Graylin says, squeezing my shoulder with his left hand, while his right still streams magic down into Marcus's chest. "But until then, we'll be with you every step of the way, Maddie."

"You won't be alone," the Silver Prince echoes. There's something about the way he's looking at me, steady, intense, that feels like an anchor.

I swallow, laying Marcus's wrist carefully down at his side. To give myself time to consider, and to have something to do with my hands, I bend and gather some of the scattered papers from Marcus's desk, carefully avoiding touching any of the sticky blue blood staining the floor.

It makes sense, I guess, why someone from another Realm can't lead Havenfall. Tensions between the magic-gifted worlds have flickered and shifted over the centuries like tides; most recently, in the nineteenth century, before the city of Oasis was built around the Byrnisian doorway, the ruinous climate of that world sometimes spilled through into Haven and the other worlds. Gouts of flame or ice or toxic, blistering wind, strong enough to fill the tunnels and wipe out anyone unlucky enough to be passing through at the moment.

Back then, Fiorden and Solarian delegates entered a secret alliance to close off the door to Byrn forever. Byrnisian delegates caught them in the act, and it sparked a battle that led to a dozen dead delegates on both sides. The Innkeeper at the time—whoever held the post before my ancestor Annabelle—stopped the violence with a hasty treaty: the door would remain open provided that Byrn weathermakers were posted there at all times to keep the passageway safe. But it's clear that the Silver Prince has never forgiven the short-lived Fiorden–Solarian plot to cut his world off from the Realms.

And Brekken. He's gone, and so are my keys, and that can't be good. It definitely doesn't look good. *What could my friend possibly have to do with this?* His face flashes through my mind, his laughing smile as he stepped away from me at my door. The lightness of my pocket where the office keys are missing. Our kiss, his hands on me, under my clothes.

It doesn't square with the boy who carried shiny polished stones or bits of brightly colored eggshells or books of poetry in his pockets, all the way from another world, just to give them to me.

My eyes blur with tears, a drop falling on a piece of paper as I pick it up, some kind of handwritten receipt. Marcus is so careful, so conscientious of his responsibility to keep the peace. *Please let him wake up.*

The Silver Prince's voice comes softly, breaking me out of my spiral of thoughts. "Madeline?"

Get it together, Maddie. People are depending on you.

I take a deep breath, stand and lift my chin. Fear rages in my chest, but I can't let that rule me. Solarians took my mother and brother from me. I won't lose Havenfall too.

"Okay," I say to the room. I meet the Prince's steady gaze, drawing some comfort from knowing Graylin is behind me. "Tell me exactly what you saw."

The Silver Prince nods and leans casually against the bookshelf, folding his arms. He doesn't seem discomfited by the Solarian corpse at his feet. "My advisor, Bram, and I were leaving the ballroom earlier tonight when we saw a Fiorden soldier heading toward the tunnels. It didn't seem right, so we followed."

I swallow hard. "And you're sure it was Brekken of Myr? The soldier we spoke to in the ballroom?"

I strive to keep my voice casual. I spoke to lots of people in the ballroom tonight. The Prince doesn't know there's anything special between me and Brekken. I want to keep it that way—I don't want anyone to know, not until I've untangled what's going on.

The Prince gives me a considering gaze. "Yes, fairly sure. Red hair and red jewels in his ears." His tone says he is *entirely* sure, even if he's trying to be tactful.

Even though I expected that answer, it's still a blow. My stomach sinks, and I lean back against Marcus's desk, gripping the papers so tightly they crumple beneath my fingers. All the feelings I had kissing Brekken float back to me, but now they're twisted and corrupt, heady joy turning to sick dizziness, the butterflies in my gut dissolving into nausea.

I work hard to keep my voice even and ask the Silver Prince, "And then what happened? What did you see at the juncture?"

"The soldier went into the Solarian tunnel." The Silver Prince drops his gaze, clear regret crossing his face. "I didn't follow. I didn't think there was any danger in it. I thought—just a dare from a fellow soldier, or a girl . . ."

I think of Marcus earlier, warning me against being seen with Brekken. If he did have something to do with this and *anyone* finds out about the kiss, I'll be shut out of talks like this, out of piecing together what happened with the Solarian door. No one will trust me to be neutral. No one will trust me, period.

"What did you and Bram do?" I ask.

85

The Prince lowers his head into his hands. Regret looks strange and incongruous on him. "I checked in the Innkeeper's office while Bram went to intercept the boy, and I found it like this." He looks up and waves a hand around, indicating the open drawers, the evidence of the place having been searched. "Then I heard a scream from down the hall. I ran out and found that *thing*—and no Bram. Just his sword." He points at the carpet-wrapped corpse; his voice trembles with righteous anger. "I slew the beast, but it was far too late. And the Fiorden boy was gone. He must have opened the door to Solaria and then escaped back to Fiordenkill."

My stomach turns over, swirling with sickness and questions. *How could Brekken have opened the door when it's been closed for almost a century? He has no reason, no ability. And yet, why else would he have been down here? Why would he take my keys?*

And that brings a whole new tangle of questions to the surface: If Brekken lied to me, how deep did it go? Was everything between us just a ploy, a setup? My throat constricts as I glance at Marcus's unconscious form. *I'm sorry. You were right.* The rise and fall of his chest is scarcely perceptible. I will him to move, to wake. But he doesn't.

"We shouldn't take rash action," I say, trying to sound braver than I feel. "We don't know enough about what happened to place blame. Not yet, anyway. We need to keep everyone calm and find a way to secure the door. Sal should look through Brekken's room to see if he left any sign of what he might—or might *not*—have been up to. And we can sweep the grounds to make sure no other Solarians escaped."

It feels like a paltry plan to me, and I expect one or both of them to push back, but neither of them does. The Silver Prince rises to his full, imposing height and inclines his head in my direction. Graylin, for his part, gives me a small nod and a sad smile.

"We'll get to the bottom of this," he says in the Silver Prince's direction. "I swear it. We'll run the summit until Marcus wakes up, and the other delegates and staff don't need to learn what's happened here tonight."

The Prince turns and gives him a long look, but still nods. "Very well. As long as Madeline is the one making decisions if Marcus is unable, leading Havenfall."

All the air seems to vacate itself from my chest. I understand why the inn needs a neutral leader, but when the Silver Prince puts it that way—

Lead Havenfall. My mind races, circling around the words. Just for tonight, but still. It's almost more than I can process.

"Whatever we do," the Silver Prince says after a few stretching moments, "we must begin now."

Graylin says tersely, "I agree," and then glances at me. Waiting, I realize, for me to weigh in.

"Sounds good," I say. "I mean, yes. Start now. Let's do it."

Ugh. Whatever a leader of Havenfall sounds like, it isn't that.

"I have to attend to my people," the Prince says, gliding toward the door. He glances toward Marcus with a strange expression on his face. It's worry, sort of, but not for my uncle—for what his condition means for the Prince. For Byrnisians. For Havenfall.

Then he's gone.

It crosses my mind to worry about him, alone in the tunnels with more Solarians potentially on the loose. But that's silly; I have the feeling he'll be protecting us, not the other way around. I push off the desk and turn to look down at Marcus again, avoiding looking at the Solarian and its blood. We'll have to do something about that, but first—

"Should we take him to the hospital?" I ask, indicating my uncle. My voice breaks.

Graylin's dark skin has gone sallow. He shakes his head a little.

"I healed all his physical injuries. The rest is magically inflicted. The humans won't be able to do anything."

Helplessness seeps through my chest. I nod, trying not to let my lip tremble, but I can't stop it. The bravado I found when the Silver Prince was in the room has deserted me now that it's just us.

Graylin notices, his eyes snapping up to me, and his brow smooths out. "Oh, Maddie," he murmurs, stepping forward to wrap me in a much-needed embrace.

"It'll be all right," he says into my hair. "Think of it as practice for when you inherit Havenfall for real someday."

Tears slip free and crawl down my cheeks. I know I shouldn't be worrying about myself at all right now, not when there could be Solarians on the grounds. But to be told to lead the inn at such a moment—I feel so small, so childish and unprepared. I expect to feel like this in Sterling, but not at Havenfall. Never at Havenfall.

"What if Marcus doesn't wake up?" I say through a sniffle.

"He will," Graylin says firmly. "But in the meantime, he'd want you to be in charge. You don't have to be perfect, Maddie, but you're ready."

"I don't know about that," I whisper, smiling to try to trick myself into bravery. Because it seems like I don't have much of a choice. Even so, I appreciate Graylin's belief in me.

He loops his arms beneath Marcus's shoulders and knees and lifts him up, and I feel myself flinch. Even though Graylin is strong and gentle, it's still unsettling to see Marcus carried like a corpse, his head tipping back, slivers of his blue irises showing through his lashes. A memory flashes through me of Marcus spinning me around by my hands in the ballroom when I was a little kid, making me feel weightless. Even through what happened to Nate and Mom, Marcus always seemed invulnerable to me, the happy king of this little kingdom. He's my only family on Mom's side, not counting her. I can't lose Marcus. I can't.

"Wait here until I get him settled, will you?" Graylin says. "Then I can take you back upstairs."

"What about . . ." I glance without meaning to toward the Solarian corpse, wrapped in the carpet.

Graylin's smile, already weak, flickers out. "I'll come back later and bury it."

I wonder if we'll ever get the blue bloodstains out of the rug. A short laugh escapes me, because it's such a trivial thing to worry about, and yet in my exhaustion it seems important. Marcus will come out of this soon, and I want him to see that I've kept this place shipshape in his absence.

We need to get rid of the body.

And I don't want to be in the tunnels alone.

"Let me help," I tell Graylin. "Please."

I walk a little ahead of Graylin on the way back to their suite, in case I need to head off any delegates out for a late-night stroll—we can't let anyone see Marcus like this. But the first person we pass in the hall is Willow as she brings a handful of security staff down the hall toward the Solarian doorway. She stares worriedly at Marcus but doesn't stop to chat.

I know that the team trailing her—the security team—is part of Havenfall's staff, but I almost never see them. They're stationed out in the woods usually, and the sight of them all gathered together makes everything feel even more dire somehow. These aren't the dissolute college kids I saw in the common room earlier. They're muscled, silent men and women, dressed in black with pistols at their hips. But, I worry they might not be enough.

Eventually Graylin and I get Marcus to their room and settled into bed. He's still out cold, and Graylin takes a moment to hit him with another round of healing magic, though I can tell Graylin's tiring. When we step back out into the second-floor corridor, Graylin locks the bedroom door behind him, and I don't know, I don't ask, if it's to keep threats out or Marcus in.

Because now we have to deal with the body.

With Graylin at my side, his head on a swivel for anything amiss, I go upstairs to a supply closet where Marcus stashes all the random crap that delegates and staff forget here every summer. It doesn't take long to find what I'm looking for: a giant, smelly duffel bag that seems to be meant for ski equipment of some kind. I send a silent apology to whoever it belongs to as I roll it up and tuck it under my arm.

Outside, the night—almost dawn now—is beautiful as usual for Havenfall. The air is pleasantly warm with just a touch of a cool breeze, the sky is spattered with stars, and a bouquet of night scents float on the wind—fresh water, pine, soil, and stone. The songs of crickets and frogs fill the air, blending with the soft rustling of pines. But it seems darker than usual, the shadows misshapen and looming. Every twig that snaps beneath our feet makes me jump and hold the shovel tighter, my heart hammering so hard it hurts. Little moonlight makes it through the trees, and Graylin is just a dark shape ahead of me, the bulging duffel bag slung over his shoulder distorting his silhouette. I don't want the Solarian's body anywhere near the inn, but still, every step we take away from the lights of Havenfall's windows seems weighted with more and more danger.

I don't do much of the actual burial—mostly just standing nearby to make sure we're alone while Graylin digs the hole, then helping him fill in the pit—but it's still an ugly, brutal business. The sound of shovel hitting dirt, and then dirt hitting flesh, makes me flinch and my stomach roil. Suddenly, as I go to drop a blade full of dirt into the blackness, my stomach heaves and the shovel falls from my fingers.

I feel like I'm going to throw up, and I don't want to do it in front of Graylin. He's dealing with enough right now; he doesn't need to worry any more on my behalf.

"Be right back," I choke out, and dash away, instinct carrying me the way we came, toward the inn. I hear Graylin hiss out my name behind me, but I don't stop. It's like my body has a mind of its own and has determined to steer me back to the safe familiarity of the inn, away from blood and dirt and shovels and blue fur.

The lighted squares of Havenfall's windows come into view through the trees—the delegates on the upper floors are asleep, but the first floor lights are always lit—and relief fills my chest, even though I know it's not really safe, not when the Solarian door is open. I'm exhausted and scared and angry and sad, and all I want to do is fall into bed. I can figure out what to do next in the morning—

Then something moves in the shadows of the garden.

I freeze, feet skidding to a halt, my breath vanishing in my lungs so I can't even shout for Graylin. I'm in the middle of the lawn, halfway between the trees and the inn, totally exposed if another soul-hungry Solarian has slipped free of its world—

But then the creature in the garden moves again and I see it's not a Solarian, but a person, stone still on the little footpath between the rosebushes. Blond hair, leather jacket, big eyes. Taya. The girl who almost hit me with her motorcycle.

"Maddie?" she calls softly, voice rising just above the frogs and the crickets. "Are you okay?"

I'm still frozen. Before I can tell her to stay back, tell her anything at all, she's out of the garden, crossing the lawn toward me.

I want to shrink away from the moonlight, conscious of the blood and the dirt on my clothes, but there's nowhere to go. I cross my arms over my chest, aware that I'm still in my now-ragged party finery. "What are you doing out here?" I ask.

Her brow furrows. "I couldn't sleep. I thought I'd take a walk. What about you?"

"Same," I say, not knowing what else to say, even though that excuse doesn't hold water considering my clothes.

One of Taya's eyebrows arches. "Sure, okay." She looks me up and down, her confused face breaking into a smile, then looks around me with an exaggerated motion. "So are these woods the hot make-out spot, then? Should I expect more company here?"

"What? No!" My voice comes out too loud, confused and angry, before I realize *that is* the most logical explanation for me being outside like this. But that just makes me think of Brekken and brings all the feelings of fear and betrayal rushing back. I step back from Taya and take a deep breath, trying to gather myself.

She eyes me warily. "Hey, no judgment," she says. "It's your life. There's a lot of pretty people here, even if there is something weird about this place."

My stomach drops. Of course, Taya got here late. Willow probably hasn't had a chance to give her the rundown on Havenfall and the Adjacent Realms. It's not only the Solarian I need to keep secret from her, it's everything.

"There are a lot of pretty people here," I agree, trying to keep it light. "But keep the making out inside, okay? At least at night. There's been . . . Some people have seen a mountain lion around."

One corner of Taya's mouth crooks upward. I can't tell if she believes me or not. "If you say so," she says slowly. "Not that it matters, anyway. I have a rule—no girls for me this summer, not until I figure out some life stuff."

"Oh?" I blink, forgetting for a second about haylofts and Solarians and shadows. "What does one have to do with the other?"

She flashes a smile, teeth white in the dark. "I have important things to do. And girls are so distracting, don't you think?"

"Everyone is distracting," I say, thinking of Brekken, then belatedly realize how that sounds. Even if it's pretty much true.

Taya laughs, and a laugh bubbles up out of me, an alien feeling after all the crying I've been doing tonight. I wonder what important things she has to do. I realize I've uncrossed my arms, they're hanging loose at my sides, and I hurriedly cross them again, hoping she hasn't seen the blood. At least it's blue, not red.

Remembering the blood, the stickiness and grime on my skin, the momentary lift in my mood deflates and dread seeps back in. How can I even think about laughing at a time like this? Graylin is still in the trees, probably waiting by the graveside for me to come back. Suddenly I feel small and ashamed, like I did at Nate's funeral when the pastor started talking about innocent lambs brought back to the fold and I laughed out loud, because Nate would have been horrified to be compared to something so boring. How everyone looked at me, aghast and pitying.

"Do me a favor?" I say to Taya. "Go in for the night. Save your walks for the daytime until we have this . . . mountain lion situation sorted out."

Her smile fades. She shrugs and turns around, then looks back over her shoulder. "Aren't you coming in too?"

I shift from foot to foot. "In a second. Go on. I'm right behind you."

She knows I'm lying. I can tell. The guardedness comes back into her face. She nods once, her eyes narrowing, then looks away and strides back toward the inn doors.

I watch her go for a few moments, then turn back toward the trees. Exhaustion is closing in on me, making my limbs heavy and making it hard to focus on anything but one foot in front of the other, the next step. *Clean up. Lock the doors.* I can't think any further ahead than that before things get vague and overwhelming.

Fix this.

8

IN MOVIES, THERE'S THAT THING when the main character wakes up the night after a disaster, and they have a moment of peace and not-remembering before everything crashes back in.

Not for me. Even before the events of last night come back to me, everything feels wrong, like a heavy, sticky gray gauze muffling everything. I woke up to my chirping phone alarm with a scream in my throat the shape of my brother's name. I'm frozen, my limbs pinned to my side and my jaw wired shut by some invisible force. Seconds crawl past, the alarm blaring louder and louder until it matches the scream in my head, until finally something breaks and I can grab my phone and hit snooze.

I drag myself out of bed, blood and grave-dirt still clinging to my skin.

When I finally stumbled back into my room just before dawn, I was too exhausted to do anything but strip off my filthy clothes and fall into bed. Now I regret it. Some of the Solarian blood has gotten on me, and it dries black and sticky, like tar. It clots my hair, stains my pillowcase.

I spend too long in the shower—not even caring about the ice-cold water; I want to scrub every trace of last night from my body. I must have only slept for a couple of hours. Exhaustion still weighs down my sore limbs and makes my head fuzzy. But I'm weirdly glad for it. It makes it easy to think simple thoughts.

After everything happened, after I first moved in with Dad and I couldn't eat or sleep or do anything at all for the crushing grief, Dad had a motto. *How do you eat an elephant? One bite at a time.* I didn't understand it at first, but it sank in a little every day, when Dad would coach me through the simplest tasks, cheer when I managed to do the littlest things—eat half a bowl of mac and cheese, brush my hair. I started thinking of the grief, the memories, as a huge shadowy elephant that stalked me through the day and sat on my chest at night. Whenever Dad said that, *one bite at a time*, I snapped my teeth at the imaginary elephant, imagining that I had fangs that could tear through smoke and shadow.

Now I know to think simple thoughts. I need to focus on one thing at a time. Otherwise everything that's happened will crash back down and crush me.

So: wash my hair once, twice, three times, scrubbing the short strands with a vengeance. Get out and return in a bathrobe to my room to assess the damage. Strip the sheets off the bed and cram them into the laundry basket. Take the book of poems Brekken gave me and shove it deep into the back of my closet, in the secret compartment I found years ago behind a loose wall panel, where I won't have to look at it.

Still, I can't help but be gentle with the book, brushing the floor clear of dust before laying it down.

That done, I pick yesterday's outfit off the floor and lay it out, my favorite velvet riding pants and the beautiful Byrnisian jacket with scale sleeves. They're ruined now. Not because of the wine, dirt, and bloodstains—even though those are extensive—but because I'll never be able to put them on again without remembering too many things. The way Brekken's eyes lit up when he saw me across the ballroom last night. The way he ran his hands carefully up the sleeves. I was so sure it was want I saw in his eyes. But want for what?

How is it only twelve hours ago I was walking down the stairs to the celebration, grinning for the joy just of being in Havenfall?

I shake my head hard, as if that will break the chain of impossible thoughts quickly spooling out. I have to figure out something to ward off any questions from the laundry team. Looking around the room, I zero in on my desk, the pens scattered on top. I grab a Bic, hold it over the pile of clothes, and snap the pen in two. Black ink flies over the sheets, the clothes, my hands. Carefully, I stick the broken pieces into the jacket breast pocket and then go to wash my hands. Hopefully, the pen's presence will explain away the dark stains of Solarian blood. I pull on leggings and a hoodie and go down to the Innkeeper's suite, feeling like a zombie.

Most people are still asleep, will be till breakfast, but I run into a few guests out and about. I hurry past them, head down. I'm pretty useless before coffee on my best days. But on the last flight of stairs, someone grabs my shoulder. Nessa, the Fiorden noblewoman I spoke to last night, dressed for a day of peacemaking in a sharp-cut silk suit.

"Madeline," she says, eyes drilling into mine. "What was that commotion last night?"

I tug out of her grip, the worry in her voice bringing back the fear, the screams. "We'll explain everything at breakfast," I say, stalling, hoping that'll put her off, and escape down the stairs before she can ask anything else.

When I knock on the door to Marcus's suite, Willow is the one who answers. She's more composed than she was last night, in a crisp blue blouse, her hair tied up with gold pins. But she still looks pale and drawn, with shadows under her eyes. She smiles when she sees me, but it's small and lacks her usual warmth. She ushers me into the living room and closes the door.

The smell of coffee and fresh-baked bread hits my nose right away, settling deep in my chest and making me feel a little less like a zombie as hunger asserts itself. Graylin sits on the sofa, a tray of food on the coffee table before him. But he looks exhausted and worried, and the hope that poked its head out of the ground when I came in slithers back down. I go over and sit next to him, dread gathering in my chest. Willow draws up a chair across from us.

"He's still the same," Graylin tells me, his voice hoarse and scratchy. "He'll take water, but nothing else." Graylin looks down, shakes his head. "It's strange. Not normal unconsciousness. It's almost like Marcus is in stasis."

"Is that usual, with . . ." My voice cracks; I take a breath and try again. "With Solarian attacks?"

"I've been reading up on it," Willow offers. "I can't find any instance of someone surviving a soul-stealing. So I'm not sure."

She and Graylin exchange glances. It occurs to me that I'm the only person in the room who has direct experience with Solarian attacks. For a second I'm back in Mom's bloodied kitchen; I flinch. *Is this what happened to Nate?*

Stop. I can't think about that.

98

"Can I see him?" I ask.

"Of course." Graylin walks me to the door of their bedroom, and hangs back at the threshold while I go in.

Marcus looks the same as he did last night. It's eerie—his chest is moving, he's breathing, but he's too still and uniform to be sleeping. I touch his hand—it's cool, with his pulse fluttering faintly under his skin.

"Hey," I murmur softly. "Try to wake up soon, okay? We all need you here."

Of course, nothing happens. All at once it's too much. It's like talking to Mom through the prison glass, useless words falling on dead air. I feel tears and panic rushing up. I stand and back toward the door, unable to take a breath until I return to the living room.

"Did Brekken say anything to you?" Graylin asks. "He's still missing, and Sal didn't find anything of interest in his room. All his things are still there." He picks up Marcus's phone from the coffee table, enters the passcode, and scrolls through it, brow furrowed in concentration.

"No," I say, my voice small. "No, he didn't. And I'm afraid I need a new set of keys. Mine have gone missing . . ." I trail off, not wanting to fill the air with even more suspicions of Brekken. The instinct to protect him is still strong, some slow-on-the-uptake part of my heart wanting to pay him back for all the times he took the fall for a vase I'd broken, or hot chocolate I'd spilled, or a delegate's toe I'd stomped on.

Willow looks at me with sadness as I return to the couch. "It could be something innocent. A misunderstanding."

But I can tell she doesn't really believe that. She hands me her set of keys and scoots a plate full of pastries and bacon in my direction. But I can't eat even though I'm starving. The idea of eating makes my stomach turn over.

"We'll have to tell something to the delegates," Graylin says.

"Their meetings." My heart starts beating fast as worst-case scenarios run through my head. During the summit, Marcus is everything to everyone, as he always says. Any agreement struck during the summit needs his signature. He smooths over any conflict and ensures that everyone is friends again by evening, when everyone gathers in the ballroom.

"Just take it one event at a time," Graylin says cautiously, coming to join us.

My eyes meet his. He looks as tired as I feel, dark shadows beneath his eyes. I wonder if he, too, only thought ahead as far as the dawn. If anything beyond that was too horrible to consider.

Lead Havenfall. It's what I wanted, what I've worked for. But I thought I'd have ten years, twenty, before it was my turn. Decades to live here and learn from Marcus all the history, the etiquette, the intricacies of interaction between Fiordenkill and Byrn that ensure that our summers see balls and not battles. I thought I'd always have Marcus.

But what's the alternative? That the peace summit ends? A strangled feeling descends on me as I imagine everyone filing back through the doorways. It would be bad enough to end the summit early, but it's no longer the solstice. Letting more than a handful of people through the doors at once could upend the balance, cause earthquakes or worse on the mountain. No. That's not an option.

"What do I have to do?" I ask.

"Write everything down. Keep good records of every meeting. Marcus didn't have to," Willow says with a slight grimace. "That memory of his is unparalleled."

My stomach sinks. Marcus has a photographic memory—paired with his charm, it's what makes him a great Innkeeper, that he never forgets an appointment or a face. Every year at the summit, merchants from both worlds bring goods to sample, and they meet with the other

Realms to strike deals that will be carried through the rest of the year. He keeps tabs on everything happening under this roof, knows the goings-on of each day like the back of his hand, always. A small, spiteful part of me is tempted to comment about how I would be more useful if Marcus had included me in the business side of things before now. But Graylin doesn't need to hear that.

"I'll tell the delegates he's sick," I say, thinking out loud. There's a croissant in my hands, though I don't remember picking it up. I rip it apart, letting the pieces scatter on the plate. Nervousness churns my insides. "I'll ask them to tell me if there's a meeting they want me at. I'll make a schedule."

Graylin hesitates a second, then nods. It's the start of a plan, but what none of us mention is that it won't help me at the meetings themselves. I don't know the politics, the undercurrents that go into every year's Accords.

"We'll go with you where we can," Graylin says. "Some of the delegates are more wary of us than others." He exchanges a rueful glance with Willow. "Either we're compromised because of our loyalty to our homelands, or we're traitors for leaving them."

Something inside my chest twists. They already carry so much. I should be able to rise to this occasion. But it sinks in, now, that the summit isn't just a party. The peace of the Realms depends on it going smoothly.

———

When the delegates gather in the dining hall, the sun is streaming down through the high, frosted-glass windows, creating squares of shimmering light on the dark wood floorboards. The kitchen staff has arrayed heaps of food on each of the round tables. Earth food like pastries, eggs, bacon, and sausage; heaps of Byrnisian fruit the color of tropical flowers; the dark, rich meat-and-vegetable broth that Fiordens traditionally drink in the mornings. Tea, coffee, even liquor mixed with juice or tea—some of the delegates like to start the party early. But I notice that few people seem to be touching the booze, like everyone is still on edge.

It could be any other morning, except for the frisson of tension in the air. Instead of the cheerful greetings and chatter that usually float over the round tables, there are whispers. I can feel the weight of stares on me. I can't stop looking at the two empty seats near the back where Brekken and I usually sit, claiming our own table so that he can tell me stories about the Fiorden nobility walking past, and I can share the gossip I learned at the bar the night before. Who's rumored to be sleeping and/or feuding with who, who got too drunk at the celebration and had to be gently escorted to their room by Marcus, who has the longest political agendas, and who's just here to party.

Part of me hopes that he'll walk in now, slide out his chair and grace me with his smile. Reassure me that he's all right, that there's some sort of explanation for where he was. But he doesn't. The chair remains empty.

I don't let my eyes rest there as people filter in. There are brightly dressed Byrnisians and more somber Fiordens. Usually they mix and mingle in a show of unity, but now it seems like they're clustering together with people from their own worlds. Even the staff, flitting among the tables filling glasses of orange juice, serving coffee and mimosas, shoots nervous glances up at the head table.

Marcus's chair is empty. I wasn't sure, when I came in, if I should sit there, but I couldn't bring myself to. I sit to the right of it. Graylin sits on the other side, and Willow takes my right.

The Silver Prince is at a table near the front, along with the Heiress—today in a purple velvet gown—and a handful of other nobles from both Adjacent Realms, observing us steadily. When we sit down, he rises and glides over to our table. When I try to catch the Heiress's eye, she looks away, and I can't tell if it was coincidental or deliberate.

"Madeline." The Silver Prince greets me, his metallic gaze skipping over Graylin and Willow. His suit—a green so deep it's almost black—gleams in the sunlight, the texture of silk but with structure that seems like it would stop blades. "Marcus couldn't join us this morning?"

I smile stiffly, trying to act like everything is fine, but I'm running on three hours of sleep and too tired and scared to really act. "Unfortunately, not yet."

The Silver Prince frowns and lowers his voice. "I've been considering how we might close the Solarian door," he says, looking from me to Graylin and Willow. "Perhaps we could attempt it at this morning's security meeting."

A security meeting? Marcus has never let me sit in on one, but I know he doesn't typically involve guests in the nitty-gritty of keeping Havenfall safe. Why would the Silver Prince be invited? All these thoughts race through my head in a second as I blink, pretending familiarity. "Of course."

I momentarily wonder if I should tell him not to come, but that seems dangerous. Starting an inter-realm diplomatic crisis is at the top of my list of things *not* to do today.

Besides, he witnessed everything that went on last night. What Havenfall secrets could be worse than that?

"I've identified a team of my best soldiers," the Prince tells me, as if picking up a conversation we've only just left off. His voice is low so as not to carry, but confident. "I haven't told them anything yet, but they stand ready if needed, to supplement the inn's forces."

Forces. He makes Havenfall sound like a fortress, not someplace designed entirely around the idea of being *open.* Someplace that's been at peace for so long that Marcus has never prioritized security over freedom of movement; he hired guards, but made sure they stayed below the radar so the guests scarcely noticed them. He's always said that having guards in every corner doesn't make for a good party. But now, thinking about the open doorway far below our feet, I can't help but feel like that was an oversight.

When the Prince at last has returned to his table, Graylin leans over and whispers to me. "It's time."

My stomach sinks, like it wants to stay where it is as I rise to my feet. A surprised murmur goes through the room, as if they didn't notice Marcus wasn't here.

"Good morning," I say, ignoring the sound. "Welcome to the first official day of the Summit at Havenfall. My uncle Marcus, the Innkeeper, has unfortunately taken ill and sent me to address you in his stead. I'm so pleased you're here."

I take a deep breath. "I apologize to any of you who were disturbed by the commotion last night. A staff member strayed through the Byrn doorway and was injured. She is being treated and will recover, but will not be permitted to return to the inn." I keep my voice bland, like I rehearsed on the walk over. Try to project calm, even if I feel the opposite. "However, until we determine that her circumstances haven't given rise to suspicion among the people of Haven, I must regretfully close off the grounds to entry and exit. No one, delegate or staff, Fiorden or Byrnisian or human, is to leave Havenfall without permission from myself, Graylin, or Willow."

Surprise and alarm play over the sea of faces. A few mutters of protest. "Again, I apologize for the disturbance and inconvenience," I say. I try to imagine what Marcus would say if he were here. "But I know it won't stop us from having an, um, festive and productive summit to celebrate the unity of the Realms."

If Marcus said that line, people would cheer, but no one does now. Heat stains my cheeks as I stammer a thank-you and sit down. Maybe people are hungover from the opening celebrations, or tired from being woken up by screaming the night before. I'll tell myself that.

After breakfast, the five of us from last night—Graylin, Willow, Sal, the Silver Prince, and myself—head back down to the tunnels to try to figure out how to close the door. Everyone is jittery. Graylin is tense, clearly anxious to return to Marcus's side even though he checked on his husband over breakfast, Willow wrings her hands, and Sal's jaw is set grimly. My palms are sweaty, my stomach set to a low, constant churn. No daylight reaches down here, and I feel like we're walking back into last night in all its terror.

Once again, the Silver Prince is the only one who seems calm, and I can't help but marvel at his easy, unconcerned stride as he walks ahead of me into darkness. A long, slender sword hangs at his side, the jeweled handle catching the lamplight. The rest of us have weapons too: Sal has two pistols holstered in his belt, Graylin and I have daggers, and Willow has her weather magic and knife. Sal's guards—three guys and one lady, all burly and dressed in black—are stationed at the juncture, but nod at Sal and part to let us through. I wonder what they think about all this. They most likely have never seen a Solarian before—as far as I know, the attack on my family was the only sighting of one on Earth for the last thirty years or so. I wonder if that would be better or worse, not to know what the monsters look like.

We continue past the juncture and into the Solarian tunnel, the stone all around us seeming to swallow the sound of our footsteps. The lamps have been relit, and Sal and Graylin carry flashlights, but it still feels too dark. Like the dark itself is alive, shifting and growing around us. Too soon we come to the end and are faced with the Solarian door, the crack in the stone with shadows swarming inside.

Is it just me, or has it gotten wider? Trying to look brave in the hopes that it'll make me feel brave, I step up and put my hands to the stone on either side of the opening.

Graylin's breath catches. "Maddie . . ." He takes a stride forward, but nothing happens, and he doesn't pull me away. A moment passes in tense silence. The stone is cold and seems to vibrate very slightly, though it might just be my imagination.

"Can we just push the stone shut?" Willow asks, her voice hesitant. "It seems almost too simple, but . . ." She trails off, looking to me. I shrug and step back. I have no idea where to start, and Willow's idea seems as good as any other.

"Okay." Now she approaches the doorway, eyes flickering over it like it's a jigsaw puzzle or sudoku board. She glances at the Prince and addresses him politely. "What is your gift, Your Highness?"

I blink and make a mental note to ask Willow later—have I been meant to address him like that all along?

He glides toward the door. "Fire." He traces long, faintly metallic fingers over the jagged crack.

"Mine is earth," Willow says. "If I push the stone on either side together, can you melt it and create a seam?"

Graylin and I retreat, exchanging curious glances as Willow and the Silver Prince take their places. The air shimmers around them, gathering magic. Her raised hands are steady as a statue. She closes her eyes and breathes out and *something* seems to swirl in the tunnel, intangible but raising goose bumps on my arms. There's an ominous creak from the stone in front of us, but then the cracked wall seems to *grow,* stretching like a linen cloth being pulled at from both sides. The faint hissing sound coming from the crack to Solaria dies in the grinding of stone against stone, and the shadows disappear from view.

Next, the Silver Prince advances, the air above his palms shimmering with heat, like a highway at noon in the dead of summer. I feel the warmth against my face as he runs his hands down the seam, and where his hands touch, the stone glows orange and sags down. *Melting*, sealing off the crack. He goes all the way down to the floor, crouching to reach, then straightens and steps back as the stone hardens and cools.

For a moment, I don't think any of us breathe.

Then there's a grumbling, cracking, spitting noise, and the floor beneath us trembles as the wall is wrenched back open. Bits of stone, still hot and smoking, tumble to the floor and scatter. One burning pebble glances off my calf, but I scarcely feel the pain underneath the horror.

Because the opening to Solaria is still there, and it's wider.

———

After we part—Graylin to sit with Marcus, Willow to the library to find anything that might be helpful, the Silver Prince to I don't know where—I walk outside, needing to clear my head.

This wasn't how day two of my summer was supposed to go. On our way out to the hayloft last night, Brekken and I made enough wild plans to carry us through the summit. We'd hike to the very top of the tallest of Haven's surrounding mountains and go sledding in June. We'd go riding in the wildflower fields outside town. We'd break into the wine cellar and drink on the roof, under the stars.

Instead, I have half an hour between this and the next meeting I need to go to, a negotiation between Lady Mima of Byrn and Saber Cancarnette of Fiordenkill, who will barter for jewels in the observatory. At two, food merchants from all worlds will show their wares in the dining room. At four, weather permitting, clothiers will have an exhibition on the lawn. I go over the schedule like a mantra, using it to keep away all other thoughts about how woefully unprepared I am.

After we left the tunnels, it was all I could do to keep my face neutral, much less contribute. The Silver Prince offered to set up a barrier of Byrnisian weather magic ringing the grounds, and he gave me a bracelet of polished crystal to wear around my wrist that would counteract it, letting me—only me—come and go freely. I don't like its weight on my wrist, don't like the feeling that anyone should be stuck here. But for all we know, more Solarians could have gotten out last night. It's not safe for delegates to be wandering around the woods or into town.

Of course, there's an even worse possibility—that if more Solarians *have* escaped, they won't stay on the grounds at all but slip down the mountain to hunt and destroy human families like mine. But there's nothing I can do about that possibility, except work to seal the door as soon as possible. There must be a way hinted at somewhere in the massive library, and if anyone can connect the dots, it's Graylin and Willow. I need to keep everyone calm in the meantime and hope that the beast the Silver Prince killed was the only one that got through.

I head outside and to the stables. It's the start of a summer day so beautiful it feels treacherous, the sun casting down gentle warmth from a glazed blue sky, the scent of pine drifting on the breeze, one big pretty lie trying to tell me everything is okay. My mind and heart won't stop racing. I want to run, to burn off some of this jittery excess energy, but even with the bracelet, I can't leave now. What would that look like to the delegates, that I run at the first sign of trouble?

Hanging out with the horses always calms me. In the musky, hay-scented warmth and dimness of the barn, I make for the stall at the far end, where my favorite pony, Kitkat, rests. Her ostensible purpose is to be a mount for delegates' children on expeditions around the grounds, but she's so obstinate and lazy that her days are mostly spent wandering and grazing. She whickers softly when I pull the apple I've carried from the dining room out of my jacket pocket and, once I let myself in, chomps it noisily, her velvety chocolate nose brushing my flat palm.

But even her presence can't chase away the tornado of anxiety whirling in my thoughts. The loft shows in bits and pieces through the cracks in the floorboards above me, bathed in soft light. I can see the stain in the ceiling where I must have spilled the wine last night. Spilled the wine kissing Brekken. The glow I felt then has been replaced by a piercing ache, a vine with so many pointless questions for thorns.

Where is he?

What has he done? How long has he been planning it?

The kiss—did he mean it? Did he mean any of it? Or has our whole friendship been a means to an end?

It felt so real. How could he betray me? How could he break my heart?

He couldn't have been plotting anything then—we were *kids*. And trying to pinpoint the threshold—the exact point when we shifted from real to not, assuming his vanishing is what it looks like—will make me crazy. But still I can't stop going around in circles. First the jolt of remembering his lips on mine, his hands on me; then the nausea of guilt and betrayal. Naïve, I was naïve. Just like when I was a kid, when I looked out the window, saw a shadow skirting the house, and dismissed it as nothing. I'm too distracted by a sunny sky, a pretty face.

And now Marcus is paying the price—all of Havenfall is paying the price.

Soft footsteps from outside the stall startle me. I didn't hear the barn door open. I straighten up hastily, swiping the back of my wrist across my eyes just as Kitkat's stall door opens.

Irritation mixed with shame shoots through me when I see Taya standing in the doorway, a pail of feed in her hands. Why is she always around during my worst moments?

She raises her eyebrows at the sight of me. Her eyes are shadowed, dark circles under them—she can't have gotten much more sleep last night than I did—but she looks otherwise put together in leggings, a plaid button up, and a soft T-shirt, the sleeves of her flannel pushed up around freckled forearms. Wisps of pale hair escape from the braid lying over her shoulder.

"I didn't expect to find the Innkeeper in here," she says, setting down the bucket in front of Kitkat; the horse nuzzles her cheek before diving in.

"I'm not the Innkeeper," I say, standing and brushing hay off my pants. I dreamed of hearing that title for so long, but now it just piles me with guilt and fear. "That's my uncle. I'm just filling in until he gets better."

"What's the matter with him?" Taya asks.

"Uh . . ." I didn't think about that bit of the lie. "Bad flu."

"In the summer?"

"Hey, it happens."

Taya's eyes narrow, as if, for the second time in twelve hours, she knows I'm lying. Somehow it was easier to lie to the whole dining hall full of delegates at breakfast than it is to lie to her in this cramped stall now.

I reach for something to put her off the scent. "Last night, you said you had important stuff to do with your life," I say, winding my fingers into Kitkat's mane for emotional support. "What did you mean?"

Something Marcus told me once when teaching me how to charm delegates: everyone loves talking about themselves. Keep them talking—always have a question ready—and you control the conversation.

She blinks. "Why do you want to know?"

"Just curious," I reply, offhand. "You're kind of mysterious, you know."

"Says the girl who materialized out of the woods at o'dark hundred last night." She eyes me, the corner of her mouth twitching up and ending the ruse of seriousness. "Maddie, are you a werewolf?"

A laugh breaks unexpectedly out of me. "Only if you're a vampire. You were out there too."

She does have the pale skin, I think absently, the dark circles beneath her eyes that are somehow kind of sexy. The tragic past, the leather jacket. I wonder where our vampire myths came from, if they were ever rooted in one of the Realms.

She smiles, steps past me—her shoulder brushing mine in the cramped space—and lifts a hand toward the small, high window set into the barn wall. In the sunlight, she turns her hand from side to side. "Not burning."

"Not sparkling either." I heave a sigh of mock disappointment. "And here I had such high hopes."

"What, regular old people aren't your type?" She does the raising-one-eyebrow thing again—not skepticism this time, but maybe a little bit of a challenge.

I shoot her a surprised look. "Why, how old are you?"

She glares. "You know that's not what I meant. I'm nineteen, twenty in October."

I've already drawn breath for another hopefully witty reply, but her last words pierce right through me.

Nate. He would have been twenty in October too. His birthday is always the second-worst day of the year, after only the anniversary of the attack, of his death in April all those years ago.

Tears spring to my eyes. I can't stay in here anymore. "Sorry," I mumble. "I just remembered I have to be somewhere."

Taya tilts her head at me, confused, but I don't meet her eyes. Just give Kitkat an apology pat and hurry out of the stables, brushing the hay frantically off my clothes because the scent reminds me of Brekken and brings it all rushing back, the memory of what we did just a few feet above in the hayloft. His touch, confident, not nervous like I was. Like he knew exactly what he wanted. And here I was, thinking what he wanted was *me*.

I grit my teeth and push away thoughts of Brekken, of Nate. I've had plenty of practice losing people I loved. And I have to get my shit together if I'm going to help run Havenfall. I know that. But right now, the seemingly constant threat of tears is back again, stinging my eyes, making pressure build in my chest and throat. It seems like the only way to keep ahead of it is to stay in motion. Outrun the panic, outrun the tears.

It's not until I'm well away that I realize how neatly Taya dodged my question about her big life plans. But that doesn't matter now. It's time for my first commitment as interim Innkeeper.

———

The observatory is all the way at the top of Havenfall's main building, a little glass dome sticking out at the highest point of the peaked roof, ideal for taking in the summer sky and the glorious mountains in all directions. Maybe it's some kind of Realms magic, but somehow the paneled glass captures all the light in the sky and multiplies it across the polished oak table. Even on the cloudiest of days, this room is bright and cheerful. On sunny days, the deep blue carpet blends into the view to make you feel like you're sitting in the sky. And at night, the windows cast thousands of speckles of refracted light over everything and make you feel part of the stars.

It was here, one night a few years ago, when I first looked at Brekken and thought, *holy crap, he's beautiful.* We'd snuck up in the middle of the night just so I could show off my knowledge of constellations, but then everything shifted under my feet. And ever since then, I've never set foot here and not thought of him, the stars in his hair.

But I'm here on business, I remind myself. Delegates book this room when they want to impress. Today is my first chance to make a good impression as interim Innkeeper.

Soon after I sit down, the delegates enter. Lady Mima of Byrn sporting an opalescent pendant the size of my fist, practically glowing against a night-black jumpsuit. And Saber Cancarnette, an ethereal Fiorden guy with hair, skin, and eyes so pale he looks like a ghost, in a long, impeccably tailored silver fur coat.

At breakfast, they asked me to sit in on their meeting, but they still look skeptical that it's me instead of Marcus. And I can't say that I disagree with them at the moment.

Graylin is there too, but he warned me earlier that he'd need to stay in the background to avoid any appearance of interfering in the meeting. He greets the delegates and gives me a quick shoulder squeeze as he sits down next to me. *You've got this,* he mouths at me, and I try to smile.

I sit with my hands in my lap, trying to stay still and inconspicuous while Mima and Saber begin their negotiations. It turns out that the jewels Fiordens wear in their ears actually originate in Byrn—which is why they're such a mark of status; only noble families have the Havenfall connections needed to obtain them. Add that to the long list of things I didn't know. I slide my phone out of my pocket under the table and peek at it for just long enough to open up a text file. I hope phones are a foreign enough concept to the traders that they won't notice me typing notes.

Mima, the Byrnisian delegate, produces a briefcase filled with a jaw-dropping array of jewels of every cut and color and size. Diamond-like stones that seem to suck in the sun and spit it back out tenfold, red gems that glow even though the dirt of the mine still clings to their rough surfaces, blue ones that seem to come naturally in intricate patterns like snowflakes, but are the color of sapphires and big as my palm. In response, Saber, the Fiorden, unrolls a small bolt of soft white cloth, to which he's sewn fur swatches in a rainbow of colors and textures.

Animals in Fiordenkill, Brekken's told me, aren't just shades of black, brown, gray, and tawny like they are here. They're blue and red and gold and green—

But there I go again with thoughts of Brekken. That won't lead anywhere good. I blink hard and try to concentrate on what's being said, the transactions.

There's no universal currency between the Adjacent Realms, so everything is done by a barter system. This year, it seems like the blue snowflake gems are in, because that's what Saber has his eye on. They haggle and negotiate and decide in the end that three cases of the gems will be transported to Fiordenkill over the course of the coming year, in exchange for seven cases of a rough, warm-looking purple fur, one case of a slinky black fur with gold spots, and two cases of a rich, lustrous red.

But just when I start to think I might get through this meeting without making an idiot of myself, Mima carefully closes her briefcase and turns to me.

"Who is running the transport channels, now that Frederick has retired?" She speaks precisely, each word delivered carefully to minimize her Byrn accent. "Who can we speak to in order to arrange this?"

My mouth goes dry. I remember Frederick, a stately old rancher from town who was in on the Havenfall secret, who helped Marcus man the transport of goods between the doorways all year round. I remember a conversation with him at the bar last year, where he told me he was retiring and moving to Florida. He must have told me the name of his replacement. It's on the tip of my tongue. But I can't remember. My cheeks burn as the silence stretches.

My phone vibrates silently in my hands. I look down out of habit and see a text from Graylin. LEE REISS.

"Lee Reiss," I say automatically. Then a memory clicks—Frederick's assistant at the ranch, a clever younger woman who always seemed to know a bit too much when she came by the inn to pick up packages in her beat-up minivan.

"Oh, of course," Graylin murmurs, as though he's just remembered Lee too. When the delegates aren't looking, he drops me a wink, and I smile weakly.

"If you want to write a letter to arrange a shipment, my lady, I'll be sure it reaches her. What's your room number?"

Mima sighs in poorly hidden exasperation. "Three forty-nine."

I stab the number into my phone and try to decide which element of today's particular cocktail of emotions is the least bad. Fear or shame or grief or betrayal. I force myself not to apologize again as we all stand up and I shake Mima's and Saber's hands.

The mountains look like a painting on all sides and the sky is as blue as Mima's gems. I wish I could soak up all this serenity and let it drown the anxiety gnawing at my heart.

This—being in the room where deals and business and politics are happening, shaking hands and having the delegates learn my name—is what I wanted. And I need to step up, or I'll let down not only myself, not only Marcus, but every single soul here, human and otherwise.

Graylin and Willow, the Silver Prince and the Heiress, Jayden and Taya and everyone else. Shit, the whole planet, if I'm being honest with myself.

I have to push through. I have to be better.

Even if it feels like the magic has turned to poison.

9

I AVOID THE DINING HALL when lunch rolls around, a time that always puts a pit in my stomach. Not like I'm not used to it from every single day in school, taking my lunch and eating alone in the library or outside, my back to the school's brick wall, looking out over the parking lot. But this isn't supposed to be my life at Havenfall. This is supposed to be the place where I belong, I'm welcome, I'm my true self.

And yet I can't face the delegates, their questioning gazes and whispers too low for me to hear. I want to not worry about anything for half an hour. If Brekken were here, he'd sneak out with me and we could take a walk through the woods or lounge by the side of Mirror Lake. But he's not here. Maybe I can help Willow with something mundane or play a game of table tennis with Taya.

But they're both occupied when I duck into the staff common room. Loud and crowded as it is, Taya is in one corner, her face mutinous.

I can't see Willow's face; her back is to me, but there's tension in her bunched-up shoulders. I drift over, acting like I'm just out for a sandwich and chips from the lunch spread set up along one wall, but straining my ears to listen.

"I was very clear that everything below the first floor is off-limits," Willow is saying coolly. Her voice low, but not low enough. I blink, my hand freezing for a beat too long as I go to pick up a PB&J. *Below the first floor?* The only thing below the first floor is the tunnels.

"I'm sorry." Taya's cheeks are a hectic pink, her posture tense with her hands stiff at her sides. "I honestly just forgot."

I'm torn between feeling bad for her and being concerned that she was in the tunnels. I'm sure Willow did tell her to stay on the first floor and above, but I saw Taya in the gardens last night too, so it seems more likely she was just wandering than that she was up to anything nefarious. And Willow can go right to DEFCON 4 when she wants to. But I know her fear—the fear we're all feeling—is probably making it worse. I decide to intervene, taking my paper plate and edging awkwardly into their space.

"Um, sorry to interrupt." I look between them. "Willow, I promised Lady Mima and Saber Cancarnette I'd help them arrange a shipment with Lee. Do you remember her address?"

Willow blinks, her eyes flickering from Taya to me. Her anger ebbs away. "Of course," she says, then glances back at Taya. "I don't want to hear about you being where you shouldn't be again, do you hear me?"

"Of course, ma'am," Taya says, perfectly charming.

When Willow turns and glides away, Taya slumps back against the wall, miming wiping sweat off her brow. "Thanks for that," she says with a crooked smile.

"No problem." But I didn't come here just to get her off the hook.

If she was in the tunnels last night at all, even if it was just an accident, I need to know why. And if she saw anything.

"So, um, you were in the tunnels?" My voice trembles a little.

Taya's smile fades. "I'm sorry. I know I wasn't supposed to be down there—"

"I'm not mad," I say. "Just, what brought you down there? They're not exactly pretty."

Dirt floors, stone walls, claustrophobia, darkness. *Shadows. Monsters. Blood.* I sit down on a battered ottoman nearby, balancing my plate on my knees, suddenly not hungry anymore.

"Nothing really." Taya sits down a few feet from me, her hands twisted together on her lap. "I—I got turned around after cleaning up the ballroom, and something just kept pulling me further down." She looks down at her hands, like she might be able to see through the woven rug, through the floorboards, down to the tunnels. "I can't really sleep in a new place until I've explored it."

Something about her voice is weary, like she's explored too many new places. But if she went down there after cleaning up from the dancing, it must have been late, after everyone else was in bed but before I saw her in the garden. Maybe she was there around the same time as Brekken, if the Silver Prince's claims about him are true.

"Did you see anything down there?" I ask. My breath comes short as she opens her mouth to respond, and I'm not sure why, not sure what I want her answer to be. If she saw Brekken. Or if she didn't.

"Not down there, no," she says. She meets my eyes squarely. "Do you want to tell me what's going on, Maddie? Because yesterday you were worried about a mountain lion, but I really doubt there's one running around in the tunnels."

I blink, startled at the sudden shift in her tone from guilt to challenge. "Um . . ."

Another classic bit of Marcus advice floats into my mind. *People can sniff out lies. If you can't share the whole truth, share whatever little bit of it you can to get people on your side.* Quickly, holding Taya's gaze, I assemble a new story in my head, fitting pieces together into something that hopefully makes sense.

"Okay, so you were kind of right that I was with someone last night," I say. True enough, but I don't mean Graylin in the woods, but earlier, in the hayloft. I don't have to fake the ashamed blush I can feel burning my cheeks. "A guy. He, um, he stole my keys." I need to pause to take a breath. It's absurdly hard to get the words out. "And then disappeared."

Taya is very still, her eyes trained on my face. When it's clear I'm not going to say anything else, she lets out a slow breath. "Well," she says, her voice quiet but still cutting through the noise of the common room. "That seems like a problem."

I swallow. "Yeah."

"And that's why you're on the lookout for anything weird."

I nod. "So you're sure you didn't see anything?"

Taya hesitates. "Not in the tunnels . . . but there was something this morning."

Her eyes cut from side to side, and my heart picks up. "What is it?"

She chews her lip for another moment before pulling a rolled-up newspaper from the pocket of her leather jacket. "I wasn't going to be a snitch, but I saw someone walking outside today, off the grounds. After you told us at breakfast not to."

My pulse races. "What did they look like?"

"One of the guests. An older lady," Taya says. "She was wearing a long purple dress and this frankly amazing hat."

She smiles, but I don't, can't. The picture forms in my mind right away. *The Heiress.*

120

"She had a big bag and this paper. She left it in the library." She shrugs as she hands it to me. "Maybe that will mean something to you. I don't know."

I unroll the paper and glance at the date. Today's. The *Briar Star.* A cheaply printed local paper that mostly features stories about the weather—consistent only in its strangeness—and yard sales and lost pets. I'm a little relieved when there's nothing in there about other-worldly monsters or mysterious, gruesome murders. But we're not in the clear yet.

There's only one place the Heiress could have gotten the paper. She went to town. But how? The Silver Prince charmed the boundary of the property. The air around the perimeter is compressed, its gravity strengthened with Byrnisian magic so strong that anyone who tries to cross it without an amulet will get stuck there, rooted in place until Marcus's guards come to collect them. Only Graylin, Willow, the Prince, and I have the charms to pass through.

So how did the Heiress get out? And what was the bag for? I hand Taya back the paper, unsure what to make of this new information.

"I don't know what's going on," Taya says, her gaze intent on mine. "But I can talk it through with you, if that helps. You can trust me."

Trust. The word is a dagger in me, though Taya couldn't know that. She couldn't know how bad my track record with trust really is.

I want to talk to someone. I've only been here a day, and I can already feel everything swirling around inside me, too tightly bottled. Graylin and Willow have enough on their minds, the delegates would gossip, Marcus is unconscious, and Brekken—my best friend—is gone. Maybe it's better to let someone like Taya in, just a little, rather than keeping everything locked up and risk it spilling over to any old delegate with too much evening champagne.

But on the other hand, it could all backfire. Humans are hard to predict, and if Taya somehow got ahold of a phone or left the inn, forgetting-wine wouldn't keep Havenfall's secrets safe.

But then, if she told anyone, who would believe her?

"There's only one way to find out what the Heiress is up to," I finally say, deciding to throw caution to the wind just this once. If I'm Innkeeper-for-a-day, I can't just sit back and wait for threats to make themselves known. "Let's ask her."

———

Taya is quiet, staying a few steps behind me as we climb the stairs to the Heiress's room. We start down the long, sunlight-dappled hallway on the top floor. There are windows on either side and only one door at the end: the Heiress's quarters.

What is the Heiress really up to? If all this had gone down a year ago, I might have asked her advice. I might have trusted her with the secret of the open door to Solaria. She's been a constant presence at Havenfall and has always been kind to me.

Brekken's face still hangs in my mind, though, reminding me that I really shouldn't trust anyone. I still don't know what happened between the Heiress and my uncle, and with Marcus still *asleep*—I think the word firmly, asleep—I have to tread carefully.

I knock on the Heiress's door, but she doesn't answer.

I knock again, a little louder, nervousness crawling in my stomach. The Heiress is known to be wrathful when her writing sessions are disturbed. But one old woman being mad at me is the least of my problems right now. Again.

There is only stillness behind the door.

I turn my head to the side and lean in close, seeing Taya shift on her feet as I put my ear to the smooth wood. She's stuck her hands deep in the pockets of her bomber jacket, shoulders drawn down and face etched into a faint scowl. On the other side of the door, I hear nothing.

The Heiress scarcely ever leaves her room except for long walks in the mornings, meals, and the evening balls and parties. Otherwise, she's always sequestered up here, working on her epic history of the Realms. She's never much cared what goes on outside Havenfall. When I tell her stories of the outside world, she just gets stressed out—all the tech, all the wars, an existence she doesn't understand. Her interest has always been here, in the inn and the relationships between the Realms.

At least, that's what I thought. A sudden idea seizes me, and I take my hand out of my pocket, my new keys clenched in my fist.

Willow would kill me for going into a delegate's room without asking, much less the Heiress's. But I can't shake the feeling that something is off. And—technically—this is *Marcus's* inn. At the end of the day, the Heiress is only a guest here—an honored guest, a longtime guest, but still a guest. And it's Marcus's responsibility—and mine, for the moment—to keep everyone safe.

At least that's what I tell myself as my fingers find the skeleton key.

"What—*okay,*" Taya says, letting out a breath as I stick the key in the lock and turn it carefully. "We're doing this?"

"It's fine," I lie. "I know her."

"Sure, you don't know her name, but you *know* her." Taya's voice is brittle. "Invasion of privacy much?"

But the lock clicks beneath my fingers, and Taya hears it too and stops talking. I step forward before she can say anything else, pushing gently on the door so it won't creak as it opens. If I'm going to do this, I need to do it fast, before the Heiress comes back from wherever she is. But then the door opens and that thought flies out of my head.

I've been in the Heiress's room plenty of times before by invitation. Pretty standard old lady stuff, if all old ladies had access to three worlds.

There is an explosion of pink and porcelain and velvet, curios from all the Realms displayed in glass-fronted cabinets, intricate lace doilies beneath bowls of shiny candy, and bookshelves crammed with dusty gold-edged books in all sorts of languages. Her belongings give the feeling of only slightly faded glamour, of luxury. The dragon hoard of a traveler between worlds.

I hardly notice any of it, though, because arranged in neat rows on her desk is a crap-ton of Haven silver.

Taya steps in beside me and pulls the door closed. She whistles, low and soft. "Damn. Did she buy out a Tiffany's?"

I drift across the room toward the desk without quite meaning to, eyes glued to the brilliant shine of the silver. The desktop is covered with teapots and statuettes, goblets and silverware, jewelry and coins and even plain ingots stamped with the word HAVEN. It all gleams, the pieces seeming to give off their own light. Next to the desk on the floor is the bag, now empty, that Taya mentioned the Heiress had been carrying.

"What is this?" I murmur.

I don't really expect an answer, but Taya's hand shoots out to grab my arm, gripping a little too tight. I turn to look at her in surprise.

"This isn't our business," she says. She looks paler than usual, freckles standing out on her face. "We should leave."

"It is *my* business." I break away from her and reach out to the desk, but stop short of touching the nearest object. It's a necklace that looks familiar.

"I . . ." I stumble, trail off. Something about this feels wrong to me. And to Taya too, judging by her stiff demeanor. And the fact that she looks like she might throw up all over the Heiress's gold-and-green embroidered rug.

I open the top drawer of the desk, hoping to find the manuscript for her book. *Maybe the Heiress is writing about the silver trade?* It's the one industry that keeps Haven afloat. Guests from Fiordenkill and Byrn wear it as a sign of status. It means you've been invited to the summit and you've traveled the Realms.

But when I look in the drawer, there's no manuscript. No book. There's money, and lots of it.

My heart speeds up, a feeling taking residence in my stomach like I'm climbing up to the top of a roller coaster. There's a jumble of U.S. dollars, Fiorden wooden coins, and Byrn glass beads, all piled together haphazardly, shoved toward the back of the drawer. It's more money than I've ever seen in my life, so much that it almost doesn't seem real. Back in the real world, where money means possibility, a tenth of this would have fixed Dad and Marla's problems forever, but nothing registers for me now except dread.

There are letters and receipts in the drawer too. I pull a handful out carefully, bills and coins and beads rustling together as I do. In the note on top, which looks half-finished, brief lines of text are written in the Heiress's careful, slanted hand, beneath yesterday's date.

I will meet you at the antique shop when the sun is highest on the third day of the summit with the money you've requested. I'll require proof that the objects do bear magic.

A familiar green wax stamp sits in the upper right-hand corner. It's the image of a great flowering tree. My stomach drops even further. It's the official stamp of Myr, the Fiorden queendom Brekken serves and which houses the door to Haven. It usually appears on official documents, letters carried out of Fiordenkill or contracts hammered out at Havenfall. Not hastily handwritten notes on scraps of paper, clearly meant to be a secret.

What the hell? One of the first things Marcus told me about Havenfall was that its magic lay in its occupants. That there were no such things as magic wands or enchanted swords or spelled treasure. People—people, not things—were precious; people, not things, carried magic.

And more than that . . . I know so little about my uncle's running of Havenfall, but I know that he would never, ever allow enchanted objects to be traded outside the inn's walls if they existed. The inn and everything in it are supposed to be secret. It's a joke between my uncle and me that what happens at Havenfall stays at Havenfall, and that's the only thing that keeps us all safe. That ensures this place can exist.

How long has the Heiress been undermining that? Maybe this—whatever this is—was what caused the rift between her and Marcus. I spread the papers on the desk, and words jump out at me: Brekken, silver, private, Innkeeper, cost. *Brekken. Brekken!*

Then something else in the drawer catches my eye. It's metal, but different from the Haven silver. I recognize it even before I reach down to fish it out of a tangle of bills.

My key ring, complete with the cat-ear brass knuckles. The keys that went missing last night. My stomach drops into my feet.

It sinks in for the first time that Brekken really did take it. He kissed me and stole my keys from my pocket. He's mixed up in this with the Heiress somehow.

For a second, all I can do is stand and stare, wishing I could forget the knowledge away, wipe my brain clean of the humiliation, the betrayal, the guilt. My knees feel weak. It's too much. My palm presses into the edge of the Heiress's desk hard enough to bleed.

Then a gasp from behind me pulls me back to reality. I whirl around, my fingers closing around the keys, in time to see Taya stumble back.

She's standing by the Heiress's nightstand, and a vase with a silver lily plummets to the hardwood floor. Its shatter is loud in the silence.

I shove the keys in my pocket and cross the room to grab Taya's shoulder and guide her into an overstuffed armchair embroidered with vines. She's pale, bordering on green. Her shoulders are trembling.

"What's wrong?" I croak, still not fully in control of my voice.

She doesn't meet my gaze. Her eyes are fixed off in the distance as she shakes her head. "I just . . . something just came over me. I'm sorry."

"Don't apologize." I take my hand off her shoulder. I want to make sure she's okay, but I'm also nervous that someone heard the crash of the vase breaking. We need to leave.

I turn and start quickly plucking up the shattered pieces of porcelain, dropping them carefully into my palm. I wrap them in tissue and drop them into a nearby wastebasket, crumpling a few more tissues on top for good measure. I hope the Heiress won't notice, or one of the maids will stop by before she does.

"Wait!" Taya's weak voice freezes me as I reach for the silver lily on the floor. She stands and takes a shaky step toward me. "That . . . that's what caused it. I touched the flower, and I felt something . . ." She trails off, her brow creasing.

I smile at her, trying to look reassuring even as worry unfolds inside me. Maybe the forgetting-wine has side effects I don't know about. "It's just metal. Just a decoration. Look, see—"

I pick up the flower and tuck it beneath the tissues in the wastebasket. I ignore the strange, uneasy thrum of the silver stem between my fingers. It has to be just my imagination. Just something that Taya's words planted. *Doesn't it?*

My phone buzzes in my pocket. Grateful for the distraction, I fish it out, but the gratefulness dissipates as I see Graylin's text message: *The Fiorden princess is here.*

"Crap." All at once, everything crashes back down on me—the papers, the keys, the Heiress, Brekken. I don't know who to trust, but I need to run this inn anyway. I hurry back to the desk and gather up the papers, but then stop, the stack trembling in my hands. I can't carry these around with me.

Taya watches me, cautious, and with her dark eyes on mine something occurs to me. It's a risk. A huge risk. But at this point, *everything* is risky. All I can do is choose the options that pose the least danger. And we've already come this far together.

"Taya, could you do me a favor?" I ask.

Her eyes turn hard, wary. It stings a little, but—fair. So far, our friendship—if you can even call it that—has consisted of me making her crash her motorcycle, appearing out of the woods in the middle of the night looking like death, giving her forgetting-wine, and dragging her up here, where she still looks like she might throw up any second. Not exactly a solid foundation.

But to my surprise, she asks slowly, "What do you need?"

I lift the papers. "There's somewhere I have to be, like right now. Can you put these in your room for a bit? I'll come by later tonight and pick them up."

I want to add *and don't read them*, but I know if she's anything like me, that would make her only more likely to do so. Plus, I'm asking for her help; it's not like I can be the one setting terms and conditions.

With her hand on the back of the chair to steady herself, she keeps her eyes on mine for another long moment. But finally, she nods and comes toward me, reaching out for the papers. "I'm in room five eighty-eight."

Relief washes over me. "Thanks so much."

Taya puts her hands on the papers—and over mine. Her skin is cool, but I can feel her pulse fluttering through her palms and fingers. "At some point, though," she says, holding my gaze, "you're gonna have to tell me what else is going on here."

I swallow and try not to blink. "Of course," I lie.

———

Taya and I part outside the reception room, the opulent private den where we entertain distinguished guests. She goes off to stash the papers in her room while I head inside. The wallpaper—a green leaf pattern with touches of gilt here and there—and the potted palms that Willow has placed around the room at strategic locations lend the feeling of standing in an enchanted forest, all dappled with afternoon sun from the skylight above. Graylin is chatting with Princess Enetta, one of the members of the Myr royal family and the head delegate to Haven this year.

Brekken told me that she's skeptical of Havenfall and the alliance with Byrn, so there were rumors that she wouldn't come at all, but she must have thought better of it.

What I don't expect is for the Silver Prince to also be there, pacing the room, looking angry.

I pause at the doorway, taking the situation in, but Graylin catches my eye and beckons for me to enter as he pours Enetta a drink. I've seen her before at previous summits, but I've never spoken to her. She's in her thirties and pretty, with skin a little lighter brown than Graylin's. Her shimmery silver-white hair is woven into a net of thin braids, and a cloak of sleek purple fur is wrapped around her shoulders. Beneath that, she's dressed in simple but elegant traveling clothes. Only the diamond-like gems climbing her ears mark her as royalty.

Once, when I was fourteen, I was morose for two weeks when I was convinced—for some reason I don't even remember—that Brekken was in love with Enetta. Until Graylin took me out to lunch to ask why

I was being so mopey, and I burst into tears and told him. He laughed and informed me that Fiorden soldiers and princesses couldn't marry.

As I hurry into the room and bow low, I silently review what Marcus has told me about the royal family. Most of the important decisions in Myr are made by the elected members of the High Court, but the royal family is still important in a ceremonial way, like the British royals. They're respected by all, revered even. Princess Enetta is beloved. So it makes me uneasy seeing the Fiorden princess's eyes follow the Silver Prince pacing. Now that I'm paying attention, I realize that her manner is serious, far from the young and inexperienced monarch Brekken told me about. My stomach clenches. *Was it possible he lied to me about Fiorden politics too? What else don't I know?*

I put on a smile as I straighten up. "Your Highness. Welcome to Havenfall."

Enetta looks at me without recognition. She's been here previous summers, but I've never gotten so close and I suppose I shouldn't be surprised; most delegates saw me as a child in years past, beneath notice.

"I'm sorry to hear the Innkeeper is unwell," she says in her melodic, faintly accented voice. "I do always enjoy his stories. Such a curious world you have here."

"He will be fine," Graylin says firmly before I can reply.

I can't tell whether it's for Enetta's benefit or mine or his own. But whatever it is, it seems to make the Silver Prince lose patience. Halfway across the room, he whirls, moving so fast that for an instant he's only a metallic blur.

"You can't know that," he says. His eyes light on me. He didn't even notice me come in. "Madeline, this princess"—the word drips with condescension—"shouldn't have been allowed through. Movement through the doors will disturb the balance of the Realms further."

I automatically step between them, surprised. He's not wrong—using the doors too much destabilizes the magic of Havenfall that keeps all the doors in equilibrium. But we knew the princess was coming late, and it's not her fault the doors have already been disturbed in the last twenty-four hours. And now he's offended Enetta.

"How dare you?" she asks, rising from her chair. She's almost as tall as he is, and her eyes seem to shimmer.

Graylin raises his hands beside me. "There's no need for unpleasantness," he says evenly, but I realize with a jolt that it's me Enetta is looking at expectantly.

"It's all right." I lift my voice, glancing around to try to address everyone at once. "Princess Enetta knows that she is welcome at Havenfall anytime. She was expected." I try to picture Marcus here in my place, try to hear the words he would use and mimic them. "The doors are safe."

My gaze locks with the Prince's as I finish the sentence. I hold it, trying to communicate to him with my eyes. *Stay calm. Keep the peace.* But he still looks wrathful. After a long, tense moment, the Silver Prince inclines his head. He sweeps out of the room and I let out a breath, careful not to let my relief show on my face.

It's not the elegant, fair solution Marcus would have come up with. But Marcus isn't here. Only I am.

10

BY THE TIME I DRAG myself up the stairs to the staff wing that night, I'm exhausted. My head aches and my limbs are heavy as stone.

I push one of the hallway windows open with a creak, desperate for fresh air, and poke my head out and stare up, trying to draw strength or serenity from the gorgeous spread of stars above me. They look like thousands of diamonds scattered carelessly over blue velvet. The music from tonight's dance still echoes in my head, an enchanting siren call. A part of me wants to keep drinking and dancing until this day is scrubbed from my head. But I know I can't do that. The delegates can distract themselves with dresses and jewels, liquor and music, but I need to keep my head clear.

I don't know how Marcus does this. After I got Princess Enetta settled in her suite and soothed her scorched pride over the Silver Prince's treatment—*you know how Byrnisians are*, I'd told her, smiling like we had an inside joke, *no manners*—I had to rush off to "hear petitions and moderate grievances" in the dining hall, per the schedule. Then to dinner and dancing. All the while I had to keep a smile on my face; all the while I had to squash down any stray thoughts that crept in of Marcus, or Brekken, or what I'd found in the Heiress's room.

She wasn't in the dining hall at dinner, and though I glimpsed her across the ballroom once or twice when she was dancing, by the time I got out from behind the bar and wove my way through the crowd, she was gone.

What reason could she or Brekken possibly have to want the door to Solaria—a dark world, a hellscape, if Havenfall's library books are to be trusted—open? And yet, how could Brekken stealing my keys and vanishing on that same night be a coincidence?

Now all the fear I pushed down all day bubbles back up with a vengeance, making my eyes burn. Fear, and anger too. Because if Marcus had trusted me sooner—if he'd let me help him with the day-to-day operations of the inn, like I've begged him to for years—I wouldn't be so damn out of my depth now.

Most people are still downstairs dancing or working, so the hall is empty. I walk quietly, though, not wanting anyone to hear me and ask what I'm doing up here. I thought of telling Graylin about finding my lost keys in the Heiress's desk, but I haven't had a moment alone with him since this morning, and besides, I don't want to heap more worry on top of his fear for Marcus. I want him to concentrate on fixing my uncle so that he can wake up and help us figure out how to seal the Solarian door so everything will go back to normal.

Please let everything go back to normal soon. I don't think I can do this.

My knock on Taya's door is soft, but she opens it right away. She smiles when she sees me, but it's a guarded, grim sort of smile. She stands back to let me in, and the door falls shut behind me.

Her room is tiny. Since she was late coming to the inn, all the other staff got to choose rooms first, and she ended up with one that's sparse, almost monk-like. Her bed is neatly made, her tattered backpack hanging off the foot of it, and a few shirts and pants are hung in the closet beside her bomber jacket. She's wearing leggings and a thin, worn Rascal Flatts T-shirt, which has to be a hand-me-down. She doesn't really seem like a Rascal Flatts kind of person.

The papers are stacked on her bedside table. I make a move toward them, but then the pressure behind my eyes rushes up again, and after a day of pushing it down, of smiling and shaking hands and assuring delegates that of course, of course my uncle will be fine, I suddenly can't hold the tears back anymore. They flood my eyes all at once and swim there, blurring my vision. With my back to Taya, I blindly grab the papers and flip through them, trying to look busy while I furiously blink the tears away. But I feel my shoulders trembling.

"Maddie." A small hand finds my shoulder. "Tell me the truth. Maybe I can help."

Her voice is kind, with none of its normal snark, and it feels like a harpoon through me. I don't turn around, don't meet Taya's eyes.

"You wouldn't believe me." The words spill out of me, too much, too fast.

"Try me. I've seen a lot of weird shit today."

"I'm sorry, Taya, but I can't." I clutch the papers to my chest and nearly knock her chair over in my pivot toward the door.

But then Taya steps past me, faster than it seems like she should be able to. She stands between me and the door, her arms slightly spread and her face deadly calm. "No," she says. "You're not leaving this room until you tell me why."

I stop, wiping my face with my sleeve. I hate that I'm crying and hate it more that I can't stop. Marcus would never let any situation at the inn get to him like this. "I can't. I really can't. I'm sorry."

"What if I told you I already know?"

That catches me off guard, my breath hitching. *She read the papers.*

"I read the papers," she confirms.

Should have seen that one coming, Maddie, I think distantly.

But didn't I? I knew it was a possibility when I gave her the papers, and I did it anyway. Maybe a small part of me wanted her to snoop, if only so I could finally talk to someone.

"So . . . what's in them?" I ask carefully, or as carefully as I can through tears and a plugged nose.

"Where to start?" she says with a laugh. "One, that there are other worlds. That there are doorways to those other worlds right below our feet." She points down, at—or past, I guess—her scuffed combat boots. "I wish I'd met your uncle. He seems like a cool guy." She's smiling, but I can't figure out the implications of it. Does she think it's a joke? Some kind of prank?

"I asked some of the other staff," she goes on, "and they told me to talk to Willow. So I did. And she told me it was all true. That she meant to tell me earlier, on the first night; that she told everyone else. And that's why everyone's just going around like everything is normal. When there's people downstairs with scales on their cheeks."

I take a deep breath, a tentative relief starting to unfurl in me. "So you know about the realms? And you don't think we're all batshit crazy?"

She shrugs, a deceptively casual gesture. She paces toward me and sits on the edge of her bed, the old mattress creaking beneath her. The lamplight does nice things to her face, easing the sharpness and the shadows.

"I have a twin brother," she says softly. "Terran. When my parents died, we were split up and put into different foster homes. I haven't seen him since I was four. But I remember the stories he used to make up."

I open my mouth, about to say something trite like *I'm sorry*, but Taya shakes her head at me to let her finish. "He always talked about a place like this, a palace that held doorways to a million worlds. So when I read those papers . . . I don't know, it seemed like fate or something."

She smiles ruefully, like she expects *me* not to believe *her*, when I'm the one holding my breath, riveted. "Ever since Roswell, I always figured we aren't alone in the universe."

She quirks one eyebrow to show me she's at least half-joking. And I feel myself smiling back through the tears drying on my cheeks.

"We're definitely not," I say after a moment of contemplative silence. "Except I guess it would be the multiverse, not a universe."

"Semantics," she says, but she smiles. "What I'm saying is that if you're crazy, I am too. I believe you."

And it's that easy, that simple to share the truth of the Adjacent Realms with another person.

I think of all the hours I spent as a little kid trying to explain it to my dad, and knowing he just thought I was making it all up. Now a weight seems to lift off my chest, just a little. It's good to be believed. To be understood.

"So now we've established that, wanna tell me what's wrong?" Taya says. She moves to sit cross-legged on the bedspread, the smile fading off her face.

"It's a long story." I swallow down the sudden lump in my throat. "Can I sit?"

Taya gestures wordlessly toward the armchair in the corner; I sink into it and draw my knees up to my chest. I tell her the SparkNotes version of everything that's happened since we arrived at Havenfall, leaving out most of the strands I still don't understand—the disappearance of the Silver Prince's manservant and Brekken. I tell her that there's a world full of monsters, the long-dormant door to that world cracked open again, and something got through.

Her eyes flicker, unreadable through it all, but she doesn't speak. Not until I tell her about the Silver Prince seeing Brekken in the tunnels.

"What if he was wrong?" she asks, resting her chin on her folded hands. "Or lying?"

I blink. Of all the questions she could ask, I wasn't expecting that one. "About seeing Brekken? Why would he lie, though?"

She shrugs. "Dunno. But you said you've known Brekken forever. I just heard a bit of your talk with this Prince guy in the reception room, but he seemed kind of pissed about the Fiord princess being there."

"Fiorden," I correct. I fiddle with a hangnail, tugging at it until it hurts. "Clearly I have a habit of trusting the wrong people. Maybe I should just assume that to be the case, going forward." A bitter chuckle escapes my lips, and a question rises in my mind: do I trust the Prince?

The truthful answer is *I don't know.* He's charming, a little too much so. Slick. But he saved his people. He leads them. If the Byrnisians trust him, what business do I have questioning him? I don't have any reason not to trust him.

"Okay, here's the thing." Taya speaks after a long moment, sounding suddenly, strangely uncomfortable. She looks between the papers and me, as if deciding whether to share something. "I read up on Solarians a bit." She reaches down and opens the nightstand drawer to reveal a book, hidden where the Bible would be if this were a regular hotel. It's leather-bound, yellowed, the embossed title reading *A History of the Solarian Realm.*

"There's nothing in there about eating people," she says. "Sucking souls, yeah, but nothing about—you know." Her nose wrinkles in distaste. "Does it make sense that there would be *nothing* at all left of the Prince's bodyguard guy?"

"There was a lot of blood," I say automatically, thinking about the horrible stickiness on my hands and clothes. But then I remember—it was blue blood, not red. Was there red anywhere? Maybe Sal or Graylin or Willow cleaned the worst of it up before I got to the tunnels?

A shudder rips through me at the thought, as I imagine red blood staining Havenfall ground. Red like in the kitchen that night. *We never found Nate's body either.*

I take a deep breath, picturing clean air filling me and shoving the gruesome thoughts away. "The Silver Prince has more reason than anyone to want to find the truth," I say, maybe a little too fiercely. "Bram was his friend."

"Okay, it was just a thought." Taya slips off the bed to pace in front of the window.

"Brekken stole my keys," I point out.

"We don't know that for sure." She gazes out at the mountaintops. "You had them and then you didn't."

"And then they were in the Heiress's room." I feel my mouth tug down, remembering.

Taya perks up. "Maybe you just dropped them somewhere, or she took them in the ballroom." She pauses, her eyes far away. "Do you think she opened the door to Solaria?"

I shrug. "I don't know how she could have. I thought only a Solarian could do it. But it seems like she's involved somehow."

And why would she be? Academic curiosity? Some kind of vendetta against Marcus because of whatever they were fighting about last year?

Fear settles cold into my insides, bringing with it the threat of memory—*bloody kitchen, broken glass*. I don't want to get sucked in, so I make myself get up and move to the bedside table, where I leaf through the papers we stole from the Heiress's room.

"Did they say anything else?" I ask, turning to Taya.

Taya raises her eyebrows at me, as if to say, *obviously*. She perches on the windowsill, her back to the moon and the mountains, her legs swinging off the edge. "I think the Heiress is smuggling something between the Realms."

I feel colder. "What do you mean? What would she be smuggling?" But the images from inside her room stick in my head. The piles of trinkets, several college educations' worth of silver just lying around. And the drawers full of cash.

Taya comes over and taps her fingers on the top page of the papers we stole. It looks like something torn out of an old-fashioned ledger, with descriptions of objects written in the Heiress's careful writing.

Silver teapot with vine handle.
Pendant with silver chain and Byrn-diamond stone.
Plain silver ring.

And so on, with eye-popping amounts of money corresponding on the other side.

That's not the strangest thing, though. Beside each object is a symbol in green ink, almost like a hieroglyph. As I run my pointer finger over the column, Taya leans over and pulls another sheet of paper out of the pile, flattening it under the lamplight.

"Here's the key to what that all means."

Sure enough, the page she's holding replicates the symbols beside the descriptions of the objects. And—my stomach drops—each one seems to represent a kind of magic from one of the Adjacent Realms. *Blood healing*—that's Fiorden. *Wind-wielding, rain-calling*—Byrnisian. *Wakefulness*—Fiorden again. And on and on. There have got to be three dozen symbols on this page.

"She's trading magic," Taya whispers, almost reverent. "Maybe that's why she would want the door open? Another world to trade with?"

"That doesn't make sense," I mumble, half to myself. Solarians are monsters; surely the Heiress couldn't be trading with them.

But that's not right. Whatever can be said about the Solarians, they were once welcome guests at Havenfall alongside the Fiordens and Byrnisians. They participated in the trading of goods between the worlds just like everyone else. They were our allies, right up until the day they turned on us.

But surely the Heiress knows they aren't to be trusted?

I sit down on the bed, my heart racing, trying to make sense of this. I've heard rumors among the delegates of magical objects before—enchanted swords or cups or rings, carrying Adjacent magic inside them. Just like on Earth we have stories of grails or swords pulled from stones. Marcus always dismissed them as old wives' tales. He insisted Fiorden and Byrnisian magic runs through its people's blood. It can't be separated from them.

But what if the rumors are true?

"Weird," I say, but instead of coming out light and airy, my voice cracks on the word. I keep coming back to the same conclusion: I have to close the Solarian door as soon as possible, to keep anyone and anything from getting out or in. As long as the door's open, the inn is vulnerable, a gaping wound right below our feet.

Taya, now leaning against the desk—it's like she can't sit still or stay in one place—looks up. "What is it?"

"It's only . . ." I clear my throat and gather my thoughts. Buying time,

I drop the papers on the nightstand and line up their edges carefully. "I still kind of can't believe that *you* believe me. About everything."

"Don't question it, or I might change my mind." Taya grins and claps my shoulder before leaning back with her hands on the desktop, tipping her head up to consider the oak-beam ceiling. "There's something strange about this place. I can feel it. And . . ." She looks down at me for a second, then up again, cheeks stained pink. "My brother always told me there were other worlds out there. That maybe we were a prince and princess of one of them, and someday we would find our way back. I shouldn't remember that. I was just a toddler, but I do." Then her smile dims. "Unless I just made it all up. That's also a possibility."

"No." The word comes out with a force that surprises me. Maybe because the way she talks about Terran is like putting a stethoscope to my own chest and hearing my thoughts about Nate. "Just because you were little doesn't mean the memories aren't real." Mine are real.

"You asked about my big life goals," Taya says. "I want to find him." She lets out a shaky laugh. "It sounds stupid out loud."

"Not stupid at all." Sympathetic pain shoots through my chest. I can't imagine what it would be like to lose a brother because of a government system, not because of a monster like I did. To know every day that he might be out there somewhere, and never know for sure. "I could help you."

I don't know why I say it. I never decided to say it. The words just come out. But I find that I can't take them back either. I just sit there like an idiot, looking up at her, still half-sure that she's going to laugh in my face any second.

She tilts her head, and it's hard to read her face. "Why would you do that?"

"Because I lost a brother too. I'd give anything to have him back." More word-vomit.

What is it about Taya that makes me lose it like this? I've always prided myself on my ability to keep my mouth shut. I never told anyone about Havenfall, except my dad, even though—or maybe because—I knew he wouldn't believe me. I've never talked about Nate because I could never share the whole truth, and lying always made it worse, not better. And now here I am, spilling my guts to someone who I met only a little over a day ago, practically a stranger.

Her face has softened. "I'm sorry. Is he—"

"Dead, yeah. Nate died."

I say the words fast like that'll make it easier, but it doesn't, nothing does. The tears are threatening again. Hastily, I grope to change the subject. I point to the papers.

"Help me get to the bottom of this, and once my uncle gets better I'll do whatever I can to help you find your brother. Terran?"

"Terran," she confirms. Her eyes on mine are thoughtful and so dark, almost black.

"Deal."

She leans forward and shakes my hand in a soft, warm grip, and then leans back, blowing out a breath like she's exhausted. "Whew. This summer is already heavier than I signed up for."

"What did you sign up for?" I ask, half-curious.

She hitches one shoulder in a shrug. "The usual. You know. Kill some time, forget about my ex-girlfriend, make some money so I can find my brother."

"Are you in college somewhere?" I ask, remembering that she's nineteen.

A guarded look flits over her face. It's there and then gone. "No. The making money thing has to come first." Her tone doesn't invite any further questions. "What about you?" she asks.

Even though there's a hint of a sparring tone to her words, I feel a smile spread over my face as I think about my master plan. "Yeah. I want to take classes online and live here."

"And what then?"

I shrug. It's become a habit to talk about Havenfall to outsiders in a deliberately casual way—letting anyone see how deep my need for this place goes is exposing a wound in my soul. People my age want money, a car, a college acceptance letter, a boyfriend or girlfriend. Normal things. All I want in the world is for Havenfall to be my home.

"Who knows?" I say lightly. "Maybe I'll take this place over someday."

Taya's gaze holds mine, and I have the uncanny feeling she sees through my blasé façade.

But all she says is, "Sounds like a good plan."

———

The next morning when I wake up, I feel just as exhausted as ever, having scarcely slept at all. Nightmares kept me tossing and turning all night, and though I can't remember them, I can guess well enough what they were about. Open doorways, tunnels hiding monsters.

Still, I drag myself out of bed, into my least wrinkled clothes—a short, long-sleeved gray dress over black leggings—and stumble downstairs to Marcus and Graylin's suite.

Just like yesterday, Willow lets me in. Just like yesterday, Marcus is unconscious on the bed. Graylin sits in a chair beside him, magic glittering between his hands.

"Marcus looks a little better," I say, too brightly, but it's true. Some of the color has returned to my uncle's face, and the rise and fall of his chest is deeper and steadier than it was yesterday.

"If you say so," Graylin mutters, not looking at me. He looks even worse than I feel. There is a sallow undertone to his skin and bags under his eyes.

Willow, circling back to me with a cup of coffee from the Keurig on the dresser, leans in and whispers in my ear. "Graylin hasn't slept at all. I tried to get him to take a break, but maybe you'll have better luck."

I nod my understanding and step forward cautiously. "Graylin . . ."

He shakes his head, still not meeting my eyes. "I know what you're going to ask. Answer's still no. He's been out too long. I'm here until he wakes up."

"Graylin." My stomach twists. Fiordens can go for longer than humans without sleep, but not indefinitely. "He would want you to get some rest."

At that, Graylin finally looks up. His expression is awful, hollowed out and heartsick and somehow—guilty. Does he feel to blame for what happened? *Don't*, I want to tell him. If this was anyone's fault, it was mine. Mine, for letting Brekken trick me. I still don't understand what he and the Heiress have to do with the door to Solaria opening, but it can't be a coincidence that it all happened on the same night.

Before I can put my thoughts into words, a knock at the door makes all three of us jump. I'm the closest, so I shrug and go to the door, but I can't help but hold my mug tighter. As if a monster like the one who killed my brother would knock. As if a face full of coffee would stop it.

But it's just a girl, one of the Boulder college kids on staff. Kimmy, I think her name is. She looks worried.

"Hi, sorry, is Marcus around?"

The bed is around a corner, but I still position my body so she can't see deeper into the room. "Not right now, but what's up? I might be able to help."

Please let this be something normal and silly. A clogged toilet or bickering delegates or wine spilled on white carpet . . .

"Jayden found a dead deer in the woods." Kimmy chews her lip. "We went out there last night to, um . . ." She trails off, reddening.

"Never mind about that." I don't mean to snap at her, but worry pushes the words out fast and sharp. "As long as you didn't go out of the grounds, that's fine. But what happened to the deer?"

"It looks like a mountain lion got it. It was half-eaten." She shudders. "But there were these weird footprints around it. Like . . ." She holds her hand out palm up, fingers stretched out. "They were huge, and had claws, but something like thumbs too. Been a long time since I was a Girl Scout, but I don't think mountain lions have thumbs."

My skin tightens. "Yeah, no." *Okay, Maddie*, I tell myself. *Stay calm. This doesn't necessarily mean what you think it means.*

"A bear, maybe?" I hear myself say. "They have five toes." I fight an insane urge to laugh.

Kimmy scrunches her eyebrows. "Maybe . . ."

I can tell she doesn't believe it any more than I do.

"I'll send people to check it out," I tell her. "In the meantime, maybe hold off on the wandering alone in the woods."

Kimmy nods.

"And tell the others too—stay inside, if you can."

Once Kimmy leaves, I turn back into the apartment. Graylin's and Willow's dark expressions echo the feeling in my chest. The tight, churning fear. That we didn't try hard enough to close the Solarian door. Because now, even though we put guards in the tunnels, something else has gotten through.

"I'm going down to the tunnel to check on things," I say. "If I'm not back in half an hour, call the cops."

It's a bad joke, and neither of them laughs. Willow rises to her feet, and Graylin a second later.

"Marcus will be fine without us for a few minutes," he says to my questioning look. "You're not going down there alone."

———

Sal and six guards—a different team from yesterday; Sal has them rotating out to keep eyes in the tunnel 24/7—meet us at the juncture and accompany us down to the Solarian tunnel. None of them saw anything unusual, and though none of us say it, I wonder if the others are thinking, as I am, about the Solarians' ability to shapeshift. How far does it go—could a Solarian disguise itself as a rat, a moth, a speck of dust? How can we guard against a threat when we don't know what form it will take?

The only sound in the tunnel, besides our footsteps and breathing, is the usual muted howl of wind through the stone labyrinth—the icy whistle of Fiordenkill's arctic breeze, and the hot, wild roar of Byrn's tempestuous gales. None of us says anything. We just walk faster into the darkness—Graylin and Willow first, side by side, then me, the guards flanking us.

When we round the corner, there's nothing but air and darkness. The crack in the Solarian door is wider still, and a terrifying orange light shows through. I think I can hear howling on the other side—whether it's the howling of wind or beasts, I can't tell.

And—goose bumps break out all over me as I see it—there are more scratch marks than before. The long, pale, curved slashes look like wounds in the stone.

My eyes follow the slashes around the crack in the door. Into the hallway. Fading just before they reach my feet. There's no mistaking the implications this time.

A Solarian beast is in Havenfall.

11

THAT EVENING, I'M CROUCHED IN front of the fireplace in the
reception room, trying to focus on taking deep breaths. The distant
strains of the Elemental Orchestra float through the halls from the ballroom, but the music is nearly drowned out by the clatter of hail on the
skylight, so heavy and loud that I'm sure at any moment the glass will
break and rain down on me.

After what we saw in the tunnels this morning, I spoke to the Silver
Prince and Princess Enetta, letting them know that there was almost
certainly a Solarian somewhere on the grounds and that we had to keep
everyone inside. The Silver Prince offered Byrnisian magic to buy me
time. The storm he spun has been raging all day, rattling the windows
and making the light dim and dull. Now it's dark, but the storm is slow
to fade. My heart stutters every time lightning lines the windows in red,
or thunder sounds in the distance. It's the first time I've been alone all

day, and the dread that I've managed to push down through today's meetings is fighting its way back up. Making my pulse race and my ribs feel too tight, like my heart and lungs are fighting for space inside me. Sweat drips down my back, but I still feel cold, even holding my hands close to the flames. Tendrils of panic have worked their way into the edges of my mind and they're pulling, pulling, pulling.

There's a Solarian somewhere near. It could be literally anywhere.

No. I can't go there. Graylin told me after the tunnels that their shapeshifting ability only goes so far. That from what he can tell from the history, most Solarians can only cycle between two or three forms that manifest over their lifetime. They can't take one glance at a person and mimic their appearance, or shrink themselves down to nothing. We'll know it when we see it. I don't need to be afraid of Kimmy hurrying by in the hall, silver meal tray in her hands; or the moth I can see on the glass of the west window, seemingly unbothered by the rain, slowly beating its wings.

But I still am.

Every time I close my eyes, I'm back in Mom's kitchen cupboard, boxes and tins and cans pressing against my back and legs, hearing Mom scream and Nate scream and smelling hot copper blood through the crack in the door. I can't see anything, just flashes of color and movement, blue fur, red blood . . .

Focus, Maddie. I don't have time to wallow in horrible memories, even if I wanted to. I reach for a happy one instead, something Dad told me to do in those early months afterward, when nightmares still woke me up screaming almost every night. *You have more happy memories than scary ones, don't you? Why give the scary ones so much space in your head?*

It's hard to think about the time before the attack, because there's always an undercurrent of fear in the memories now—like I should have known such happiness couldn't last. But I think about walking to the bus stop at the end of the street, clutching Mom's right hand while Nate holds her left, cotton puffs swirling down all around us like summer snow. I think of the dinosaur costume she made me for Halloween and how big and brave I felt with claws and the tail that swung behind me. I think about lying underneath the Christmas tree with Nate, peering through the string lights woven through the branches that looked like a red-and-green galaxy.

When my head feels clearer, I let out a slow breath.

I need to be stronger than this. There's a monster somewhere on the grounds of Havenfall and a hundred people around me who are counting on me to keep them safe. Even if they don't exactly know it yet.

Footsteps sound outside, and I straighten up as the door to the hall opens and Graylin, Willow, Sal, the Silver Prince, and Enetta all file in. Graylin is holding what looks like a bolt of dark leather. The lines of his face seem more deeply drawn than ever before, and I feel a twist of sorrow. Graylin loves poetry and music and Marcus. He shouldn't be holding what I know he's holding. But his jaw is set as he deposits the bundle on the nearest coffee table and carefully unrolls it, the contents gleaming in the low light.

He's brought a collection of weapons from the old armory room on the second floor, weapons that my whole life up till now have just been for show—more a museum exhibit than anything, but not anymore. Willow and I each receive a curved, slender short sword; Graylin and Enetta both get belt holsters with gold-filigreed Fiorden revolvers—light and elegant, rain- and snow-proof and fitted with capsules of poison instead of bullets.

Brekken and I used to play-fight in the woods as kids, pretending to be Fiorden soldiers, sparring with wooden swords or firing BB guns at empty pop cans balanced on tree stumps. Hoisting a weapon feels different now—it's heavy, slippery in my sweating hands as we make our way down into the tunnels. Tomorrow we'll go out to try to find the monster; tonight we'll try again to seal the door so no more can escape. Byrnisian magic didn't work, but maybe Fiorden magic will. They can heal flesh—maybe they can heal whatever's amiss with the doorway too.

It's hard to tell if anything about the doorway has changed since yesterday. The orange light is still there; shadows still flicker and shift on the other side. This time it's Graylin who steps up, along with Enetta, and they stand with their eyes half-closed and their hands against the stone. They're very still, but I can almost feel the slow pull of their magic, the current. Graylin told me once he could feel the movement of water beneath the earth if he looked for it, the same way I can touch someone's throat or wrists and find a pulse. He said the mountains were living things just like him or me, different but no less alive. I wonder what the mountains are telling him now.

After a few minutes of silence—well, silence except for the ominous hum from the other side of the door—Enetta moves. She takes a small knife from her sleeve and makes a shallow cut along the back of her arm, then touches her fingers to it and dabs blood on the wall.

"Um." My voice quavers. Blood makes me queasy, and even though it's only a little—and almost invisible in this dark tunnel anyway—my body reacts, a shudder gripping me for a moment. "What are you guys doing?"

Graylin starts to say something, but Enetta cuts him off, irritable and urgent. "Now."

They start speaking in low, unified voices, too quiet for me to make out the words of a language I don't recognize. The Silver Prince shifts his feet, drifting closer to the wall and closer to me, and I feel the heat of him in the cold tunnel.

Then a kind of charge seems to pass through the air, ghosting over my skin, and the shadows behind the door stir more than usual, waving like seaweed in a tide pool. But after a moment, they lie relatively quiescent again. Graylin turns and Enetta steps back, a hard frown on her face. Whatever they tried, clearly it didn't work.

"I don't like this," Enetta says coldly. She keeps her eyes on the Solarian doorway, drumming bloody fingers on the wall in thought. "I did not bring my people here to put them at risk. If Havenfall has ceased to be safe, the Fiorden delegation will return to Myr forthwith."

My stomach drops. "Didn't you feel anything?"

If the Fiorden delegation leaves now, days after the solstice, it could disrupt the balance of the doorways. And worse, almost, is the thought of the summit ending early. A centuries-long peace ending because I couldn't keep things together for a few days in Marcus's absence.

"There was a ripple," Graylin says, stepping away and rubbing his forehead. "But the doorway didn't respond to our blood."

An idea hits me, and my mouth goes dry, but my words are already spilling out, a surfeit of fear whittling down my ability to think first, talk second. "Try it with my blood."

Graylin's head shoots up, his eyes shockingly hard. "No," he says.

I feel, rather than see, the Silver Prince move. Step closer.

"It might work, Graylin," he says, uncharacteristically gentle. "I don't pretend to be an expert on your magic, but if *whose* blood matters . . ." He glances sidelong at me. "It's a good idea. Maybe the Innkeeper's blood will accomplish something."

"I'm not the Innkeeper." I correct him hastily. "But I am of this world. Maybe that matters?"

I meet Graylin's gaze, willing him to understand. *This is for Marcus. This is for everyone.* But I don't wait for a nod of approval before I step forward and hold out my arm to Enetta. At this point, my skin is crawling from nerves. I would do almost anything if it meant us getting out of here faster.

Enetta sighs and draws a thin red line across the back of my arm. The sting is quick and unexpected, like a doctor who tells you to count to three and sticks you on two. My breath catches, but Enetta already has me by the shoulder and is propelling me forward, gently in spite of her brusqueness, and she lifts my arm to rest against the cold polished wall.

The charge sweeps the air again and the shadows burst into a silent frenzy—not seaweed this time, but more like tentacles, alive and reaching. It's all I can do not to jump back as they stretch and wave out of the cracked doorway, licking at the air.

But after a few tense breaths, they retreat through the doorway. The door doesn't close.

Still, it's something.

"We should try it with Solarian blood," I say, surprising myself with my calmness. Maybe it's just that I've burned up my stores of fear, but no one else needs to know that. "We'll gather a hunting party tomorrow to bring it down, and once we have it, try this again."

I take the handkerchief Graylin passes me, using it to blot the little bit of blood off my arm, and turn to face Enetta. "Princess, if that doesn't work, you and your delegates can return home if you wish. But please, give me one more day to fix this. If we have your warriors' help, I bet we can kill the monster in time for tomorrow's ball."

The flattery works. The princess nods. When I stand up, a ray-of-sunshine smile has broken through the clouds on Willow's face. Graylin looks relieved, and the Silver Prince is watching me, looking thoughtful and faintly impressed.

Despite everything—the fear still running through me, the weight of responsibility, the awfulness of this whole situation—a quick thrill of pride blooms. Maybe I really can do this.

In the entrance hall, we part ways toward our respective rooms, the inn now quiet around us. The dancing is over, though the storm rages on outside. But as I start up the red-and-gold-carpeted staircase toward my room, wanting nothing more than to put my headphones on and drown out the world, someone lays a hand on my arm. The Silver Prince.

"Maddie," he says. The first time he's used my nickname. "Can I speak to you privately for a few moments?"

I blink. Did I make some mistake, some misstep in the tunnels? But then the Silver Prince smiles, a different kind of smile than the stately, gentle one I've seen on him so far. This one is small, subtle, maybe even a little conspiratorial.

"Of course," I say, hiding my nervousness. A talk with the Prince is something you don't turn down. "Where should we go?"

"Follow me," he says without missing a beat.

We take the stairs up, a boyish spring in the Prince's step. I'm tired to the bone, but he seems in good spirits, more animated than I've ever seen him.

"What are you so thrilled about?" I ask—quietly, so as not to wake the delegates in the rooms we pass. "We didn't fix the doorway."

"But it responded to your blood," he shoots back, and his smile is huge and real. "We're that much closer to closing the door for good."

Somehow, we've reached the top of the stairs with me scarcely noticing. The glass-paneled door to the observatory is before us, and I hesitate, thinking suddenly of Brekken, but the Prince charges ahead. After a moment, I follow, feeling unmoored but light in his wake.

In the observatory, the sound of the rain drumming against the glass dome is loud, almost too loud to speak. The glass-enclosed space is uncharacteristically dark, the rain blocking any light that the enchanted glass could refract. Heavy fog wreathes the inn and the mountains, above and below and all around us. There's no moon that I can see, and fat raindrops smear the windows and drip down.

But when the Silver Prince raises his hands, it all stops at once. The rain evaporates from outside the glass, and the clouds scoot away above our heads, leaving a small, perfect circle of clear night sky. Yet the rain continues everywhere else, forming opaque shimmering walls on every side. I feel like we're in a tall, slender cathedral, a cathedral with fog for a floor and rain for the walls and a roof made of stars.

"How did you do that?" I whisper, awestruck in spite of myself. "I thought you had fire magic."

The Silver Prince strolls to the wall and slips out of one of the scarcely visible doors there, stepping out onto the narrow balcony. I follow and feel another rush of wonder as I see—but don't feel—the rain, stopping precisely a few feet away. The stone of the roof beneath us is wet and shining, but we are dry. Moonlight glitters on the Silver Prince's scaled cheekbones.

"I am not content only to protect Oasis, to keep the storms away from the city walls. I want to create a world where Byrnisians can thrive," he says. A shooting star winks over his head. "In ten thousand years, I want to be remembered as someone who plumbed the uncharted reaches of magic to save his people."

I glance at him, surprised to hear his ambition stated so baldly. Yet it's noble, isn't it? A spark of recognition goes through me, quickly followed by the now-familiar guilt and sadness. A week ago, if you asked me, I might have said something similar about my someday-leadership of Havenfall. Ten thousand years might be a stretch, but in a hundred years I'd want whoever lives at the inn to remember my name.

But that dream is evaporated now. At this point, I'll count myself lucky if we get through the summer without any more murders.

I lean out over the low wall surrounding the balcony, stretching my hand to try to touch the wall of rain. Too far—vertigo rears. Almost faster than I can see, the Silver Prince is at my side, his fire-warm hand closing around my shoulder and pulling me gently back. He gives me a small, sad smile, like he understands my desire to feel rain against my skin.

"Wait. Look."

He reaches up and a little piece of storm cloud detaches from the mass and floats our way, rain gusting down. Bits of lightning flicker silently through it. In a moment, the water hits my palm, warm and urgent.

"What uncharted reaches do you have in mind?" I ask. I think of the silver in the Heiress's room. I don't know if the powers she referenced in her records are real or if she's just scamming clueless humans, but what the Prince is doing right now is far beyond the scope of one element—suggesting that Marcus is at least somewhat mistaken about the limits of magic. The Silver Prince doesn't answer for a moment. I look over at him to find him looking back, an odd, calm, curious expression on his face.

"I'm glad I could come to the peace summit at last," he says. "I grow more and more convinced that magic is not something unique to each of our peoples, but a single force that flows through all the worlds." He turns his hands palm up as they rest on the stone wall, and tosses more tiny bolts of lightning between them, like a cat playing with a ball of yarn. Sparks gather between his fingers. "Think of the solstice—a long day here, an eclipse in my city, an aurora in Fiordenkill. There is something that governs us all, that exists everywhere. We can tap into it in our natural-born ways, but perhaps there are other ways too."

"Like objects?" I ask, faking casual. I'm not quite ready to tell him what I found in the Heiress's room, if only because it shows how little control I really have over the inn. But maybe the Prince's theory of the multiverse can still shed some light on her hoard of silver.

"Objects, yes." He grins at me, the lightning from his hands reflected in his eyes. It's so dark out here, yet he seems fully illuminated, like what moonlight and starlight there are have settled on his skin. "Or perhaps there's a way for humans to access it. Or for anyone in any realm to travel safely, the way Solarians can." His eyes flutter closed for a moment. "Don't tell Enetta I said this, but I dearly wish to see the Fiorden aurora in my lifetime."

I laugh, but beneath that, the Silver Prince's words open a deep pit of longing in me. How many times have I wished for exactly that? To explore other realms, especially Fiordenkill? Brekken has told me so much of auroras, bridges carved of shining ice, great wolves that can run so fast they don't break the surface of the snow. I always thought I would have to be content with seeing them via the pictures his words painted, and through my dreams. What if there were another way?

"I've always wanted magic," I say, adding a laugh to balance out the longing I'm sure he can hear in my voice. "I think all humans do."

I try not to think of the fact that I also always dreamed of seeing Fiordenkill with Brekken at my side. I doubt even the Silver Prince knows of magic that can undo a betrayal.

"I think you already have it." The Silver Prince's eyes gleam and, as if to emphasize his words, a pair of meteors slashes through the sky above him. In my tiredness, it seems to me they look like portents. But of what, I don't know.

"I can't help but think it fate that our reigns should coincide like this," the Prince goes on. He brushes the back of my hand with his fingers, and it startles me enough that I don't think to correct him. I'm not a ruler, just . . .

Just what? A caretaker? A substitute—

"Innkeeper," the Prince says softly, as if he can read my thoughts. He smiles. "We will put this Solarian in the ground, and then we will find a way to break through to the power that lives in you."

12

I USUALLY LOVE THE RAIN—THE gentle patter of it on rooftops
and how it makes the light steady and unchanging from dawn to dusk.
Like white noise, it quiets my always-racing mind, makes me feel cozy
and protected. When it rains in Sterling, Dad never asks why I'm not
going out with my friends. I can stay curled up under the covers, watch
old movies and forget about everything else for a while, like the world
has paused its turning just for me.

But it's been raining so long and hard now that everyone at Havenfall is getting antsy, including me. Anxiety bubbles in my gut as I creep
down the stairs, careful not to step on any of the spots I know to be
creaky, though if the delegates can sleep through the rain pounding on
the windowpanes, a loud stair step probably won't disturb them. It isn't
yet dawn—when our hunting party will go out in search of the loose
Solarian—but I've been awake since four, the machine-gun rattle of rain

on the roof yanking me back every time I slipped toward sleep. I should have known it was a lost cause. It's probably a good idea to get something in my stomach anyway before I go out in the woods after a monster. Even if my gut is already churning, I need all my strength.

All I want to do is turn around and run back upstairs and lock my door behind me, close the curtains and wait for someone braver, stronger, *better* to deal with the loose Solarian, the open door, the Heiress's secrets—all of it. Every cell in my body screams to find a safe corner, curl up, and hide with my back to a wall and wait this all out. The natural thing to do when there's a predator loose and you're the prey.

While Graylin spent his spare hours yesterday pouring healing magic into Marcus, Willow was in the library, researching other ways we might try to close the door. But until she hits on something, all we can do is post more guards in the tunnels and, in the meantime, try to hunt down this beast before it starts hunting us. Graylin and Willow and Sal, the Silver Prince and Enetta, and the security staff will all be part of the hunting party. I can't ask them to risk their lives and not go into the woods myself. We have to find the Solarian and end it. We can't fail. I can only pray it's still on the grounds—not gone down the mountain, not escaped into the world to kill someone else's sister, someone else's brother, shatter someone else's life into irreparable shards.

Someone crosses by the stairwell a ways down from me and I freeze. It's a middle-aged man with pale yellow hair and a furtive way of moving, coming from the direction of the front door and going toward the meeting rooms. He's there and gone across the hall before I even fully register it, but something about him makes me stop walking.

It's not that I don't recognize him. There are plenty of people here I don't recognize, new staffers or delegates whose names I haven't gotten around to learning, though Marcus would scold me for that. No, it's because I *did* recognize him. But from where? His walk—head down, shoulders bunched up—set off a skin-crawly feeling in me. And the memory of his leering smile . . .

It hits me. The guy from the bus. The one with the newspaper, who tried to chat me up on the way into Haven.

What is he doing here? And how did he get past the Silver Prince's boundary charm?

Before I can think too much about it, I change course, turning not left toward the kitchens but right, after the man. A creepy dude on a public bus is bad enough, but a creepy guy in my inn, before dawn, today of all days—I don't like it. I want to know what his business is at Havenfall. As I turn the corner, I just see the tail of his shabby coat disappearing around the next one. Careful to tread lightly and keep my distance, I trail him across the first floor. The rain masks the sound of my footsteps.

Soon enough, the man vanishes behind a door in a back hallway. It's one of the meeting rooms, disfavored by the delegates because it's small and plain with no windows. I pause at the end of the hall, ready to duck back behind the corner if need be and wait to see if he'll come back out.

He doesn't. And when I listen closely, I think I can hear a low, muted murmur of voices from inside the room. Goose bumps rise on my arms—he isn't alone. Maybe he does have a legitimate reason to be here, but I have a bad feeling. Slowly, silently, I drift closer until I'm standing right in front of the door, and the voices resolve into clarity.

"—apologies for dropping by unannounced like this," says the man from the bus in a greasy, obsequious tone. "But I wanted to ensure that you were still prepared for the drop-off tomorrow, given your missing associate and these new . . . circumstances."

"I am."

I bite my knuckles—a nervous habit—and a good thing, because my hand muffles the gasp that escapes when the Heiress's voice comes through the door. It is cool, clipped, stately, and unmistakable with her strange, rich-person accent.

"I am not afraid of one stray beast," she says.

Cold shoots down my spine. *She knows.* How? To avoid panic, we haven't told any of the delegates that there's a Solarian on the loose.

The man's voice turns low, wheedling. "You've got to understand. I have buyers waiting for this stuff." A little bit of urgency creeps into his car-salesman spiel as he goes on. "So I just want to make sure—"

"Consider yourself assured, Whit," the Heiress cuts in. "I will be there at the appointed time with what you've asked for."

In another context, her clear disdain for him, Whit, might have made me smirk. But instead, my heart is racing, my stomach churning, as I lean closer to the door. This drop-off they're talking about must be related to the one referred to in the papers Taya and I stole, if not one and the same. *And who is the missing associate the guy mentioned?*

A sour taste fills my mouth. Even just in my own head, I don't have the heart to think his name. Images flash through my vision. *His smile when he kissed me. My key ring in her desk.* Whatever Brekken was doing with my keys, it must have been connected to the Heiress's smuggling operation. And the fact that she knows there's a monster on the grounds makes me even more suspicious that they had something to do with the door opening, as well. But I still don't know *why.*

I push away those thoughts. It seems obvious that the Heiress is selling Adjacent Realms artifacts to an outsider, a human. A sleazy one at that. If this gets out—if it hasn't already—it could expose the inn. It could destroy everything my uncle has worked so hard to preserve.

The anger in my gut builds so fast and hot that I don't realize the voices have stopped. I don't register the footsteps coming toward the door until it's too late. I leap back and turn down the hall, but don't have time to escape before the door swings open and the Heiress storms out, creepy bus guy—Whit—two steps behind her.

They both stop short when they see me. I pivot toward them, hoisting on a fake smile and hoping it looks like I was just passing by. Deep down, though, I know the Heiress isn't stupid. She may be a lot of things—a liar, a backstabber, a con—but not stupid.

"Madeline," she says, her voice brittle. "What are you doing here?"

"I live here," I say. I mean for it to come out light, a joke, but my true feelings sneak in and it drops from my lips hard and sharp-edged. *This is my home.* "What are *you* doing here?"

"Just some summit business," she says, words airy, but there's strain below the surface.

"Oh?" I look pointedly toward Whit, waiting for an introduction. "Bit early for that, isn't it?"

If he recognizes me from the bus, he doesn't show it. He glances rapidly between the Heiress and me, a sheen of sweat growing on his face.

"Yes," the Heiress says, edging away from me down the hall. "Sensitive business."

Anger rears up under my skin, and I step closer so that she stops moving. "My apologies, Lady Heiress," I say, hoping my tone communicates just how *not* sorry I really am. "But as you know, my uncle is still indisposed, so I'm carrying out the Innkeeper's duties in his stead. And the protocol says that all new visitors have to be approved by the Innkeeper before they enter the grounds."

I have no idea if that's a real rule, but it seems like it should be. Add that to the list of things I need to ask Marcus when he wakes up.

The Heiress's eyes are wide, surprise and indignation chasing each other across her softly lined face. "I'm sorry, Madeline," she says eventually, sounding wounded. "But I—"

But whatever she's going to say is lost when an earsplitting clap of thunder from outside rattles the windowpanes.

It snaps me back to myself, and I yank my phone from my pocket, look at the time. 5:33. Shit. The hunting party—we were supposed to convene in the entrance hall at 5:30 sharp.

I look at the Heiress, pouring all the coldness and authority I can muster into my voice. "I have to go. We'll talk later."

"Madeline!" Her retort is sharp, but it fades into nothingness behind me, because I've already turned on my heel and walked away.

———

The sun is usually rising by now, but the heavy clouds prolong the night, so all we can see outside is fog and the raindrops splitting against the windows. The Silver Prince is the first person I see when I skid into the entrance hall. He's pacing along the far wall, a small flame dancing above the palm of his upraised hand. As he walks, he twirls the flames around his fingers like a one-handed cat's cradle.

"Maddie," comes Graylin's voice from my right. He hurries toward me and deposits two objects in my arms. A chain mail shirt, I realize, lifting the heavy thing by its metallic sleeve. And a Fiorden revolver, carved with snarling wolves. Graylin already has one strapped to his hip, and I see the glint of metal under his fur cloak. Around the room, Willow, Sal, and Enetta are also donning armor and weapons. The beautiful antique side table with pearl inlay, the one Annabelle was said to have treasured, is piled with guns and swords and knives. It's silent except for the rain and clanking of chainmail, dark except for the torchlight that makes shadows dance along the wood-paneled walls.

Once everyone is dressed and has their weapons strapped on, Willow makes the rounds, handing us each one more thing from a cloth pouch at her waist. A Byrnisian whistle, sleekly carved from what looks like onyx.

"We'll split up in the woods to cover more ground," she explains, raising her voice just enough to be heard above the rain. "The gravity barrier has likely stopped the Solarian from leaving the grounds, so we should expect to find it. But whoever does, they are not to attack the beast alone. Blow the whistle, and the rest of us will come to aid."

Fear roils my insides as Graylin opens the front door, and the rain and wind and sound of distant thunder gust into the hall. Outside, against the dim not-quite-dawn, the pine trees dance frantically in the wind.

Graylin catches my arm as I go to file out, the rest of the group already spreading out over the lawn, shadowy figures disappearing into the rain. "Maddie," he says, voice rough from lack of sleep. "You don't have to do this. No one is expecting you to."

"I know." I smile at him as best I can and walk outside, flinching at the freezing rain that immediately splatters my face. "But I'm not doing it for anyone else." *I'm doing it for Havenfall.*

Graylin and I part ways on the lawn, and I don't let myself stop and think, but plunge straight into the trees. I can do this.

I know these woods. Brekken and I played here as kids, too many hours to count spent dodging between the trees, turning sticks we picked up off the ground into swords and wizards' wands, chasing squirrels and pretending to be Byrnisian warriors after a squall-storm, or crouching very still in the undergrowth, imagining ourselves Fiorden hunter-warriors. I've spent days alone out here trying to catch glimpses of foxes or deer, wandered the grounds after dark to see a meteor shower or the night-blooming Byrn flowers Willow planted in the woods.

I have never, not once, felt afraid here. But now I am nothing but fear. It crawls under my skin, feeling like it's going to burst free any second, changing the familiar shapes of the trees and bushes into shadows strange and threatening. At least the overhang of leaves stops most of the hail. Small animals scuttle through the undergrowth and the distant shouts wrap around me as thunder shudders my bones. I listen for a whistle, but the woods seem to swallow sound, like a stone sinking through water without leaving a ripple.

The woods are dark, the light level more like twilight than sunrise with the swollen gray rain clouds. I cut in the direction of Mirror Lake, so that the ground slopes slightly downward under my feet.

And something blue flashes up ahead of me. As my head snaps up to look, my foot catches on a root and all at once I'm sprawling, hitting the ground hard on my ribs and elbows and rolling. The carpet of dead leaves and pine needles absorbs the blow, but not by much, and stars burst in front of my eyes as the back of my head slams into the earth. A coppery taste fills my mouth as I roll back around and heave to my feet, grasping for the whistle and blowing it. The shriek cuts through the air, blasting my ears.

Another flash of dark blue through the trees, and terror spills through me. *It's here.*

I stagger backward. Hail spatters the ground around me. The blue flash was maybe twenty yards away. My hand flies to my waist but I feel only my belt, the sheath light and empty. *Where's my revolver?*

I see it lying on the ground to my left, just as the Solarian bursts into view up ahead.

It roots me to the ground, the sight of it. And shockingly the first word that pops into my head as the Solarian freezes ten yards away from me is *beautiful*. It has a long, tiger-like body. Shifting muscles under fur the blue-black-gray color of an arctic ocean. Eyes like flames.

Lots of things that can kill you are beautiful. A high cliff. A lightning strike. A freezing cold night on the mountains.

That doesn't change the fact that this is the same kind of monster that dragged my brother away, leaving me and Mom nothing but blood on the floor and my life snapped in two. *Before, after.*

The beast and I lock eyes. I can see the intelligence there, the cunning. It's faster than me. Bigger. Stronger. It could rip me in half if it decided to.

It's not moving now; maybe it doesn't think I'm a threat. That gives me a chance. Just one small sliver of light. Shoot the thing. Get everyone the hell inside.

Fear weighs me down like ice. Tells me I can't move, that I'll die if I do. But there's nothing else for it, no one else in sight. And besides— this is my job. This is what Marcus would do, anyway. If he sent people out into the woods after a monster, he would lead them. He would fight.

I take a slow, deep breath, careful to make it silent, not show my body moving. My blood roars in my ears, blotting out all other sound.

I dive for the gun. I hit the ground hard, but my fingers close on metal. I twist to see blue and flame bearing down on me.

Aim.

Shoot.

The Solarian's scream drowns the echoes of the gunshot. It's the same scream I heard from my bedroom that first night, but now it's right there, and the gun clatters to the ground because I've clapped my hands over my ears. I can't stop myself. But the monster is already gone, crashing a path through the underbrush. The scream is gone, but echoes bounce through the trees, inside my head.

I sit up shakily. My ears ring and my chest aches and my blood races through me so fast I feel like it's going to jump out of my skin. But after a few seconds, everything around me is silent. The woods are still, all life fled or hidden.

Until Graylin bursts from the shadows and stops in front of me, knife in one hand and revolver in the other. His alert gaze sweeps the clearing and lands on me on the ground, and his eyes widen. He sheathes the weapon and kneels next to me.

"What happened?" he asks, taking a moment to blow the warning whistle. His eyes scan me from head to toe, and I know he's checking for injuries.

"I—" My voice shakes. I scoot backward to sit against a tree and stay there, trembling, my hands clutching air. I strain my ears for more distant screams or movement. "I shot the Solarian, I think." Scared it off, but clearly didn't slow it down.

It's okay, I tell myself, knowing I'm lying to myself, but it's all I can do with the adrenaline still rushing through me. Someone else will finish it off. And besides, my ankle throbs—I must've twisted it and not realized—and my ribs ache when I gingerly prod at them. Bruised, or even cracked, I can't tell. It's not like I could have given chase, anyway. Shock and exhaustion push my fear down to a low, muted buzz—ever-present, but not overpowering—as I pull myself together and Graylin loops an arm around my shoulders. I don't strictly need help, but I'm glad for his closeness on the way back to the inn.

When I stumble out of the woods, I see that Sal and the Silver Prince are under the gazebo with a couple of the security guards, Ricky and Kara. They're all looking at something, their backs to us, and I give Graylin a worried glance as we head over.

My heart drops when I see what they're looking at—*who* they're looking at, sitting on one of the damp benches with her head in her hands, her blond braid trailing over the shoulder of her jacket.

Taya.

"Hi there," she says weakly.

"What are you doing here?" I blurt out.

The Silver Prince steps forward, looking furious. His jaw is tight, his silver hair shining with rainwater. "I was on my way to respond to the whistle when I ran into this servant," he spits, and I cringe at the word. "She claims she was out walking in the woods." He looks hard at Taya and then from me to Graylin. "Did either of you see it?"

"I did," I say shortly, not wanting to think about my failure to take the Solarian down. After I let it get away, it found Taya—it must have been sheer dumb luck that the Prince was there, and it didn't kill her. "I shot at it, but I guess not straight enough."

I feel sick as everyone looks at me and I try to figure out how to do damage control. I *told* Taya to quit it with her midnight strolls. But I also lied to her about why—that stupid mountain lion story which she probably saw right through. Why did I expect her to stay in when I hadn't told her about the real danger?

Taya and the Silver Prince lock eyes, which only makes me feel worse.

"I just saw the Solarian down by Mirror Lake, so it must be close," I say to the Prince, trying to break the tension. "I'll handle Taya," I add, not needing to fake the glare I shoot her way.

"Inside." I turn to her. "Come on, it isn't safe out here."

She nods, mouth pressed into a thin line. Suddenly I realize how oddly she's sitting, hunched over with her left arm in front of her. How she's slow to stand. She's hurt. But she doesn't say anything, just falls into step beside me as we walk back toward the inn. Fear climbs bitterly up the inside of my throat as we walk. I offer an arm, but she shakes her head, jaw set.

"I'm fine. Just need to sit down for a bit."

"What are you even doing out here?" I ask her, shaking rain out of my eyes. "This isn't a midnight walk, more like a midnight swim." I try to keep the annoyance out of my voice, but it's hard. Her inability to sit tight like everyone else at the inn just made me look like an idiot in front of the Silver Prince. Like I can't even keep our staff inside for a few days, much less run the whole inn.

"Looking for the Solarian." Her eyes flash defiantly, cutting off my argument before I can make it. "And I found it."

"What?" Shock pulls the word from me. "How do you even know about that?"

"I put two and two together. It wasn't hard." Irritation and pain mix in her voice. "You told me the door was open and that there was something dangerous on the grounds. I can shoot. I can fight. I want to help, even if it got me first this time before running off. You promised to help me find Terran. I can help you with this."

I flinch at the memory. It seems like a dumb, empty promise now, in the daylight. Why did I promise Taya to help get her brother back when everything is falling apart around me? Will we even live that long?

"But you're hurt."

Taya nods, not meeting my eyes. "I guess I do need to work on those shooting-and-fighting skills." She pulls her jacket closer to her body. "I'd say it's just a scratch, but unfortunately that's not actually the case."

I still catch a glimpse, a mess of shiny red at her shoulder, and my stomach drops.

Wordlessly I take the lead, steering her inside to a heated back porch that Willow has converted into a temporary infirmary. The healers must still be outside. From the porch, we can see the town of Haven laid out beneath us like something out of a toy train set, untouched by the storm. It looks strange to see the sun on the distant buildings while thunder still shakes Havenfall's foundations.

Taya sits down on one of the white-blanketed beds, clutching her shoulder and staring hollowly out the glass walls at the valley and the town below us. I go to the cabinet to get the first-aid supplies, my stomach clenching. I wonder what she's thinking. Probably she's wishing she'd never come to the inn.

All I wanted was to get away, get out of Sterling, spend my summer hiking the mountains, dancing in the ballroom, studying with Marcus, kissing Brekken. And now everything is so screwed up, and I can't see a way to make it right. *One bite at a time, Maddie,* I tell myself. Fix Taya—that's all I can do right now.

Fix Taya. Kill the monster on the grounds. Close the Solarian door. Wake Marcus up.

She slides off her jacket as I approach, and I stop dead, all the blood rushing out of my head.

It's worse than I thought. Way worse. It looks like something has taken a chunk out of her shoulder. The whole arm and upper back of her blue T-shirt is stained red, and I think I can see the white glint of bone somewhere in there too. The first-aid stuff clatters to the ground as I reach out for the couch to keep me from falling. The world spins a little. Maybe it's a good thing I didn't eat breakfast, because it would be coming back up now if I had.

"Oh," Taya mumbles, looking down at her shoulder. "That's . . . I didn't realize . . ."

A tumble of swear words falls from my lips. "You didn't realize your bone was sticking out of your shoulder?"

How did she even walk up from the woods? This isn't a matter for antiseptic and stick-on bandages. I can't just stitch this up. She needs to go to the ER. But no, I can't send her away without giving her forgetting-wine first. And no way I'm doing that in her current state.

Still cursing, I yank my phone out of my pocket and stab at Graylin's icon, hold it to my ear while I pace.

Ring . . . ring . . . He's probably still out in the woods.

"Hey." Taya's voice is soft and slow, her eyes sluggish as they follow my movements. "How come you got to keep your phone?"

"Innkeeper's niece, remember—"

But then Taya's eyes flutter and she slumps to the side. I rush over and drop beside her, propping her up against the headboard before she topples into the bed, shuddering as I feel the warm slickness of blood on my hands.

Keep it together, Maddie.

She sags against me, then blinks in confusion and straightens up.

"Sorry," she mutters, her voice far away, drifting. "I don't know what happened."

Graylin hasn't picked up; when the call goes to voicemail, I hang up and try again. This time I get him.

"Maddie? Are you okay?"

"I'm okay," I say. "I'm in the infirmary with Taya. She was hurt by the Solarian. Could you help? Or send another healer?"

A pause. "So just to confirm, you're not hurt?" Graylin asks.

At another time, I'd roll my eyes, but right now there's no room in me for anything except worry for Taya.

"My ankle's a little messed up, but I'm fine. Can you please hurry?"

I hang up and rotate to face Taya, keeping a hand on her arm as I do, trying to ignore the blood under my palm. We can't both faint.

"Help is coming," I tell her, feeling horribly ineffectual. "I need you to stay awake until then."

Her eyes are lidded. "So-lar-i-an." She draws out the word, lingering over the strange syllables. "Why do you call them soul-devourers?"

"Because that's what they do."

I don't want to talk about that, don't want to think about my close call or how the monster is still out there. I stick some pillows on either side of her. She's getting blood all over the bed but that doesn't matter, doesn't matter. Needing to move, I get up and rush to collect the scattered contents of the first-aid kit. I can at least get her ready for the healer.

I return to her side and sit down carefully again, not missing how Taya sucks in her breath as the mattress shifts beneath her. I look her over, swallowing to get my dizziness under control. The Solarian's bite has ruined her T-shirt, shreds of fabric clinging to the wound with dried blood. I need to clean it out, I realize distantly.

"I think I have to cut your shirt to clean this out," I say, trying hard to keep the hysteria out of my voice. "Is that okay?"

"Why?"

"Because I need to disinfect—"

Taya shakes her head once, and then winces at the movement. "Not that. That's fine. I meant why do you think the Solarian wants to kill us?"

I chew my lip as I take the scissors from their plastic case. "I guess it's hungry."

"What if it just wants to be left alone?" she mumbles.

I ignore this, taking Taya's arm and extending it as gently as I can, but it still makes her jaw flex and her lips thin as she holds back the pain. "I'm really sorry."

I cut from the hem of her sleeve to her collar, careful to avoid her braid and the soft skin of her throat. The back side of her shirt flops down when I make the final snip, exposing a black bra strap and a dusting of freckles on her shoulder blade, but the front side stays where it is, glued in place by blood.

The copper smell threatens to send me back to Mom's kitchen, Nate's blood spreading over the floor, me useless and helpless in the cupboard. But that's not me anymore. I'm not a child—I can't be a child about

172

this, for Taya's sake. I bite the inside of my cheek to chase the faintness away and unwrap gauze and antiseptic.

"The Solarian beasts are intelligent," I tell her, mostly to give myself something to focus on besides the blood. "I know that much. Brekken said they have all sorts of wild technology in their world. Maybe they see us as so far beneath them that there's no difference between us and deer."

Taya speaks slowly, like even in the haze of blood loss, she's choosing her words carefully. "What was it like when you saw it today?"

I shake my head as I dampen the cloth with antiseptic and screw the cap back on. "Terrifying."

I hope my bullet did its job, hope the Solarian is in pain right now. Payback for doing this to Taya. My hands shake.

Calm down, focus on something positive, I hear Dad say in my head. I close my eyes briefly and call up memories of Nate—not the kitchen, not the end, but other times. Playing together on the little hill behind our house, racing down with flattened cardboard boxes for summertime sleds so often that the grass started growing sideways. Nate helping Mom bake brownies, his head barely clearing the top of the counter as he stirred a bowl of rich brown batter. When we played hide-and-seek and I would hide in the same place every time—curled in the nook behind the old tweed couch—but he'd always look everywhere else first and still pretend to be surprised when he found me.

Carefully, I peel the ragged edges of her T-shirt away from the wound. Taya's breath hisses out through her teeth. Then I lift the damp cloth, its harsh chemical smell stinging my nose.

"I'm sorry," I say, and my words have a weird sort of echo in my own ears. Like it's someone else talking, telling me: "This is going to hurt."

13

ANXIETY COATS THE AIR OF Havenfall for the rest of the day.

Sal still has people out patrolling the grounds, has for almost sixteen hours straight now, but nobody's seen the monster since it bit Taya and I shot at it. I think we've managed to keep the hunting party a secret, but the delegates know something is wrong. I saw it in their frowns and darting eyes at breakfast, after I left Taya in the infirmary and dragged myself to the dining hall to stammer through announcements. All through the day as I sat in on meetings and negotiations, I heard it in the whispers that trailed after me, even if I couldn't make out the words.

The beast is still out there, and the door is still open. I couldn't find the Heiress anywhere today, so no answers on that front, and Marcus is still asleep. Nothing is fixed.

Now the Elemental Orchestra is playing in the ballroom like every evening, but even from my bedroom I can hear that the strains of music are more subdued, less joyful than usual. I've skipped out on tonight's celebration to sit up with the Heiress's papers, to try to make sense of the hundreds of lines of cramped writing. It reads like nonsense. Oblique references and dates and times with seemingly no connecting thread.

But now, after catching her meeting with Whit, it seems increasingly important to figure out what the hell she's up to. And one thing in the documents is clear enough. A list of dates and times next to a Haven address. The antique store. A meeting, happening tomorrow morning.

I text Willow and Graylin, telling them that I'm feeling sick and probably won't be able to make it to breakfast tomorrow. Guilt stabs through me as I do. I know the delegates will have more and more questions the longer we keep them cooped up inside, and by ditching the inn, I'm leaving it to Graylin and Willow to field them. But I don't want them to worry about me while I get to the bottom of whatever the Heiress is doing—and maybe get some clue as to how to close the doorway to Solaria. If the delegates find out it's open, we'll have a riot on our hands.

It's hard to get to sleep, with threats both below in the tunnels— the door—and outside—the beast. I can't decide what would be worse: if it's still on the grounds somewhere, or if it's slipped past the guards and escaped into the mountains. If it's here, everyone at Havenfall is endangered. If it's elsewhere, the whole world is.

And weighing even heavier on my heart is the fact that Marcus is still unconscious. Last time I checked in on him he looked better, his breathing even, and the color in his cheeks made it seem like he was simply asleep. But he still wouldn't wake up. I sat with him, talked to him, and even shook his shoulder. Nothing. Graylin's been alternating between helping me with meetings and healing Marcus, but he seems wrecked, his eyes drooping through our meetings even as his posture stays always perfect. I don't know how long he can go on like this, I don't know what kind of magic he's using on my uncle, and I don't really want to ask about it either. Because that would mean . . . I don't want to think about what we'll do, either of us, if he doesn't wake up soon.

———

I dream that Brekken and I are walking along one of the high mountain paths above the inn, not holding hands, but close enough that our fingers graze together with each step. The sky is blue above us, the valley green, Mirror Lake like a disk of silver far below. Brekken turns to me, and I dimly remember that something is wrong, I'm supposed to be angry, but I can't remember why. He's so lovely, his eyes so bright blue they might be holes to the sky, his hair and smile dazzling. He leans in for a kiss, and my heart starts to gallop, my breath whipping away in the mountain breeze.

But when I lift my hands, I don't feel his sharp jaw dusted with stubble, his cool skin and short hair. Instead, my fingertips meet a warm throat and fine, soft hair that falls freely around my hands. The breath brushing my face smells like flowers and spearmint, and when I open my eyes, the ones looking back are brown, not blue. Taya blinks and cocks one eyebrow, and I realize my fingers are still knotted in her hair when the ground beneath us vanishes.

Suddenly we're falling, falling, the world becoming a terrifying vacuum of sky and pines and jagged mountains. They rush up around us, sharp as swords, and I close my eyes, brace for the impact . . .

Then I land and I'm in a cupboard. The cupboard, glass shattering somewhere outside. But I'm not a little kid. I'm sixteen, and my elbows and knees ache where they're pressed against the wooden walls. Someone is screaming outside, begging me to save them. When I call out and bang on the doors, nothing happens. The walls just constrict tighter around me.

I wake up confused, my heart beating painfully fast, and I'm tangled in my sweaty sheets. The scream of metal on metal and the cold embrace of water reverberate in my mind, new ingredients in the familiar nightmare cocktail.

Sitting up, I let out a shuddering breath and glance at my phone. It's the middle of the night. And if the dream told me one thing, it was this: I have to follow this lead with the Heiress all the way down. Brekken is mixed up in it too. I need to know the truth or I might never sleep soundly again.

And the other part of the dream, with Brekken, with Taya—what was that about? Sure, she's attractive, even with her rough edges and hard questions. If we crossed paths in Sterling, I might flirt with her, if I was feeling especially brave that day. But my heart has always belonged to Brekken.

Maybe it's because I've been worried about Taya after leaving her with Enetta's healers; maybe this is my subconscious telling me to check on her? I pull on a hoodie over my leggings and tank top and pad downstairs.

I'm on my way to the infirmary, but something stops me when I'm halfway across the second floor—the door to the library is open, a lamp on inside. I glance through the doorway. Taya's curled on a couch by the picture window, her pale hair almost glowing in the lamplight. The window behind her is black, nothing visible outside. The thought of what could be out there in the dark makes my heart beat faster, but it doesn't seem to trouble Taya.

I pause in the doorway. I expected her to be asleep in the infirmary; I expected to just poke my head in, confirm she was all right, and get back to bed. I feel suddenly self-conscious about my rumpled hair and ragged hoodie. But before I can retreat, Taya looks up at me. Raises her eyebrows.

"Hey." She smiles. She looks tired, the shadows under her eyes pronounced, but a thousand times improved over last night. She wears a black long-sleeved shirt and skinny jeans, and there's no sign of her horrible shoulder wound.

I step in and slide the door shut behind me, not wanting to wake anyone else. The only sound is the rain outside and the faintest buzz from the lamp. The smell of paper and books is a comfort and a sting all at once. I've been avoiding the library. It was here, last year, when I finally realized Brekken might feel the same way about me as I did about him. We were cooped up because of a summer thunderstorm, bored and restless, taking turns reading to each other out of *Outlander*, exaggerating the sexy bits and trying to get the other to blush. Until I tensed up during one of the action scenes and Brekken oh-so-casually reached over and took my hand.

I stopped reading and turned to him, and I'd never really understood before then how eyes could sparkle, but his were definitely doing all the things I'd only ever read about. Sparkling, glittering, smoldering. The air between us was suddenly charged somehow. We might've kissed then if a gaggle of bored Byrnisian delegates hadn't charged in at the exact wrong moment.

Taya clears her throat, snapping me back to the present. "What's up?"

I blink, willing the heat on my cheeks to fade away. "Shouldn't you be resting?" I ask, crossing the room toward her.

Taya lifts her right hand from the book, stretching her arm out in front of her and rotating it. "No need. This magic stuff is pretty cool." She meets my eyes. "Couldn't sleep either?"

I shake my head and perch on the arm of the couch. I look down at the book she's reading—something that looks Byrnisian and relatively recent, with shiny ivory filigree spreading over the brown cover. It's called *The Silver Prince*.

I laugh in surprise. It's startling to think that the Silver Prince I've met—the man who I think, I hope, is starting to see me as more than Marcus's little niece, as someone to respect—is the subject of whole books. Though of course it makes sense; he's impressive enough.

"Anything in there I should know about?" I joke.

But Taya's not laughing. Her brows draw together as she glances between me and the book. "Guess I was just curious, after I had the honor of meeting him in the woods today," she says quietly. Her eyes flicker up. "Maddie, doesn't something feel . . . off to you?"

"About . . ."

"Just—*him*. The Prince." She shakes the book.

"Um . . ." I remember last night, how the Prince took me to the observatory and told me his theories about magic in the calm heart of the storm. "Not really? I mean, he's intense, but . . ." I think of the shooting stars flashing over his head. "I think he means well."

"He said something about you, something weird. 'She's perfect. She'll save us.' "

My face heats with a mixture of pride, surprise, and discomfort. "That sounds like a compliment, honestly."

It feels good to know that at least one person at Havenfall other than Graylin has faith in me. Especially now that, more and more, I don't have faith in me—to find the beast, close the door, stop the Heiress's smuggling, fix everything. Keep Havenfall safe. But I don't like the direction this conversation is going.

"What? Don't you agree?" I mean for it to sound teasing, but it comes out weighty and breathless, almost pleading.

"You know I do. It's just . . . the way he said it." Taya seems to grope

179

for words for a moment, then sighs and looks down, setting the book aside. "Sorry, it's nothing. So why are you awake?"

I feel strangely hurt and defensive. "Nothing. Just nightmares, the usual."

"I get that," she says, gently. "Do you want to talk about it?"

I'm about to shake my head, but something stops me. My usual answer to that question is *hell no*, but if anyone would understand, it's Taya. I take a breath, trying to get past the feeling that something is sitting on my chest, cinching my ribs, stopping me from a full inhale.

"I told you that a Solarian killed my brother, right?"

Taya nods, looking not surprised, but troubled. "And you saw it."

"Sort of." I look down at my hands twisted in my lap. "I was home with my mom and Nate one night when I was five and he was eight. We were baking brownies."

I rub my eyes, as if that will chase away the memories flashing behind them. But it doesn't. I see the scene so clearly: Nate in a red kid's apron, pouring brownie batter into a pan with the utmost serious concentration. I remember stirring the batter of another bowl, sneaking licks of the spoon while Mom's back was turned as she checked the oven.

"But then we heard a window break." I speak slowly at first, careful, but with Taya's silent attention on me, the words come faster and faster. It feels good to talk, good to be listened to. When I was with Brekken, he was an open book, he told me everything and I told him everything. We knew everything about each other. It's weird, now, to try to explain something so massive to someone new. The dark wound that my whole life has grown around, healed over, but which still festers deep under my skin.

"Mom put me in a cupboard, but there wasn't enough room for both of us. I guess the Solarian got there before Mom could find another hiding spot. I . . . I heard it attack Nate and I just froze." This is where I would choke up, usually, but right now I feel hollow, empty. Like there's a pit in my chest instead of a heart and lungs. Maybe the nightmare wrung the last bit of feeling from me. "If I'd left the cupboard earlier, if I'd tried to distract it . . ."

But there's no *if*, only *after*. After, my memories become fragmented, scattered moments as sharp as loose razor blades: our front yard washed with red and blue police lights, a funeral without a casket and without Mom. Sitting in the front row between Dad and Marcus, too numb to cry. The stares and whispers at school, the sitting alone on the swing set, watching the other kids run around with their friends and sisters and brothers. After, every good memory I have of Nate comes with a counterweight, the memory of his scream.

"You were a kid; it wasn't your fault," Taya says. "But . . ." She casts her eyes down, uncertain. "You didn't see any of it? How did you know it was a Solarian?"

My stomach drops. "I saw a little through the doors. Blue fur and orange eyes."

"And your mom didn't say anything?"

I shake my head. Now the grief is starting to creep back in, the shadow elephant. "Our neighbors called the police, but they didn't get there until after Nate and the monster were gone. When they did get there, Mom told them she killed Nate. And she's been saying it ever since."

Her eyes widen. "Why? Even if the police wouldn't believe that the killer was a monster from another world, why would she say she did it?"

"We've never talked about it, but I think . . ." A lump forms in my throat and it's hard to talk. "I think she was trying to protect Havenfall. She was afraid that someone *would* believe her. And the secret of the realms and the doorways would get out."

181

Taya looks horrified. She tries to school her face into neutrality, but her voice shakes when she says, "That's noble, I guess." She doesn't look like she believes it.

"But it meant I lost her too," I whisper. "And now that's been the party line for so long, I think even she's forgotten it's not the truth."

No remorse. That's the phrase that kept coming up in the trial and on the news. From the outside, the case looked murky—no body, no history of violence, no explanation. If Mom had fought back, said she was innocent, maybe people would find some other explanation. Even if she shouted from the rooftops that it was a Solarian, an insanity ruling would keep her off death row.

But instead she stuck by the first and most important lesson Nate and I got as children. *Havenfall is our secret. You both must always protect it.*

Soon, she'll give her life to protect that secret. And sometimes I feel like she's already given her soul.

14

EVENTUALLY, MORNING COMES. I WAKE UP in my room exhausted from the witching-hour heart-to-heart with Taya, with a lump of dread already fully formed in my chest about the task ahead of me.

Pale morning light streams through my windows. Birds sing outside, and somewhere a woodpecker drills away at a tree, *thudthudthudthudthud*. A memory wells to the surface of my mind. Once, when I was thirteen, a woodpecker landed on my windowsill and started going at the wall as if all the bugs in the world were hidden inside. I ran and brought Brekken back to my room to see it up close, the bright red plume of his head, the black-and-white-striped wings. I watched the grin unfurl across Brekken's face, and though he'd been in my room a hundred times before, that was the first time it made my stomach flip to see him inside, sitting on top of my old quilt.

One bite at a time. Dad still tells me that all the time, and it's become my mantra these past few days. I can only do one thing at a time. *So you'd better choose carefully, and whatever you do, do it well.* I shoot him a quick text before silencing my phone and shoving it into my backpack. *Miss you.*

Right now, my One Bite is hauling out my old bike—the jeep can't get through the Silver Prince's gravity barrier—and pedaling down the winding road to Haven, with the hope of catching the Heiress in the act of smuggling. I know she's trading magic artifacts—or what she claims are magic artifacts—but I still don't have the first guess as to why, or how she's getting out of the grounds.

Is it for money? The Heiress has always seemed so grand, so above all the petty concerns that drive the rest of us. But maybe not. Does she want the notoriety? Even if only 3 percent of people in the wider world believed a story about Havenfall, that would be enough to make the leaker famous—and enough to ruin us. Neither of these motivations seems to fit the Heiress, though, no matter how I turn them around in my head.

The Silver Prince's storm, meant to keep everyone inside Havenfall, only stretches to the grounds' borders. When I slip through the increased-gravity barrier, holding my breath against the feeling of weight crushing my lungs, the rain stops; the woods beyond are dry, as is the road. By the time I reach town, it feels intensely strange how normal everything is. I've only been at Havenfall for four days, but it seems like weeks we've been cut off from the world.

In town beneath the ridge, it's just another lazy June morning, the start of a bright day. Haven wakes up in the slow rhythms of summer. People in bathrobes or sweats drift onto their front porches, smoking or sipping coffee. Somewhere I hear a radio playing Willie Nelson. One stooped old man is feeding chickens in front of his house; a middle-aged woman walks an ancient, rotund beagle down the cracked sidewalks. Ms. Douglas arranges cookies in the window of the town's lone café; Lisa at the general store emerges from inside as I pass and flips the wooden sign on the front door to Open.

Shutters open in windows.

Birds sing in the trees.

But a slow dread is gathering in my stomach all the same.

The antique shop, where the drop-off is supposed to take place at 8:30, is at the far end of Main Street. It's 8:10 now. I pull off at the still-closed gas station and lock my bike to a broken pump, out of sight from the road. There, I sit for a few moments, taking deep breaths and going over what I need to do. Intercept the Heiress. Stop this deal before it goes down, and make her tell me what the hell she's doing.

The Heiress used to be like family. But that was before she went behind Marcus's back and undermined Havenfall's secrecy for some quick cash, put the doorways at risk, and exposed all the Adjacent Realms to discovery. It's a betrayal almost too big to fathom.

At a quarter after eight, I leave my bike and set off toward the antique store, skirting the back of the gas station and the small cow field that sits between the two buildings. My boots leave marks on the dew-damp grass, and big-eyed cows look up at me inquisitively as I pass.

It seems peaceful, but anxiety prickles the back of my neck, and I can't stop myself from glancing a few times toward the woods. The Solarian could be anywhere. The people on their porches, the guy and his chickens, the lady and her chubby dog—they're all in danger as long as the monster is out there. I'm in danger too. I have to fix this soon.

And then, just as I'm slipping into a copse of pines running along the side of the antique shop, I hear hooves from the road.

It's not actually that unusual to see people on horses here in Haven—there are plenty of narrow, windy, rocky paths where cars can't go. But the Heiress had better hope most of the townspeople are still asleep and not looking out their windows, because her grasp of modern fashion is . . . not great. This morning she's wearing her usual riding outfit: elegant leggings, a tunic, leather boots, and a flowing green cape that drapes over the back of her chestnut horse as it trots down the road. And a cowboy hat.

I have to swallow an incongruous bark of laughter as I step out of the trees and into her path. But it dies fast as the anger bubbles up inside me, heating my face.

The Heiress jumps at the sight of me, yanking the horse to a placid halt. "Maddie," she says, and shock tinges her voice. "What are you doing here?"

"Trying to find out what *you're* doing here," I growl.

Some of the color leaves her cheeks. "Madeline, this really isn't a good time." She has a black linen bag slung across her body, bulging with something that looks heavy.

"A good time for what?" I glance up and down the road to make sure we're alone. I'm having a hard time keeping my voice down. "How long have you been running this little one-woman black market?"

The Heiress tugs on the reins, a quick, violent motion to bring the horse trotting over to the side of the road, opposite the antique shop. I stalk after her.

"Quiet," she hisses over her shoulder, her eyes darting to the storefront—still quiet, closed, the small parking lot empty—before drilling back into me. "Listen to me, Madeline. This isn't what you think. And it's certainly not a one-woman affair." She dismounts, ridiculously graceful for someone her age, landing lightly on the pavement. "But we can't talk about this now. It's not safe."

"Because you're meeting that guy Whit. That buyer. You're pawning off stuff from the Realms."

"No, actually."

The Heiress comes toward me. I don't back away, even though part of me wants to, and she opens the bag a few inches so I can glimpse inside. I expect to see silver, but instead I see green. The Heiress is carrying a crap-ton of cash.

"*I'm* the buyer," she tells me, enunciating each word. "I'm recovering artifacts sold away from Havenfall long ago. I'm bringing them *back* to the inn so they'll be safe. So can you please make yourself scarce and we'll talk about this later?"

"No," I say, planting my feet, trying to hide that her words have taken me off guard. *Then who sold them in the first place?* "If that were true, you wouldn't be sneaking around. Marcus would have known if something like that was happening."

At that the Heiress laughs, short and harsh. "You think I'm the one who brought this trade to Haven?"

My stomach drops. "What do you mean?"

"I mean that there are many things your uncle has kept from you."

The anger roars up under my skin in a heartbeat, like embers sparking to life. "Marcus would never do something like that. Havenfall is his whole life. Literally his whole life." I step forward. "He would never put it in danger like this—"

A faint rumble makes us both look sharply down the road. In the distance down the mountain, a rusty nineties station wagon is making its winding way up toward town, the sun reflecting off its tan hood.

The Heiress grabs my shoulder, making me jump. Her cowboy hat falls off into the dirt and she ignores it; her strong fingers dig in like claws. "Listen to me, Madeline," she says again. "The purchase I'm about to make—it has to go through. Hide and watch in the trees if you want, and I'll explain everything after. I swear it. But you must let me do this."

There's something new in her tone now, a ragged urgency. Her rich, throaty voice has always been the only part of her that really has seemed centuries old.

"Think," she tells me, one hand on the reins and one on me. "If I were the orchestrator of all this, why would I have left Havenfall for so long? It was my home too, and the center of the trade besides. Why would I have left the black market's black heart?"

I don't know what to say to that. I can scarcely process anything she's said. She's accusing Marcus of being involved in this, somehow. Just the thought makes rage race through my veins.

But she's buying, not selling. The idea of hanging back and watching feels so wrong, but the thought of letting Whit carry away any piece of Havenfall is even worse. It makes my skin crawl. If my goal is to keep Realms objects safe and secret in Havenfall, I need to let this deal go through.

The station wagon chugs up the road, closer and closer.

"Okay," I finally say. I jerk free of the Heiress's hand and back away, toward the trees opposite the antique shop, where there's a clear view of the window. "Fine. Do what you have to do. But then you're going to tell me everything."

15

I FEEL STUPID, HIDING IN the trees like this. This isn't a child's game. I should be in there with the Heiress, and yet here I am, on the outside, waiting.

Earlier, someone opened the antique store and let both the Heiress and Whit in. All I can see now is their shapes in the lighted window. Occasionally, the Heiress breaks from their huddle to pace the floor, the hem of her cloak one misstep away from knocking over all the dusty silver and porcelain and bringing the whole place tumbling down. A buzz in my pocket makes me jump.

I fumble for my phone to put it on silent. See that I've gotten a text from Dad. *Miss you too sweetie!!*

I ignore him. No time for that now.

———

Finally, finally, Whit leaves and drives away. The Heiress comes out and we head to the twenty-four-hour diner in tense silence; she's leading her horse on foot down the side of the road.

She has her cloak balled up under her arm, worry and annoyance creasing her usually serene face. It's starting to get hot out, but my insides feel cold as ice with anger and confusion.

Inside the diner, the girl at the hostess stand—maybe fifteen, brown ponytail sticking out of a green O'Connor's hat—looks uncertainly between us when we come in, clearly picking up on the tension, although she doesn't bat an eye at the Heiress's strange outfit. She seats us at the big booth in the far corner and leaves the Heiress and me to stew in our solitude, the expanse of speckled plastic table stretching like an ocean between us.

The Heiress is glowering, clearly agitated, waves of distress and irritation rolling off her. She gazes out the window at Main Street, and I can't tell if she's lost in thought or avoiding my gaze or both. But I'm not going to let her off the hook that easy.

"So." I put my elbows on the table, leaning forward so she's forced to meet my eyes. "You said that this wasn't what I thought it was. Fill me in. What is it really?"

The Heiress turns her gaze on me finally, looking like she'd rather be somewhere, anywhere, else. Without makeup, she looks even older, softer. She has a heart-shaped face, a sharp chin, and eyes that are still gray and clear and piercing.

"What do you know?" she asks me.

"I found some papers in your room." There doesn't seem to be any point in talking around that bit now. "I know you're trading magical artifacts. Enchanted things."

"I wouldn't have thought a modern girl like you believed in such things," the Heiress says, witheringly. "Everyone knows the magic of the Adjacent Realms is bound to its bearers. Only people carry magic."

I feel my hackles go up. "It doesn't matter if the magic is real. You're telling people it is." My anger, held at bay while I hid in the trees, is rising rapidly now. "You told that creepy-ass dude from earlier that magic is real, and it can be found at Havenfall."

The Heiress's eye twitches when I swear. She might not understand the slang, but she understands my tone just fine.

"I've told him nothing he didn't already know," she said. "There are many who know the true nature of Havenfall. Humans all over this world of yours. There always have been."

My face must betray my shock, because she tilts her head at me.

"Come, Madeline, did you really think a place such as this could truly be a secret? This is the nature of magic. The green children of Woolpit. Canneto di Caronia. The Fairy Flag. I could go on. There are always leaks, but the world doesn't end."

I wait for her to say more, but she doesn't. My mind races. If I take her at her word—that magic really can be bound to objects . . . what does that mean? I think of her room, glittering with dusty trinkets, and I skim over Havenfall's grounds and perimeter and everyone who walks through its doors every day. Marcus trusted his people, and I trusted him. How could he not have known about this? Or worse, how could he have known and done nothing about it?

"It predates Marcus's term as the Innkeeper," the Heiress says, reading my face. "It predates even my time there. Secrets—and magic—always find their way free."

My head feels like it's spinning as I try to wrap my mind around this new information. "How many people are involved?" I whisper. "How many have had their hands in this?"

"It's hard to say," the Heiress says calmly. "Hundreds. Maybe more than a thousand."

"That's—" Anger and fear twine together inside me. "A thousand? How are you so relaxed right now?"

"We're still here, aren't we?" she retorts. "The inn is still standing. And I'm on your side of this. I am trying to right the wrongs."

"You don't understand! There's no such thing as an open secret in this world!"

I clench my hands hard under the table, nails digging in. *How can I make the Heiress understand a world full of cell phones with cameras and microphones? The Internet?* "Everyone talks about everything online now. If you don't keep something a total secret, everyone will know soon enough."

"Ah, but you forget that humans are selfish creatures," the Heiress says evenly. "If there's something to be gained by it, they will hold their tongues."

I bite my own tongue as the waitress approaches with our food: a chicken sandwich for me and coffee and scones for the Heiress.

She breaks off a corner of the scone and eats it delicately, then makes a face. "Too sugary."

That's a joke between us ever since I was a little kid. I'd bring her some Haven food to try, and she'd pretend not to like it. But I'm in no mood for games right now, nostalgic or not.

"How long has this been going on?" I demand.

The Heiress's face stays placid. The unshakable calmness in her voice somehow angers me even more. "I don't know. Before either of us was born. As long as people have been crossing through the doorways, I expect."

"And you're trying to put a stop to it. By buying the objects back up . . ."

"And returning them to the Adjacent Realms where they belong," she finishes for me. "Yes, that's the idea. I've used their magic to get past the barrier on the grounds."

"Then why didn't you tell Marcus a long time ago?"

For the first time in our exchange, a flicker of emotion shows. The Heiress's face falls, only slightly, and only for a second. But I don't miss it.

"Madeline," she says slowly. "I'm going to tell you something, and you're not going to want to believe it, but you must. It's true."

Dread fills my insides, heavy, cold. "What is it?"

She looks me straight in the eyes. "Your uncle knows about the trade," she says. "He is the seller."

———

I don't believe it. I can't believe it. Even after we return to the inn, when the Heiress brings me back to her room and shows me papers with Marcus's handwriting on them, I can't believe it.

And yet . . . there's no other explanation. No other reason I can think of that would explain the existence of letters in my uncle's distinctive slanted handwriting, promising buyers riches beyond imagining, Havenfall silver infused with magic. Long lists of names and mailing addresses, each one noted next to what they purchased, when, and for how much. The records go back decades, since before I was born, since Marcus took over Havenfall from my great-great-grandmother. There are copies of receipts for silver objects passing hand to hand. This time I can't deny the Heiress's claim. She was buying. And my uncle—my uncle who I trust more than anyone else in the world—was, is, selling.

The Heiress sits patiently and pours us tea while I go through the papers, watching me steadily. My gut churns. My body is slow to accept the truth even as my mind is forced to.

"So that is what your big fight was about," I say finally, letting the papers flutter from my hands onto the desk. "You were trying to get the objects back, and Marcus—he was—"

"Selling them," the Heiress fills in, when my voice breaks. "Yes." There's no satisfaction in the words. Just a quiet sadness.

"And that's why you left."

The Heiress nods again. "For a while. But . . ." She looks out the window at the mountains, the wrinkles deepening around her eyes. "I came to realize that Havenfall, and the sanctity of the magic within it, was more important than my pride. That it would be better to let Marcus think I'd made my peace with his doings, and then do what I could myself to remedy them."

I look down, blinking hard. *How could he do this?* Havenfall is home—that's even truer for him than it is for me. Marcus spends all year on these grounds. I can't remember the last time he left.

That you know of.

Because if these papers are to be believed, he's been traveling all over the country, selling off Havenfall silver bound with the magic of the Adjacent Realms. There are names of drivers, people he trusted enough to make shipments. But sometimes, when he was dealing with a particularly rare magical object—a vase that bore Byrnisian tide-magic, or a watch carrying the Fiorden ability to manipulate emotions—he would make the trip himself. To Denver, Phoenix, Seattle, Minneapolis. Even farther afield sometimes, New York, Vancouver, Mexico City. There are flight receipts, itineraries. Marcus is nothing if not meticulous.

"How did you get all this?" I ask the Heiress in a hoarse whisper.

I don't really want to know, don't really care how these records ended up in the Heiress's desk drawers, but it's an easier question to put into words than the ones really weighing on my mind. Namely, why, why, why, and why didn't he tell me?

194

The Heiress doesn't answer my question, but counters it with a demand of her own. "Before I tell you anything more, Maddie, I need your word that you won't divulge any of this to your uncle."

"I couldn't tell him if I wanted to." I'm not thinking. The words just spill out. "He's still unconscious."

While the Heiress's expression softens a little, her gaze stays on me, waiting, expectant. "When he wakes up, then. You mustn't tell Graylin or Willow either. They don't know about this. They don't need to."

I want to argue. I want to tell her that he's my uncle—how could I promise her that? But the papers seem to whisper to me from where they rest uneasily in my lap. Telling me that Marcus was keeping secrets, dangerous ones, from me and from everyone else. Maybe he doesn't deserve my loyalty.

He's my family, one of the last people I have. Dad doesn't know about half my life, Nate is dead, and Mom's soon to follow.

But Marcus lied.

"Okay," I say, and though my voice is shaky, I mean it.

The Heiress must see the truth in that word, because after a long moment of looking at me, she nods. "All right, then," she says heavily. "There's one more thing I need to tell you. Brekken of Myr stole these papers from Marcus's office."

The name hits me like a fist of ice to my chest. When my voice comes out, a beat too late, it sounds like I've been punched too. "Brekken?"

The Heiress nods. "He was helping me." Her voice gentles. "I know you two are close. He loves this place as much as you do, and he would do anything to save it."

"What happened to him?" I whisper. "Where is he?"

The Heiress looks down at her hands in surrender, like an old, defeated queen. "I don't know," she says. "He fled back to Fiordenkill, but why, I can't say."

That night comes flooding back to me. His kiss. I remember the heat of his lips on mine. His skin was cool, but his lips were warm, as if touching me set something ablaze in his soul.

So is this why Brekken was down in the tunnels that night, to go through Marcus's office and steal these papers? If what the Heiress is saying is true, he had nothing to do with the Solarian door opening. The Silver Prince was wrong; Brekken is innocent. That should be a comfort to me, but I can't forget that even if Brekken's cause was noble, he still used me. I thought he always told me everything, that I knew him better than anyone. Instead, he had this whole plot, a secret life I hadn't an inkling of. He took me to the stables, kissed me stupid, and stole my keys.

I push the thought away. I have plenty of more important things to worry about, like where Brekken is now. Maybe he crossed paths with the first Solarian in the tunnels and fled back to Fiordenkill for safety? Or maybe—my stomach clenches—Marcus caught Brekken snooping before the Solarian showed up, and Brekken had to run. In any case, the Heiress doesn't know about the open door to Solaria—hopefully she believes the beast on the grounds wandered in from outside—and I don't trust her enough to tell her. Quickly, I look back down at the desk, so she won't read anything on my face. The papers take up fully half of the polished wood of the desktop, the rest taken up by a jumble of silver objects.

"What do these do?" I ask the Heiress, pointing to the silver, more to fill the silence and give myself time to think than because I really care.

She smiles sadly, like she knows I'm not actually looking for an answer, but humors me anyway. "I don't know. They're a Fiorden shipment I just got back. I need to test and catalog them."

But my gaze has already been pulled back to the correspondence.

There are years and years of it. I read enough already to know that she's telling the truth about Marcus's involvement, but it would take days to read through the stack of documents. I know I should read every single piece of paper. I need to understand, but the thought makes me so tired.

All I want to do is crawl into bed and wake up to find everything is back to normal. I'd go downstairs and listen to Marcus make the breakfast announcements. I'd spend my day hiking the grounds or trying to eavesdrop on meetings or sneaking out with Brekken. I'd practically be a guest of the inn. Everything would be out of my hands, and I'd experience all the beauty and grandeur of the summit from the sidelines. I wouldn't understand the weight that comes with being at its center.

Instead, I'm the Innkeeper for now, and I hate it.

Something on the papers catches my eye, and my finger traces the ink on the page. A name: Sylvia Morrow.

Mom.

Her cell phone number is listed beside it. It's still the only number I know by heart, the only number I could dial in my sleep. Forgetting to breathe, I scan up to the top of the page. The heading says HOSTS.

What the hell does that mean?

I look up at the Heiress for explanation, when a knock from the hall makes our hands freeze, our heads swiveling toward the door.

The Heiress's eyes dart toward the papers, and she gestures at me to put them away. I hurriedly cram them into the still-open desk drawer and shut it, careful not to let it slam. Then I take a cup of tea from the side table and hold it mid-sip, like we've just been in the midst of a casual chat, as the Heiress opens the door.

Taya is standing in the hall, one hand raised to knock again. She sees the Heiress first and takes a step back, starting to apologize—but then she sees me in the room and freezes, her eyes darting between the old woman and me.

"Good afternoon, Heiress. Maddie, hi," she says, clearly confused to find me here. "Graylin's been looking for you all morning. We've checked everywhere."

I get up and busy myself with the tea tray. The rows of Fiorden silver glint invitingly at me from the Heiress's desk, especially a silver dish with a gold inlay of a winged snake wound around a staff, like you see on the signs of doctors' offices. The familiar symbol—I can't remember what it's called, something Latin?—snags my attention, and I instinctively seize the moment to slip it from the table into my jacket pocket. Even as I do it, I'm not sure exactly why. Maybe to know what all the fuss has been about. To figure out how the magic works.

"Thank you for the talk," I say to the Heiress, carrying the tea tray out into the hallway.

When Taya and I are on the staircase and out of earshot, my shoulders relax for the first time in what seems like ages.

"What's going on? How are you feeling?" I ask Taya beneath my breath.

She shifts her feet. She still looks pale and tired, just like last night, but there's something else buried there too. Shock. Fear.

"We have a problem," she says darkly.

A groan escapes through my gritted teeth. "What is it now?"

Taya looks right at me. "News got out about the Solarian on the grounds. And that the door to Solaria is open."

16

SOMEONE IS SHOUTING IN THE reception room. "It only makes sense!" he yells.

Standing alone in the hallway—Taya's gone to find Graylin—I recognize the voice as belonging to Lonan, the Silver Prince's associate who traded gossip with me at the bar my first night here. His words are blunt and heavy, weapons that will shatter our fragile peace if I don't disarm him and defuse the situation. I reach for the door, my breath coming fast.

"We didn't open it," Princess Enetta shoots back. Her anger suffuses the air, echoes ricocheting from wall to wall. "I already told your Silver Prince—"

She falls silent as I burst into the room. The door bangs off the wall and bounces back. I catch it with one hand and shut it quietly behind me, heart racing.

Lonan and Enetta face each other in front of the fireplace, a gaggle of concerned-looking delegates hanging back behind the circle of arm-chairs. The fire pops and flares dangerously, and maybe I'm imagining it, but the ground seems to tremble a little. The air crackles with tension and magic.

Lonan's gaze moves to me and stops, cold. "Madeline," he says. His voice is no longer loud, but flat and unnerving. "What is the meaning of this? Why didn't you tell us that the door to Solaria was open? That there was a beast on the grounds?"

My breath, already ragged, vanishes in my chest. All eyes in the room snap to mine.

"It was for all of our protection," I say in a rush. "We didn't want to cause a panic. I've posted guards outside the door at all hours, and we're in the process of resealing the door right now."

My voice breaks on the lie. I must sound as hollow as I feel.

It's a shitty excuse. Even I know that. Now that I'm pinned under the weight of their shock and searching gazes, all the reasons I had for keeping the news hidden evaporate from my mind. *Didn't the guests of Havenfall deserve to know they were in danger? What kind of stupidity or arrogance does it take to hide something like that?*

"And this Solarian monster in the woods," Lonan goes on. "Did it come from outside, from Haven, or did it come through the door?"

"I don't know," I whisper.

Their expressions are withering. I've never felt more useless, not even when I was a child at Havenfall. Not even the time when Enetta's father Elirien caught me playing hide-and-seek with Brekken under the dinner table and reprimanded us in front of the entire delegation. I've never felt more unworthy to fill Marcus's shoes, to take his place as Innkeeper.

"I will meet with the Fiorden delegation this evening," Enetta says, raising her voice to address everyone in the room. "And if they decide that they wish to leave, we will do so."

Betrayal shoots through me. Enetta knew the door was open, but now that everyone else does, she wants to take her delegation and go? "But . . ."

The word sounds high and wild. I stop and take a breath, imagining stripping the jagged panic from my voice like bark, until it's smooth and featureless. *Take a breath, start again.*

"Your Highness, with all due respect, I don't think that's a good idea. The magic of the doorways is delicate, as you know. An early exit by the Fiorden delegation could disrupt things. It could cause the Solarian door to open further."

"And then we will be in our own world, ready with our army to meet anything that should come through," she counters. "Not trapped here like . . . like . . ."

"Sitting ducks," I supply, my voice popping out of its own accord. Again I feel the crazy urge to laugh, like at Nate's funeral.

Now both Enetta and Lonan are scowling at me. They think I'm mocking them. I try to project a neutral expression, something appropriately contrite for keeping secrets from them, but not overly panicked. Something that says *I'm sorry, but I know what I'm doing.*

Judging from the level of emotion in the room, it doesn't seem to be working. Where are Graylin and Willow? Why is Marcus still asleep? *I need you*, I think, willing him to hear me wherever he is.

The door to the hall slams behind us, and I turn around. It's Taya.

"Maddie," she says, ignoring the imperious glares of the delegates. "You're needed at the infirmary."

Marcus? "Is it Marcus?" I ask without meaning to.

Taya's eyes flicker around to all the delegates, and my heart sinks.

Whatever information she brings, she doesn't want to say it in front of them. Not a great sign. I take a deep breath.

"Okay," I say, and look back at the delegates and Lonan and Enetta. "We can—we will—talk more about this later," I promise them. "Just please don't do anything rash in the meantime. I swear to you I'll fix this."

The vow lands with a thud in the room. No one's expression changes except for Princess Enetta's, whose face hardens. And she's right. I put her people in danger. That's the worst part—that she's right.

Taya doesn't ask me what happened in the reception room as she leads me to the infirmary, and I don't ask what's waiting for us there. I know not talking won't fix anything, but I need the respite. We use the twisty, narrow, back employee-only hallways, thankfully empty of delegates and staff. I have pretty much zero comfort to offer anyone.

But any shred of relief dissolves when we step into the infirmary. Graylin's standing inside with a handful of other Fiorden healers. They are gathered around a form on the bed that seems very small. Too small. My stomach drops and my breath vanishes.

The crowd divides for a second as people shuffle around, and I see the patient—Max, a human, a busboy. Crap, he can't be more than fifteen. He's covered up with a white blanket, his face pale and breathing shallow.

"What happened?" I demand as I rush over, Taya a step behind me.

Graylin is the one who answers. He and the rest of the healers hover their hands over the boy's body. Magic shimmers beneath them like distant rain.

"I don't know," he says hoarsely. "We found him on the grounds."

I catch a glimpse of Taya's face, and it's a mirror of how I feel—confused, terrified. Horror curdles my insides.

"Is he going to be okay?"

Graylin's mouth flattens. He pulls the blanket back for a moment, just enough for me to see the thick bandages wrapping Max's thin, pallid torso.

"He'll live, but it's bad. This is a magic sleep, to help with the pain until we make more progress."

"What do you think happened?" Taya asks quietly.

"The Solarian?" I guess.

Graylin considers, his lips pressed together. "Maybe. But his injuries are different from Marcus's and yours, Taya. He's been slashed."

I open my mouth to say something else—I don't know what—when the earth seems to shudder and groan beneath our feet. It's over in a heartbeat, but everyone looks up at once and Graylin's eyes fly wide.

"What the hell was that?" Taya asks in a low, husky voice that shows she's scared.

Graylin looks at me. "The doorways."

———

Graylin, Taya, and I rush down to find chaos in the tunnels. Fiorden and Byrnisian delegates swarm the juncture, the lamps on the walls barely enough to illuminate them, so it appears at first like just one seething ocean of bodies. Shouts echo off the stone, layering over each other until it's all a jumbled mass of sound and panic. I want to hide away somewhere, curled up with my hands over my ears, until this is all over. But I can't. I can't.

"They're going through! The Fiordens are going through!" someone screams when we stop in the entrance tunnel.

A knot of Fiordens at the front of the crowd has clustered around the tunnel mouth to their world, shouting at Sal, who they've pressed up against the stone wall. A few of the soldiers who joined yesterday's hunt have gone farther down and formed a line across the hallway, weapons drawn, as if to catch anything that might come from around the bend of the tunnel and the Solarian door past it. Through the tangle of noise, words and phrases float to my ears.

You can't keep us here.

Let us pass!

Graylin has his hand on my arm, protective, but I pull free and dart through the crowd, panic making my ears buzz, requiring that I move. I can't hang back and watch this. I throw elbows until I'm at the front of the crowd and step up in the gap next to Sal, turning to face the Fiordens' wrathful gazes. The door is not far behind us. An aching, cold, snow-scented breeze plays at my back, ghosting over the nape of my neck. Like it's beckoning me through, inviting me to step across to a world where I might freeze to death in a matter of minutes, but at least that's better than getting torn open by a Solarian's claws and teeth. Or an angry crowd. I wonder where Brekken is now, somewhere in that cold universe.

I don't know what I'm going to say, but I have to say something, because when I raise my hand, the crowd quiets all at once. I feel their eyes on me like heat-seeking missiles. Marcus would know what to do, what to say. But he isn't here. Just Sal. And me.

"I hope you know what you're doing, Mads," he says under his breath.

"Delegates," I begin, willing my voice not to shake. Then I realize that wasn't loud enough, so I try again. "Delegates. I'm sorry I didn't tell you about the door to Solaria. I feared exactly this."

Silence. I see Graylin's face and Taya's at the far end of the tunnel, but the crowd is pressed too tightly for them to come forward.

"I get that you're scared," I say. "I'm scared too. And with my uncle sick, I haven't made all the right choices. But the last time Solarians threatened Havenfall, we beat them by coming together—"

"Not before the ice lovers allied with them!" someone shouts, using a derogatory Byrnisian nickname for Fiordens.

An angry ripple cuts through the crowd, and I see hostile glances shooting from face to face like wildfire, like infection. Tension churns in the air.

"That was over a century ago," I say, trying for calm. "I know the Fiorden delegation is as committed to peace as any of us. Aren't they?"

That last bit comes out with the hint of a challenge, directed at the Fiordens gathered around us as we block the door. The courtier Nessa is closest, and I hold her gaze, my head high. For a second I think I've convinced them, that I've won.

Then Nessa draws her sword—her pretty jeweled sword that I always thought was just ornamental—and lunges for the doorway.

Sal shoves me out of the way, his extender baton coming out just in time to meet the sword with a sharp crack. The people around us barge ahead, though, and when Sal spins one way to counter Nessa's blow, a middle-aged delegate darts behind him.

The door ripples and there's a *fwoom* sound like a drumbeat at the bottom of the range of human hearing, and a blast of icy air and starlight, and the delegate is gone.

That's all it takes. Nessa's sword flashes and blood flies; Sal cries out and stumbles back, clutching his shoulder.

The clatter of his baton on the stone floor opens the floodgates.

Everyone surges forward at once, and I grab on to the rough stone wall to avoid being pushed through the Fiorden doorway. Bodies shove past me, indistinguishable in the rush and the noise. People shout and scream in three languages. I yell at them to stop, but no one hears me; if it weren't for the scrape in my throat and lungs I wouldn't be sure I was speaking at all. I can't move, can scarcely breathe. I don't know what to do.

Then lightning—*lightning*—branches across the top of the tunnel, searing my vision, leaving a forked trail of light behind my eyes. Heat scalds my upturned face, and the *boom* an instant later resonates in my chest and sends dust raining down. The noise dies at once, as suddenly as if someone pressed a mute button; everyone turns to the top of the tunnel, where the Silver Prince stands silhouetted against the light of the upstairs hallway.

In the still and the silence, I notice that the crowd is thinner. Some people are on the ground; some people are hunched and trembling; some people are gone. In the panic, how many people went through to Fiordenkill?

"Enough," the Silver Prince calls, and his voice echoes the thunder. His gaze finds me and he beckons. "Madeline."

A part of me resents being summoned in my own inn, but I am too shell-shocked to do anything but obey. The delegates who remain in the tunnels, sweaty and pale and wide-eyed, separate wordlessly and I walk up, past Graylin and Taya, to stand by the Prince's side. He lifts a hand and points, past the doors to Fiordenkill and Byrn, into the darkness toward Solaria.

"*There* is the enemy," he says, voice dark and scary and commanding. "We suffered through a decade of war to learn this lesson, but it seems some have forgotten." His eyes drill toward the Fiorden door, the delegates still lingering around it, frozen in the act of trying to get through. "As the Innkeeper's niece has said, only in unity will we triumph over them. We must preserve the peace at any cost."

That's not precisely what I said, but I'm not about to argue. The delegates are listening to the Prince in a way they didn't listen to me.

"If anyone else attempts to go through the doorways, they will be arrested," he says. "My soldiers and I are working with Madeline

Morrow to close the Solarian door. Rest assured that you will be protected in the meantime."

He takes a step back, putting me at the forefront, exposed before the crowd. I feel so small, young, weak, but the Silver Prince continues.

"It bears repeating that you will all consider Madeline Morrow vested with the full duty and authority of the Innkeeper. She is the Innkeeper."

The gaze of the crowd turns to me in the dark of the tunnel. I stand up straight and take it, but my eyes prickle with tears.

It's what I always wanted to hear.

And it feels completely and utterly hollow.

17

THE RISING MOON SHINES THROUGH Marcus's window, the windowpanes casting cross-shaped shadows on the hardwood floor. The lamp on the bedside table seems dim and paltry by comparison. The mountains outside seem alien, cast in silver, like something out of a black-and-white photo. Marcus looks the same as he did this morning, his breathing shallow and quiet. But now, instead of Graylin, his visitors are me and the Silver Prince.

An hour has passed since the chaos in the tunnels. The staff and the delegates—at least the delegates that didn't flee to Fiordenkill—are in their rooms, kept there by a curfew the Prince laid down. Leftover adrenaline still trickles in my veins, making my heart race and my limbs ache to jump, to move, to do something.

I'm aware of the Prince like I would be of a live wire in the room. He's been sitting quietly with me, waiting for me to be ready to talk, but I don't know how I can. I'm grateful that he stepped in earlier, I guess, or all the Fiorden delegates would have fled instead of just a third of them.

I couldn't have stopped them. I know that. But I feel . . . diminished somehow, after seeing the Silver Prince step up and take charge. Yet I don't feel any safer. It would be crazy of me to think of the Prince's actions as a power grab . . . but I can't help feeling that way. Taya's words from when she found out about the realms bounce around in my head. *What if he was wrong? Or lying?*

I guess at the end of the day I don't. But I do know that I need the Silver Prince on my side. Alone, I have no strength. No power.

"Have you ever seen someone recover their soul after a Solarian attack?" I ask, gesturing at Marcus's almost-still form.

The Silver Prince shakes his head. "It's strange. In all the other cases I've seen, the victims have either recovered by now or . . ." He trails off tactfully.

"He'll wake up soon," I say, the words slipping out in my exhaustion like a fevered prayer. "He's the Innkeeper, not me."

Because I need you . . . and I have questions.

The Silver Prince looks questioningly at me. On edge as I am, it catches me off guard, and I blurt, "What is it?"

He speaks slowly, measured, weighing each word carefully. "I had imagined you might aspire to the role yourself, permanently. Was I mistaken?"

My cheeks burn with a mixture of shame and hurt. If this were a fairy tale, maybe my not-so-secret ambition to be Innkeeper could have sent Marcus into his sleep. But this isn't a fairy tale, and I always thought Marcus meant for me to take his place someday.

"Not now," I say firmly. "And not like this. Not for years, not until he wanted to retire."

My stomach churns as I remember what the Heiress told me, about Marcus's involvement in the magic black market. *Why didn't he tell me? Was it because he didn't trust me, or because there were things he didn't want me to know? Or both?*

"Even so . . ." The Prince's words are quiet, but each one still lands heavy in the almost-silent room. "I think you're underestimating yourself, Maddie. I think you could be a great Innkeeper. Maybe more than Marcus ever was."

A harsh bark of laughter escapes me. It's loud and makes me flinch, and I press a hand to my mouth, but of course Marcus doesn't stir.

"Better than him?" I whisper incredulously, when I have control of my voice again. "I've been in charge for less than a week and everything's falling apart."

"Because of decisions that he made." The Prince's glittering eyes cut to Marcus. "He built a tower on sand. That it has now started to fall is no fault of yours."

A trickle of cold goes down my spine, mirroring the edge of a chill that's suddenly appeared in the Silver Prince's voice.

"What do you mean?"

The Silver Prince turns on his chair to fully face me. The light of the lamp doesn't seem to reach him; the moon reflects off his silvery skin and hair, catches the slight scale pattern ridging his cheeks.

"You love the inn for what it is, not for how it can profit you," he says. "The magic, the possibilities, the doorways. This life has been cruel to you, and so you take comfort in the knowledge that other life is there, even if you cannot access it. Byrnisians are much the same."

Something in his voice is sharp, like a razor floating in honey.

"Marcus feels the same way," I tell the Prince, defensive.

"Possibly," he replies, eyes steady on mine over the bed and Marcus's form. "But you must know that he is not practical like you. He looks for good where there is none. He used to believe the Solarians could be redeemed. Even when it risked the peace of the Adjacent Realms. Even when it put his family in harm's way."

I don't understand what the Silver Prince is trying to tell me. I've never heard of Marcus looking kindly on Solarians. Why would he, after what happened to Mom and Nate?

"What do you mean, his family?"

"I mean the attack on your mother and brother," the Silver Prince says, softly surprised. He looks down at Marcus, and now his eyes are cold. "Everyone knows it happened because your uncle invited a Solarian into the home. He tried to shelter it, and it killed your brother."

My blood is icy water in my veins, and my voice comes out a hoarse whisper. "Where did you hear that?"

The Silver Prince dips his head, his eyes cutting to my uncle's pale, blank face.

The ice water turns to ice itself. I can't move, I can't think. For an instant, I'm in the cupboard again, Nate's scream searing into me and leaving a burning brand on my heart. Then—

"You're wrong," I choke out.

Sympathy looks odd on the Silver Prince's face, unnatural. "Maddie, I'm sorry. I thought you knew—"

"I need to be alone right now," I say.

I instantly regret it. The Prince is the most powerful person here, possibly the only person keeping us from total chaos, and I need him. But he doesn't appear angry. He doesn't move either.

I feel sick, feel emptied out as I stare down at Marcus. Even in sleep, his face is so familiar, so safe. Every summer, he's come to pick me up at the crossroads, and when I saw him through the bus window and watched the smile break out over his face, that's when I knew I was safe, I was home.

He is compassionate; he's always thinking of others first. Is it possible that what the Silver Prince is telling me is true, and that his boundless kindness extended even to Solarians, the monsters who killed my brother?

There was the sound of breaking glass. There were a million shards sparkling on the linoleum kitchen floor. But thinking back now, I can't remember if I heard the window break *before* Mom shoved me into the cupboard, when we were still just a normal family baking brownies, happy and together, or *after*, when the monster dragged Nate's body through and into the night.

Could Marcus have *let* a Solarian in?

We were his family, Mom, Nate, Graylin, and me. We were supposed to come first.

But now Nate is dead and Mom is locked away from me forever, and he's wasting away, and there's a monster out there in the woods. If the Prince is telling the truth, Marcus's foolish kindness has already demolished half our family, and might finish me and Graylin off any day now.

How could he have let the monster in?

"I'll leave you be," the Silver Prince says, snapping me back to the present. His voice is calm as a frozen landscape, without a touch of anger. "When you're ready, come find me. We need to address the defection of the Fiorden delegates."

"What can we do about it?" I ask, my voice raw. "They're gone."

"Exactly, and there must be repercussions." His voice turns over from authoritative to gentle again. "This is the second time the Fiordens have betrayed Havenfall. Remember Brekken."

"I remember," I say, because I don't want to hear more about Brekken from the Prince. I know he thought he was acting for a good cause, stealing my keys to investigate Marcus's involvement in the magic black market, but it still stings fiercely that he didn't tell me. That he didn't trust me. That he left me.

"We all want to believe the best of intentions in others," the Prince says. Sitting still as a statue, casting a shadow even taller and thinner than he is, he seems older, more the eerie, powerful magical being he is. "But it's not always the truth."

Even if he doesn't know Brekken's real motivations, he's not wrong about me. I trust too easily, too soon, and now that flaw has put in danger not only me, but the whole inn and everyone in it. I feel frozen.

"What should we do?"

The Silver Prince's lips pull up in a small, regretful smile of acknowledgment. "Fiordenkill must face sanctions," he says. "They've disturbed the balance of the doorways, and the Solarian door has opened wider. My elemental soldiers have it blocked off with a barricade of iron, but if more Solarians come through, even that may not hold." He leans forward, elbows on his knees, seeming to see straight into my soul. "So what do you think is an appropriate price for the danger they have put us all in, Innkeeper?"

I close my eyes, trying to think. "There's not much I can do. I can't prohibit entry back into Havenfall or cut off trade. Not as long as they're part of the alliance in the Accords."

"Alliances can be changed." He speaks quietly, but every word is clear on the still air. "Treaties can be changed."

For a second, my heart seems to stop in my chest. "Cut Fiordenkill out? But the Three-Realm Alliance has stood for a hundred years."

"A hundred years is not so very long a time to some of us," the Prince says. "And what else can we do? Would you bring back the executions, which your great-great-grandmother used to impose upon traitors?"

My breath catches in my throat. I didn't know my ancestors had killed people. I have a sudden vision of standing on the lawn with a sword in my hand, someone with copper penny hair kneeling before me with their head down, and my heart lurches so violently I have to lean forward and put my head in my hands for a second.

"I need time to think."

He glides to his feet and to the door. "Time is scarce, Innkeeper."

A shudder of mixed thrill and disgust goes through me at the word. "I will get you an answer soon. I swear."

"Very well," he says. But his eyes stay on me. "Don't doubt yourself, Maddie. You have what Marcus doesn't. You're strong enough to make hard choices in service of a greater good."

Then he's gone.

I want to cry, but I can't. The tears aren't there, and they won't come. It's like someone's scooped my insides out and left me empty except for dust and echoes.

I sit hunched over with my face in my hands, still except for my slowly beating heart and breathing that hurts with each inhale. That's how Graylin finds me when he walks in, yawning, a few minutes later.

Graylin stops for a second when he sees me. Then his shoulders loosen, and he comes over and sits by Marcus. Graylin was supposed to be taking a nap, but he doesn't look very well rested.

"How is he?" Graylin asks, running his fingers over the back of Marcus's hand. The words, though, sound moot, not something he expects an answer to.

I can't tell him what the Prince said about Marcus fostering Solarians. Not when Marcus isn't awake to explain his side of the story. Graylin is already carrying so much; I can't put this on him too.

My voice comes out croaky. "He's not getting any better."

A silence.

"No, he isn't," Graylin says at length. "At least, not that I can see."

"Isn't there anything else we can do?" I ask desperately. Of course I want Marcus to get better. But I also need answers. About the silver trade. About Solarians and my mother and Nate. And Marcus has those answers. He must.

"If there was, I would have done it already." Graylin's voice is a mirror of how I feel. Brittle, like the slightest blow could break us entirely.

When I shift in my chair, my spine makes a muffled crack. My muscles ache. I feel old, and that makes me think of the Heiress again. I still need to ask her why my mother's name appears on Marcus's list of HOSTS. I think about the magical objects in the Heiress's room, the rows of gleaming silver things marching over her desk like ants, and the ledger with the tightly scrawled descriptions of the magic each one had. Magic like healing.

I reach into my pocket and my fingertips meet cool, smooth metal. I pull out the silver dish I took from the Heiress's room and hold it up for Graylin to see. The one with the inlaid gold symbol of two snakes wound around a winged staff. I googled the symbol yesterday—it's a *caduceus,* something to do with Asclepius, the ancient Greek god of medicine. Maybe the Fiordens have their own versions of our myths, or maybe our ancient stories have permeated all the realms. Maybe they made their way to us from another world long ago.

But however the symbol of medicine came to be stamped on this hunk of silver, it can only be a good thing, right? The dish looks almost ordinary, except for the faint glow that seems to rise off the metal, visible only now that it's dark. I still don't understand how it's possible for magic to live in such a mundane object. But why not try it? It's not like things can get much worse.

Graylin looks at it and blinks. He straightens, like he's coming fully awake. He sees the glow too.

"What is it?"

"Um . . . Brekken gave it to me a long time ago," I improvise. "He said it had Fiorden healing magic." If I can't protect anyone from real danger, at least I can shield Graylin from this whole tangled mess a little longer. Let him focus on healing my uncle so we can learn the *actual* truth.

Graylin breathes in sharply when I put the dish in his outstretched hand. He holds it up to the lamplight, turning it this way and that, looking for I don't know what.

"Well?" I ask.

Graylin's brow furrows. "I don't understand this," he says, half to himself. When he looks back at me, there's something wary in his gaze. "You said Brekken gave this to you?"

I nod, hoping he doesn't see the lie on my face. Marcus would, but Graylin's always let me get away with more. Saliva pools in my mouth but I make myself not swallow.

"The magic is there. I can feel it."

Graylin turns the dish over and over, and I catch quick slashes of reflection in it—the dim lamplight, Graylin's brown face, guilt in my own eyes. "But I don't understand how it was bound here. It feels . . . alive."

I shrug, careful to keep my face expressionless. "Who knows. But do you think you can use it?"

"I can, but the question is whether I should." Graylin lets his hand drop and looks hard at me. "Maddie, Brekken betrayed us. You know that."

No, he didn't, I want to say.

Marcus did.

I can't meet Graylin's eyes, so I look down at my hands instead, fidgeting against my jeans. "I know. But if there was something wrong with the magic, couldn't you feel it?"

"Maybe." His voice frays, agitation creeping in. "But I don't know where this came from. I don't know anything anymore. I thought I could heal Marcus myself and look what's happened—"

His voice cracks, and he falls silent, closing his eyes and taking a deep breath. I can't seem to breathe as I watch him try to collect himself.

There's a very specific kind of splintering feeling that comes with seeing the people you trust fall short or fall apart. They are the ones who are supposed to take care of you. I've felt it twice in a major way, with Mom and with Marcus, and a hundred lesser times, whenever Dad was too tired to see that something was wrong, or my teachers ignored the ugly chants that followed me around the playground. I know it's not Graylin's fault; I can't expect him to stay calm and collected when his husband won't wake. But I still feel very alone in this moment.

After a long time, Graylin speaks. "I'll try to use this magic." He closes his fingers around the dish, his eyes flickering between it and Marcus. "But no promises."

"Of course."

Suddenly, a new wave of exhaustion rolls over me, stronger than any of the ones before. If I stay here any longer, I'll keel over in my chair, and I won't be any use to Marcus then. Not that I am now, but still. I stand.

"Get some sleep," Graylin tells me as I head for the door. "It'll be okay."

But he doesn't sound convinced.

———

I'm walking back to my room when I catch a glimpse, out of the corner of my eye, of movement outside the window. Instinctively, I freeze, then inch closer, keeping to the side of the frame so that if whoever—or *whatever*—is on the lawn decides to look up, they won't see me.

My heart contracts when I see a familiar small figure skirting the trees, her pale hair shining in the moonlight. Taya. She looks over her shoulder every few seconds, and sticks to the shadow of the trees, like she doesn't want to be seen. She has some kind of tool or weapon in one hand, but I can't make it out at this distance.

Hot anger curls suddenly through my insides. She knows the Solarian is on the loose. It's already attacked her. She saw what happened to Max. So what is she doing? Without wanting to, I imagine her lying in the infirmary, bandaged and unresponsive.

My heart lurches, and before I can think, I'm running down the stairs, through the entrance hall. There are guards at the front door, two of Sal's guys who look at me with concern, but I wave them off and they let me go. How did Taya get past them? The Byrnisian dagger and Fiorden revolver that I carry now at Graylin's request bounce awkwardly against my hip.

The grounds are damp from all the Silver Prince's manufactured storms during the last few days, fog clinging to the ground and shrouding the distant mountains; but the night is clear and the stars shine overhead. I get out onto the lawn just in time to see Taya vanish into the woods. Knowing that the guards are probably watching me, I make myself walk, not run, after her.

Once I'm among the trees, the night noises billow up around me, much louder than on the lawn. Frogs, crickets, owls, wind in the pines. Somewhere far off, there's a plaintive howl, a howl that might be a dog, a coyote, a wolf even.

I stop just past the tree line, not wanting to go farther in without knowing where Taya is, or to yell and advertise my location to whatever else is lurking in the woods. I stand very still, hold my breath and listen for any noise that doesn't belong to a night on the mountain.

Then I hear it. A sound that is now burned into my memory forever. The metallic, rhythmic *thump* and *whoosh* of a shovel and dirt.

What the hell?

My eyes adjust to the dark as I start walking again, trying to be careful where I put my feet, to be as silent as I can. I recognize this spot, I realize with a sinking feeling. I'm nearing the same place where Graylin and I went my first night here. Just like then, the forest noises die down in the clearing, like even the bugs and frogs and owls know that something is deeply wrong.

Taya. Taya is standing in the clearing, shovel in her hands. Even though it's obvious what she's doing, it still takes a second for my brain to put it together. To process. A pile of soil beside her and the shovel flashing in the weak moonlight.

Just like when I found her in the library last night, part of me wants to walk away. Leave and pretend I never saw anything at all, that nothing has to change between us.

But I can't. Because she's digging up the Solarian.

"What are you doing?" I ask. It's only a whisper, but it cuts through the air in the silent clearing. Taya stops, her head snapping up. There's dirt and mud on her face and in her hair.

She doesn't move, doesn't even blink when I walk up. Not until I grab the shovel and pull it from her, my hands shaking; then her hands fall and she takes a step back from me. She's shaking too, and I don't know if it's from cold or fear or something else entirely.

I give voice to the only thought my mind has room for. "What the *actual* hell, Taya?" I keep my eyes on her pretty face, avoiding looking into the hole in the earth she's created. Not wanting to see how deep it goes, or what might have been uncovered.

"I'm sorry," she says, and her voice sounds too loud in the still night—high and trembling. "I had to check something."

"Check what?" Horror is crawling over me like a second skin made of ice, the cold seeping through my veins and into my heart. "How did you know where we buried the Solarian?"

I drop the shovel and take her arm. Pull her back and away from the grave, toward a sideways log at the edge of the clearing. I sit, pulling her down beside me. Even through the thick material of her bomber jacket, I can feel her shaking.

"I didn't find the grave," she says, the words broken up by ragged breaths. "Max did. He told the staff about it and that's when he was attacked."

Cold drops down my spine. "What are you saying?"

"I don't think the Solarian attacked him," Taya says. I'm still trying not to look at the open grave, but Taya can't seem to tear her eyes away, and it's hard not to follow her gaze. When I do, just for a moment, I catch a glimpse of dull orange scales and my insides heave, the world lurching around me.

Max is awake now, Graylin told me earlier. He won't talk about what happened to him, no matter how Graylin tries to draw him out, but his soul hasn't been stolen.

"Look," Taya says. She holds something in her lap—a dagger as long as her forearm, finely made, but coated in mud and old bloodstains. My head spins. I feel sick as Taya rubs at a spot of dirt on the hilt with her thumb, exposing an unfamiliar sigil. A five-petaled flower wrought in gold.

"It's Bram's knife," she says, after a moment of silence. "Not the Prince's."

I look between the knife and her face. She looks terrified and like she hasn't slept in days, but I can't read much beyond that, her brown irises turned black by the moon. "I don't get it," I whisper. "So what? Why did you dig up the body?"

"The Silver Prince was wrong about Brekken, wasn't he? What if he's wrong about other stuff too, like what he saw the night the doorway opened? Or what if he's lying?" Taya's eyes burn. "Maddie, I don't think a Solarian in the woods is the real danger here." She raises a hand and points back toward the inn, where we can just see the lights of its windows through the trees. "I think it's in there."

"You can't be serious." I want to laugh—I would, except for the grim expression on Taya's face. "I'm pretty sure the Silver Prince is the only thing between us and total chaos."

"Max went white when the Prince visited the infirmary." Taya's words are dark. "I saw it. The kid was terrified of him."

I feel like the ground is pitching beneath my feet, the way the earth heaved when the Fiordens flooded back into their world. "He's a scary guy, okay. He has strong magic, that's not a reason to hate him."

"That's not what I'm saying," Taya hisses. "I'm saying *don't trust him*, for God's sake. Do I have to spell it out for you what happened to Max?" She points an accusing finger toward the fresh-turned grave. "No one else knew about this body except you and Graylin and the Prince. And I can't see Graylin ordering an attack on a kid."

"If you want to say something, just say it." I don't have time for this. I only came out here to keep her safe, and now it feels like she's shitting on every action and choice I've made as Innkeeper.

"Fine." Taya takes a deep breath, sets her jaw. "I think the *Prince* opened the door to Solaria. I think he found a beast somewhere else, or lured it through, and he's using that threat as a distraction while he takes over the inn."

Genuine shock jolts through me. I almost laugh, thinking she's joking. But her eyes are round, her face dead serious. "And the Solarian is just, what?" I ask incredulously. "An innocent victim?"

I hear Taya's teeth grit together. "Maybe . . . ?" She nods in the direction of the inn. "How long did Solarians live there in peace with everyone else before everything went to hell? Maybe they're not really monsters. Maybe they fight back when someone threatens them, like, oh, everyone else in the world."

Somehow, though I don't remember deciding to stand, I'm on my feet, my nails cutting painful half moons into my clenched fists.

Nate was never a threat.

"You're wrong," I say, hearing my voice come out quiet and cold. "Or you're lying."

She stands up too, eyes narrow. "I'm just trying to help," she says, articulating each word like a razor blade. "Seeing as you don't exactly have everything under control as it is."

Fury shoots through me. "Leave, then," I say. "I'm trying my best, but if that isn't enough, I don't know what to tell you." I almost tear off the crystal bracelet the Silver Prince gave me, the charm that lets me cross the gravity barrier, and snap it in two. I shove one half toward her. "Take this and you can go home if you want. At least then I won't have to follow you around and make sure you don't get yourself killed."

She takes the broken bracelet but not the bait. "You could leave too," she says softly. "Leave right now, with me. We can figure it out—"

I make my voice as icy as I can. "Not in a million years. This is my home. If you want to go, go."

Taya's face goes white, her mouth flat.

"Maybe I will," she says, and turns and walks from the clearing.

18

AFTER A FEW HOURS OF restless sleep, I give up and let my feet take me where they want—to the Heiress's room.

The inside of my head is an obstacle course, full of things that I don't want to think about and yet can't avoid, each collision a fresh jolt of pain. Brekken's disappearance, the fight with Taya, what she said about Max. The silver trade and the fact that Marcus is still unconscious, or the Silver Prince's claim that Marcus made a deal with a Solarian and invited it into our home the day Nate died and Mom's and my lives fell apart. Whatever the Heiress knows about all this, I need to know too. Maybe it has something to do with the HOSTS list?

When the Heiress's door opens under my knock, she doesn't seem surprised to see me. She stands back to let me pass, and I crash into one of her fluffy armchairs, pull my knees up and wrap my arms around them.

Images flash through my mind: the crowd and the chaos in the tunnels, the bright glimpse of Fiordenkill and the shudder of magic as the delegates scrambled through, the Silver Prince standing in Marcus's room and telling me to make a choice. And Taya turning her back on me, the mud and moonlight in her hair as she walked away. It feels like there's something sitting on my chest, getting heavier and heavier every minute, making it hard to move.

The Heiress lets me be for a while, puttering around the room and putting away her silver trinkets, tucking them in cabinets and shutting them in drawers.

"I heard what happened in the tunnels," she says, looking sidelong toward me as she lines up rings in a velvet-lined box. Her face and voice are carefully neutral. "I felt the disturbance. The . . . unbalance."

My face burns with the memory of it. How I stood paralyzed and watched the Silver Prince fix the problem I couldn't.

"A third of the Fiordenkill delegates are gone. I—"

My voice breaks, and I put my head down on my knees, not really wanting to share this with the Heiress, but needing to tell someone. "Marcus would have never let this happen."

Even as the words escape, though, the question of guilt twists my insides again. Can I still look up to Marcus, if what the Silver Prince said is true? If my brother is dead partly because of him?

Partly because of me too.

The Heiress comes over and lowers herself into the chair across from me. "Marcus isn't here," she says, gentleness and sternness playing tug-of-war with her words. "When he wakes, maybe he can explain everything to us. All the choices he's made. But until then, we must make choices of our own as we see fit."

I hear what she's saying to me. There's no use wallowing. Get up and face the music. And she's right. But I can't. I feel like the weight of four worlds is pressing in on me from all directions, trapping me here in this chair, motionless, useless.

The ledger, the one I know carries my mother's name, sits on the polished desk. I nod toward it. "Marcus's records say my mother was a host," I say, trying to stop my voice from shaking. "What does that mean?"

"I don't know." A silver chain still sits draped over a molded porcelain hand on a side table, and she plucks it up, drawing it meditatively through her fingers. "I know she held magical objects for Marcus. Bought and sold them. But 'host' does seem an odd word to use, doesn't it." She lifts her eyes to mine. "Have you spoken to your mother about this?"

I shake my head. The thought did cross my mind. It's Wednesday, visiting day at Sterling Correctional Facility. I could take Marcus's jeep and be there in a few hours. But I can't leave Havenfall in so much chaos, and more than that, the idea of facing my mother's dead eyes on top of everything else right now feels unbearable. I used to love her mismatched eyes. I wished I had one green one like her, instead of two plain brown ones.

I ask the Heiress, "Do you think she was in on whatever Marcus was doing?"

The Heiress shakes her head, eyes sad. "I couldn't say."

"The Silver Prince told me my uncle was making deals with Solarians." The words rush out of me. "He said Marcus invited one into our house. The one that killed Nathan."

"No one knew how dangerous they were back then," the Heiress says gently, and I think of Taya last night, questioning if they were dangerous at all. "For centuries they attended the summit with the rest of us. You can still visit the abandoned wing and see proof of that. If Marcus had sympathy for them, he wasn't the only one." She sighs. "But then things changed. As they always do. Even then, Marcus still thought they were like us. He believed they were misunderstood and should be saved, not banished. But as Innkeeper, it was his job to be neutral . . . at least in public."

"It just seems so hard to believe." I rub my eyes—I don't have any tears left to cry, but they still ache somehow. "And that doesn't explain why she and Marcus never told me about any of this, afterward."

"They may have felt guilty," the Heiress says. "Or perhaps they felt it would put you in danger if you knew. I don't agree with every-thing your uncle has done, Maddie, but I know he loves you. Your mother too."

But the words feel hollow when they land in my chest. I want to believe the Heiress, but I can't. With so much chaos and blood around us, I can't give my family a free pass. I cast around for a change of subject.

"The book you're writing," I say finally. "Is it really a history of Havenfall?"

The Heiress laughs softly and shakes her head. "No," she says. "No, that is not my book to write. Maybe it will be yours, someday."

"Then what are you working on? When you've had all those people up here for interviews?"

"Magic." The Heiress lets the silver chain slip through her fingers and pool in her palm. "I want to know the nature of it, how it manifests across the worlds. Fiordens have their healing and natural gifts; Byrni-sians have control over the elements; Solarians have their shapeshift-ing. Some of that magic has been bound up in these objects."

She leans forward and lets the necklace fall, a slipstream of silver between her fingers. She catches it at the last moment and leans back. "But I don't know how. All these objects—they've been at Havenfall for as long as anyone can remember, or Marcus or I have brought them back from elsewhere. I don't know how they're created. I've never seen one made. I believe there must have been a people, from one of the worlds now closed off, who had the power to bind magic to matter. But I don't know which one."

I think of the tunnel, the dozens of dead doorways, dark portals leading nowhere. "How will you ever find out, if the people are gone?"

Her eyes flit back and forth between me and the necklace. "I don't know if I will. History, even the history I was there to witness, slides quickly out of my grasp when there is no one else to remember it with me. And now I'm trying to write about something I haven't even seen; everything I know comes to me secondhand."

She smiles, though it's more sad and tired than genuine. "Things would be much easier if your Brekken were still here, you know. He was supposed to be making the trades while I stayed here and did the research. Now I have to go down into town tomorrow and deal with that dreadful man . . ."

My Brekken. The words sink into my heart like a fishhook and tug. I know now that he was fighting a good fight. Working with the Heiress to bring the magical objects safely back to the inn. But the hurt of my stolen keys is still raw, tangled up with my shock and disbelief that Marcus would allow the black market to fester. And I don't know if I'll ever even see Brekken again. In the roller coaster of the last few days, that hasn't really sunk in—but now it hits me, all at once. He's my best friend. I love him, and he's gone.

I push the thoughts away before I can go too far down that road.

"What time are you going to the antique shop?" I ask her, trying to steer us away from topics of Brekken and leaving and guilt and regret, back toward practical, safe ground. "I can get you some security—"

But a knock at the door cuts me off before I can finish the thought.

The Heiress snaps to full alertness, her head turning in the direction of the door, her spine going army-straight. She catches my eye and points to the wardrobe in the corner.

I stare at her questioningly. Even with the curfew, there's no rule saying people can't visit each other's rooms. But as she makes a stabbing motion for emphasis, something inside tells me not to argue.

I stand quietly, pad over, and slip into a world of perfumed fur, silk, and velvet just as another knock comes and a man's voice sounds.

"Lady Heiress?"

I reach out and pull the wardrobe mostly shut just as the Heiress goes to the door and opens it.

"Lady Heiress."

I don't recognize the voice, but the man's accent is Oasis. One of the Byrnisian delegates, maybe.

"The Silver Prince asked me to tell everyone of importance that the Solarian beast has been captured."

I suck in my breath without meaning to, the Heiress's floral perfume that clings to her coats scratching my throat. But I guess the messenger doesn't hear me, because he keeps talking.

"Everyone is invited to come view the beast in the ballroom, if they wish."

"It lives still?"

Even from here I can hear the skepticism in the Heiress's voice.

"The Prince is deliberating with his advisors on what to do next. He plans to interrogate the beast."

"Then I wish him the best in that endeavor," the Heiress says, crisp and cool.

The door shuts. I hear her footsteps tread close, and then the wardrobe opens, blinding me for a second.

"Well?" she asks me as I stand there amidst her coats, a sneeze caught in my lungs and my heart beating fast with mixed relief and terror. "I suppose you'll want to go see this beast?"

———

When we get to the ballroom, there are already more than a dozen delegates there—mostly Byrnisians, but a few of the remaining Fiordens too, and a handful of human security guards. Sal and his team of guards are standing in a circle in the middle of the room, facing outward to keep the small crowd back.

Behind them I see the tops of iron bars, rising and converging. I can't see much else, but my body knows. It tells me in the racing of my heart, the sweat gathering at my palms and trickling down my back, and the sick twisting in my stomach.

Solarian.

Predator.

Enemy.

The Silver Prince stands off to the side, talking with Willow. He catches my eye when the Heiress and I walk in and gives a small smile. Not proud or elated, just a small acknowledgment of me, as if in catching the beast at last he is doing only what's expected of a leader of Havenfall. That's what he wants.

He lifts his hand and gestures toward the cage, an invitation for us to come forward, and the crowd parts as if by magic.

My feet seem to have a mind of their own. They carry me forward. This isn't like the encounter in the forest, when adrenaline and the need to fight kept true fear at bay. Now I only feel fear. I sense everyone's eyes on me and I know people are looking, waiting to see how I'll react. The ballroom around me is dim and fuzzy, and sound becomes muted, like it's reaching me through a wall of water. The only thing that's clear is the monster in front of me.

The Solarian.

The cage wall cuts up my view of it, thick metal bars interspersing a long curve of blue fur. The monster is on its side with its back to me, its blood-matted fur crushed against the polished tile floor. Muscles ripple under its skin as it breathes, but the motion is shuddering, trembling. Its head is tucked against its chest, its tail lying limply on the ground. Its shoulder is wounded, torn open by some jagged blade, and I can't look too long at the wet blue-black flesh beneath without feeling sick. Smears of blue blood mark the floor around the Solarian, and, I realize, trail all the way from the door of the ballroom. There are blue footprints on the tile where the crowd walked in Solarian blood. It's on my shoes.

Has the Prince dragged the Solarian in all the way from the forest? Why has he brought it here for us all to gawk at, rather than locking it up secure in the tunnels? Why didn't he just kill it?

Guilt spears through me, and I check those thoughts, digging my fingernails into my palms. If I've learned anything over the past week, it's that my gut can't be trusted. My instincts lead me wrong. The Silver Prince was the one, in the end, who finally brought the beast down, and if he thinks we can learn anything by it, I can't let my squeamishness get in his way.

That would make me no better than Marcus, forgetting what the Solarians really are. And with the beast captured, at least that means Taya is safe. For all my anger with her, I'm glad about that. Hopefully she's on a bus by now, headed somewhere far away from here.

I turn to find the Silver Prince, only to realize he's already right behind me. I didn't hear him approach at all. I feel a drop of sweat slide down my spine, but I force myself to get it together.

"Thank you," I say, gesturing blindly to the Solarian. "For getting the job done."

I hate how I sound. Weak, trembling. No one would look at the two of us and think I was the Innkeeper.

But the Silver Prince just nods with his usual graciousness. "I thought the hunting parties might have been scaring it off, so I went to the woods alone."

And sure enough, I can see the toll the fight took on the Prince. I see the scratches of branches across his face, and the way he's favoring his left leg. He went after the beast alone. He risked everything to do what I couldn't.

And all at once, I know what has to come next.

Being the Innkeeper means doing what's right for Havenfall no matter what. Even if it shames you. Even if the words taste soap-bitter on their way out.

"I've made my decision," I say. "I'll write Fiordenkill out. I'll accept your alliance."

19

THE SILVER PRINCE CALLS A council meeting afterward. He invites me to come, but I make up some excuse about checking on Marcus. I know it's a coward's way out, but I can't stand the thought of sitting next to the Prince in Marcus's office and pretending I still have anything under control.

I can't stop thinking about Brekken—about how he would feel if he knew what I've just done. The severing of our official alliance with Fiordenkill feels more than just political. It feels like I've cut off a limb. All the dreams I've had of one day seeing Brekken's home with my own eyes—the aurora's curtains of light in the sky, the great wolves that fly across snow without breaking the frozen surface, the ice palace blazing with reflected stars—vanished. With the signing of one page of paper, the shake of the Silver Prince's hand, I've slammed the door on my oldest friend, burned the bridge between our worlds. I've given up on the last person who really knew me for me. Who *loved* me for me.

Or so I thought.

I feel sick.

It takes everything in me to walk, not run, from the growing crowd in the ballroom. With the threat of danger gone, the delegates are laughing and gasping at the caged Solarian, or exclaiming over the Prince's brave deeds. The mood in Havenfall has definitely shifted.

But all I can focus on is the smell of blood, the blue stains on the floor. The violence of it. I keep my back straight and my chin high, but I need to get away. From the Prince, from the Solarian, from everything. Why is it that the whole scene disgusts me? That the sight of the Solarian is burned behind my eyelids? Why can I imagine its gaze boring into mine?

People pass me, smiling and laughing more than I've seen in days, on their way to see the Solarian. I hoist a smile onto my face, but I keep my eyes to the ground and walk faster so no one stops me.

When I see Willow on the other end of a hall, I take a sharp left, weaving through the staff halls instead. I can't face her. I can't face anyone. I dearly wish Taya were here. I feel like she'd get it if anyone would—but she's not here. I drove her away. Where was she even going? Did she get there safely? It causes a stab of pain to think that after everything, I didn't even get her freaking number.

When it's finally quiet and I allow myself to look up, I find myself in the Solarian wing. I glance over my shoulder to see the stairwell entrance with its hastily made covering, the one pine board that always hung loose lying in the dust. I don't even remember taking it down. The floral wallpaper around me is peeling with age, revealing warped oak beneath, and the light filtering down from the skylights above is choked with dust.

I look ahead again, afraid to go any farther, but something stops me from turning back.

"What the hell is wrong with you?" I whisper to myself, like that'll help. The Solarian is caught; we'll figure out a way to reseal the door; Havenfall is safe. I should be happy. It shouldn't matter that it was the Silver Prince who brought the monster down. I'm not that vain to prioritize my own pride over everyone's safety. I can't be.

No. There's something else, something deeper and ugly. Something I'm afraid to look at too closely.

Pity. Pity for the Solarian, caged and bleeding.

I push a breath out through my teeth, disgusted with myself. That beast almost killed me. It took a bite out of Taya's shoulder; it's the same kind of monster that killed Nate. Yet it still turned my stomach to see it caught.

No one knew how dangerous they were, the Heiress said.

Marcus didn't. But I do.

I've never liked it up here in the abandoned wing. The air feels thick with ghosts, and I almost imagine I can still smell the blood that was spilled all those years ago. This hall's floor plan is the same as the one where I live a floor below, but the doors are taller to account for occupants' beast forms. The doors are all closed, but I can imagine Solarian guests waiting just behind them.

My eyes are drawn to the door that sits above my own. The carpet of dust in front of it is thick, perfect—no one's been inside for years, maybe decades. I'm sure Willow doesn't know how dusty it is up here, that she just takes the staff at their word that they've cleaned.

The dust reminds me of Nate. When we were little kids and the first snow would fall, we would scramble over each other in our effort to be the first out the door, the first one to mark the clean spread of white with our footprints.

Without really meaning to, I turn the knob. The door isn't locked. It creaks and opens under my touch into shadowy dimness.

I go inside, feeling like someone is pulling puppet strings attached to my limbs. I don't know what I was expecting as my eyes adjust. It's just a bedroom, the same as mine, but without all the trappings of a life, the desk and books, scattered clothes and blankets that make my room mine, the documentation of me.

It's weird to think of a Solarian living here. I know they spent most of their time at Havenfall in their human forms, but I can't picture that, just the beast I saw in the woods and in the cage. I can't imagine such a creature choosing instead to look human, moving through these small rooms and narrow halls, knowing all the while that the power of claws and teeth is living inside them. It makes me wonder if maybe there's a grain of truth in what Taya said before they left. That maybe the Solarians were just like everyone else; that maybe they only wanted to be left alone.

But that doesn't explain what happened to Nate or the gruesome incident that caused the door to Solaria to be sealed in the first place.

I sink down on the bed, the dark blue coverlet dusty but neatly tucked in. The floorboards creak exactly the same way as they do in my room below. And suddenly, something occurs to me.

There is a small space in the back of my closet, an alcove created by some oddity of the plumbing, too small for any real storage but big enough to hold—and hide—whatever my secret treasures were each summer. Books stolen from the Sterling public library, punk rock CDs passed down from Marcus and an old Walkman from Dad, shiny black stones from Fiordenkill that Brekken gave me. Nate's jacks, pretty leaves, and Brekken's poems. I get up to see if this room has it too.

The closet is empty, but I can see that the same floorboard hangs crookedly, secured by one loose nail. I pull my canvas jacket sleeve over my fingers and use it to grab the nail and wiggle it free.

And then I stifle a gasp.

A five-sided box sits in the hiding space in the floor, its lid covered with ornate carvings. It's formed from something that looks like wood except for its rich dark purple color, kept away from the dust and still shining.

Moving fully on autopilot now, I carry the box over to the bed. It's heavy. I set it down, the mattress sinking beneath it with a small puff of dust.

It opens with only a soft protest. Inside, a thick silver bangle rests on a bed of velvet. I take it out and turn it over. It's beautiful, simple, with a subtle braided pattern in the pearlescent Haven silver.

Then I see the note. A small envelope of fine cream paper, tucked into the fold of the velvet.

Guilt trickles through me as I reach for it, but I push the feeling away. Whatever this is, it belonged to a Solarian. They lived here and they killed people. That is their legacy. Whoever—whatever creature— left this, I don't owe them any privacy.

But the handwriting I unfold looks human. Old-fashioned, the paper yellowed, the script hurried and slanted, almost running off the page.

Annabelle,
   You were right to want the door closed. I'm sorry for everything that's happened. Keep this safe; a part of me is bound to it. It may be the last bit of me to survive.

There's no signature. But—Annabelle.

That's my great-great-grandmother's name.

A part of me is bound to it.

It hits me all at once, so suddenly it's like someone told me the truth long ago and I just forgot it up until now.

It's not some long-lost people who have the power to bind magic to silver.

It's Solarians.

Shock wipes my mind blank as I stagger from the room and force my way out of the Solarian wing, stumbling down the hidden staircase at the back of the hall. I've lost time wandering the Solarian rooms. Soon, the Heiress will be meeting with her contact, Whit, in town. I have to let her know what I've found.

As I burst into the cool evening air, heading to the stables for my bike, I feel the weight of the bangle around my wrist, the broken talisman that lets me through the Silver Prince's perimeter stuffed in my pocket. The silver seems to thrum with power, sending electric tingles into my bones and up my arm. Maybe I shouldn't have put it on.

I bike the narrow path that leads through the trees on the far side of the garden, sure that at any moment the Solarian will burst through the trees, but it doesn't. I stop at the perimeter, the place where the air blurs, the line where the forest shimmers, like a mirage coming off a baking hot highway. I grip the handlebars of my bike tight and take a deep breath, and then step forward.

The air thickens around me and in my lungs, and my body grows heavy, and each step is a herculean effort, like I'm dragging myself through quicksand. My heart thuds painfully hard just to push blood through my veins. I squeeze my eyes shut, hating the feeling of the pressure clamping down on my skull.

But then it's over. The crystal bracelet the Silver Prince gave me must carry magic too, somehow. And I didn't even think to give it a second thought before now.

My mind races as I steer the bike down the mountain faster than I should. My heart hammers. At one point I almost hit a tree when a doe darts into my path. Later a pothole jars me so hard that I taste blood after biting my tongue. It's like the universe is conspiring to keep me from catching up with the Heiress. But I must. I have to tell her what I know before she messes with any more of the silver.

I don't fully understand what I read back in the Solarian wing, but the basics are clear enough. The silver objects may carry magic from all the worlds, but the binding itself—that's Solarian. And from the letter—the letter written from a Solarian to my great-great-grandmother, the Innkeeper—it sounds like the binding causes something of the Solarian to remain . . . inside the object. Like a cross between a Horcrux and Aladdin's magic lamp, only with monsters instead of genies. And the Heiress has been touching this stuff, handling it, surrounding herself with it.

This still goes against everything I know about magic. I always, always learned that magic was limited to its carriers. Fiordens can heal. Byrnisians have their elemental magic. And Solarians can shapeshift. It's not supposed to be transferable. And yet, would the Heiress, would Marcus be so serious about the black market if all they were doing was cheating unscrupulous buyers out of a few bucks in exchange for ordinary silver? This has to be about more than just money. Solarians must be involved somehow, binding real magic to buy and sell.

And if the objects carry some part of the Solarian in them, then . . . what does it mean that Mom's name is on a list of HOSTS? What does the Silver Prince's accusation mean, that Marcus trusted Solarians too much, was trying to work with them?

My skin prickles. I don't understand what's going on, but I know that the Heiress is in danger. She needs to know what I know.

It's hot in town, even though the sky is gray with clouds. It's like they're a blanket, trapping in the June heat. Hot enough to drive everyone inside, I guess. The streets are empty, making the drone of insects on the air seem extra loud. Closed window shutters all around make me feel like I'm in some Old West ghost town. A dog barks somewhere, the sound echoing in the quiet. Soon sweat has soaked through my long-sleeve T-shirt. I can't seem to get enough air, as if the Silver Prince's barrier has clung to my skin.

I almost miss the turnoff to the antique store and yank my handlebars to the left, sending up a spray of gravel. I check my watch. 3:41. Good. Hopefully I can intercept the Heiress before her contact gets here and explain to her what I found, what I think is true. She can't know about the objects' connection to Solaria, or she would have never allowed them to change hands. My skin crawls when I think of them flowing out of Havenfall, circulating in the wider world.

I park out back, so the bike's hidden, and enter the antique store through the rear door. A bell chimes overhead when I enter, but the shop is empty.

All the lights are off. Sunlight filters in through the front windows, but shadows line the shelves, clinging to the myriad objects perching there. Stacks of old-fashioned china, chipped mugs, porcelain figurines. Knit sweaters and blankets, Christmas ornaments, dolls and toy cars and action figures a few years out of date.

Sweat dampens my palms as I look around, my breath sounding loud in the silence. So many ordinary things, but now it all holds an air of subtle menace. How much Solarian magic has passed through this place? Before this summer, magic was something for me to believe in, hold on to, a glimpse of something shining and *more* in a mostly boring and unfeeling world. But this . . . this feels dark. Oppressive, violent.

A door at the back of the shop catches my eye. There's a dark staircase leading downward, but I can see a light at the bottom. My hope rises that it's the Heiress. I pad over and walk down, testing each narrow wooden stair for creaks before I give it my full weight.

The staircase opens into a narrow basement room with a dirt floor and cinderblock walls. It's noticeably colder—I can't help but shiver—and the light, from a bare bulb flickering against the ceiling, doesn't reach the far end of the room. There's nothing here, and I'm about to turn around and go back up into the summer warmth when a flash of movement, low to the ground in the dark, makes my heart stop.

A face materializes on the other side of the room. Not the Heiress. It's too pale, the eyes too big. My heart is concussive in my ears as the person comes closer to the light.

Holy shit, it's a kid. A little girl, maybe eight or nine, though it's hard to tell because she's so short and skinny. Her hair is in two dark braids and she wears rolled-up jeans and a Haven T-shirt. Her feet are bare on the cold dirt. A cuff around her ankle chains her to what I can now see is a radiator against the far wall.

My blood's frozen. Coldness ripples through my body. I feel every bit as afraid as when I faced off with the Solarian in the woods. More than that. I want to run, I want to flee, because something is obviously deeply, deeply wrong. But I can't leave her here. My blood roars.

It takes me too long to realize why her head snaps up, why her gaze focuses on something behind me and her eyes widen. Too long for the *clomp* of footsteps on the stairs to register. By the time it sinks in and I whip around, the strange man is already there, blocking my way out as he stares thoughtfully at me.

He is chalk-pale—Byrnisian, I realize with a shock, the faint pattern of scales ridging his forehead. I expected a human or even a Solarian. But no matter what, I know he's not a friend.

I launch myself toward him. I don't know what else to do, I just know that if a strange man gets you in his basement, you might as well kiss the world goodbye. But he just raises his hands and a wind bursts into existence, crashing through the small room, knocking me off my feet.

I sail past the girl and hit the wall hard. Pain explodes through the back of my head as I fall in a heap to the floor. The world spins and pulses around me, and I try to get up. But then the man is there, ripping the sleeve off my shirt in one violent motion and tying it around to gag my mouth. I swing my fists weakly, but they don't connect with anything. Another moment, and there's the ripping sound of duct tape tearing off a roll. And I'm attached to the radiator too.

Fear is a distant thing. I can't focus on the man as he walks away. His movements are too fast, so I look at the girl. Crouching in the opposite corner, looking at me with those big dark eyes. Eyes that seem familiar somehow.

But I only have a moment to consider it. Because then the door at the top of the stairs slams shut, and my consciousness swims away with the light.

20

THE WORLD COMES BACK TO me slowly. The first thing I'm aware of is a murmur of distant voices. One of them familiar. The second thing is a strange light, glowing through my closed eyelids.

I force my eyes open. It hurts. Something's crusted them shut so that opening them tugs at my lashes, and more—my head aches, aches like the worst sinus headache I've ever had and then some. My body hurts, too, like I've been beaten up, and a sick feeling of fear pervades everything and for a moment I can't remember why.

Then all at once I do.

I try to bring my hand up to clear the gunk out of my eyes, but pain stops me. My wrists are duct-taped together, connected to a chain that clanks against something else metal when I move. I force my eyes open anyway and the cellar beneath the antique shop swims into view. The bare bulb on the ceiling, still off. The cold, useless radiator I'm chained to. And the girl. The light is coming from her, or rather, something she's holding.

A spoon?

That doesn't make sense. But that's what it is. She's holding a silver spoon, round end up like a torch, and it's throwing off a faint pale light—enough so that I can tell she's crouching as close to me as her chain will allow, concern scrunching her little face.

Great. She can't reach me, and I can't speak.

"*Neru galtiya?*" she asks, tripping slightly over the words, a tentative whisper.

I shake my head, racking my brain for what language that could be. It doesn't sound like Byrnisian or any of the Fiordenkill languages I know of. Something about her presence is unnerving. It might be that I'm not used to being around kids, that they remind me too much of myself and Nate, of things I want to forget.

"Sura," the girl says, pointing to herself.

I try to respond with my name, but the gag makes it impossible.

We regard each other for a long moment. I make a questioning sound through the gag, but she just shakes her head and points up at the ceiling, warningly. Her hands are free, though it hasn't seemed to help her much.

The voices, though. One, a woman's, is so familiar. My mind is sluggish and fickle, curling up like a snail in its shell whenever I try to think about anything too hard. But that female voice. Aristocratic now, haughty, but I remember it being gentle, careful, even when it was telling me hard things.

The Heiress. I came here to help her, to save her, and now I'm captive and she's in as much danger as ever. The old guilt stampedes through me all at once. No matter what I do, I can't save anyone.

I try to yell. The gag vibrates between my teeth. And maybe it filters through, because it seems like the conversation upstairs falters for a second. But then something happens to the air in the room. All at once, it seems to vanish, as well as the air in my lungs.

I can't breathe, and panic spills through me. I yank at my bindings, but only succeed in making the radiator clank. Then the air rushes in. I fall back, stunned and terrified, and I swear I hear a male voice above murmur something about old pipes.

Sura reaches out with the glowing spoon, apparently to catch my attention. She holds my gaze and then lifts her other hand in the air, making a swirling motion like she's gathering cotton candy from a machine. Soft light seems to stream from her skin, and a slight wind ghosts over my face, a threatening echo of the breath-stealing Byrn magic from a moment ago.

A shiver races through me. What is this?

She tips her hand, seeming to pour the light over the spoon, and it glows brighter for a moment. Suddenly, I remember the note I found in the Solarian wing, the note and the bracelet given to my great-great-grandmother.

Keep this safe; a part of me is bound to it.

Cold sweeps down my spine, and I want to yell at her to stop, but the cloth in my mouth muffles my voice. Sura grips the spoon tight, her knuckles white in the dark. When the glow is gone, she tips back against the wall, her eyes fluttering shut like whatever magic she just performed has drained her. I get the eerie feeling that the light was a part of her, that she's just given up something important. This magic feels cruel.

Then she opens her eyes and holds my gaze as she tosses the spoon gently in my direction.

Confused, I scoot toward it, because it's clear that's what she means me to do. In a weird way, I'm grateful for the puzzle; it keeps the sick terror at bay, letting me forget the fact that I'm tied up in a basement and no one in the world, except for this girl, knows where I am. But now a different, quieter, stranger fear is building, deep in my bones.

I reach out awkwardly with my bound hands and pick up the spoon. It's hot, almost too hot to touch. It thrums under my fingers in the same way the bangle did—the bangle I'm still wearing—but this time it's too strong for me to be imagining it. The faintest breeze stirs the fine hairs on my arms. There's nowhere for it to be coming from, except—

Magic. This girl harnessed our captor's Byrnisian wind-magic and bound it to this spoon.

Which means . . .

My body gets the message before my brain does. My head snaps up, and I scramble backward until my bruised shoulders hit the wall, sending pain radiating down my back. My breath comes fast, my heart hammering all over again. Sura watches me steadily, her face unreadable.

They're shapeshifters. They can look human.

The girl—the *Solarian*—continues to watch me, and as the moments pass, her face falls and grows sad. Instinctive sympathy twists my insides. But no, she's not human, maybe not even a child. My mind is spinning as I try to see past her eyes, see what lies beneath.

She doesn't look like a monster.

Think.

The monster that killed Nate, what did it look like? I only caught glimpses from my hiding place. I try to wind my memory back to what happened before the moment when Mom shoved me in the cupboard and shut the door.

A memory of old terror creeps in. Another time when I had my back pressed against the wall. The front door to our old house, shuddering and bulging as something pounded on the other side. A bitter taste floods my mouth.

The Silver Prince said that Marcus invited the Solarian into our home. Why then would it have had to break in? Whether it looked human or had claws and fangs, I must have seen it. Heard it. Why are my memories so jumbled, so full of shadows?

Sura looks away from me, her jaw tight, and something in the gesture reminds me forcefully of Taya. My chest clamps, and words bubble up in my throat, some apology or explanation. The girl across from me is a Solarian. Yet she's a captive, too, and a *child*. There's something alien about her, but I can't keep looking at her and remain afraid. She is so small. The feeling presses down on me that I'm missing something crucial, the key that will fit into all these mysteries and pull them together. A tear, then another, snakes down my cheek. I'm on the edge of something, understanding hovering just out of my grasp, but chances are I won't live long enough to reach it.

Right on cue, the cellar door opens and heavy footsteps descend. My stomach drops. There are no more voices from upstairs; the Heiress must be gone.

I missed my chance, I think distantly as the Byrnisian wind-wielder comes into view, Whit at his heels. The blond man startles when he sees me.

I slip the spoon up my remaining sleeve as the Byrnisian man nods and tells Whit, "Kill her."

It's not those words that ignite my fear again, but the idea that I'll die and then no one will know the Solarian girl, Sura, is here. That she'll stay a captive in this dark, cold space forever and it'll be my fault. My fault, my fault, my fault.

I lash out, but maybe I hit my head harder than I thought earlier, because my limbs don't go where I tell them to. It's more of a weak flail than a blow. The Byrnisian catches my wrists easily and hauls me upright.

The last thing I see as they drag me from the room is the little girl's eyes, wide and sad.

———

I expect to panic, but instead something in me goes numb, leaving my head clear and calm as Mirror Lake.

As Whit took me from the antique store, it was like I was hovering outside my body, witnessing everything that happened from some distance. Whit dragging me up the stairs, the awkward negotiation of space as he tried to steer me through the antique shop's narrow aisles. In a moment of surging spite, I slammed my shoulder into a shelf full of antique dinnerware, sending a cascade of rose-patterned plates and teacups and crystal to the ground in a crash. That earned me a bunch of oozing, stinging cuts on my calves from the scattering porcelain and Whit's sweaty hand clamped down on the back of my neck. But it made me feel momentarily better.

Now, Whit doesn't speak as he propels me out the back entrance, past my bike and toward that dingy tan station wagon. No one is around but a cow, watching curiously from the adjacent field. I want to try to yell anyway, but Whit has a jackknife. He holds it open, close to his waist, semi-concealed but ready to strike. He's visibly nervous, sweaty, his eyes shifting ceaselessly around.

If my hands were free, I could take him, maybe. At least I'd have a chance. But there's no give to the duct tape. Maybe I could try to bash my head against his, but that sounds like a good way to get stabbed—and then, *shitshitshit*, he's opening the trunk, shoving me in. Pain blasts through me as I land hard on my side. I find my voice, scream through the gag, but the lid has already slammed shut and closed me in hot darkness.

Mixed sweat and tears trickle down my face, burning my eyes, as somewhere another door slams and the car vibrates to life. Where is he taking me? He has instructions to kill me, so why didn't he do it there in the antique shop? Will Marcus, the Heiress, Brekken, Taya— will anyone ever learn what happened to me? And the kid, Sura, in the cellar. Does anyone else know she's there? Or will I doom her too when I die?

I can't measure time by the dark and the heat and the rumble of the road. I can tell the car is climbing; I feel the slope of the mountain, the popping in my ears. We must be getting closer to Havenfall; that's the only place higher up than Haven. Maybe the guy has had an attack of conscience. Maybe he's taking me home. A slim hope, but I have to take what I can get.

When the trunk opens, though, I don't see the inn, just blue sky and the tops of mountains and trees. It takes a minute for my eyes to adjust to the light, but when they do and I realize where we are, horror fills me all over again.

The lake. The station wagon is backed up onto the bridge. Whit faces me, an arm's length away, his knife held up to my throat.

He's still sweating, some kind of battle going on in his eyes. His gaze keeps flicking between me and the knife. If I could speak, I would beg him to let me go. But I can't, and if the bad angel wins, I don't want his face to be the last thing I see.

Instead, I turn my head and look at Havenfall across the water.

All the chaos inside hasn't touched the place's beauty. It stands tall, proud, wood and slate and glass gleaming in the summer sun. Too far away to see in the windows, but I hope that inside, peace and safety will eventually return. I visited Marcus this morning and he looked better, his skin seeming to glow with health. He'll wake up. He'll get things back up and running, and even if it takes the Silver Prince's guiding hand in the meantime, that won't matter as long as everyone is safe.

And I guess this isn't the worst place to die.

"*Goddamnit*," Whit mumbles.

I dare a glance at him. Try to find the humanity in his shaking hands, shifting eyes. It occurs to me, calmly and distantly, that I've thought about things the wrong way. The difference between monsters and people—it's not a divide between Solarians and humans, or anything like that. It's what we do. And this guy is toeing the line. I widen my eyes, trying to speak to him that way. Trying to keep him on this side of the light, because I have to.

"I can't do this," he mutters, and pushes me into the lake.

21

I HIT THE WATER FACE-FIRST, pain, shock, and cold enveloping me in an instant. Panic fills me up, pressing at the inside of my skin as water presses from outside, pushing the air out in a cascade of bubbles tumbling upward, a useless scream. I should have taken a breath before. I didn't. I twist around and the sunlight spirals around me, growing fainter and fainter.

Don't let the scary thoughts in, Dad says in my head. I feel small again, automatically trusting the words of anyone who's bigger than me. Dad, Marcus, the Silver Prince, Mom, Nate.

Nate most of all, Nate who would still be alive if I had been braver.

I'm sorry, I tell him, and water spills into my mouth. His gaze in my head softens. *Forgive me.*

But then his face dissolves and resolves, the little boy gone and replaced with someone nineteen, gorgeous, scowling. Taya. Something about her has always reminded me of Nate, I realize. The fire they both share. *It's not your fault, dumbass. Nate would want you to live. So live. Fight.*

And suddenly there's something else there under the panic. Rage, blossoming like a mushroom cloud, sending heat down my limbs into my numb fingers and toes. The water erupts into bubbles all around me, suddenly hot like fury spilling out of my skin. A burning feeling races through me, echoing the heat in my lungs as my air runs out, and suddenly the duct tape around my wrists and ankles comes free. Before I even realize it, I'm kicking, tearing the gag out of my mouth. The water around me is churning, swirling like the mouth of a volcano. I'm out of air, and the vacuum of my chest aches, screaming at me to open my mouth and inhale, water be damned. My vision is warped, white lights dancing across my eyes, but I attack the water, following the direction of the bubbles, until my head breaks the surface.

Sunlight and air scald my face, my eyes. I drag the air down, coughing and spitting in my effort to get as much in my lungs as will fit. Above the wild drumbeat of my heart in my ears, I hear the growl of a motor, and I turn around in time to see the station wagon disappear over the crest of the road, gravel spraying in its wake. The sky above, framed by treetops and ice-capped mountains, has never looked so blue or so beautiful.

I tread water for a minute to make sure he's gone, and then swim for shore, my teeth chattering as the remnants of terror and adrenaline work their way through me. I crawl up the gravel slope, under the bridge where no one will see me, and pull my legs to my chest, trying to breathe, trying to think. The lake and the woods are calm and quiet, ill suited to the storm of fear and rage and confusion rampaging inside me.

The Solarian girl. The Byrnisian man. Whit, shoving me off the bridge like a sack of unwanted kittens. The knowledge that if I were

251

underwater for a minute longer, I would have passed out, I would be dead.

My arms still smart from whatever happened in the water. I push my remaining sleeve up and look down at my skin, expecting to see redness and burns. But instead it's pale, covered in goose bumps, unharmed except for a blossoming bruise around my wrists from pulling against the tape. The tape itself is gone. My phone is gone, somewhere at the bottom of the lake probably. But something else presses into my bicep from underneath the rolled-up sleeve. I reach in and extract it.

A spoon. The one the girl in the antique shop gave me.

It's still warm, almost hot in my hands. I can feel the thrum of magic still within it. I didn't use it all to escape my binds. I think back to Sura crouching over it. Wait . . .

Another chill, one that has less to do with the cold, rips through me, my teeth clattering together. She looked so human. But if I'm right, only one people have binding magic. Solarians.

I left her there. Left her in that cellar. I remember how her eyes drooped, how she shuddered when she enchanted the spoon, like it took all her strength. Like it took something out of her.

Not the enemy, something in me whispers.

Solarians are cunning, I remind myself. They were members of the summit, until they weren't. I shouldn't feel pity for one. But she gave me the spoon. The spoon that somehow ignited underwater and tore through my bindings.

And besides—it wasn't a Solarian who gave the order to kill me.

I stare at the twin images of Havenfall before me, the real thing and the one reflected in Mirror Lake. Taya's plea from yesterday echoes in my mind.

Leave right now, with me.

But even though everything is so terribly wrong, the inn still calls to me. *Omphalos*. Where else would I ever go?

———

A Byrnisian delegate, a woman named Kel, is standing guard at the front door when I trudge out of the woods. She's traded in her delegate fashion, though, for military dress, wearing breastplates made of overlapping, gleaming red scales over a loose black tunic and leggings. Her hand goes to her sword hilt when I come out of the trees; then I see her recognize me and do a double take.

"Innkeeper?" she says incredulously.

I can't stop the laugh that bubbles up, scraping my throat painfully on the way out, my vocal cords still raw from my near-death experience. The title feels so false now that I've broken a hundred years of tradition and allied with the Silver Prince. And by the looks of it, he's already flexing his new authority. I think about the man in the antique shop again; I commit his features to memory. What will it mean if the Silver Prince knows him? If he doesn't?

All I want to do is take a long, hot shower and then sleep for a week. Or sit down with Graylin and Willow, spill everything, and let them tell me what to do next. But I'm not a little kid anymore, and these problems won't go away by dumping them on the grown-ups to fix. This is on me.

As I run, drenched and shaking, up the stairs, the only thing I can think is: this is royally *messed up*. Twisted beyond all reason.

When I open my door, the room beyond is dark and still, just as I left it. But no—something is off. A presence, a movement in the darkness, like a cold wind over my skin. I thought I was all out of fear, but it roars back up, I'm plummeting again. I grab blindly for the light

253

switch but it's too late. A hand closes around my mouth, stifling a scream.

The door slams behind me and suddenly, my back is against the wall, and I'm staring into a familiar set of eyes.

Brekken.

22

THE WORLD SEEMS TO GO absolutely still. Like my heart has stopped beating, my nerves stopped firing. Brekken looks sharper than when I last saw him, harsher. Like the intervening days have carved away at him, leaving his cheeks hollow, his eyes burning. His clothes are dirt-stained, his hair damp, color high in his cheeks.

"What have you *done*, Maddie?" he whispers, toneless. His hands are on my arms, not tight, but tense, like I might fight him off. Should I fight him off? I stare at him, unable to reconcile the clash of feelings rushing up in me.

On the one hand, there's the fear, the anger—he *lied* to me. I was so wrong to trust him. And yet relief and joy are welling up too. He's safe, he's *here*. I blink hard, swallowing, trying desperately to catch up with the current moment. "You came back."

"Because you broke off the alliance." There's anguish in his voice, and anger too, simmering beneath the surface. He smells like ice. Instinct tells me to defend myself, explain. That's what the Maddie of a week ago would have done. But instead I step away, outrage prickling along my skin. "A lot has happened since you left. What have you even been doing?"

He takes a breath, but then, as I back away and light from the setting sun hits me, his eyes go wide. They travel over me, and whatever he was going to say seems to dissipate as he takes in my wet clothes, the bruises. "Maddie, what happened?" he chokes out after a moment.

My voice comes out too loud and on the edge of cracking. "Someone tried to kill me."

The rage that ripples through his clenched muscles, the fierce flash of his eyes, is enough to burn a hole through the door behind me. "Who? Are they at Havenfall?"

I take a deep breath. "This asshole named Whit. And no." *But,* a small voice in my head whispers. What about the Byrnisian man who gave the order to kill me? What's his deal, who is he working for?

Brekken swipes his hair back from his face, letting out a pained breath. "I'm sorry I snapped at you. You're right, I don't know what's happened. But we'll fix it." He steps forward, his hand coming up to gently cup my cheek. I stare up at him, frozen with confusion and doubt, but wanting nothing more than to lean into his touch.

Then something barely perceptible feathers my skin. The touch of something invisible, soft and warm and lighter than air. It spreads up from my lips, over my face, through my hair. And when it lifts, the pain in my head—the heavy pounding from hitting the cellar wall, the car trunk floor, the surface of Mirror Lake—it's all gone at once.

Technically, Brekken's my *enemy* now, I realize. But with the healing magic, a feeling of being loved and cared for crashes into me with the impact of a semitruck. No matter what's happened, where he's been, I know Brekken loves me. And even though I'm still angry and confused, still full of a thousand questions, a strangled gasp escapes me, and I'm moving forward without deciding to, launching myself into his arms.

I didn't realize just how hard I missed him, or how much I really thought I'd never see him again, even if I didn't let myself admit it. But now, he's here. He's here. And before either of us has a chance to explain anything more, I kiss him, our mouths crashing together, even as tears are streaming down my face.

"These past days, with you gone, without knowing if you were okay . . ." Words spill out of me when we part to breathe, my throat closing up with emotion. I have one hand in Brekken's hair, one on his waist; he's still cradling my face, and the effects of the healing magic combined with his kisses make me suddenly dizzy. I sway on my feet and a soft noise of alarm escapes Brekken's lips. He guides me backward, sitting me on the bed and kneeling in front of me. Tears shine on his upturned face, and I'm not sure if they're mine or his. And before I know it, I'm leaning forward and kissing him again, the snow smell surrounding me like a blizzard without cold. A whiteout.

Brekken's hands move over my cheeks, down my arms, to my waist. Slow, gentle. "Maddie," he breathes, hoarse, then lets out the breath. His pupils are blown wide in the gathering dark. "Let's first deal with the fact that someone tried to kill you, yes? And then we can do this for as long as we want, and be safe doing it." His hands move in small circles on my waist, and when I try to kiss him again, he pulls back a little—teasingly, but with seriousness in his eyes.

A growl of frustration dies behind my teeth. The problems outside the door to my room are so vast and tangled, and I'm so unequal to them. He's right, obviously, but he doesn't understand that he's asking for something impossible.

And there's more: doubts and shadows in my mind, momentarily shoved aside by adrenaline and desire, and now slinking back. I don't want to wait because the truth is, I don't know what I want. I don't know how I feel. Everything about this feels right, and yet, only days ago, I was flirting with Taya, learning of her past with a curiosity that I haven't felt in a long time. I think of the quirk of her mouth, the angry slump of her shoulders and the way she snorts when she's annoyed, which is often. I think of the burning sadness in her eyes, the secrets. And I know that I can't just fall back into Brekken as if nothing has changed.

Everything has changed.

I've changed.

"Okay," I whisper, voice ragged. "Okay, let's talk. Starting with, where have you been?"

"The palace at Myr," he replies, cracking his old half smile, though it feels more like an attempt to comfort me than anything else. "It's a long story, but I never meant to leave you, Maddie, I promise."

"I know," I say. I scoot aside on the bed, pull him up to sit beside me. Questions battle for dominance on the tip of my tongue, the weight of everything I've learned over the past few days pressing in—the complicated web of guilt and double crosses and no answers.

Marcus and the Heiress, Brekken and the stolen keys, my mother the host, whatever that means.

The kid in the antique shop basement and the spark between my fingers when I touched the metal she'd enchanted.

How she trapped wind magic in the spoon, how it ripped through the lake later, burning my skin and setting me free. How binding the magic took something out of her, from her.

"The Heiress told me what you were doing, about the black market," I say haltingly. "I know Marcus was selling magic objects, and the Heiress was buying them back, and that my mom was involved somehow. And I think . . ." I stumble, suddenly feeling unsure of myself, but Brekken's steady gaze on mine encourages me to go on. "I think that Solarians are also involved. I think they're the ones who can bind magic."

Brekken is holding my hands, and his thumb has been absently tracing circles on my palm. But now it stills. His brow is furrowed, his face grave in the dim light. I look at him carefully, thinking of the multitude of silver objects covering every surface in the Heiress's room. The thought of every single one of those objects passing through a Solarian's hands makes me shudder. And I can't tell if it's because of my old fear of Solarians—or because of Sura in the antique shop. She was clearly held in that basement against her will, monster or no monster. *I have to get her out,* I think distantly. As soon as it's safe, as soon as we figure out what's going on.

Brekken closes his eyes briefly, then opens them again and he looks at me. "You're right."

My breath freezes in my lungs. Despite everything I've seen, part of me still expected to be wrong. Wanted to be wrong. How badly I want there to be some benign explanation, for him to tell me that Solarians in this world are an anomaly, monsters far away in the night and not right beside us, woven through this nest of secrets.

"Maddie," Brekken says in a careful, soft-edged voice. His thumb traces down mine as he speaks, a comforting gesture. "I was investigating the black market in Fiordenkill, and . . . the Solarians—I know you hate them, I know—"

"Brekken," I cut in. Because I don't want to be comforted, I don't want to let my childish fears cloud my judgment now that so much else

I thought I knew has been turned upside down. "Just tell me what you know about the Solarians. About all of this. Please."

He takes a long breath and lets it out again. "They can bind any kind of magic," he says. "They can capture Fiorden or Byrnisian magic and tie it to an object. Metal usually; silver is best." He looks down at our entwined hands. "Anyone can use the enchanted object just by touching it and commanding the magic loose. I don't completely understand how it works, but . . ."

A poisonous-sweet thrill goes through me, like the ache of sugar in my teeth. I wasn't going crazy earlier. I did unleash magic from the spoon. I remember the rush of power all over again, the feeling of the world opening to me. But I know, too, it's not a fairy-tale magic. It has a cost.

"I was supposed to be in Havenfall this whole summer, buying artifacts for the Heiress," he murmurs. While the hesitancy a moment ago felt like he was trying to cover his words in Bubble Wrap, now it just sounds like he's choosing them carefully. "Then the Silver Prince caught me in the tunnels the night we kissed."

I nod, my lips pressed together. "The same night the Solarian door opened."

Brekken's eyes fly wide. "The Solarian door—open?" he echoes. His eyes lift up, past me, like he can see through the ceiling to the room above. "And one got through?"

"Right." I squeeze his hands, trying to keep him on topic. "So you didn't see it happen? You didn't . . . open it?"

Brekken shakes his head slowly. "I had no idea." His eyes go distant, his brow furrowing like he's attempting to put something together in his mind.

"I don't understand . . . ," I begin, hunting for the right words. If

Brekken fled back to Fiordenkill before the door even opened, what went wrong between him and the Silver Prince? "Why did you run?"

A shudder passes over Brekken, a shadow flitting across his face, a tremor in his fingers. "I saw something I shouldn't have," he whispers. "Do you remember the Silver Prince's bodyguard? Bram?"

I nod, another shudder ripping through me. The one who got eaten.

"He was a Solarian," Brekken says. "Maddie, I saw him shapeshift. The Prince ordered Bram to transform into his beast form, and then he stabbed him. I just froze. I saw everything from Marcus's office."

My mind feels blank, wiped clean with shock. Bram. Even though I only met him once, I can see him clearly, as if he's standing in front of me. Pale and silent, lifeless eyes, like a living shadow.

Taya asked me how there could be nothing left of Bram, not even bones. I didn't think about it, didn't listen to her. If Brekken's story is true . . . it means that Bram's body wasn't eaten. It was lying on the office floor that night, wrapped in a carpet. It's rotting in the woods now.

Which means . . .

My brain is slow to process it.

The body—the Solarian body—that *was* Bram.

"Bram was a Solarian," I say slowly. I'm reeling now. "And the Silver Prince—killed him?" I whisper. "But why?" At this moment, *why* feels like the only word I can remember.

"Good question," Brekken mutters. "I asked him that too, when I snapped out of it and ran over to try and stop him. But he just laughed and turned his sword on me."

His gaze lifts up and off me; his eyes grow distant. "Maybe it had something to do with opening the Solarian doorway. Some kind of dark magic. I just remember all the blood."

Blood. I think of the day Graylin, Willow, Enetta, the Prince, and I tested the door with Fiorden magic. How the stone seemed to stir under my bloody fingers.

"He wanted the door open," I whisper, the pieces of the story shifting in my mind, scraping against each other like tectonic plates. "The Silver Prince wanted chaos at Havenfall. So he could take over the inn. He must have known Bram was Solarian. He knew what it would look like when we found the body."

Brekken's mouth becomes a flat line. I see the faintest shimmer of anger in his eyes. "What about Marcus?" he asks. "Surely your uncle wouldn't let that happen."

My heart and stomach sink together. "You haven't heard. Marcus is . . . ill. He's been unconscious since that night."

Brekken's mouth dropped open. "How? What happened?"

Tears burn at my eyes. "We thought a Solarian had gotten him, eaten his soul." I look down, like I could see right through the floorboards to the first floor and into the ballroom with the Solarian's cage. I imagine the fiery eyes I saw in the woods fixed on me, sending shivers down my spine. "But I don't think that makes sense anymore."

Brekken follows my gaze. "There's another Solarian, isn't there?"

"Yes, but that one didn't come through until the next day. Whatever happened to Marcus happened that first night."

Brekken blinks, leaning his head against mine. Tiredness tugs my body down, like the Silver Prince has turned up the gravity for the whole inn. I wish I could wrap my arms around Brekken and both of us sink down into the mattress, sleep until this whole mess has magically fixed itself.

"The Heiress always says the Innkeeper is bound to the inn," Brekken says, his words slow and halting. Curled against him, I feel the vibrations in his chest as he speaks "Maybe the Solarian door opening impacted him somehow."

"We don't know how to close it," I whisper. "Graylin has been trying to heal Marcus with the black market magic, but it's not working."

Brekken's body stiffens abruptly. Surprised, I sit up and look at him, in time to see the color flooding from his face.

"What's wrong?"

"I . . ."

For the first time tonight, maybe the first time ever, Brekken looks totally at a loss. He runs his hands through his hair, looks around at my darkening room, as if the answers he seeks are written on the walls.

Sick dread settles into me.

"I learned something about the black market when I was in Fiordenkill," he whispers. "The Heiress just wanted to keep the objects safe. To keep magic out of the hands of people who would abuse it. She wanted to bring all the silver back to Havenfall. But she didn't know . . . there was a reason your uncle was selling the objects, Maddie."

The cold spreads up through my chest and limbs. "Brekken, what is it?"

"Marcus was trying to save the Solarians," he says. "They're not beasts, Maddie. They're people."

As his words sink into me, I brace myself for the shock to hit. But it doesn't. And I realize on some level, I already knew.

"What about the sealed door? The treaty?" I whisper. But I don't need Brekken to answer that either. *There has always been war; that doesn't make us all monsters.*

Brekken shakes his head. "I don't know what really happened in that fight," he answers. "But the door closing trapped innocent Solarians in all the worlds, and traders in Byrn and Fiordenkill and Haven are still taking advantage. Capturing them, stealing their magic. That's who Marcus was trying to save."

He takes a harsh breath. "Because the Solarians are dying. Because every time a Solarian binds magic to matter, a piece of them is bound too. There's a word—*selu*—it means soul, spirit, their essence, whatever you want to call it. There are kidnapped Solarians all over the Adjacent Realms, binding magic—and themselves—to things, and it's killing them."

He stands, paces, and I stand too, panic filtering slowly through every cell in my body.

His voice cracks, shadows flickering in his eyes. Whatever he saw in Fiordenkill, it's clearly ripping him apart inside. "Marcus would track down these objects and 'sell' them to safe houses, where the mercenaries couldn't track them. Then the hosts . . ."

Hosts. Mom? My fists clench, nails pressing into palms.

"Somehow the hosts would release the *selu* and put the Solarians back together," Brekken finishes. "I don't know how. I didn't know any of this until the night I left. The Heiress thought—she told me—we were righting Marcus's wrongs."

His voice sounds distant, like we're standing on opposite sides of a chasm. And yet it's close, too, closer than breath, closer than my own thoughts. Like he's speaking from inside my chest.

Because didn't I know? Didn't I know that it cost Sura to enchant just that little spoon, to give me the magic that would save my life? The object is heavy in my pocket now. Does it contain a sliver of her soul? Did she part with a piece of herself for my sake?

But before I can explain everything that's coming together in my head, there's a pounding at my bedroom door, and then it bursts open by force, slamming violently against the wall.

"Traitor!"

Brekken whirls around as three Byrnisian soldiers materialize in my doorway. The seconds go by in stop motion, slow and hyper-fast all at once. They're inside before I can even form a thought, hauling Brekken back, wrenching his arms behind him.

"Take him to the tunnels," a cool voice says.

The soldiers drag Brekken away, his eyes are boring into mine, and then the Silver Prince is standing in front of me in my otherwise empty room. I feel out of my body again, like maybe nothing is real.

"You still love him," the Prince observes.

There's no warmth in his voice, no emotion at all, just a detached, almost academic curiosity. There's none of the compassion he showed me when we spoke at Marcus's bedside. Or the closeness—or was it flirting?—in the observatory. This is the Silver Prince from the books in the library. And something comes back to me, distant and quiet, but carried on the currents of adrenaline from this morning's murder attempt. He told me that not everyone has good intentions.

Eerie calm descends over me. I have to lie.

"I didn't know he was coming back," I say.

"It looks like you were glad to see him."

"Good thing I held him here for you," I retort, refusing to give him an inch.

There's the note of a challenge there, but the Silver Prince doesn't call me on it. Just smiles, faintly.

"Perhaps you're developing better judgment, then. I wondered, when I saw that staffer flee. Taya?"

Cold seizes my heart, and I flinch before I can stop myself. "What does she have to do with anything?"

Is he angry I didn't dose Taya with forgetting-wine? How does he even know her name?

"She is a liar," the Prince says with an icy smile. "Call it an intuition.

Rule long enough, and you'll understand. You're young—it's all right to have trusted wrong."

Cold spills through my veins. But now it's there because I want it to be. Protective, powerful, like a Fiordenkill wind that drives enemies away.

"You're right," I say, holding his gaze. "I trusted wrong this whole time."

23

AFTER THE SILVER PRINCE LEAVES me alone, I head straight down to the tunnels.

When I reach the juncture, four Byrnisian guards are already there, Sal's human crew gone. One Byrnisian is stationed in front of each of the three tunnel mouths to Fiordenkill, Byrn, and Solaria, and one stands in front of the tunnel to Tiria, a dead world, where the Prince must be keeping Brekken and the Solarian beast.

I don't recognize the guards from the summit, but everything about them says *professional*. They hold metallic staffs with sharp ends, and they look at me when I enter. Behind three of them—the tunnels to Fiordenkill, Solaria, and Tiria—a dull steel web stretches over the tunnel mouth, blocking the way. The Prince might not be able to close the door to Fiordenkill, but he can stop anyone from coming or going.

Anxiety makes sweat prickle my palms, but I stand straight, trying to sound calm and authoritative as I address the man guarding the opening of the Tiria tunnel.

"I'm Madeline Morrow. The Innkeeper. Here to see the Fiorden prisoner."

The guard is a tall man with white hair and a greenish cast to his skin. He steps forward and regards me skeptically. His staff glitters in the low light as he leans down, and I can't help but tense, the memory jumping into my head of the Byrnisian man in the antique shop, the wind magic that whipped up out of nowhere and flung me against the wall.

I can feel the magic coming from the guard now, as well as from the other guards at my back, which is strange because before this summer, magic never felt dangerous. But I raise my head so the guard can see my face. I try not to let my worry show, though I'm nothing but fear inside.

For Marcus. Havenfall. The Solarian girl, Sura. Taya. Brekken.

He examines me for a moment, and then stands back wordlessly. He lifts the staff an inch and taps it against the stone floor, and the metal barricade blocking the Tiria tunnel mouth starts to retract, the strands of iron snaking back into the stone.

The part of my mind that's still me, that's not numb with shock and fear, wonders how that works. Do the Byrnisians control the metal in the mountain too?

The glitter of a key ring on the guard's belt catches my eye. I'll need his keys to break Brekken out.

"Will you walk down the tunnel with me?" I ask the guard. I don't really have to fake the tremor in my voice.

The guard's jaw tightens in exasperation, but he nods and walks beside me into the dark tunnel. Staying half a step behind him, I reach surreptitiously into my pocket until my fingers find the enchanted spoon. When I was drowning, calling on the magic felt instinctive, but now I have to concentrate to call up the wind magic the little girl captured and channeled into the spoon. I will a wind to start up, and a short, strong gust sweeps up the other end of the tunnel.

The guard tenses and he steps forward, his hand going to the sword at his left hip. It's my chance. I already have my dagger in hand, and I reach out with it, cutting the leather cord that secures his keys to his belt and grabbing them when they fall before they can make a sound.

For a split second, just a moment, I feel a rush of power. We come into sight of the bend in the tunnel, and I touch the guard on the arm. "Thank you. I can take it from here."

I clench my left fist tight, hiding the stolen keys. How long do I have before he notices?

The guard appraises me. "All right. Careful—the Solarian's cell is down here, too. You'll have to pass it first."

Alone, I walk into darkness. The metal grate reappears behind me, locking me in. There are no torches, and it's becoming harder and harder to see with every step. The temperature drops, too, and I shiver, my clothes clinging to my damp skin.

Up ahead, everything is quiet. *Is Brekken really down here?*

As the light from behind me fades to almost nothing, I put my hands out, guiding myself along the wall. My eyes adjust slowly, just enough for me to see the vague shape of the tunnel. Deeper, deeper, until—

Stone turns to metal under my left hand, and I know this is another iron web. Something moves behind the bars, paler than the dark stone, and I stop. My heart is in my throat and my hands are shaking.

In the darkness, I can hear ragged breathing, but I can't tell if it's mine or someone else, something else.

I see a light emanating from its cell, a light so faint as to hardly be there at all. As I approach the metal bars, I see it's from a plastic star, like a night-light or key-chain lamp. It's lying on the ground on the other side of the iron web. Lying between the paws of the Solarian.

I think distantly of the Solarian delegates that summered at Havenfall in centuries past. How sometimes they'd run through the woods in their beast forms, and other times they'd be all but human, sleeping in the same little eaved rooms as everyone else, eating in the dining hall, talking politics, dancing in the ballroom. Not monsters at all.

The beast is watching me. There's something so aware in its posture. In how it holds its left foreleg tenderly close to its body. In its eyes.

Those eyes that look so. Damn. Familiar.

And just like that, something clicks. One more tectonic plate groaning into place, just a fraction of an inch, but in that instant my whole world warps.

My knees give out. I catch myself on the gate, threading my fingers through. The Solarian fills my vision, the only thing in the world.

"It's you." My words stumble out, a ragged whisper. "It's you, isn't it?"

The Solarian blinks. Black, blue, black again. Immeasurable sadness in the look she gives me.

And then smoke streams over her body, dark as ink, coming from nowhere I can discern.

When it clears, Taya is lying on the stone.

———

Her hair spills over the ground, the lightest thing in this dark tunnel.

She is naked, battered, and when the strange smoke dissipates, her eyes are closed.

I don't even realize I'm moving, unlocking the door with the guard's keys. Although my mind is still blank with shock, I yank my T-shirt over my head and drop it by her. In my jeans and cami, I run farther down the hall, softly calling out to Brekken.

There's a moment of nothing, then the snick of a match flaring and an oil lamp flickers to life. My heart jumps so violently I almost think it's going to tear out of my chest as yellow light illuminates the contours of Brekken's face.

He's sitting against the far wall of another makeshift cell. He drops the spent match and looks up at me.

"Shh," I say, moving up to the iron net separating Brekken from me, and I put my hands on the cold metal, too finely woven to put anything more than fingers through. I unlock the cell door. "Your cloak," I gasp.

He doesn't argue, his face pinched with worry as he swings off his fur cloak and opens the door to hand it to me.

Taya has raised herself into a sitting position by the time I get back. She looks terrible, gaunt and so pale, with bruises marring her face, torso, and arms and legs. But there's a determination in her expression like nothing I've ever seen, hard and permanent as if carved out of marble, and a faint glow lights up her eyes like oil slicks. Black, no color, and every color at the same time.

I open Taya's cell door and slip inside as she slumps forward; I lunge toward her and support her shoulder with one hand, pushing the shirt and cloak into her arms. She holds them to her chest, but doesn't move any farther. Her head is down, her back heaving as she tries to catch her breath, and I can feel her heart pounding where my hand supports her shoulder, like her heart lives right under the surface.

"It's okay," she whispers after a long moment, even though her voice sounds like she's swallowed steel wool. "I'm okay."

She straightens, and I back up from her and retreat into the tunnel so she can get dressed. My mouth is dry as sand, chills chasing each other across my skin. My heart feels like it's about to leap from between my lips.

Until Taya's voice comes softly. "I'm good."

I turn around slowly, terror and shock coursing in equal measure through my veins, as Brekken cautiously comes to stand beside me. Two words take up all the space in my head, pushing out everything else, the memory of how to breathe, my own name.

Taya.

Solarian.

She's wearing my big T-shirt with Brekken's cloak over her shoulders. Holding it closed with one hand and supporting herself against the wall with the other, Taya gives us both a tight smile, her eyes lingering on Brekken.

"I'm Taya. Nice to meet you."

Under other circumstances, I'd laugh at the look of total confusion on Brekken's handsome face. After a moment, he collects himself and takes a step toward her, reaching his hand out, then seems to think better of it and stops, giving her a nod instead.

"Brekken of Myr."

Silence falls, none of us knowing what to do next. Taya looks at me now, really looks at me for the first time, and there's a question in her eyes, burning just as bright as the fire I saw there a moment ago.

"So," she says, her tone determinedly casual. "It seems like I'm a Solarian."

"I'm sorry I shot you," I blurt out.

Her lips twitch. "I'm sorry I scared you." She takes a shuddering breath and glances at the wall to her left—in the direction, I realize with a chill, of the Solarian doorway, if you drilled straight through the tunnels.

"How long have you known?" I ask carefully.

"Not for sure until yesterday." She smiles, but without any real feeling to it. "On our second day here, I felt drawn to the tunnels; I bribed one of the guards to let me down to see them. And when I was in front of the Solarian door, I blacked out; there's a few minutes I don't remember." She extends her hand, like she expects to see claws there.

I remember coming across Willow castigating her in the common room after she went to the tunnels. The claw marks we found outside the Solarian door.

"That started happening more and more," she says, eyes distant. "I could feel myself changing, but I thought I was just dreaming or hallucinating. I can't control it. I just know I have to get outside when I feel it coming on. Some kind of instinct."

She meets my eyes, her gaze pleading. "I had no idea what was going on, Maddie. It had never happened before."

She looks normal; she looks shaken. But something is different. I can feel the power coming from her, the magic, just as strong as from any Fiorden noble or Byrnisian soldier. It feels like sparks, like a light, burning, invisible snow falling over my skin. It feels alien, and yet I want to get closer, want to open my arms and feel as much of it as I can.

But no. I have to think. "The door opened wider after you came down here," I say. "Do you think that was you?" If the open door is what's disrupting the balance and keeping Marcus unconscious . . . If Bram's blood opened the door, could Taya close it?

Taya looks between us, shrugging; Brekken bites his lips, eyes fixed on her.

"You clearly have strong magic," he says, his tone polite even as his voice trembles slightly. They both look at me, waiting for me to weigh in, but I have nothing. Shock has wiped my mind clean of words.

"Maddie," Taya says. Her voice is quiet but ragged, urgent. "I didn't mean to lie to you. And I didn't hurt Max."

I take a deep, centering breath. "I believe you," I say, and I do. Maybe I shouldn't, and my mind is racing with other questions, but I do believe that much. "Why did you go to the door?" I ask her after a moment. A weird, unsettled feeling stirs my stomach. "Do you want . . . do you want to go through?"

"No." But Taya sounds less certain of this.

She slides into a sitting position on the floor, and Brekken and I instinctively follow suit. The stone floor is cold through my damp jeans, and distantly I'm still aware of the guards' presence somewhere behind us, but that all feels unimportant right now in comparison to the words trickling from Taya's lips.

"This world is my home," she says, reaching down to toy with a speck of dirt from the floor. "All that stuff I told you about foster care, about Terran, that was true. My life is here, my brother is here. My parents never told me we were Solarian. I don't even know what that means really. I thought I was just like you."

Brekken is the next one to speak. "What about before that?" he asks, carefully. "What do you remember of where you came from?"

She looks down at her hands, her lips pressing together. I think of everything she's told me about her family. Their car going off a bridge. The parade of foster homes. Her twin, Terran, and her determination to find him.

"My brother was like me," she says slowly. "I remember he told me once we were special, magical. We were just little kids, but I think he knew somehow." Her white fingers twist around each other in the dark. "We lived in Nevada until I was three. Then our parents died and Terran and I went into separate foster homes. Everything was normal, or normal enough, until I got here."

In my head, I hear Brekken's voice. *Every time a Solarian binds magic to matter, a piece of them is bound too.* I see the girl from the antique shop slumping against the wall. A sense of dark foreboding and a question gather in my chest. I'm not sure I want to know the answer, but we're short on both time and options, so I make myself ask it anyway.

"Do you remember any weird objects from when you were little?" I try my best to keep the fear out of my voice. "Objects made out of silver, especially."

Taya tilts her head at me. "Like jewelry?"

"Anything," I say, deliberately casual. "Jewelry, yeah, or trays or pens or marbles. It could have been anything."

She blinks at me. "Actually, now that I think about it, yeah," she says at length. "My brother, Terran, had this set of jacks."

My breath halts.

A faint, joyless smile curves Taya's lips. "He was obsessed with them."

Her words hit me like raindrops and slide off, their meaning not sinking in. Nothing sinks in except for the tiny pinprick of pain under my collar, so slight that I almost never even notice it anymore.

The place where one of Nathan's old jacks, strung on a silver chain, rests below my collarbone.

"When you two were separated . . . ," I whisper.

Brekken must hear something off in my voice; I see him glance at me out of the corner of my vision, but I can't tear my eyes away from Taya. Can't stop scouring her face for clues, as if I'll be able to find something in the dark of her eyes beyond even what she remembers.

"Who took him when you were separated?"

Her brow furrows. "Two social workers," she says with a small shrug.

I can tell she doesn't get why this is important. I almost don't either. But urgency fires my blood; memories swim to the surface, but whenever I try to grasp them, they slip through my hands back into the shadows.

"It was so long ago," Taya says, holding my gaze.

She places her hand over mine, and I take it gratefully, glad for something to hold on to. Her skin is hot, almost to the point of burning, but I twine my fingers through hers and let the warmth flood me. It's like she knows I need something to ground me, can tell that the earth is coming apart beneath my feet.

"It was two social workers, a man and a woman," she says. "They told Terran and me they were brother and sister, just like us. But that we couldn't stay together, or bad people might find us." She breaks off and blinks, a tear slipping down her cheek. "That never made any sense. Why would anyone be after us?"

Brekken is the one who answers. "Because you were Solarians," he says, very gently. He glances at me and back to Taya. "There are those who hunt your people for their magic. And you would have been easier to find together than apart."

She shakes her head, subdued. "Still." The hurt is fresh in her voice, swimming right under the surface.

"The social workers, do you remember their names?" I ask. Maybe I can cross-reference them with the Heiress's list of hosts, figure out who took Terran and where.

Taya shakes her head again. "But . . . the guy social worker was short, with curly hair and glasses. And the lady—I remember her because she had different-colored eyes. One was brown and one was green."

This time, it's not just my breath that stops. Everything stops.

My heart, my thoughts, the ground under me. For a second, the world shorts out in buzzy silence, the snow on an ancient TV screen.

Because she just described my mother. Marcus and Mom.

"And then what happened?" I ask, even though I already know the answer, deep in my bones, in every cell of my body.

I'm still holding Taya with one hand, but I reach out for Brekken with the other, feeling like I might float away if I don't hold on to both of them.

Nate never looked like the rest of us, not stocky and broad-shouldered like Dad or freckled and brown-haired like Mom. He was slender, grace-ful, with blond hair and dark eyes and a mischievous grin. Mom used to call him her little changeling.

So many different threads are tangled together here. Mercenaries. A secret trade in magic and souls. Corruption and stolen children.

It really wasn't my fault.

Time has slowed down. My heart crashes against my ribs as Brek-ken wraps his arm around my shoulder. Cool, familiar—it should be reassuring. But I can feel the tension in him, hear his intake of breath a couple of seconds after my own when the realization hits him too.

"The man took me," Taya says. "He took me to the foster family. I remember he was nice, even though I was terrified." Pain colors her voice; she looks down. "And the woman took my brother." She looks up at me then, her eyebrows drawing together. "What's wrong? You look like you're about to have a heart attack, Maddie."

Her fingers move around my wrist, playfully checking my pulse before braiding together with mine again. But I can't laugh. I can't think. I can't breathe.

"There's a word in Solarian," Brekken says softly. "*Nahteran*. It means 'soldier.'"

"I don't understand." Taya looks back and forth between us, her brow furrowed, her eyes lingering on my face. "What does that have to do with . . ."

"Nate," I whisper, more of a breath than a word.

I can tell the moment she understands. I can tell because her hand goes rigid in mine, her spine snaps straight, and her eyes fly wide. They drill into me.

"You don't mean—"

"We have the same brother."

24

EVEN AS I SPEAK THE words, my heart reacts faster than my mind. Something like helium gathers in my chest, and Taya's eyes are on mine, wide as coins, and I feel like we're on the edge of something, but my thoughts come in bright, sharp fragments.

Mom and Marcus, working together to save Solarians imprisoned by the magic trade.

A pair of social workers who looked just like them, collecting Taya and Terran after their parents died, splitting them up and shuffling them off, apart but safe.

Mom on the list of hosts for kidnapped Solarians.

Taya, nineteen, just like Nate would be.

Mom's little changeling. My older brother who I loved more than anyone in the world. Who never looked anything like Mom or Dad or me, with his fine blond hair and dark eyes.

My older brother, whose body we never found.

And the jacks that seem to be almost buzzing against my collarbone.

"He isn't dead," Taya says with certainty. "I would feel it if he were."

My first instinct is to be bitter. Tell her *you don't know that*. But though I open my mouth, I find that nothing comes out; the words have dried up.

All at once I understand the metaphors I've heard all my life and always written off as cheesy. A thing with feathers, sure. A baby bird fallen out of the nest, unmoving for so long you thought for sure it was toast, stirring and blinking an eye. Hopping to its feet, ruffling those feathers, and improbably—impossibly—taking flight.

Part of me never fully believed that Nate was dead. And Mom knew! She knew this whole time. That he was adopted. A Solarian. And that he didn't die that night, but was kidnapped. That he might be alive.

I don't get the chance to put any of this into words, though, because a voice floats down the hall behind us.

"Innkeeper," one of the guards calls. "Are you all right?"

Footsteps accompany it, not yet around the bend.

Brekken lets go of me to reach for a sword that isn't there. He swears under his breath. Taya has gone still as I leap to my feet.

"I'm all right!" I call loudly, hoping I sound casual.

I turn back to the other two, wild hope and fear playing a game of tug-of-war with my heart. *Nate might be alive. Alive!*

But before we look for him, I have to free Brekken and Taya. I need to deal with the Silver Prince, after playing right into his hands for so long. Even knowing, now, that he's willing to kill.

"I'll get help," I tell Brekken and Taya in a whisper. "I'll come back for you—"

"Don't worry about us." Taya surprises me with the intensity in her voice. "We'll be fine."

She reaches out again and squeezes my hand once before getting up and returning to her cell, pulling the unlocked door closed. The hope in my chest burbles a few notes of birdsong.

"You still have allies here, Maddie," Brekken says. "I've heard what the delegates say about the Silver Prince for years now, even the Byrnisians. They're frightened of him. They'll stand by you if you take back control."

"Either that, or they'll side with him because they're scared." There's a tremble in my voice, and I struggle to say the next words. "But I'll try."

Because there's no other choice.

I don't say that last part, but we all know it's true. It hangs in the air between us as Brekken turns and walks back to his cell.

"The guards haven't come back here yet," Taya says. "They have to eventually, unless they plan to starve us, I guess."

"Taya." My voice comes out soft and anguished. "I . . . I'm sorry."

She is my friend. And a Solarian. A week ago, the idea would have sounded insane. And I can still feel the place in my gut where the hatred for Solarians used to live, a hot, bitter engine driving me. But now it's hollowed out, dried up. All I can think about is fixing this so we can find Nate.

I've failed both of them so badly, but at least Brekken made his own choices that led him into an underground cell. Taya had no idea what she was walking into. Yet somehow she's still smiling at me through the bars, and suddenly all I want to do in the world is pull her out and take her somewhere safe and far away.

"Stay here for now," I whisper instead. "I'll try to draw the guards away, and then you and Brekken can escape."

Another question is lined up on the tip of my tongue, but I don't want to ask it, not now when she still looks so vulnerable. But I know I need to.

"The change," I whisper hesitantly. "Do you think you could control it, now that you know the truth?" The beast's claws and strength might come in handy once they have to run.

Something shutters behind her eyes. She shakes her head. "It comes out when I'm angry or scared. I'm not in the driver's seat here."

I think of the montage scene in every superhero movie I've ever seen, where her powers switch on once the hero accepts herself. I think of Dad's advice, *why give the scary thoughts so much room?* But I know it's not that easy. I know you can't always get away from the dark things. I know how they follow you, invade every thought.

"It's okay to be angry," I whisper. "You're right to be angry."

———

I double back and unlock Brekken's cell, then return to the juncture, hoping to sweet-talk the guards into skipping away for five minutes. I try for a neutral look, hoping they don't notice my change of outfit or the missing keys, and then I realize someone else is standing in the passageway to the main part of the inn. My stomach drops.

It's the Silver Prince.

Now that I know what he's capable of, it's hard to imagine a time and then I wasn't afraid of him. My whole body reacts, skin tightening, muscles go rigid, heart kicks up into a drumroll.

The guards move to flank him as I enter the juncture. He stands tall, filling almost the whole tunnel. His pale eyes are trained on me.

"Maddie," he says, pleasant enough, but there's an undertone of ice in the word that shoots mirroring cold through my bones. "I see you've found our prisoners. And my guard's missing keys."

The keys are closed in my fist. My arm goes leaden. I don't remember what standing naturally feels like, what it should look like.

"What?" I say, scrunching up my face in pretend confusion. "What do you mean?"

I don't like the Silver Prince's smile. It says he hears my lie, but doesn't care, because he has me backed into a corner. Dead end.

"So, what should we do with the prisoner?" he asks.

More goose bumps rip out across my bare shoulders and arms. I walk toward the Prince and his guards—even though my instincts tell me to run the other way. If I can get out of the tunnels into the main inn, in the company of others, I can figure out some way to get the guards out of the juncture. But here there's nothing but stone and darkness.

"I haven't decided," I say as I walk, trying not to blink too much, trying not to show that I'm lying. "Let me talk to Graylin and see what he thinks. I'll let you know . . ."

My stream of babble dries up, because the Silver Prince moves into my path. Blocking my way out. I wish I could call back to Brekken and draw strength from his voice, but I don't dare.

"I don't savor the idea of putting how we deal with the soldier in the hands of another Fiorden," the Prince says.

His tone is still light, conversational, but his eyes cut through me. I feel naked, like he can see through my skin and flesh straight to all my weakness and lies.

But I lift my chin, thinking of Brekken and Taya hidden down the tunnel behind me. If I fail in this, what will happen to them?

"Willow, then," I say. "Is that acceptable?"

The Prince laughs, a cruel sound. "A woman rotting away here for so long she doesn't remember what it is to be Byrnisian? No, I don't think so."

The hostility in his voice is less disguised now. That can't be good.

I let the hurt I feel show on my face, so that the rage doesn't peek through. If I can't talk my way around him, maybe I can get him to dismiss me. Convince him that I really am the child out of my depth that he apparently thinks I am.

"I don't know what to do," I say softly, and it's not difficult to let the edge of tears in. "I need to talk to Graylin and Willow."

I take a step forward, but the Prince doesn't move out of my way.

"Excuse me," I say, holding the Silver Prince's gaze. Willing my eyes to communicate: *I am still the Innkeeper. Let me pass.*

"Madeline," he says, a smile on his face that doesn't make it to his voice. "You must know I can't let you leave."

Panic blankets my mind in cold, white fog. I try to dart forward, but two of the guards grab my arms, holding me tight enough to bruise. I kick and yank at them, but it's immediately clear it's no use.

"Carve another cell," the Prince says to the guard to his right. "Throw her in—"

But then I hear the clang of metal behind me, and Brekken is out and on the Silver Prince like a whirlwind.

I've never seen him fight before, and it's transfixing.

Broken glass—the lantern?—flashes in his hands as the Silver Prince's sword comes out. Brekken swings away from him at the last moment, though, pivoting in an instant toward me and the guards.

They're caught by surprise—blood flashes; someone cries out. Abruptly, the grip on my arms is gone and I drop, lunging out of the way as Brekken pulls one of their swords from its hilt and spins around, getting in between me and them.

"Maddie, run!" he yells, but the Silver Prince is stalking toward me, murder in his eyes.

Then I see something from the other end of the tunnel, something that makes me freeze with instinctive fear.

Taya in monster form is quick and fluid as blue fire. She bursts into the light and leaps clear over Brekken and the guards, over me, going for the Silver Prince. Her claws catch on his shoulder and he bends backward, the two remaining guards leaping out of the way. One runs for the juncture; one lunges at Taya and gets a slashed thigh for his trouble. He goes down, but then the Silver Prince is rounding on her with his sword. Taya snarls and raises a blue paw, catching the blade on her claws. Sparks light up the dark.

The spoon is lifeless, dead in my hands. Nothing happens when I try to call on the wind again. But then I remember I have more magic. The bracelet I found in the abandoned Solarian closet. It sits heavy on my wrist, but when I close my eyes and concentrate, I can feel the magic, a subtle current, but alive and dangerous.

I don't know what kind of magic lives inside it. But I squeeze my eyes shut tighter and will it to come loose.

Heat and light burst all around me. I open my eyes to see flames exploding outward from my palms. For a heartbeat, everyone stops fighting. Brekken, Taya, the Silver Prince, and the three guards, our seven faces made demonic by the fiery light.

Brekken leaps out of the fire's path, light as a fox, but the guard after him isn't so lucky. As he lunges for Brekken, the fire swarms up over him like a living thing and he goes down screaming. Horror freezes my mind.

Then the Silver Prince cries out a word in a language I don't understand. He raises his hands toward the ceiling, sweat dripping from his temples.

Rain materializes out of nowhere at the other end of the hallway and blasts into my face. It doesn't kill the fire, but steam fills the hall with a hiss. I reach out, trying to find the wall, when the rain hardens into hail. The impact, a million little blows on my skin, makes me lose focus and the fire dries up. I cry out, whirl around, and throw an arm in front of my eyes, but that's no respite. The rain beats down on my bare shoulders, cutting through my thin cami. The water collects, white, on the stone floor. It forces me to step back toward the juncture.

A high war cry cuts through the fog, and a moment later Brekken barrels out, a broken-ended iron rod in his hands like a crowbar.

Adrenaline and hope drive me, making my limbs move seemingly of their own accord. Shielding my eyes with one hand, I stand and face the Prince through the steam.

Flames spring from my outstretched fist, lapping the juncture and bathing us all in greenish-blue light. I see Brekken kneecapping a guard in one smooth motion, sending him down. Taya fights the Prince in the background, trying to drive him toward my flame. My heart thunders in my ears; it takes all my will to keep the flames up, but I do. Somewhere deep below all the fear, my heart thrills at it. *Magic.*

I see out of the corner of my vision that the north wall seems to be swelling, a dark, shiny surface turning in places to frothy white. At first, I can't understand what I'm seeing, and then when I do—it's *water*, a wall of water—it's already crashing down on us. The flames die with a hiss and an explosion of fog, blinding me. Icy-cold water hits me at the waist and I stagger into Brekken, terror like I felt at the lake crashing down on me all over again. His hand finds my wrist but then is torn loose.

"Hang on," I hear him gasp, and then he's gone.

I call out for Brekken, but the fog has already swallowed him up. It's in my burning eyes, my lungs. I grab at the wall and hang on, the current tearing at my legs.

"You're not enough, Maddie!"

The Silver Prince's voice emanates through the fog. It's terrifying, like he's inside my head. Tears streak down my face, but I instinctively don't make a sound.

"Havenfall deserves someone strong at its head," he calls out. "Power wants power, Maddie Morrow, and you're not enough!"

Even though I know he's just trying to bait me into doing something stupid, anger rises to the surface. "Oh yeah?" I call back, trying to mirror his coldness, but my voice shakes. "Why's that?"

"You're weak," he almost sings, everywhere and nowhere all at once. "Under your rule, the inn will fall and everything will be chaos. Let me take over and remake this place into what it ought to be. Not just a crossroads. A throne room. For all the Realms."

"Fat chance," I spit, pulling my dagger from my waistband. I wish I could send more flames his way, but my stolen magic is spent, the bracelet cold and dead on my wrist. "Havenfall isn't about power, it's about peace."

"It can be whatever the Innkeeper wants it to be. But only if he is strong enough to seize it."

I can't see him, but I can tell from his voice the Silver Prince is smiling.

"It's not mine to keep or surrender." I know I'm rising to the bait, but fury pushes my words out. "Havenfall doesn't belong to me. I belong to it. We all do."

He laughs. "A pretty thought, Maddie. But I will have the *omphalos*." The next words he speaks are louder, closer. "I would offer you a place at my side, but I think that would be more trouble than you're worth."

"Screw you—"

But then another sound fills the tunnels. An unearthly howl of wind, growing louder over the course of a heartbeat until it's upon us, slamming me against the wall and clearing the fog instantaneously away.

Willow is sprinting toward the juncture from the staircase, hands flung wide, wind whipping at her hair. Graylin is beside her, dagger drawn, Brekken on her other side. The Silver Prince is just a few feet from me, long daggers in both his hands.

He turns to face the staircase, a faint smile playing over his face. For a stretching instant, everything is still. His shout seems to echo in the juncture, cling to the walls and slither from tunnel mouths just like the fog he created.

I will have the omphalos.

Spears of ice fly together in the air toward Brekken, Willow, and Graylin. Brekken's sword whips through the onslaught, shattering shards everywhere. The hailstorm beats at them, but Willow raises her hands, grimacing, and the air in front of them shimmers.

There's more movement behind them, though it's hard to hear over the rattle of hail and howl of wind, the juncture crackling with weather magic. Through the shimmering air, I see people flooding from the upstairs hallway to come to a stop behind Graylin, Willow, and Brekken. The rest of the delegates. Wide eyes, mouths hanging open.

A few people draw blades, and my heart sticks in my throat as I realize they're mostly Byrnisians. Will they attack us to help their prince?

"You're outnumbered," I rasp to the Prince, hoping I sound braver than I feel. "I am the Innkeeper. And I want you to leave."

I clench my fingers tighter around the knife, trying to figure out what to do. A little voice in my head whispers *kill him*—step forward and put my knife in his throat—but I'm afraid of what will happen when this stillness is shattered. Willow won't be able to keep up her wind shield forever. Everyone I'm responsible for is gathered in the tunnels. Everything hanging in the balance.

The Silver Prince moves suddenly, his limbs blurring in the dark. Before I can so much as draw breath, he's behind me, dagger blade resting lightly against my throat.

The hailstorm fades into nothing, chunks of leftover ice plummeting and melting into the water that swirls around our ankles. Suddenly the only sounds are my own harsh breathing and the pounding of my heart, the lapping of waves against the wall and the arctic crackle of ice, and a low humming that seems to be coming from the Solarian doorway. Brekken moves toward me, but the Prince cocks his head and Brekken freezes. Graylin looks stricken. The dozens of people in the main tunnel are silent. Too far away to do anything.

In the tense stillness, I can feel the Silver Prince's heart beating at my back. *What is this all for?* I want to ask him. But, maybe because I'm reasonably sure I'm about to die, the words don't come out.

"Where's your Solarian?" he says in my ear, mocking. I swallow, the dagger cutting slightly into my skin. Warm wetness trickles down. I don't know where Taya is.

But I see Graylin's face across the juncture. See his eyes focus somewhere behind me, along with everyone else in the space. The Silver Prince turns around, rotating me with him.

Taya stands beyond me, deep in the Solarian tunnel. She's human again and bloodied from the fight, blood streaking her arms and trickling from the corner of her mouth. Wreathed in fog, she's standing right in front of the doorway, framed in its eerie light. The crack in the Solarian door is wider than ever. Its orange light spills over her, making her look cast out of gold. Her hair flies in all directions; her arms are slightly raised as if in self-defense. Her back is to the door, and her eyes are wild.

And the doorway is *reacting* to her, seeming to expand and contract with each heave of her chest. Flashes of different, unearthly colors play around the edges and cracks into the world beyond. I catch glimpses of a blazing golden sky and a hill gleaming with buildings.

Her world.

Taya's chin is high and her eyes are fire. Even though she's soaked through and gaunt and shivering, knee-high in the Prince's flood, she stands straight and strong. She's beautiful and terrible bathed in the Solarian light. It's hard to believe I ever thought she was human. She is tied to the door and the door to her. I know it at the cellular level. The power rolls off her like the rays of the sun. As tangible as the fire and hail.

The Silver Prince's mouth is still frozen in a cruel smile, but his eyes are wide. He is afraid. He is afraid of Solaria, just like I used to be, but I know fear can be as volatile as gunpowder. I want to go to Taya and pull her away from the door, away from the precipice it feels like she's balanced on, but the Prince still has his knife on me.

"Go back to Oasis," Taya tells the Prince. "Or I'll bring this whole place down and you'll never have your throne room."

Her words are trembling, like she's bearing up under a great weight. She raises her right hand high, and her palm is bloody. When she places it against the stone, a shock wave tears through the tunnels, the ground convulsing beneath our feet.

I twist away from the Silver Prince as we both stumble in the moment before I hit the ground. The Prince lunges toward Taya, but the ground heaves and he tumbles backward into the juncture, the knife clattering away. I seize it when it skitters in my direction and shove to my feet, getting between him and Taya, so he's halfway between us and Brekken's sword.

"Go!" Taya snarls. The earth continues to tremble, thrumming like a living thing beneath my shoes. If I closed my eyes, I could be standing in the aisle of an ancient, rickety bus as it climbed up a mountain.

The Silver Prince stands stock-still for a seemingly endless moment, waging war with his eyes.

But then he breaks.

He turns and shoots into the Byrnisian tunnel, so fast he's a blur. The door opens before him, and I see a fiery orange sky, a broad metallic wall. And then he's gone, the ground convulsing as one last gust of angry wind whooshes through the juncture.

Relief fills me, and I feel a grin spread across my face as I look at Brekken. For a second, he grins back. But then the smile falls away, quick and sharp as ice cracking.

"Taya!" he yells. "Get back—"

I whirl around as the earth seizes once more, so violently I fall to my knees. The Solarian door flares up, wide open for a heartbeat, spilling blinding gold light. I see Taya's silhouette in it, hair flying in all directions, face tilted up in wonder or horror.

Then the door slams shut, and she's gone.

25

THAT NIGHT, THE MOUNTAIN TWILIGHT spills lavender light over Brekken's face through the windshield of the inn's jeep. We're parked in front of the pizza place in town, waiting for them to carry out our order—*as many pizzas as you can make.* The radio plays, too soft to make out the words to the song, just enough to fill the silence.

This is the kind of stuff I didn't think about when I was a kid dreaming of becoming the Innkeeper. How people need to eat even when the earth has literally shifted under your feet, even on a day when several people have tried to murder you and you've watched your friend evaporate into another world. Even when you don't know if Solaria sucked her in or if she meant to go, and you don't know which one would be worse.

Even when Nate—and I can hardly even form the words in my head—Nate might not be dead. Even when most of your kitchen staff has fled the inn and the idea of pouring a bowl of cereal for yourself, much less figuring something out for fifty confused and scared and angry delegates, feels unfathomable. Even then.

So, pizza.

"Taya will be all right, you know," Brekken says, looking over at me from the passenger seat. "That's her world."

"We can't know that," I reply, keeping my eyes ahead, watching the pizzeria's neon sign flicker against the darkening sky.

I've cracked the windows, letting in the sounds of crickets and frogs and wind through the pines. It feels absurdly peaceful down here, impossible to believe that only a half mile of road and a few hours separate this from the hail and fire and blood of our battle with the Silver Prince. Part of me just wants to keep driving until I'm back in Sterling. There are no choices to make there. No one else who will get hurt because of me.

You've hurt people in the real world, something in me whispers. The old voice of guilt—*if you had screamed, if you had done something, Nate wouldn't be gone.*

But it wasn't my choices that hurt my brother, I know now. Someone broke into our house. Someone *took* him. Not one starved soul-devourer, but a conspiracy too deep and dangerous to comprehend then.

And too big for me to fight now. Soon. But not now.

"We don't know anything about Solaria. It could be a wasteland," I say to Brekken. Even though I know that Solarians—at least some Solarians—aren't evil, it's hard to erase the image I built up in my head for so many years. That Solaria is a world of darkness, of hunger and monsters. I don't want to think of Taya there. And *Nate.* My brother—not my biological brother, as I always thought, but still my brother. A Solarian, all along.

Brekken looks steadily at me, an unspoken question in his eyes. I look back and smile, but it feels like someone is playing tug-of-war with my heart.

He looks exactly how I remember him from our first night here, just a little more worn, a little sadder. Even dressed in jeans and a Boulder T-shirt borrowed from Jayden, playing with the tab of his Coke can, he looks like a soldier, his posture straight and his copper hair neatly combed. Strong. Safe. Like I could bury my head in the space between his neck and shoulder and shut out the world.

He would let me. He would protect me. I could lean over the dashboard right now and press my lips to his cheek and chase everything else away for a little while. I could turn back time and be the girl kissing him in the hayloft, feeling nothing but light and want and the summer stretching out ahead of me like a trail of sun on Mirror Lake.

But something has shifted between us. I want to kiss him, want to feel his arms around me, but there's a sharp edge buried in the longing. I know all the secrets were him trying to protect me. I know he and the Heiress thought Marcus was supplying the black market by smuggling the silver objects out of Havenfall, before he knew what they really were— fragments of captive Solarians' souls—and maybe Brekken thought my loyalty to my uncle would win out over doing what was right.

But still, it's a lot to get used to. Everything could have been so much simpler if he'd just told me. Trusted me, his best friend.

And Taya. I see her behind my eyes when I blink. I don't think even kissing Brekken could chase away the image of her leaving, no matter how much I might want it to. It's a waste of energy worrying about her, seeing as there's not a single thing in the world I can do to help her, to find her. But I can't stop wanting to try.

"She's a Solarian," he says. "If anyone can make it there, she will."

I nod and blink to smother the nascent sting of tears. I have to believe him. I don't have a choice. I can't help Taya—at least not right now, when there are people here that need me to have my head in the game.

A knock on the window makes my heart stop for half a second. I whip around, my jumbled mind half-expecting to see the Silver Prince, but it's just a frazzled-looking Jorge, the Pizza Palace owner, shoulders hunched under the weight of two bright red insulated delivery bags. Behind him, two apron-clad kids carrying more pizzas stare warily into the jeep as Brekken hurries out and pops the trunk. I get out, too, and follow Jorge inside with my wallet.

"Big party?" he asks as he rings me up.

I fake a smile, but even as I do it, I can feel that it must look more like a grimace. "The hotel refrigerator broke. Everything went bad."

The irritated lines on Jorge's face smooth out into sympathy. A handful of other patrons in the eighties-themed restaurant look curiously on as I hand over Marcus's credit card.

I try not to look at the eye-popping price as I do the math for a tip. At some point, I should probably figure out where the money to run Havenfall comes from. But that's a problem for another day.

Dark has started to fall by the time Brekken and I crest the hill leading back to the inn, the lilac twilight fading into the color of plums or bruises. I press the brakes so we can take it all in. The moon is rising, bright as a new silver coin, and balanced between it and its Mirror Lake reflection is Havenfall, an indigo silhouette against the sky.

Even after everything, Havenfall still takes my breath away. The shape of it is so familiar, I could draw the lines freehand in my sleep. But as wind sweeps over the mountain and ruffles all the trees at once, an invisible current eddying around the inn, it feels different too. Bigger and darker, shadows reaching out from it like something alive.

It *feels* alive. I can almost sense the pulse of energy from beneath the earth, the tunnels far below like veins. Even after everything, Havenfall still stands, beautiful and dangerous. Even if I couldn't see it before, it was always dangerous, but that doesn't lessen the beauty.

Omphalos.

The center of everything, the heart. A home for people from all the worlds. If I'm strong enough to keep it that way.

Brekken reaches out and rests his hand on top of mine on the gearshift, and a spark of electricity travels through me. I doubt anything could stop his having that effect on me. His grip is gentle but strong, warm. For a moment, before we start driving again, I turn my palm up and let our fingers interlace, our palms press together. I don't know what it means, but I know that somehow, we are bound together. That our story is still unfolding.

I have two months left of summer, two months to pick up Havenfall's scattered pieces, to rebuild the delegates' trust in me that I've burned away. Two months to decide what my next steps will be. There's so much to do. Whatever strength Brekken can give me, I need it.

———

As the delegates gather for dinner, I peek into the dining hall through the back door. Even if I'm not ready to face everyone just yet, it seems prudent to make sure the guests aren't rioting. Through the open doorway, I see pizza boxes strewn over the grand tables. The familiar smell of melted cheese and grease is a small comfort—one that never fails to make me feel like I'm four again. I imagine Mom cutting up my pizza into little bite-size squares. What would she think if she could see me now?

I can tell her, I realize, a spear of guilt and grief over lost time lancing through me. Ever since I arrived at Havenfall, ever since the sentencing, I've thought of her as if she's already dead. I took her silence as surrender. But that's not the Mom I remember, or the woman I read about in the Heiress's files. She was a player in this game, working together with Marcus to save the captive Solarians. I have to tell her I know the truth. I have to tell her that Nate could still be alive.

I understand now that what happened to Mom and Nate wasn't my fault, but there are so many things I've done wrong since then. Writing Mom off as a lost cause. Not looking hard enough for the truth about Nate. But I can't let myself sink into a morass of shame. If I want them back—my heart races at the possibility—I need to keep moving forward. Starting by winning over the delegates tonight.

The remaining guests cluster near the front of the room, eating half-heartedly while they await my announcement, their eyes constantly flickering to me at the front table. At a table a few yards away, Brekken cuts a piece of pizza into small pieces—just like Mom used to do for me—and puts the plate in front of Sura, the Solarian girl from the antique shop. She's sitting between Brekken and the Heiress now, wide-eyed and flinching at every noise, even though the hall is quieter than normal.

While the healers tended to me and Brekken after the fight with the Silver Prince, we explained to Graylin, Willow, Sal, and, crucially, the Heiress what we had learned about Solarians and *selu* and the silver trade. I stayed as calm as I could, careful not to let any anger at the Heiress into my voice. She was horrified at her mistake. It wasn't her fault—she didn't know that the silver she was buying held slivered bits of stolen souls—and more pieces of *selu* are in traders' hands because of her actions.

After Brekken and I related the truth, the four of them drove straight to the antique shop to free the girl and bring her here. Watching her now, though, her wide blank eyes and careful movements make my heart twist as I think about how she gifted me her magic, her *selu*.

Can it be restored to her—can all the Solarians who have been harmed by the traders be restored? I hope so, but I'm not sure. I wonder if the legend about Solarians stealing souls is just another way their own history has been twisted against them.

I tear my gaze from her and look over at the other tables. Part of me wants to smile at the sight of these elegant, otherworldly delegates peering discreetly over at the human table to see how to eat a slice of pizza. No such thing in the Adjacent Realms, I guess. But the larger part of me is worried over the fact that there *is* a human table. That in this atmosphere of uncertainty and suspicion, everyone has separated and is sitting with their kind. The Byrnisian delegation fills an entire table, while the remnants of the Fiordenkill delegation and human staff, sitting apart at different tables, look especially motley in comparison.

They all know what happened with the Silver Prince—from his plot to control the inn to murdering Bram to his attack on Max. I have a new plan. Graylin and Willow were skeptical, but secrets and lies got us here. I couldn't justify any more. It won't be long until we hit the two-week mark, where the worlds will align and allow people to come and go through the Fiordenkill and Byrnisian doorways. If the delegates leave, they leave.

And they still might.

But there's one more thing I have to do before I get up in front of them and make my case.

26

WHEN I SLIP INTO MARCUS'S room, my heart leaps with joy before I fully process what I'm seeing.

Marcus is sitting up. His eyes are open.

A thousand emotions crash into me at once as I run over to the bed-side. Graylin manages to jump out of the way just in time.

He's been getting steadily better since the Solarian door closed. Still, he looks strange. There is a frantic color buzzing in his cheeks, and his eyes are unnaturally bright and yet slow to focus on me.

But I push the doubts down to make room for the utter joy, dizzy-ing joy and relief that I have my uncle back. Whatever comes next, fighting the Silver Prince, putting Havenfall back together—we will figure it out. I'm not alone anymore.

"Hey there," he says, his voice smoker-gravelly from lack of use.

I plop down on the side of his bed, looking up at Graylin to make sure I'm not dreaming. He nods at me with a strange, strained smile, but maybe I'm not seeing clearly because my eyes are filling with happy tears. I blink them away and turn back to Marcus.

His hand reaches out and touches my chin, his expression uncertain. "Sylvia?"

"I—" What he's said takes a second to sink in.

Sylvia. Mom's name.

"No, I—I'm Maddie."

The song in my heart hiccups, but I try not to let it show on my face. He's been out for a week. It's probably normal to be a bit confused.

"What year is it?" I ask jokingly.

Marcus's brow creases. "Why, it must be . . ."

Worry spikes in my heart. "Never mind." I grab his hand and hold it between both of mine. "How are you feeling?"

"Good," he says, holding my gaze. "But warm. Too warm."

I notice for the first time that it's freezing in here. The window AC unit is cranked way up. But Marcus is sitting on top of the covers, wearing a T-shirt and jeans, his face flushed like he's in the tropics.

I slide off the bed and go over to the AC unit, but it's already turned up to the max. Just standing near it makes goose bumps rise up and down my arms. I mess around with the dials for a second, trying to compose myself, when Graylin comes over.

"He's been like this for half an hour," Graylin says quietly. "I'm sorry. I couldn't think how to tell you."

"What's wrong with him?" I ask, my voice coming out croaky.

Two hours ago, after the fight with the Prince and Taya vanishing and before Willow came to tell me that Marcus was awake, I felt empty, numb, my feelings quota for the day wiped out. But I guess there's always room in my heart for more fear.

"I don't know, exactly," Graylin says, each word soft and careful. "But Willow has a theory."

"I'm listening."

Graylin takes a deep breath. "The silver-magic I used changed him."

Guilt and panic stab through me. I was the one who told Graylin to use the enchanted objects.

"Changed him how?"

It takes Graylin a moment to answer. "I think they've made him not entirely human."

For a moment, my mind is utterly blank.

That's not possible, I want to say.

But after everything that's happened in the last few days, nothing really seems impossible anymore.

There are so many things I need to ask Marcus. But now isn't the time, not when Graylin just got his husband back and the delegates in the dining hall are all waiting to hear from their Innkeeper. So I settle for just one question. "Did you know Nate was a Solarian?"

Marcus blinks again, but not like before—his eyes go distant and I can tell he's remembering. "I did," he says quietly.

"And he didn't die. Traders took him." It spills out before I can stop it. Okay, more than one question.

He flinches, nods, and more guilt floods in. That was the worst night of Marcus's life too—he effectively lost his sister and his adopted nephew and, I'm realizing just now, watched all his efforts to help one Solarian child burn to the ground.

But I put my hope down for so many years, and now it's roared back with a vengeance. "If he's alive, I'll find him."

"If he's in this world," Marcus says. He closes his eyes and presses the heels of his hands into them. Graylin comes over to drop a kiss on the top of his head.

I have more questions, but I swallow them. Before I can learn the whole truth about Nate—*Nahteran*—and Mom and the Solarians and the silver trade, I need to get through today. With the Prince gone and the immediate threat with him, I can take time to piece my life, piece Havenfall, back together.

Even if it'll never be the same.

———

Back in the dining hall, I nibble halfheartedly at a slice of pizza as Graylin taps his fingers nervously beside me. He's not totally sold on what I'm about to do. I can tell. But we need to find out the truth about the silver objects and the bound magic.

We need to find Taya and figure out what happened to Nate. And how to fix Marcus.

It all comes back to the same place. The same world. The same door.

Another *omphalos*.

I keep trying out words and phrases in my head, looking for the right combination that will ease everyone's fears and bring back the authority and trust in me that the Silver Prince usurped. But my thoughts are scattered and slip quickly away. Images keep butting in, driving out organized thought: Brekken kneeling in his cell, trying to keep the light alive; the Silver Prince, coming toward me with rain and hail swirling at his fingertips; Marcus awake, delirious, asking for cold; Taya silhouetted in the Solarian doorway, broken and fierce and brave.

What would she tell me now?

I feel a smile creep onto my face, because I know the answer right away. *Just do it. Don't think too much. You've got this.* I hope she—or at least the version of her in my head—is right.

No one's been talking much, just a scant murmur of conversation across the tables, but even that quiets when I push my chair back and stand up. The half-empty hall feels hollow, and I'm momentarily seized by a childish urge to yell out just to hear the echo.

"Good evening," I say.

Project, as Marcus would say, I remind myself. "Thank you for being here."

A few scattered nods, but mostly just stares.

"Some of you have heard that I was attacked earlier today inside Havenfall," I say haltingly. "And that the attacker fled. I'm sorry to have to tell you, officially, that the attacker was the Silver Prince of Byrn."

They know this. I know they know. Yet somehow the silence seems to plummet even deeper when the words escape my lips. Like no one in the room is even breathing.

"There was a Solarian on the grounds of the inn—who returned to Solaria and closed the door to Haven—but she did not kill Bram or attack the staff member," I go on, willing my voice not to shake, even though I couldn't keep it steady even when I was just practicing in front of the mirror alone in my bedroom. "That, too, was the Prince."

A few people around the room gasp.

"He blamed everything on the Solarian," I say, my voice gaining strength as my anger reignites inside me. "He wanted to incite chaos so that he could assume control of Havenfall. It was the Solarian who saved us and forced the Prince to flee back to Byrn. I don't know if he'll return or try again. But I want to say . . . I want to say that I know things have been frightening lately, and I haven't always made the right choices as Innkeeper. But we're safe now, and I want to remind you that the principles Havenfall is built on—neutrality, nonviolence, cooperation—they still stand."

I take a deep breath. Listen to the sound of my own heart. "If the Silver Prince does return, he will be considered an enemy. But I don't want to make an enemy of Byrn or this delegation. If any of you want to return, now, you're free to go. But I hope you'll stay. Stay and help me rebuild the trust between the worlds."

More murmurs. People exchange glances or look down at their plates. My senses seem fuzzy, the sound of the room staticky in my ears, faces blurry. But maybe that's a good thing. If everyone looked skeptical, I don't know if I could go on.

"We will be scrapping the Accords and crafting a new treaty starting at noon tomorrow, in the observatory. Anyone who wishes to have a voice in writing it is welcome to attend."

Muttering, louder than before, erupts. Someone gets up from the Byrnisian table and walks from the hall. The door closing seems ten times louder than normal. My heart skips a beat, but I force myself not to react. To hold steady.

"Our goal," I call, "is to build a new alliance that incorporates people from *all* the Adjacent Realms, anyone whose goal is peace. Including Haven. Including Fiordenkill. Including Byrn. And including Solaria. The war with them is long over, and the survivors have been blamed for others' violence. Our quarrel with them is over, and now is the time to work on healing."

As soon as I sit back down, dizzy with nervousness and exhaustion, the room erupts into chatter. It washes over me, less a collection of distinct words than a tide of feeling: anger, confusion, relief, hope.

There are so many voices at Havenfall, so many different directions this delicate balance could tip. The Silver Prince told me I wasn't strong enough for this. That the inn would decay into chaos in my keeping. And maybe he's right.

But I know, too, that I'm not giving up, not walking away. As long as I'm the Innkeeper, official or not, I'll be whatever Havenfall needs me to be. I will *become* strong enough. Whatever it takes to make this place safe again, home again.

Home to anyone who needs it, with its doors open wide.

ACKNOWLEDGMENTS

THERE ARE SO MANY PEOPLE without whom *Havenfall* would not exist. Thank you to my wonderful editorial team of Cindy Loh, Hali Baumstein, and Claire Stetzer; publicity/marketing forces of nature Erica Barmash, Faye Bi, Beth Eller, Phoebe Dyer, and Courtney Griffin; fantastic production editor Diane Aronson and proofreader Katharine Wiencke (thank you for putting up with my inability to keep a timeline or outfit straight!); and to everyone else at Bloomsbury who's had a hand in bringing this book to life. Thank you, too, to all the publishers abroad who had faith in me and *Havenfall*, especially Rebecca McNally, Mattea Barnes, and everyone at Bloomsbury UK; and Leo Teti and the whole Puck team. And many, many thanks to Sarah Baldwin, John Candell, Donna Mark, and Peter Strain for an absolutely gorgeous cover!

Thank you to everyone on the Glasstown Entertainment team past and present—especially the always-wise Lexa Hillyer, publicity badass Emily Berge, and editor extraordinaire Deeba Zargapur; you all have made me a better author and I appreciate you! And thank you to everyone in my extended support system, especially Stephen Barbara, Lyndsey Blessing, and Pete Knapp. I couldn't do it without you!

I'm so grateful for my friends and colleagues navigating these writing and publishing trenches with me, including (but not limited to) the Curtis Brown crew, Celine Aenlle-Rocha, Liz Trout, Ronnie Alvarado, Mark Oshiro, Arvin Ahmadi, Dhonielle Clayton, Zoraida Cordova, Laura Sebastian, and Patrice Caldwell. And special shout-out to Alexa Wejko; I still remember the phone conversation with you when the scattered seeds of ideas about mountains and magical hotels started to fall together into an actual story.

Thank you always and forever to my family, who are my best cheerleaders and my strongest support. You're the best!